Shadow's Messenger

T.A. White

To Morgan– Thanks for challenging me to aspire to further height

Chapter One

Late. And I fucking hated being late.

Even if this job hadn't been reliant on me delivering the goods on time, I'd still be pissed about missing the deadline.

Damn the accident on Fifth. When would people learn texting and driving just don't mix? The resulting fender bender backed everything up for miles. If I hadn't been on my bike, there would have been no hope of me making the destination on time.

I leaned forward and pedaled harder. Three years in the military had reinforced the habits of a lifetime. Fifteen minutes early; you're on time. You're on time, you're late. And if you're late, well, you might as well just start pushing.

These days being late carried worse consequences than muscle failure. That's why even with my thighs burning in protest and my chest heaving, I stood and pedaled faster.

A right and then a left and I'd be there. I could make it. No reason to tarnish a perfect record.

I veered around a stopped vehicle and narrowly missed an oncoming car before jumping the curb and making the last turn. I braked hard, hopping off at the same time. No doubt I left several drivers in my wake, cursing my existence.

No time to put a lock on the bike. Not my first choice when in the Short North. Though a trendy, upscale destination just outside the Columbus downtown, bikes were still a popular target for kids and vagrants looking to make a quick buck. In high school, my boyfriend and his friends used to come down here and egg cars. Why was anybody's guess.

I was rushed for time so I had to pray that my beat up old bike would escape attention. I yanked the seat off the bike. Hopefully, that would delay a would-be thief long enough for me to complete my business.

Adjusting my messenger bag, I checked the name of the store against the one in my notes. Right where I was supposed to be.

Located in an old brick building off High Street, the name 'Elements' was etched in silver lettering complete with one of those flourish things at the end. The shop window had an attractive display of a skeleton in a top hat, holding a glass titled 'Potions' while sitting on a funky patterned sofa.

The brief ding of a bell announced my arrival as I stepped into a maze of touristy candles, gothic necklaces and other paraphernalia I didn't recognize. The small aisle was narrow and overgrown with items just waiting to be knocked over. I clasped my bag tightly. It would not be a good idea to break anything in this place.

A witch owned Elements. Getting on her bad side was something I'd prefer to avoid.

I made my way over to the woman next to a cash register. A skull candle sat next to the change tray. It was actually pretty cool. I wondered how it would look in my kitchen.

The girl wore all black and her face was coated in way too much makeup. Her blond hair was plastered to her head and pin-straight with a severe part in the middle. She didn't look up as I stopped before her.

"Delivery for Miriam," I said.

The girl flipped another page in her magazine, not acknowledging me. I didn't have time for this. There was less than a minute to get the package into its owner's hands.

As the girl turned the next page, my hand darted forward, stopping the page from completing its movement.

Slowly and precisely, I said, "Delivery for Miriam."

A pair of washed out blue eyes, rimmed in bright blue eyeliner, lifted to mine. With the disdain only the young could summon, she nodded at a door hidden behind a purple curtain embroidered with black and silver beads.

"Thanks."

I didn't know why I bothered. The girl had already returned to her magazine.

I moved as quickly as I could, without running, through the store. I'd learned on my first job for Hermes Courier Service that running would not be tolerated. Appearing rushed was a good way to get fired. I needed this job a lot more than it needed me so I was stuck moving at a snail's pace when every ounce of me screamed for speed.

The curtain led to a staff room complete with fridge, microwave and laminate table. Even with the time constraint I couldn't help blinking dumbly at the blond seated at the table calmly flipping cards.

Not what I had expected of a store owned by someone belonging to the Coven.

It was even less expected to find the proprietor playing what looked to be Solitaire.

"Miriam?"

"Yes?"

"I have a delivery for you." I stepped forward and pulled my phone from my pocket.

With a swipe of my fingers, I pulled up the delivery verification app and held the device out to her. She rested her forefinger lightly on the screen until it beeped. Before sliding it back in my pocket, I glanced down to make sure it said confirmed. Even more important, the words still showed green. It meant I'd made it in under deadline. If I hadn't, it would have turned red, and I'd have been screwed.

"You cut it close," Miriam said, already turning back to her game.

Pausing in the act of pulling the package out of my bag, I grimaced. No kidding.

"Another minute and I could have solved my ingredient shortage," Miriam said, eyeing my body with an appraising eye.

Oh. That would have been unfortunate. And probably painful.

I'd never had that as a consequence.

3

Hermes Courier Service was special. Its owner guaranteed satisfaction of service. Things like merchandise reaching its intended destination in one piece, and more importantly, on time. Failure resulted in a penalty clause kicking in, usually at the client's discretion. This was normally something simple, like working as unpaid help for a predetermined length of time, but the penalty could be anything the employer wanted. The more expensive the job, the nastier the penalty.

I'd never been late so I hadn't bothered to inquire about this job's penalty clause. I may have also been more interested in the money.

"Right," I eventually said, handing over the small package. It was no bigger than a deck of cards and wrapped in brown paper and tied with red twine.

As always, I had no idea what was in it.

The witch set down her cards and took the package from me. Dressed in jeans and a bright yellow shirt, Miriam was different in almost every way from the girl watching the front counter. Except the color of her hair. Miriam's makeup was done with a light hand and flattered her large green eyes. If I met her at a bar one evening, I would have assumed she was a young professional only a couple of years out of college with a normal job, something like a graphic designer. Of the two, the girl out front seemed more likely to be a witch.

"Not all of us embrace the human's depiction of us," Miriam said.

I shifted back and eyed the witch warily.

Miriam looked up from her game with a sardonic lift of her eyebrow. "I didn't read your mind, if that's what you're thinking."

Since that's exactly what I was thinking, I didn't feel much better even with her assurance.

"Your face is surprisingly open for a vampire."

Crap. That was supposed to be a secret.

"Relax." Miriam turned back to her game and flipped another card. "I wouldn't be much of a witch if I couldn't tell if someone was supernatural or not."

While slightly more reassuring than the thought of Miriam being a mind reader, it didn't solve the issue of her knowing I was a vampire. I wasn't exactly in hiding but I also wasn't 'out'.

Miriam didn't give me time to dwell on what I should do or if I should even do anything. "What news do you bring me, courier?"

I settled down to the second half of my job. That of acting as a verbal news source.

One of the things I'd learned since my involuntary transformation to one of the fanged was that the different species of the supernatural world didn't play well together. It was kind of like the Hatfield's and the McCoy's only with many more families.

Information was a prized commodity. My job allowed me to go anywhere as long as there was a package to be delivered. This gave me unique access that Hermes' clients were willing to pay for and pay well.

"Another human family was found murdered."

"I could have learned that from the human media. Tell me something I couldn't find out for myself." Miriam stared down at her cards with a frown.

"There's been talk of a task force being put together."

Miriam snorted. "There's always talk. Nothing ever comes from it. Everybody will want to be in charge but nobody will want to donate their people for it."

"I don't know. Fear does funny things. They might be willing to set aside differences to get to the bottom of the murders and disappearances."

Everyone was spooked. I could see it in their eyes, hear it in their voices. The last time I'd seen something similar I'd been in a war zone.

It had started with disappearances at the beginning of summer. Mostly from the smaller enclaves. The ones who weren't strong or under the protection of someone strong were the first to vanish. A few dryads from the Park of Roses gone in one night. From there the perpetrator moved on to the bigger groups. A sorcerer found smoldering in his bed. A few shifters torn apart like they were ragdolls. Shifters were strong too. Anything that could do that was not something you wanted coming after you.

It wasn't limited to the supernatural world either. Humans were being slaughtered in their beds. Police were horrified at the grisly remains but helpless to figure out who—or what—was doing it.

5

The only common thread in all this was that nobody knew anything about what was doing it. Not species, gender, or name. Nothing.

I lifted one shoulder. "If a few more disappear, it might give them incentive to work together."

Miriam propped her chin on one hand. "You're so young."

I mentally snorted. I hadn't felt young in a long time. Not since I'd come back from war. And not since my entire world view had been readjusted to include things that went bump in the night.

That was rich coming from her. She didn't look any older than I did.

"How old are you?" Miriam asked.

What could it hurt to humor the client?

"28."

"And how long have you been a vampire?"

I pretended to think about it. It was mostly for show. I knew exactly how long it had been.

"About two years."

Miriam turned back to her game. "Once you've been part of our world a little longer, you'll see we never really change. The different species will never successfully work together. Too much bad blood between us."

Right. I didn't agree, but it also wasn't my place to argue with a client.

Miriam waved a hand, dismissing me. "Ask Angela for your payment."

Guess my job here was done.

Before turning to go, I paused. "If you move the black nine to the red ten, you can clear a spot and move a king there."

I was through the curtain moments later, stopping only long enough to get my payment from the Goth girl, Angela.

My bike was right where I left it. Missing a seat of course, but that was easily fixed.

Pushing off, I headed home. It was just after midnight and that had been my last job. There'd been fewer deliveries to make than normal. I had hours of free time stretching before me. I'd miss the cash but it was nice to have the rest of the evening to myself.

Being a vampire had its advantages. Long life and near miraculous healing being among them. The hours? Not so much. Only being able to go out at night severely limited my free time. I'd always loved summer but found myself wishing the past few months would fly by. Having less than eight hours of dark to move around had been challenging both personally and professionally.

It's one of the reasons I worked at Hermes. The owner might be a complete troll but at least he understood my special needs. More than I could say for most potential employers.

With fall firmly upon us, it meant lengthening nights and more time to work and play.

Now that I had a rare night off, I planned to take advantage.

Hm.

What should I do first? Most stores were closed, so that was out. It was a weeknight so my old friends would be firmly asleep. Same with my family. I could go for a bike ride. But I did that most nights, all night. I wanted to do something different. Something I never had time for.

Who was I kidding? There was nothing to do at this time of night. It was kind of sad really. A rare chance down the drain.

Might as well head to the grocery store for my shopping before heading home. Maybe I could watch a few episodes of Firefly on Netflix before dawn.

Yeah. Vampirism was really paying off for me.

* * *

The grocery store was mostly empty at this time of night. Only students and the rare frantic parent walked its fluorescent lit aisles. There were maybe five people total in the store, including the stock boy, cashier and me.

I wheeled past the produce aisle and headed for the meat section.

Not all of the myths about vampires were true. Thank God. I could still eat, which considering my life-long love affair with food was a blessing. Never to taste chocolate or the black raspberry ice cream from Graeters? Might as well kill me where I stood.

Food didn't carry the same nutrients as it had before. Mostly it passed through my system doing nothing to help. Too much of it would make me sick, but in moderation I could still eat some of my favorites as long as I was careful.

The one exception was red meat. I could eat as much of that as my stomach could hold. I think it had to do with the blood and iron content, but I'd never had anyone to ask. All I knew was it hit the spot in a way even black raspberry ice cream didn't.

And the rarer the better. Yum. I think I drooled.

Two years ago I'd been returning with my unit from Afghanistan. I was a 25V, a combat camera for those in the civilian world. I, like so many of my fellow soldiers, was eager to hit the town after 362 days locked on a FOB where the closest I got to alcohol was what was in my mouthwash, and the height of entertainment was watching dust storms blow in.

That night was where my life took a serious detour from the path I'd planned for it. My night began like so many other young twenty somethings. I met a stranger. He was cute. I was horny as fraternization is strictly forbidden while in country and I've never been one to break the rules. I've always had an irrational fear of jail, and it didn't really matter if breaking the rules would actually lead to a jail cell. At least back then. Now, most nights I break three laws before midnight.

That's the only excuse I have for lowering my guard for some strange man when I'm normally extremely cautious. So cautious that friends have accused me of being unreasonably paranoid when it comes to men.

Not that night, though. That night I had to be wild and carefree and in love with being home. The world was my oyster and nothing could touch me. I'd survived a year in a warzone getting shot at, after all. The states were a cake walk after that, right?

Not so much.

It was quick when it happened. I didn't even see it coming. He'd isolated me from my friends without me even realizing it. Before I knew it, I was held tightly against him and his teeth were in my neck. Then I was discarded like so much trash. Woke up the next night lying on a gurney being wheeled to the morgue. I scared the daylights out of the attendee when I sat up in my body bag.

There were a lot of screams exchanged between the two of us before it was assumed the doctors had made a mistake in pronouncing me dead on arrival.

The authorities were called. My statement was taken and then they called my military chain of command.

Lucky for me, the captain on duty owed me big. Even luckier, he was part of this new world I suddenly found myself in. He's the one who got me put on profile, allowing me to stay in my room during the day and ultimately processed out of the military. That last one I'm still not too happy about, but it couldn't be helped. What good is a soldier who's useless from the time the sun rises to the time it sets?

He even got me the job with Hermes. Not that that's saying much, but it keeps me from having to move back in with my parents.

I pulled a tub of cottage cheese out of the display case and eyed it with uncertainty. I used to love cottage cheese, but ever since my change it tasted funny.

Shrugging, I put it in my cart. Just because I bought it didn't mean I had to eat it. People from my old life still stopped by now and then. They'd expect me to have some health food in the fridge. It's what the old me would have done. I was careful to show them what they wanted. It was safer for everyone that way.

The bottom of my cart barely littered with items, I headed to check out. Being in the grocery store was depressing me tonight. It reminded me of all the things I'd lost. I hated getting maudlin. What's done is done. Truthfully, most nights being a vampire wasn't so bad.

My sneakers squeaked against the linoleum as I wheeled my cart over to the cashier, bypassing the self-pay kiosks. The ones at this store tended to go a bit buggy after midnight. Even if they worked perfectly, I would have chosen the cashier. I needed human interaction.

I placed my groceries on the belt and wheeled my cart to the other end. The cashier's face was bored as he slid each item over the scanner. He was a college kid, his face all sharp angles and so incredibly young.

"That'll be $21.06."

I handed him a twenty and a five dollar bill. He took it, hitting the cash button on the register. It beeped but didn't open.

"What?" The cashier looked slightly more alert now. He hit the button twice more. "Come on. Not again."

He felt along the register, the boredom now completely gone from his eyes and his motions becoming slightly more frantic when he didn't immediately find what he was looking for.

"Oh no. No. No. No. My manager will kill me if I've lost the key again."

Out of the corner of my eye, I saw a pair of translucent wings disappear behind one of my plastic bags. Pixies. Great. I'd have to avoid this place for the next few weeks until the little bastards moved on.

Pixies were the magpies of the supernatural world. They tended to appropriate things that interested them only to discard them soon after. A lot of times when humans misplaced things, it was pixies at work. They love mischief and helping someone "lose" an item is right up their alley.

On one of my first jobs, a few managed to stow away in my messenger bag. I was new and still trying to figure this whole world out. I didn't know to guard against the pests. Hell, I hadn't even known what they were. They'd made life impossible in my home for nearly two months before they got bored and moved on. More than a year and half later, I still found things they'd hidden in the most random places.

I was not going to chance them hopping a ride again.

Taking pity on the cashier, I pointed to the bags. "Have you checked the bags yet? You may have placed it over there."

The cashier rounded on me, "The key never moves. It should be right here."

I held my hands up and motioned for him to calm down. "Hey, just trying to be helpful. Obviously the key has moved. Might as well check the area thoroughly before panicking."

Rolling his eyes to make it obvious he was just humoring me, he rustled through the bags.

"I don't see-" His voice trailed off and he held up the key.

He looked at me suspiciously. I shrugged.

He didn't say anything as he unlocked the drawer and gave me my change.

I smiled and told him to have a nice day as I grabbed my bags and walked out. As soon as I was through the doors, I dumped everything on the ground and shook the bags out. I inspected every item thoroughly before putting them back in the plastic bag.

Groceries taken care of, I headed home. My apartment was a one bedroom walk up located right outside the campus district. I'm about eighty percent sure the rickety wooden staircase leading to the second floor entrance wasn't up to code.

My place was small, and while the area wasn't rough it also wasn't nice. Most of my neighbors were college kids or grad students.

Things went missing around here all the time so I hoisted my bike onto my shoulder and carried it up the stairs. A porch light illuminated the steps, not that I really needed it. Vampirism came with improved night vision. I'd say I had the vision equivalent of a cat if I knew what that equivalent was.

At the top of the landing, I propped the bike against the rail and reached into my mailbox. Pulling a cinnamon spice container out, I shrugged off my bag before emptying its contents on to the wooden landing. I liberally doused everything with the cinnamon and shook it a few times over my bag.

A soft sneeze, and then something darted past me, faster than my eyes could track.

Ha. Served the little bastard right.

Pixies disliked cinnamon. It affected them much like ragweed affected humans only about three times worse. They wouldn't linger long in an area that contained it.

11

It was one of the most effective, low cost methods I'd found for warding off pests. Much cheaper than a charm from a witch and just as effective.

Satisfied no other pixies lurked in my items, I dumped everything back into the bag and wheeled the bike inside, propping it inside the entryway.

My kitchen was small, just a fridge, stove and microwave, with barely any counter space. Since food was optional for me, I didn't really need counter space any more. It only took a few minutes to pack away my groceries.

I grabbed a wine glass out of the cupboard and fished a bottle from the fridge. The dark liquid was mesmerizing as I poured it into my glass. I unconsciously licked my lips, my stomach rumbling. I was already anticipating that first sip.

The blood tasted cool and crisp as it slid down my throat. I could practically feel the tissues soaking up the liquid. In seconds, it was gone.

I set the glass down, licking my lips free of any blood. God, I'd really needed that.

A stray spot of red drew my eye to the counter. I stared at it transfixed. I must have spilled a drop.

My eyes drifted to the clock. 1:07. I didn't have it in me to walk away from that drop, but I could wait. I had enough discipline for that. Five minutes. If I ever wanted to have full control of myself, I needed to start exercising will power.

I could do this. No problem.

My finger tapped against the counter anxiously. I let go and crossed my arms in front of me. My eyes never strayed from that drop.

Imagine the worst craving you've ever had. You know, the kind you get for that last piece of pizza after a stressful day at work. You've been thinking about it all day and remembering how it tasted last night and imagining the hot cheese on your tongue, the springy dough as you bit into it. Now take that craving and magnify it by a factor of about ten. That might give you some idea of what it's like to crave blood.

I'd be tempted to compare it to how a junky feels staring down their next fix, but I've never done drugs so I can't be sure of that.

Either way, blood was addicting and damn near impossible to resist. I was determined though. I was getting better at fighting temptation too. When I'd first been brought over, I would have licked that drop away almost as soon as it hit the counter. I also would have licked the entire glass in an attempt to get every speck of the life giving nectar.

These little exercises in self-restraint were torturous but oh so necessary. One day it might even save someone's life.

And time.

The five minutes were up. I forced myself to use my finger to swipe it up rather than just licking it. My tongue darted out to catch the drop. My eyes closed in bliss. So good.

I recapped the bottle, putting it back in the fridge where it had plenty of company.

Feeling good now that I'd had a top up, I changed into a pair of pink flannel pants and a loose t-shirt before grabbing a bag of chips and settling onto the couch.

What should I watch tonight? I'd just finished a sci-fi show last night and was in the mood for something different. Drama? Nah, I needed something a little more light hearted than that.

I navigated to one of the funnier shows on my list and sat back, prepared to follow Nathan Fillion around as he solved crime while keeping up a running stream of banter with his female costar.

Chapter Two

The odor of burned meat called me from my death-like slumber. Under that smell, another one tantalized and teased. Drool pooled in my mouth. Whatever it was promised relief from this fire consuming my throat.

Someone was in my apartment.

My eyes still closed, I held myself still while every instinct urged me to track down the source of the temptation.

The sound of fat sizzled on the stove.

My gums ached. The fangs starting to slide out. My fingers clenched around my pillow as I wrestled with my inner hunger. My thoughts spiraled down to blood. Need. Thirst. My skin suddenly too tight for my body. I shivered.

"Aileen, you up yet? It's nearly eight pm," my sister said from the bedroom doorway. "I know how much you like to sleep, but this is ridiculous. Even for you."

I didn't answer, curling tighter into a ball.

I would not eat my sister. I would not eat my sister. No matter how obnoxious I found her sometimes.

I held myself very still, afraid that even one small movement would cause me to snap.

At last, her footsteps receded down the hall.

With the promise of yummy, warm blood fading to more tolerable levels, I cautiously uncurled from my ball.

Shit. What the hell was she doing here? I'd told everyone in my family that drop-ins were not welcome under any circumstances.

Didn't matter right now.

I needed to focus. I sat up and slid my feet to the floor. The craving was growing every moment that smell teased my senses. I needed to get to my wine bottle and top off. Once I'd taken care of my hunger, I wouldn't be tempted to drain my sister.

Yes. I just had to get to the blood, then everything would be alright.

I shuffled down the hall, moving as slowly and carefully as my eighty-year-old, arthritic grandma. Even with my focus rapt on the fridge, I could hear Jenna's heartbeat. It was such a lovely sound. I could dance to it, swaying to the rhythm.

Before I'd realized it, I was several steps closer to her. I stopped and gripped the counter, my fingertips digging into the cheap vinyl.

I refused to eat my sister. I backtracked, heading for the fridge. This night would not begin in a bloodbath.

The fridge's handle was cool in my hand, I opened it and bent down to find nothing. I shuffled the few items inside around to be sure. Nope. It wasn't there.

"Where's the wine bottle?" My voice was rough and harsh to my ears.

There was a moment of silence. I resisted the urge to look at Jenna. I couldn't be sure I wouldn't attack her.

"Jenna?"

"I thought we could do without the wine tonight."

She thought. I rested my forehead against the freezer door. The fridge handle creaked ominously in my hand.

"You thought? And why is that?" My voice was flat.

"Mom's right. You have a drinking problem. Ignoring it will only make things worse."

"Where is it?"

There was a pause. Jenna took a deep breath. "I threw it out."

I screamed, a low sound of pain and rage. My fist flew at the freezer, the skin on my knuckles splitting and healing almost simultaneously.

Jenna backed away from me, fear in her face. I bore down on her, fury giving the room a red tinge. I thrust my face close to Jenna's.

15

"This is my God damn house. You do not come into my house and throw shit away. You don't get to do whatever you please."

Jenna's eyes welled with tears. "I was just trying to help."

Trying to help? She was going to get herself killed.

I steeled myself against her tears. In the past, I'd always been a sucker whenever she pulled them out, caving quickly. She couldn't afford for me to do that this time.

"You were not invited here, yet you throw my stuff away and think to lecture me. Who the fuck do you think you are?"

Jenna's eyes fell from mine. She stared at the head of lettuce in her hands. I closed my eyes and counted backwards from ten.

"It's in the bathroom," she said softly.

Without a word, I whirled and headed for the bathroom, locking the door after me. She'd stashed the wine under the sink. If I'd been in possession of my faculties, I could have just sniffed the damn thing out. The hunger and close proximity of Jenna's tempting blood had short circuited my senses.

Tilting my head back, I drained the bottle in three huge gulps. I could practically feel my parched cells soaking up the life giving liquid, soothing the fire inside. Lowering the bottle, I caught sight of the stranger in the mirror. Dark circles under her bloodshot eyes, pale translucent skin. I barely recognized myself. Worse was the look of starved desperation on my face. It was a look that said I'd do anything for my next fix. No wonder my family thought I was an alcoholic. My actions in the kitchen certainly had done nothing to allay that image.

The worst thing about being a vampire, and the part I hated the most, was the blood lust. The craving turned me into someone else. Something else. Something dangerous.

The stranger in the mirror bowed her head. Hiding wouldn't change things. It never did. Being depressed and cursing my fate wouldn't either.

I corked the wine bottle and placed it gently in the trash before picking up my tooth brush and giving my teeth a good scrub.

Time to go see if I could salvage the situation with my sister.

The good news was that I'd always been territorial when it came to my stuff. I once glued every drawer in my room shut to prevent my sister from borrowing my clothes. I wore the same outfit for nearly a month before our parents instituted a new set of rules where everything in my room was off limits unless I said otherwise. It hadn't mattered to me that I'd been stuck in the same clothes. It was the principle of the thing. It helped that I'd also sentenced her to the same fate by gluing her dresser drawers closed as well.

She knew exactly what my reaction would be to her coming in and throwing something of mine away. It's why she hadn't dumped the contents and why she'd cooked me a meal. She was hoping to get on my good side. She had just underestimated the depth of my reaction.

I dressed before heading back to the kitchen where I leaned against the counter, watching as she set the table. She avoided looking at me as she moved around my space.

A stranger wouldn't be able to tell we were sisters. Jenna took after our mom, both were on the shorter side with bright blue eyes, and blond hair that had reddish highlights, whereas my hair was dark brown with a reddish tint when the light hit it just right, and my eyes were closer to gray than blue.

I should probably start with an apology. No reason to damage our relationship further.

"How did you get into my apartment?"

On the other hand an apology might encourage her to do it again.

She gave all her attention to setting the table as if this was a test and setting the fork down just so would make everything better. "Your landlord let me into the apartment when I told him I was your sister and wanted to do something nice for you."

"Did he now? I'll have to speak with him about letting strangers into my place."

Jenna set the plates she'd been loading the steak onto down hard. "What is wrong with you? I'm your sister, not some stranger off the street."

"There's nothing wrong with me."

"Yes, there is. You've always been territorial, but you've never been physically violent."

I straightened. "I wouldn't lay a hand on you."

"I didn't know that," Jenna said. "You scared me. You backed me against the wall and acted like you were going to hurt me if I didn't tell you what you wanted to know."

This time it was me who had trouble meeting her eyes.

"You won't even let us come to visit you."

"You know I don't like it when people just drop by. I've told you and everyone else to call before you come over."

"Why? So you can make up some excuse to get out of a visit?" she said.

"That's not true."

She gave me a look. The one our mom used to give us to let us know she was on to our game. "The last four times I've called to set up lunch or a movie you've always had some reason why you couldn't get together."

Well yeah. Vampires couldn't go out during the day. At least this one, anyway. I couldn't tell her that, though.

"Of course I have an excuse. I work nights. Day time is when I sleep. Sorry I don't interrupt my sleep schedule to keep you amused."

She ignored the sarcasm. "Why are you even working in that job? You have a degree. Mom and Dad didn't put you through college so you could be a delivery girl. You still have the GI Bill if you need more education."

"Is that why you're here? To talk to me about my job?"

My baby sister was lecturing me about my life decisions. Great. A thought occurred to me. "Did Mom put you up to this?"

"No, of course not."

I could tell by the way she avoided my eyes that she was lying. I stayed silent. She'd never been able to resist talking if one of us just waited her out.

"So what if she did," Jenna burst out. "She's worried about you."

My laugh was harsh. "Of course she is. I'm not on the path she planned for me."

"You know it's not that," Jenna protested.

I arched an eyebrow at her. We both knew that wasn't true. My mom had been disappointed in me ever since I had graduated college and decided to join the military and fight for my country, instead of going on to get my law degree.

"Tell her and everyone else that I'm fine."

Jenna voice was sad when she asked, "Are you? The first thing you did when you woke up was head for the wine. You got violently angry when you thought you couldn't get your fix. You know what that's a sign of."

"Spare me the sanctimonious preaching Miss Unwed-Mom."

Jenna looked like I'd slapped her. She bowed her head and adjusted the plates. I shouldn't have said that. I'd gone too far bringing Linda into this. Linda's father was Jenna's only mistake. He was a married businessman who knocked her up and then refused to take any responsibility for his actions.

"Jenna, I'm sorry."

Jenna held up a hand, stopping me.

"Whether you want to admit it or not, you need help."

"And we're done." I pushed away from the counter and grabbed my jacket from where I'd thrown it over the couch. I'd heard this speech before.

"I have to go to work. Please see yourself out and leave the key on the counter."

"What about dinner?"

"Not hungry."

"But-"

"Put it in the fridge. I'll eat it later."

I grabbed my bike and headed out the door, not even bothering to lock it behind me. The door only slightly muffled the sound of crying. I pressed one hand against the cool wood.

"I'm sorry, Jenna," I whispered. But this is something you can't help me with, and I can't explain without putting you and myself in danger.

19

Every point she made was valid. What she hadn't said, but what everyone in my family was thinking, was that I'd come back from Afghanistan changed. They attributed it to some form of PTSD or a problem with alcohol. They thought I was having trouble adjusting to civilian life again and that my job was a symptom of my problems.

They were wrong, but I couldn't explain that without revealing what I was.

The number one rule of my new world was to keep its existence a secret. Breaking that rule meant death for everyone involved. Since I didn't want to see my friends and family die, that meant sucking it up and letting them think what they would.

My phone chimed, signaling I had a new text.

I dug it out of my pants pocket, thankful I'd had the presence of mind to grab it when I was getting dressed. Without it, I wouldn't know what jobs Hermes assigned me.

The message said, 'Come into the office. Now.'

Huh. Most jobs were assigned by text. It meant I only had to go into the office when I needed to fill out paper work which was rare. In fact, I think I'd only been into the office five times in the nearly two years I'd worked for Hermes.

Guess I was heading in.

* * *

Thirty minutes later I parked my bike in front of an old brick building in the Warehouse District. The area was a little run down and many of the buildings around here were abandoned, but recently there'd been a resurgence of interest in this part of town. Luxury housing companies started buying up the warehouses and converting them into high end apartments. Young professionals were willing to pay top dollar for the open floor plans, exposed brick and an old feeling.

I doubted Hermes office building would be among that revitalization. Hermes' owner, Jerry, was old, though you'd never know it to look at him, and he didn't like change. That's what I'd heard anyway. I'd only met him a handful of times since coming back to the city.

I walked around the building to a door with a keypad next to it. That was new.

This might be a problem. I didn't know the code.

My phone chimed. The text message had 4649# on it.

Convenient.

I looked around but couldn't see any cameras or people watching. Not that I really expected to. The few times I had met Jerry he had really embraced the whole creepy 'I know what you're thinking before you do' air of mystery.

I inputted the code and wasn't particularly surprised when it lit green and the lock clicked open.

The inside was at total odds with the run down exterior. The enormous expanse looked taken care of and well lit. Lights turned on one by one, highlighting a raised dais in the middle of the warehouse. Despite the fact there were no internal walls, the dais looked like any high end office with a nice rug covering wooden floors, and several leather chairs arranged in front of a cherry oak desk.

I blinked, noticing the stern mountain of a man bent over the desk and the red headed woman standing next to him with an armful of papers.

My steps echoed in the wide open space as I headed toward the quasi office. Neither of the figures at the desk turned to pay me any attention, continuing with their work as if they couldn't hear my approach.

Reaching the dais, I paused, unsure of the protocol. There wasn't a door to knock on and it seemed rude to just step up onto the wood. Last time I'd been called into the office, it hadn't looked like this. There had been actual rooms with walls.

"You may have a seat." Jerry's low base voice rumbled through the air.

I stepped up, my footsteps almost instantly muffled by the thick woven rug. There were four chairs to choose from. I picked the closest.

Jerry and his assistant, a woman I hadn't seen before, kept working, leaving me fidgeting in my seat.

Was I supposed to initiate the conversation? He had summoned me. Not the other way around.

"Blood," the red head said suddenly.

I jerked, barely stopping myself from holding my hand up to my mouth and huffing. Did my breath stink? I'd brushed this morning but perhaps hadn't taken as much time as I should have given the drama going on in my house. Some species in the supernatural world had a heightened sense of smell and could detect when you rushed your hygiene.

"Would you like me to get you a bottle of blood?" she enunciated slowly when I didn't respond.

Oh. Jerry must have told her what I was. That was the second time in as many days that someone had ambushed me with the knowledge.

"No. I drank before I came."

Her face didn't shift expression, but it felt like she sniffed disdainfully.

Naw, I was being paranoid.

"Aileen," Jerry rumbled, "how long have you been with us?"

Slightly thrown by the shift in topic but hoping the question would lead to me getting more responsibility and by extension more money, I answered, "Just under two years."

"Twenty months and twelve days," the woman inserted.

"That sounds about right," I answered slowly.

If they knew down to the day, why bother asking the question?

"How do you like things so far?" Jerry leaned back in his chair, the leather creaking under his bulk.

I fumbled for an appropriate response. Somehow I didn't think either of the two would appreciate the word 'ok'. "It's interesting."

Jerry tapped a folder in front of him. "Looks like you have a perfect record in your deliveries."

I opened my mouth to respond but was cut off by the woman. "You cut it close last night."

"Yes, there was an accident on Fifth."

"We don't need excuses," Jerry said.

That was a familiar refrain from my days in the military. I almost let it pass, but I wasn't in the military anymore. I didn't have to play by its rules.

"It wasn't an excuse; it was an explanation. As you can see from my record, I ended up making the delivery on time."

Both stared blankly at me.

"Am I in trouble for something?" I asked.

"Should you be?" the woman asked.

I could feel my temper rising and took a deep breath. Anger made me hungry. Hunger made me dangerous. I was pretty sure Jerry could wipe the floor with me if it came down to it.

"I don't know," I said. "But it's certainly starting to feel like it."

"You're not in trouble, Aileen," Jerry assured me. "We're just trying to determine if you're qualified for a job with special circumstances."

Intrigued, I asked, "What sort of job?"

"The kind where you don't ask questions," the woman said.

Ignoring her, I spoke to Jerry. "Why haven't you reached out to one of your other couriers?"

As much as I would like to think my hard work had earned me this chance, I knew better. All of his other couriers had been doing this much longer than me. They were also much more powerful than me and didn't come with as much baggage.

"They're otherwise engaged," Jerry said.

"Ruth?"

"She's on her way to Beijing."

"Harry or Catriona?"

"Harry's on bedrest after an encounter with a siren and Catriona is out on a different delivery. Everyone is out."

"So it's not that you think I'm qualified, it's that I'm your only choice."

His lips tightened as he dipped his head in a small nod.

I sat back. If Jerry was willing to risk his company's reputation on me, this job must be important. That meant danger. And lots of it.

"How dangerous?"

"Your cut would be $10,000."

"So life threatening then."

Jerry grunted.

I'd never made more than $500 on a job. I was lucky to get away with a few broken bones, and minor cuts and bruises up and down my entire right side on that job. I couldn't even imagine how dangerous a $10,000 job would be.

My brain couldn't help tallying up the bills I could pay with that sum. I could even put a little away for a rainy day. Get some breathing room.

"Think I'll pass."

As welcome as that money would be, I couldn't spend it if I was dead.

The two exchanged a look. The woman tilted her head at me and nodded. Jerry sighed and picked up a pen, twirling it between his fingers.

"Refusal isn't really an option at this point," he said.

I stiffened. "Since when?"

"The fact is that you weren't hired under our normal methods," the woman inserted, taking over for Jerry. "Our shielding you from detection could have extreme consequences for us."

I looked from her to Jerry then leaned back, slinging an arm over the back of my chair. For all that he was the boss, Jerry looked trapped. His face said he wanted to be anywhere but here.

"Uh huh," I said slowly. "And?"

"We need you to start bringing more revenue to the table," she said crisply. "In essence, you'll start by being assigned higher profile jobs. We expect you to complete those to satisfaction."

Right. Higher profile jobs. I.e. more dangerous, life threatening jobs.

The slow burn of my temper kicked up a notch. I didn't need the money or this job bad enough.

"Guess that means I'm fired then," I said.

"No, no, that's not what we're saying," Jerry hurried to insert.

"What are you saying then?"

There was another shared glance. Once again the woman took the lead, "We would like you to take this job."

"Pass."

The woman's face turned dark, and she opened her mouth to speak. It was quite entertaining to watch. Made my smart ass comment worth it.

Jerry got there first. "Aileen, I would take it as a personal favor if you were to do this job."

That might change things.

One thing I'd learned since my transformation was that favors carried more weight than money. A favor from an influential or powerful being was worth a lot. They could be collected and called in at the owner's leisure. You never knew when something like that would come in handy. It's how I got this job in the first place. If it hadn't been for that favor the captain called in, I would be in a very different place. One not quite as comfortable and one that definitely would have meant letting my family think I was dead.

"Any limits to this favor?"

"Nothing that will put this organization at risk."

"Not a very useful favor then," I observed.

"You're not really in a position to negotiate," the woman said. "Think of what would happen if word of your existence got round to the wrong people."

Vampires were rare. Very rare. We were supposedly powerful, though you couldn't tell that from me, but we took time to grow into that power. For the supernatural world, I was basically the equivalent of an infant.

Vampires also existed in clans or families. It was practice that if one of the vampires in a clan managed to successfully turn a baby vamp, their progeny would be raised in the clan for one hundred years. It was basically an indentured service. A sort of 'hey, thanks for totally disrupting my life. Now let me devote the next hundred years to your interests and goals and pray you don't get me killed in the meantime.'

Not really something I wanted any part of. I'd had enough of being the good little soldier while in the Army. Don't get me wrong. Being a soldier was one of the best, most worthwhile things I'd done. It gave me discipline, made me grow up and opened my eyes in ways that most civilians will never experience. I wouldn't change a minute of it even if I knew I'd end up as a vampire, never again to sit on the beach roasting myself under the summer sun.

Besides, I'd never been much of a joiner, the sole exception being the Army.

"So you're threatening me now?" I asked, looking back at Jerry.

"No, that's not what we're doing." He quelled the woman with a look. "I'm asking that you step out of your comfort zone to do me a favor."

He must have been pretty desperate to push like this. It made me wonder why he didn't just do the delivery himself or send the woman. I still hadn't quite figure out what she was but from the confrontational way she positioned herself at his shoulder I assumed she had some power. That or she just wasn't afraid of the baby vamp.

It would be a mistake to take this job.

"Fifteen thousand and no limit on the favor."

"You-"

"Done," Jerry said firmly.

I nearly whistled in appreciation. Hadn't really thought he would go for my conditions.

He selected a folder to the right of him and slid it over to me. Though her face hadn't changed expression since I sat down, the woman's presence nearly boiled with frustration. It was unsettling. Most people, their eyes shift, their mouths smile or tighten. They fidget or gesture. This woman could have been a statue.

I couldn't figure out what she was. Not a witch. For all their power, they were very human in appearance. She didn't have the same feel as a shifter.

"This has all the information you need. The pickup is near Easton. You need to be there by ten or the punishment clause will kick in."

"And that is?"

"That's between you and the client. You'll get more details from him once you make the pickup."

Already I was rethinking my agreement in taking this job. It was a quarter after nine now. It would take me nearly an hour to ride my bike all the way over to that area of town.

Before I could protest, Jerry reached into the desk drawer next to him and withdrew keys. I caught them before they could hit my head.

"Take Cherry. Your bike isn't going to be fast enough for this job."

I stared at him wordlessly.

What sort of job was this? And who the hell warranted this level of caution?

The keys were scarier than the veiled and not so veiled threats of before. Cherry was Jerry's baby. She was a candy apple red 68 Ford Mustang GT/CS, hence her name. I'd never heard of Jerry lending her to anyone. He did, however, break every bone in a gnome's arm when he had the audacity to touch Cherry's paint with his dirty hands.

I stood. Jerry's attention shifted back to the paperwork in front of him.

"And Aileen, I don't think I have to tell you to bring her back in the same condition I lent her to you in."

I nodded quickly. "Of course."

My footsteps echoed in the warehouse as I stepped down from the dais and walked away. My priorities for that money had shifted. It was now earmarked for a down payment on a car. I never wanted circumstances to force me to borrow Cherry again. My luck was just not that good. Hopefully, it would hold out for the night and I could return the car to Jerry undamaged.

Chapter Three

"I'm here to see Mr. Barret," I told the receptionist, who was busy typing.

"Name."

"Aileen Travers."

"He doesn't take walk-ins. Please schedule an appointment and then come back," she said without lifting her eyes from the computer.

"He should be expecting me. I have an appointment for ten."

The clacking of the keys paused, and the receptionist finally looked up. She scanned me skeptically. I fought not to fidget. I couldn't help being a bit self-conscious in my tight athletic spandex pants and bright yellow fleece. I'd thrown a beanie over my hair before I left the house, and I was wearing my fingerless gloves. I'd dressed for riding my bike in fall. It was hardly the professional attire she was probably used to.

She pulled up a screen on her computer. "There is only one appointment for ten."

"Yes, it should be for Hermes Couriers."

She arched one eyebrow. "You're with Hermes?"

Nobody ever believed I was with Hermes. I didn't know what it was about me that caused such doubt.

I reached into my messenger bag and pulled out my employee ID, holding it out so she could see.

"Please take a seat until you're called." She pointed one long finger at a trio of uncomfortable, modern looking chairs.

I checked my watch. It was 9:50. I had ten minutes before the pickup time. I could wait and hope he consented to see me before the deadline. On the other hand, this could be a test to see if I had the assertiveness needed for this job.

I'd never been one for waiting.

Ignoring the protestation behind me, I walked over to the double doors and pushed them open. Since there was no real attempt to stop me, I assumed I'd made the right choice. It was easy to find my way as the double doors led to a hallway, which led to a conference room unlike any I had ever seen.

It was nearly the size of a basketball court, which by itself would have been amazing considering this building didn't look big enough to house a room of that size. The show stopper, the thing that made me catch my breath and drew my attention upward, was the night sky twinkling on the ceiling. It wasn't a projection or painting either. The clouds actually moved, obscuring some of the stars. The moon looked so close and bright that I felt I only needed to reach out my hand to touch it. The sky was as beautiful as any I had seen in the mountains of Afghanistan. Better because I knew it should have been impossible to see from this room or even in Columbus. Too much light pollution here to see the sky with this clarity. If not for the four walls surrounding me, I would have sworn I was standing in a field far from the city staring up.

I'd always had a thing for the stars. Once upon a time I wanted to be an astronaut or at the very least an astronomer. If not for my very real deadline, I could have spent hours staring.

"Magic," I said softly. It was impressive. Probably more than any I'd yet seen.

"How very astute," a voice said from right behind me.

I jumped and whirled around.

No one was there.

I searched the shadows, for the first time noticing that much of the room was hidden from me. I should have been able to see into every corner of this room as if it was daylight.

Looks like magic was good for more than turning a ceiling into the sky.

"A vampire." I turned again only to find nothing. "I knew Jerry had one on the payroll but never thought he'd send one to work for a sorcerer."

Sorcerer? Great. Nobody played well with sorcerers. No wonder Jerry had been desperate for me to take the run. His other couriers had probably refused or made up some excuse to get out of this.

All sorcerers cared about was gaining power. Things like ethics never really bothered them. Most were extremely powerful and not afraid of throwing their weight around.

Sorcerers were scary, but nature had balanced that by making them extremely rare. Only about one person in a couple million possessed the gene needed to become a sorcerer. Even then, it required years of study and discipline. Most never even awoke to their power.

Right now, I knew of only two sorcerers in Columbus. One was assumed dead. A victim of the unknown baddy plaguing the supernatural community.

Didn't even know what the delivery was and already I was beginning to hate this gig.

He had to be throwing his voice or something. No doubt he was trying to intimidate me. I wouldn't play his game. He wanted to appear like he was invisible? I'd treat him as such. No need to jump and turn for his amusement.

I turned my eyes back to the ceiling. It went against every instinct I had to deliberately ignore the presence of a potential hostile, but it would be impossible to spot the sorcerer unless he wanted to be seen.

"Tell me about the job," I said.

I wanted the particulars so I could get this run started. The sooner it was over, the sooner I could get back to ferrying things around for less terrifying clients.

And I would never again accept another job without all of the details.

There was a long pause. The weight of his regard fell on me, sizing me up as a scientist would a rare bug. I held still and tried to project more confidence than I currently felt.

"No, I think not," the voice said.

I started. "What about the delivery?"

"I have no need of a vampire. Tell Jerry to send another."

My mouth dropped open.

What? He'd barely met me. How could he assume on the basis of a glance that I wasn't up for this?

"Jerry's not sending someone else. It's me or no one," I said. Inside, I was seething. I hadn't exactly been thrilled about this gig, but I'd be damned if some sorcerer who was too afraid to let me catch sight of him was going to tell me I couldn't do it.

The indefinable presence, which had been retreating, rushed back. It was odd, but I felt his power brushing against my skin just as surely as I would have a breeze. It buzzed and tingled. I'd never felt anything like it.

"If I say I want someone else, he will send me another."

I let a smirk show. "Nope. You get what you get. You don't like it; you can use another service. It's in the contract you signed."

There was a pause where I could feel the presence consider.

"You did read the contract, didn't you?" I wasn't able to resist injecting a little sarcasm into the proceedings.

The power briefly whipped against my skin. I winced as the sensation edged towards pain. Guess he hadn't.

"Fine. Have it your way. I was trying to be nice, but it was obviously a wasted effort."

Looked like I'd won this little skirmish.

"Since the baby vamp has decided she wants to play ball with the big boys, I'll indulge you. Don't complain to me if you get broken."

"What makes you think I'm barely turned?"

Did I have a sign on me saying "baby vamp"?

The voice scoffed. "Please. You practically scream it. It's in the way you move, the lack of power you project. You're so new you're practically still a human. I bet one blow to your heart would be enough to kill you."

His hand touched the back of my neck. I whirled only to be met with thin air. Again.

I touched my neck. The warmth of his hand lingered.

"Do you want this package delivered or not?"

"Why wouldn't Jerry send someone else?" the voice abruptly asked.

I wasn't ready for the question and took a moment to answer.

The voice sighed. "Nobody else wanted the job, I bet."

I don't know what made me offer up the excuse Jerry had given me. "He said everyone else was already out on assignment."

He could make of that what he would.

"The message needs to be delivered by midnight. Denise has the location and item. See her on your way out."

I blinked. Guess that meant I'd gotten the job. I turned to go.

"It is absolutely vital the message be delivered by midnight. If you fail to meet the terms of the contract, your punishment will be to act as my familiar for fifty years."

I sucked in a breath. That was a very long time.

"I trust that won't be a problem."

I could feel the voice smirking.

Too late to turn back now.

I smiled. "No, of course not."

I wouldn't let it be a problem. The only way that clause kicked in was if I failed in my assignment. I just needed to ensure I didn't fail.

"I hope not. Let me be clear. If you fail, I will make your next fifty years feel like the worst pits of hell."

"Guess there's not a moment to lose then."

I strode out of the room. I'd make that delivery on time even if it killed me. My next fifty years were riding on it.

* * *

Denise's directions led me to a bar on High Street just north of Clintonville. It was a small hole in the wall called Lou's Bar and had been around since anybody could remember. I must have passed it a hundred times over the years, always with the intention of returning sometime to get a drink when I had a spare moment. I never did and now I had to wonder if that was because of the very cleverly hidden 'keep away' charm I could feel even from where I was parked a block away.

Werewolves. And from the noise coming out of the place, I'd guess there were a lot of them.

I looked at the address one last time. I was in the right place. According to my directions, I needed to get to the office in the back of the establishment. That's where I'd find one Franklin Wade. He was the one I needed to sign for the package.

What could a sorcerer want with a bunch of werewolves? As far as I knew, there were no special ties between the two sects. Werewolves tended to keep away from outsiders. They preferred the company of their pack. I'd only met a couple of lone wolves in passing. Jerry employed one, but the wolf kept mostly to himself so I'd never been able to get any good intel.

No use standing around debating the possible connection. There was still a half hour before the deadline, but I wanted this done and over with.

I stepped out of the car and turned the key in the lock. The car was old and lacked some of the modern conveniences of a car made in the last decade, such as manual locks. I wasn't taking any chances with Cherry.

Putting my hands in my pocket, I strode up to the bar. Two men stepped in front of me before I could get in the door.

"Private party," the bigger of the two said.

They were both mammoth size, towering over me by nearly a foot. I wasn't a small woman, standing at five feet seven inches, but these guys made me feel downright tiny by comparison. They were about two of me wide.

I gave them my most professional smile. "Delivery from Hermes for a Franklin Wade."

They shared a look. I waited as patiently as I could, feeling the smile turn stiff and unwieldy on my face.

"Hand it over then," the smaller one said, reaching for my bag with one oversized mitt.

I touched the messenger bag and stepped back to avoid him. "Whoa. No one touches the bag but me. You know the rules. The only person who gets the package is the person it's intended for."

"Little human, you are not getting in here," the big guy rumbled.

Finally. Someone who thought I was human.

"Then call Wade out here. I don't care where the delivery is made as long as it's done."

The smaller one's eyes turned amber, and suddenly it was a wolf looking out at me from the human face.

I froze, not wanting to incite him to possible violence. I would be lying if I said a part of me didn't wish I had just given him the package as he requested. The two of them seemed like fine, upstanding werewolves. I'm sure they would have gotten it where it was supposed to go.

No. I couldn't do that. Besides the fact that it would violate Hermes policy, it would be impossible to hide from the Hermes app on my phone which was designed to register delivery to the right person.

He leaned forward and sniffed, drawing a lungful of my scent into his lungs.

"Doesn't smell of deceit," he told the other one.

Discreetly, I sniffed at my collar. All I smelled was me. What did deceit even smell like?

"I'll go see if I can find him," the smaller one said.

The big one grunted and slid over to more fully block the doorway as the small one ducked inside. Sound poured out and was cut off as soon as the door closed again.

"That's a pretty impressive sound dampener," I said.

The man watched me silently.

After another moment of awkwardness where he glared at me and I looked everywhere but at his eyes, I said, "Great talk."

I checked my phone. I'd wasted five minutes trying to get into the bar. That left me fifteen minutes to make the delivery. I tried not to think of all the things that could go wrong in those next fifteen minutes. Things like if he wasn't in the bar or if they couldn't find him in time. It had sounded like it was packed in there.

The small one stepped out, the noise level rising and then dropping once the door closed again. No one accompanied him.

"Couldn't find him."

"That's not possible," I said. "The directions said this was the place."

"Don't know what to tell ya. I didn't see him in there."

I looked over his shoulder. "Maybe if I could just take a look."

I stepped forward only to be brought up short by the big one's hand hard against my shoulder.

"Not gonna happen. No humans allowed."

"Great. I'm not human."

He looked me over skeptically as if to say 'could have fooled me.'

The other one said impatiently, "Doesn't matter what you are. You're not getting in here. Only pack or friends of the pack allowed. You're neither."

"But-"

A low growl rumbled from the big ones chest. I shut my mouth and stepped back. Both of their eyes shimmered amber. I didn't think I was imagining things when it looked like the bones under their skin rippled, as if they were planning to rearrange themselves.

Holding up my hands, I backed further away. They waited until I was on the street before going back inside.

This was not good.

I checked my phone again. Seven minutes left.

He had to be in the bar. It was my only hope. If he'd left, I had no way of tracking him so I'd assume luck was on my side and the smaller werewolf had simply missed him in his walk through. Maybe he'd been in the bathroom.

That meant I just had to find another way into the bar. Easy. Right.

These places always had a back entrance. I think it had something to do with the fire code. There had to be two exits to an establishment of this size. I'd just work my way back there and see if it was as well guarded as the front.

It took only a few seconds to walk around and find the alley the bar let out on. I crinkled my nose at the strong odor of decay. I didn't know what they were putting in their dumpsters, but it smelled foul.

I was in luck. Nobody challenged me even when I pulled open the door, which thankfully wasn't locked, and made my way inside.

It was a little surprising, actually. For people who didn't want any outsiders in their bar, they didn't do a very good job of securing the perimeter. I expected some type of lookout in the rear entrance given the giants at the front. Maybe they thought the keep away charm would dissuade persistent strangers.

The smell of blood stopped me. My fangs lengthened as the first sharp tang of iron hit my senses. I found myself turning towards a door midway down the hall as if in a dream. The blood called to me. I could practically taste it.

I opened the door and stopped short, shocked out of my bloodlust.

A dark haired man knelt over a figure on the floor. His sharp blue eyes met mine, pinning me in place. I couldn't move, my thoughts scattered and unable to assemble as his gaze held me spellbound.

A distant part of me noted the fangs protruding from his mouth and the puddle of blood spreading out from the body on the ground. A body that was currently in several pieces.

The scrape of a shoe in the hallway distracted me enough to break the stranger's gaze. The smaller of the front door werewolves stared at me in surprise.

"How did you-?" His eyes shifted to amber as he lifted his nose to sniff at the air. "Blood."

In the next moment, he shouldered me aside and let loose an eerie howl at the sight of the body on the ground.

The man with the beautiful blue eyes was gone.

In the next moment, someone grabbed the back of my jacket and threw me into the wall behind me. My head banged hard against the plaster. I saw stars. I didn't have a chance to do much more than blink before a snarling face was in mine. The owner of that face lifted me off my feet, bringing me still closer.

Growls filled the hallway as men and some women caught the scent of what was in the room.

This wasn't looking good.

"Murderer," the half transformed face lisped at me.

He raised one furry, clawed hand. If that landed, I didn't know if I could survive. I kicked out, landing a solid blow against his stomach. He grunted, his grip loosening.

"Enough." The voice came from the room, halting the half-man in front of me. "Brax will want to see her."

My captor turned back to me, a row full of very sharp teeth on full display. Seeing the intention in his eyes, I tried to duck as one fist caught me on the side of my head. Darkness rose up to greet me.

*   *   *

Ugh. My head felt like an elephant was tap dancing on it. Blood coated my tongue. Please tell me I hadn't hit the bars and snacked on one of the college kids. The ensuing hangover would last all night. I hated being hung over.

I opened my eyes to find myself the focus of several sets of angry glares. Oh right. The knowledge of the body and the very angry werewolves came rushing back to me.

Hah, this was so much worse than a hangover.

My head protested as I drew myself up to sitting. That must have been quite the blow he gave me if my enhanced healing hadn't fixed it. By the pounding in my head, I was guessing a normal human wouldn't have survived. At least not without brain damage.

Score one for being a vampire.

I was leaning against a wall in the bar area. Someone had turned the lights on full and the juke box off. At least twenty or thirty people were crammed into the room. Lucky me, it was standing room only. A few even perched on the bar.

Despite the various hostile glares aimed my way, I found my attention drawn to the man sitting calmly at a table directly in front of me, my messenger bag at his feet. Power rose off him, coating my skin like a warm blanket. He was like a bonfire on a cold night, full of life saving warmth that beckoned you but would burn if you got too close.

"You're not human," he observed.

When growls met my attempt to stand, I settled back down. Guess I'd be seated for this conversation.

"Never said I was," I told him. "Actually, I'm pretty sure I specifically told your doormen that I wasn't human."

His gaze shifted to the small giant from before. The man gave a slight dip of the chin.

"Did you kill my man?" the alpha asked. That's the only person this could be. He spoke with too much authority and assurance to be anyone else. Maybe one of the enforcers but I doubted it with the way the pack had created a small oasis of space around him.

"Of course I didn't," I said. "Besides the fact I didn't even know him, I don't have the strength to do what was done to the body."

"Lie," the big guy said. "He's the man you asked for at the door."

"That was Franklin Wade?" I asked. A stony face gave me the answer. "Crap."

This was not good. My already bad position just got worse.

"I don't suppose you'd be willing to sign for a delivery in his stead as Alpha?" I asked.

Growls rose from the crowd gathered around us.

The man stood and walked towards me. He crouched and leaned close, sniffing me.

"Not human," he growled.

Claws slowly slid out of his fingertips, gouging the wood floor on either side on my legs. It was one of the scariest things I'd ever seen. Made more terrifying by the perfect control with which he did it and the fierce, ice blue gaze that remained fixed on mine.

"Yes, but that doesn't mean I killed your man. Look, I'm with Hermes. I picked up a package earlier tonight with instructions to deliver it to Lou's Bar where a Franklin Wade was supposed to be waiting."

I pressed myself hard against the wall behind me. It wouldn't save me, but it kept me from curling into a sweat soaked ball.

"How did you get in the back?" The voice that came from him was human only in the fact that it used words. The tone was guttural and so deep it vibrated in my bones.

"I walked through the door leading to the alley."

"Impossible," the big guy from the front door said. "We have people watching that entrance. They would have stopped you."

"There was no one there when I came in. I didn't sense anyone until I smelled the blood."

The alpha's eyes sharpened. "Then what?"

I didn't think he wanted to hear about how I momentarily lost control and was on my way to drink down the owner of that tasty smelling blood.

"I went to see what was wrong and saw a man standing over the body. Then your guy over there startled me and when I turned back the man was gone."

"Declan?"

The small giant's face was thoughtful as he said, "I saw her standing outside the office door and recognized her from earlier. Then I smelled the blood and ran into the room. I didn't see any man."

"There was definitely a man," I said.

"She could be lying," a woman said from her perch on the bar. Her hair was curly and wild around her head. It matched the feral beauty of her face.

"Look, I assume with all the sniffing you guys have been doing that you can smell if I had Wade's blood on me. Given the way Declan happened upon me, I wouldn't have had time to hide the blood from your senses."

"Could be magic," someone else said.

"Or she could have a partner."

"What reason would I have to kill your pack mate?" I asked.

"That is a good question," the alpha said. "What did the man you said you saw look like?"

That was easy.

I struggled to remember.

"Uh. He had blue eyes."

His face was blurry in my memory.

"Brown hair?" I couldn't help the question in my voice.

Why couldn't I remember? Maybe the blow to the head had rattled my brain more than I thought.

"She's making this up," the woman said. "She can't even come up with a convincing description."

"Oh. Fangs."

I think. No. I was eighty percent sure.

The alpha's mouth tightened.

"A vampire would explain why she can't remember very clearly," Declan said. "He would have been able to cloud her mind."

I didn't know they could do that. You would think Jerry or even the Captain would have clued me in. I could have been practicing all along. It would make paying my rent so much easier.

"A vampire didn't kill Franklin," the alpha said.

That cleared me. If I was willing to reveal what I was. I'd like to avoid that if at all possible. Especially with a vampire now in the mix.

Fifty years in service to a sorcerer or a hundred years shut up in a vampire clan. I'd pick neither.

"Look, you can check with Hermes. They can verify my story."

"Oh we will," the alpha said. "That still won't clear you, and in the meantime you'll be our guest of honor."

He stood and walked away.

Wait. He didn't understand. I climbed to my knees but was grabbed roughly by my arms before I could make it any further.

"Wait, you don't understand. I need someone to sign for that package. I'll be in a lot of trouble if I don't deliver it."

The two men who had hold of me began dragging me out of the room, ignoring my struggles.

No, it couldn't end like this. No way was I going to let myself end up as a sorcerer's stooge.

"Please. I just need my phone and a thumbprint."

The alpha ignored me as his men pulled me away. My eyes landed on the clock. 12:03.

I went limp. It was too late. They picked me up, holding me suspended between them by my arms.

I let them carry me out of the room, down the hall and into the basement. They threw me into a cell. I flinched as the door clanged shut. I didn't say anything as they walked out, talking about the Buckeye's chances of winning the next game.

Fifty years. I couldn't believe it. After all my hard work staying off any of the major player's radar, I'd signed away half a century of my life for a measly fifteen thousand dollars.

Could I even be held accountable if the person I was making the delivery to died before the deadline? No, of course not. That would be ridiculous. Not to mention impossible. I was a vampire not a necromancer.

The sorcerer would just have to understand that I put in a good faith effort but was prevented from doing my job by forces I couldn't control.

I looked around, hope giving me renewed purpose. This was an old building. The basement was small, damp, and surprisingly well fortified. It held at least four cells that I could see. It looked like they pounded the bars into the ground and then poured the cement in after them. There were even bars on the ceiling and against the cement blocks of the foundation.

I grabbed one and yelped. The skin on the palm of my hand was angry red and blistered. Silver. They'd coated the damn things in silver.

Who did that? For that matter, what kind of people had cages in their basement? Not normal ones, that's for sure.

Looked like I wasn't going anywhere for the moment. At least there wasn't a window in here. I wouldn't want to fry in the morning sun.

I settled down onto a cot in the middle of the cell. There were no blankets or pillows but at least they'd provided a place to rest. Such nice captors.

The hours crawled by at an agonizing pace. There was nothing to do but worry. I passed some of the time by singing all the Army cadence's I knew. That didn't last long as I'd forgotten a lot of them in the short time I'd been out. Trying to sing any song I remembered didn't last long. My memory had always been kind of bad when it came to remembering lyrics. After the fifth repetition of 'The Itsy Bitsy Spider', I gave up on singing.

I laid back on the cot and stared at the bars above me.

I'd met a vampire and hadn't even realized it until the werewolves pointed it out to me. How sad was that?

My knowledge of this world was exceedingly small even after two years. Some of that was because I had no reliable mentor. Everything had to be picked up on the fly. It didn't make for a well-rounded education.

On the other hand, I'd made no real attempt to further my understanding, preferring to bury my head in the sand. What I didn't know couldn't hurt me. Or so I told myself.

That truth wouldn't hold for much longer. Not knowing about myself or the spooks around me was going to get me hurt or killed. I needed to find someone I could trust to teach me what I didn't know.

For better or worse, I'd picked this way of life when I decided against declaring myself to the clans. I needed to own that decision. I didn't survive a year in Afghanistan being shot at with mortars and dodging IEDs, and then live through my transformation to vampirism to let my ignorance get me killed now.

If I got out of this in one piece, things would have to change. I'd have to make more of an effort to learn about this world. It was the only way to keep myself safe.

The heavy thud of footsteps distracted me from my thoughts.

Heat bathed my skin and lightning snapped at my fingertips as the alpha's power preceded him down the steps.

I remained reclining with my arms folded behind my head. The picture of relaxation.

He came to a stop in front of my cell.

The silence grew between us.

So, Mr. King of All He Surveys, what did you discover?

The scent of blood clinging to him told me exactly what he'd been up to in the past few hours.

"What are you?"

Huh. Of all the things he could ask, I hadn't expected that one.

"Didn't your mother ever tell you it's rude to ask that?"

Common etiquette among the spooks discouraged that kind of question. Some species were rare and hunted by the others. Also, it was a sign of status and power to be able to determine what brand of freak you were.

Maybe he wasn't as powerful as I'd assumed.

"Didn't yours tell you it was rude to break into someone else's home?" he asked.

"I didn't know bars counted as homes now." I sat up on my elbows, giving him a pitying look. "Was the recession a little tough on you? Forced you to bed down in a bar?"

"Smart mouth from the one in a silver cage."

I looked around me. "True. Wonder how long it will be until Jerry finds out you have physically assaulted and detained one of his couriers while on a delivery. Wouldn't want to be you when he does. I'll take my cage and smart mouth over his wrath any day."

"I have no proof you're a courier. Only your word. Someone found you standing over a body killed in much the same way as several others found this summer."

I rolled my eyes. "I wasn't found standing over the body. I was in the doorway leading to a room with the body. Big difference."

"Who asked you to deliver the message?"

"Ah, ah. That's privileged information."

"Your intended recipient is dead. That excuse no longer holds weight."

I sat the rest of the way up, folding my legs under me. "My client still lives. And while he does, that information remains secret unless he instructs me otherwise."

He folded his arms across his chest and pinned me with a glare. I'm sure it was the same kind he gave to many a rebellious pack member. They probably quelled and showed their belly to signal their submission to his superior will. Me, it bounced off barely registering as a glare.

"Tell me about what was in the package."

"Privileged."

He snarled. I couldn't help the smile that spread across my face. He'd kept me in here for hours. It felt good to get some of my own back.

I figured the only reason he was down here asking me questions was because he couldn't get my bag open to get at the message. It wouldn't open for anyone but me. It's how Jerry ensured the contents of a delivery remained confidential even in the event of a mugging. He also probably couldn't break through the security both technical and magical on my phone.

"You were willing to have me sign for the package. How is this any different?"

Wondered when he would get around to that.

"But you didn't sign for the package. Because you didn't, you can't see what's in it."

I got a little thrill from being able to throw that back into his face.

"I'll sign now."

"Nope. It's too late now. The delivery deadline has come and gone."

There was no point in telling him the deadline had passed even before I'd asked him to sign for it in the first place.

"We could torture you," he said.

"You could, but it wouldn't do you much good. That bag won't even open for me at this point."

His face looked like it was chiseled in stone. Didn't like that, did he?

Good. Perhaps he should have signed for the damn package when he had the chance.

My last statement was complete bullshit of course. I could open the bag anytime I wanted. I just wasn't in the mood to cooperate after sitting in here all night.

"Tell me again how you broke into my bar."

"I've already told you this. Again, I didn't break into anything. I turned the knob and walked in."

"You saw nothing?"

"No. I saw nothing. There was no one guarding the entrance. I didn't even realize anything was wrong until I smelled the blood."

"Did you sense anything? Smell anything?"

I pushed down my frustration, knowing it was pointless to give into it. Besides the fact I was convinced the alpha would look at me with that blank expression that said I was a child if I threw a tantrum, it would serve no purpose and get me out of here no faster.

"Again, no, I didn't sense anything."

But I did smell something.

"You've thought of something."

He stepped closer to the bars.

I thought it was the dumpster, but maybe it had been something else. It had smelled of dead and decaying things. I thought a raccoon or something had died in it or behind it.

"How bad does your dumpster normally reek?" I asked.

"That's it? Our dumpster smelled?" He didn't seem convinced.

I sighed. "Look, I may have smelled something, but I can't be sure. That area was pretty ripe, but I don't know if that's normal."

"I smelled nothing unusual when I checked earlier."

"Perhaps whatever was there left right before I passed through," I said, thinking aloud. "Did you ever find out what happened to the guards who were supposed to be on duty?"

"They both said they were relieved by someone but can't remember who."

That didn't help much. What I needed was to get back to that dumpster to see if it smelled the same.

Metal scraped against metal. I looked up to see the alpha holding a key in one gloved hand.

"What's this? You're letting me go after all that?"

Not that I planned to complain if he did.

He gave me a sharp toothed grin. "We're going to test your theory and see if the smell was in your imagination or not."

Oh. That made a lot more sense.

"I warn you. If you try to escape, my wolves will rip you apart."

"Ah. How nice of them. All of your guests must feel so at home with your hospitality."

He took me by the arm, his grip firm but not painful. "We're werewolves. We don't have guests; we have dinner."

How comforting.

*   *   *

The alley looked much the same as it had when I passed through earlier. The only difference being the four werewolves eyeing me like I was a juicy rabbit they'd like to pounce on.

I took a deep breath.

That was the other difference. The foul odor I smelled on my way in was gone. I couldn't believe I thought it was the dumpster. I'd been so focused on finishing my delivery on time I'd missed a vital hint that something was not as it should be.

It occurred to me that it was a good thing I hadn't been any earlier. I must have missed whatever did this by scant minutes for the smell to be that pronounced.

"Anything?" the feral woman from the bar top asked.

"Yeah. The thing I smelled when I came in is gone."

"How can we be sure she's not making this up?" a strange wolf asked.

"We can't," Declan said, examining the surrounding area. He took a careful sniff of the air. "Even if whatever caused the smell is gone, I should still be able to catch something."

For that matter, the smell should have continued into the bar. It hadn't. At least I didn't think it had. It's possible I hadn't noticed the difference.

I examined the alley. There had to be something they'd missed.

"Could they have had a dampener?" I looked up to find four sets of eyes once again on me.

Brax was the one to ask, "What do you mean a dampener?"

46

I straightened and looked around. The woman and stranger looked disgruntled and suspicious, while Brax and Declan regarded me with a steady gaze.

"Like what you have in the bar but instead of hiding sound it hides smell."

"Then how would you have been able to pick up the scent," the woman challenged.

"Proximity? Bad timing? A sound dampener can hide sound, but if you get too close it doesn't work. I assume something that hides smells would work the same way. I could have just come through the alley right after the murderer left the bar."

Declan looked over at his alpha, "It could explain why I didn't smell blood until she opened the office door. We should have smelled something the moment he was wounded."

I shrugged at the skepticism the others aimed my way. "It's what I would use if I wanted to murder someone in a bar of super sniffers."

Brax bent his head and rubbed his jaw. "Shit. That would mean a witch is involved in this somehow."

No one looked happy with that assessment.

He tilted his jaw at me. "Return her to the cage then report back. We need to compare this to the other scene now that there's possible new information."

The woman nodded and glared at me, tilting her head toward the bar when I didn't move fast enough.

Guess they were done speaking with the captive. The other three had already walked away, leaving just the woman and me.

The sky was beginning to show the faintest signs of sunrise. It was a barely discernable lightening of black. Given my present limitations, I'd had a lot of experience guessing when that pesky ball of fire in the sky was going to start playing havoc with my life. Didn't want to get caught out without cover. By the looks of things, I had an hour, maybe an hour and a half, before dawn.

I might not get a better chance. I needed to make my move now. If I waited any longer, they'd know what I was when the sun rose.

There wasn't a window in the basement to light me up, but the coma like slumber would be a dead giveaway to anyone with half a brain.

I couldn't let her put me back in the cage. I was never going to be able to get out of that. Not unless I learned how to pick a lock in the next hundred steps.

Bolting wouldn't work either. As a werewolf she'd probably beat me in speed. At least I assumed that was the case since Brax trusted she was strong enough to escort me back to the cage.

Or did he? Perhaps he was counting on me seizing this chance so he could trick me into lowering my guard. He could be waiting for me to lead him back to my client. It would be the sort of thing an experienced hunter would do. Track its prey back to its den.

No. I couldn't think like that. I'd psych myself out of taking any action. Remaining wasn't an option if I wanted my secrets to stay secret.

My moment came on the stairs leading to the basement. I waited until she nudged me to continue down into the dark before twisting to the side and sticking my foot between her legs. I timed it perfectly. Waiting until right before she completed a step.

It threw her off balance and allowed me to help her tumble down the stairs, leaving me standing at the top. I don't care how fast or strong you are. I just need the right leverage to take you down. Of course, if I'd mistimed my move by even a little, it'd be me taking the tumble.

Chapter Four

I was out the door and in the alley before she even finished falling. A howl rose from the basement.

I cringed. It was so loud.

I needed to get to Jerry's car before her racket alerted the pack. I ran in that direction.

Another howl rose. You would have thought the basement would at least muffle the sound a little. From around the block, several other voices lifted in answer.

I ground to a halt. At least a few of them sounded like they were coming from the direction I needed to go.

Shit. They'd catch me before I could reach the car. Or worse they'd catch me after I got in the car and damage it trying to get me out.

Okay, new plan. I'd leave the car behind and return for it later.

Decision made, I wasted no time in changing course, taking off between two buildings, running through several backyards and hopping more than one fence.

Two streets over I nearly ran headfirst into a pool, swerving at the last minute and yelping when a shadow flew past me, landing in the water with a splash. The smell of wet dog and the sound of yips told me the shadow was a werewolf. I hadn't even seen the beast until it missed me.

They were hunting me. Needed to move faster.

I leapt another fence. It was near impossible to listen for the sound of pursuit over my own clumsy fumbling. They probably didn't even have to use their noses to get my scent. They could just listen for the elephant currently stomping all over someone's rose bushes.

The smell of my own blood rose to greet me when one of the thorns scratched me. Great. Another way to announce my presence. Why didn't I just run along shouting, "Here! Here!" and save them the trouble of tracking me?

Seeing a dumpster behind an apartment complex, I darted towards it. The smell was not pleasant. Not nearly as bad as the murderer's smell but not a perfume I wanted on me either. It would do the job. I jumped in and stomped on the bags a few times then hopped back out.

I paused before running off again. Wouldn't they be able to still tell it was me? My scent marker led directly to the dumpster. By simple process of elimination, it would be easy to tell that the dumpster smell running away from the site was me.

I didn't know how sensitive a werewolf's nose was. All I had to go on was urban fantasy fiction books. They all seemed to think the nose was pretty sensitive. Just like a working dog's. They could sniff out bombs and drugs. Stood to reason a werewolf's nose could do something similar.

I was overthinking this.

The roof wasn't that far up. I could take it and drop onto the other side of the building. Might confuse them for a little bit.

I took a running start, hopping onto the dumpster then leaping up to grab a window ledge. I used it to hoist myself up and over to a drain pipe that I used to climb to the roof. My bad ass ninja skills strike again. I should try out for America's Ninja Warrior at some point. I'd be a natural.

Once back on the ground, I took off, doubling back several times to disguise my trail as much as possible before dawn. I had no idea if it was effective or not. Most evasion tactics I knew were designed to evade humans not dogs.

Near dawn, I found an abandoned building to hide out in. I didn't want to go home in case I led the wolves' right to my door step. If was I still free and alive tomorrow, I'd take the chance.

The basement felt like the safest place to find shelter from the sun so it was with considerable reluctance that I headed down there. You'd think given my status as a big, bad vampire that I wouldn't be afraid of whatever monsters might lurk in the dark. That wasn't the case. I was just as afraid as I'd ever been. Maybe a little bit more.

The ground was hard as I waited for the last bit of night to fade. As the blackness on the inside of my lids rushed up to claim me, I could only hope I'd done a good enough job hiding my trail.

* * *

"Are you kidding me? A basement?"

I came to wakefulness with a start.

"What are you doing down here?"

A kid, no more than sixteen or seventeen, glared down at me.

I looked around in confusion. I was still in the basement. A dim light flickered overhead. Last night it wouldn't turn on no matter how many times I flicked the switch.

"Well?"

The teenage boy was looking at me expectantly.

Was he talking to me?

Naw. He'd have to be beyond stupid to confront a stranger in a basement.

Unless he was a teenage punk who got his kicks messing with women he thought he could bully. Well, he'd be in for a surprise then. I was feeling kind of peckish after all the activity last night.

"Well, what?" I finally asked.

Now that I thought about it, why wasn't I hungrier? Yesterday I was nearly willing to rip apart my sister to get to all that lovely blood. Today, a slight pang of hunger. Maybe I was getting a handle on this appetite of mine.

"Why the basement?" he asked, sounding very put out.

I looked around and shrugged. "It feels safe."

He rolled his eyes. "Whatever. It doesn't even matter. After the way you've screwed up, you'll be lucky to sleep anywhere but six feet under from now on."

I paid closer attention to the boy. He was tall and gangly, as if he'd had a growth spurt and now didn't know what to do with all the extra length. His face was nice enough. He'd probably be a handsome man in a few years. Right now, he was all angles and bones with a beautiful pair of green eyes.

He spoke like I knew him, but he didn't look at all familiar.

"Do I know you?" I asked.

He frowned at me. I fought a laugh. He probably meant for me to be intimidated, but after the alpha's stare from last night, he just seemed kind of comical.

"Do you know me?" he semi shouted. "I'm just the guy whose delivery you screwed up."

I straightened. He had to be some type of supernatural. "I'm pretty sure I'd remember if I had ever done a job for you."

"Does this ring a bell?" his voice deepened and the room darkened as if someone had dialed down the light. Shadows flew from the corners to wrap around him like a cloak, rendering him invisible.

"The sorcerer is a kid?" I asked.

This was weird, even for this world. How could a sixteen year old boy have enough power to scare an entire city to such an extent that they didn't even call him by name? Just the Sorcerer, like Cher or Madonna.

The shadows flew apart leaving the boy standing there glaring at me in affront.

"I'm not a kid. I'm over fifty years old."

I blinked. Impossible.

"Uh huh."

His lips turned down giving him a mulish expression. The air charged and an arc of green light snapped from him, zapping me and sending me flying into the cement blocks behind me.

My head knocked against the wall. Lights exploded behind my eyelids. I slid to the ground. I could barely move and everything hurt. It felt like someone had frozen my lungs, making it impossible to draw a full breath.

That's how I found out that vampires didn't really need to breathe. That didn't stop my lungs from trying though.

I managed to get a look at my chest, expecting to see charred flesh. There were small singe marks on my shirt, but it and the flesh below were whole and undamaged.

Everything in me hurt. It felt like I'd stuck my finger in a high voltage socket, only maybe worse. My mouth tasted like old pennies.

When I had enough saliva in my mouth to speak, I asked, "What the hell?"

He shrugged, not looking the least bit guilty. "I felt like you needed a little help to process my appearance."

More like torture.

I drew myself up to sitting. My legs didn't feel quite steady enough to attempt standing.

A soft green light gathered around his hands. "Do you need another demonstration?"

"Alright. Alright. I believe you. You're the sorcerer."

The light dyed.

"Still doesn't explain why you look like a sixteen-year-old kid," I muttered.

A tiny light, no bigger than a hair, nipped at my leg. It felt like a vicious pinch.

"You don't need to know," he told me, drawing himself up to his full height and giving me another glare.

Guess he was a little sensitive about how young he looked.

"You owe me fifty years of service for failing to meet your part of our arrangement." The cracking in his voice ruined his attempt at intimidation.

I'd been afraid that was coming. I had planned to talk with Jerry to clarify what happened if the recipient was dead before delivery before speaking with the sorcerer again. Looked like that wasn't going to happen.

"Guy was dead when I got there." I'd just have to figure this out myself. He couldn't hold me to the contract if the guy was already dead.

"Impossible."

It didn't seem like he was talking to me. Instead, he stared off into space, the fingers of one hand tapping against his chin.

"Went to the bar like you asked. Even snuck in the back entrance when they said he wasn't there. I smelled blood and when I went to investigate I found your guy lying on the ground, dead, with a vampire crouched over him."

That brought his attention back to me. The room became silent as he sunk back into thought. I waited.

"This is the absolute worst possible scenario," he muttered.

I wondered what he'd hoped to accomplish with his package. Had it been the reason the recipient was killed? Or was it just a weird coincidence?

"Alright, give it to me."

I looked at him blankly.

"Give what to you?"

"My package," he said impatiently.

"Um. I don't have it."

I'd left it and my messenger bag behind when I escaped from the werewolves.

The air pressure built and little arcs of dark green light darted through the air. I pressed myself against the basement wall. I did not want to get hit by one of those things again. Once had been enough

"I need that package." His voice went deep and eerie like he was speaking from a great distance and yet right next to me at the same time. Power throbbed through every word.

"Your package is safe. It's still in my bag."

The power lifted a little and backed off. It wasn't much, but at least I could breathe again.

"What is to stop someone from simply going through the bag and taking what's there?"

"It's keyed to me. They've already tried and couldn't get through. It's safe until we get my bag back," I told him.

The green light faded until just a few fairy lights darted around his hands.

"Looks like we are at an impasse," he said. "You failed in the task I gave you, and worse you left my item behind to save your own skin. This is not the type of service I expect from a courier from Hermes Courier Service."

He had me there. Jerry was going to be furious over the cluster fuck of last night. I might have had ground to stand on if I'd managed to snag the bag on my way out.

"What are we to do about this?" he said.

I eyed him. Although he had a serious look on his face, I could tell he was just seconds away from cackling like some two bit storybook villain.

Playing along, I asked in a dead pan voice, "Yes, what are we to do?"

He clapped his hands. Was that glee on his face?

"I'm so glad you asked."

Oh boy, I didn't have a good feeling about this.

"You see, even though you failed to deliver my package and then left it behind, I'm willing to overlook everything as long as you're willing to perform one minor service for me. I'd even be willing to forgo the punishment clause and put a good word in with your boss."

I perked up at that. Maybe this situation could be turned to my advantage after all.

I shouldn't get ahead of myself. This service could be anything.

"What would I have to do?" I asked.

He smiled at me. "Nothing much. You just need to help me recover an item and find a murderer."

"A murderer? Oh no. You're on your own with that."

Who did he think I was? The police? No way did I have the skills or physical power to apprehend a murderer. Most spooks in this world could tear through a baby vamp like tissue paper.

"Is that so?" he asked.

"It is."

He nodded and the green lights winked out. I let go of the breath I was holding. I didn't think it would be that easy. I thought there would have been a bit of an argument from him. Pushing, slapping, and maybe zapping me with that green lightning from before.

A slicing pain radiated from my chest, coursing down my limbs, paralyzing me with agony. The pain froze my arms and legs and I fell onto my back jerking slightly. I couldn't move no matter how I begged my body to obey me. All I could do was gurgle. A high pitched whine escaped me.

"I guess I'll take my fifty years of service beginning now."

What was he doing to me? It was difficult to think with the pain ripping my senses apart.

"I've never kept a vampire before. I'll have to think of the best ways to put you to use. This will take some thought. You're so young and you don't have much power. It would be entirely too easy to break you. Yes, this is going to take some considerable thought."

He smiled down at me, delighting in all the plans he had going on in that little sorcerer's brain of his.

The pain abruptly shut off. I drew in a sharp breath. Even the absence of pain hurt in a weird, aching way.

He crouched down next to me. "Of course, you can make this all go away by agreeing to help me out."

Yeah and I could just give up on living a long and healthy afterlife while I was at it.

"No?" he asked.

The fingers of his hand flicked. The pain turned back on, made more intense by the absence of before. I shook and whined as it coursed through every nerve ending. It was akin to the feeling of being hit by a thousand lightning bolts at once. Blood trickled out of my ears.

It turned off. I sobbed for breath.

"How about now?" he asked.

"You're crazy," I gritted out.

His eyes were deadly serious as he said, "What I am is desperate. You help me out and this can all go away. Otherwise-"

The pain came back, the strength of which bent my back nearly in half as I arched and jerked. It dissipated almost at once.

"Okay, okay," I shouted when he lifted his hand again.

I couldn't take fifty years of this. I had to take the offer and hope the added time would give me a way out of my predicament.

"I'll do it. Just stop whatever you're doing."

I must have imagined the sigh of relief he gave. That or whatever he'd done had busted my eardrums and was making me hear things. There couldn't be much out there that scared the big, bad sorcerer.

I dragged myself up to sitting, not wanting to have this conversation lying on my back. My dignity was already smarting from the smack down I'd got from the teenage looking sorcerer.

"Great. I knew you'd agree. I just had to incentivize you."

Oh, he'd done that alright.

He started to help me to stand but backed away when I smacked his hands and glared.

I wiped the blood from under my nose. Whatever he'd done must have given me a nosebleed in addition to the ear bleed. "Tell me exactly what I have to do."

Suddenly he seemed every inch the teenager as he rushed to explain. "Okay, well, I'd hoped to have the werewolf help me in this, but since he's dead, you'll have to do."

"What was in the package?" I didn't need to hear how I was his emergency choice.

"It had information about all of the murders and disappearances that have been happening since the summer. I was helping the werewolf figure out who's been orchestrating all of this. We were close too. He was supposed to send something back with you. It was something he said was the cause of everything that's happened." He stopped in his recitation and looked at me hopefully. "I don't suppose you saw a package lying around addressed to me?"

I shook my head. All I'd seen was a pile of broken limbs, blood and a piercing set of blue eyes. There could have been a house sized package lying next to all that with the sorcerer's name scrawled on it in big block letters, and I never would have noticed.

He looked disappointed.

"So this killer you want me to find. It wouldn't be the person who has been running around town killing supes all summer would it? The same one that's been on the human news, the one killing and hiding the bodies of all those people?"

"That's the one."

He was crazy. Totally crazy.

"You're crazy. No way am I going after that guy. He'd squash me like a bug. One of my life goals is to not be killed by dismemberment. You might as well get back to the torture part of things."

"You're not going to die." He thought a minute and shrugged. "Probably. Anyway, it's too late now. You've already agreed."

"I take it back."

He frowned at me. "You can't do that."

Ha.

"Watch me."

He gave me a pitying look. "No. You really can't do that. Check your arm."

I looked down at my sleeve covered arm but saw nothing.

He rolled his eyes and grabbed one arm. I flinched back.

His grip tightened, pulling me forward. "Stop that. I just need to show you the mark."

He rolled the sleeve up on my right arm, exposing the forearm. There, on the underside of the arm about an inch or two below the bend of the elbow, was a pale silver tattoo of a stylized lion wrapped in thorns. Looking closer, I realized the tattoo wasn't silver, or at least not only silver. It had purple glints in it, almost like someone had embedded metallic purple thread in the dye.

Where did this come from? I would have remembered if I'd gotten a tattoo like this.

"What the hell is this?"

He sighed. "It's a sorcerer's bond. The mark announces and formalizes any agreement you've entered into with a sorcerer. Once you've completed your task, it'll disappear. How can you not know this? Honestly, I'm amazed you've survived this long."

I gaped down at it. Sorcerer's bond? I'd never heard of such a thing. And when did I enter into any sort of agreement?

"When you said 'I'll do it. Just stop whatever you're doing,'" the sorcerer said.

I grabbed him by the shirt and pulled him close, letting my fangs slide out. "Are you reading my mind?"

He scowled at me and gently touched the tattoo. The skin caught fire and I screamed, shoving the sorcerer away from me.

"Of course not. Your face said everything I needed to know. You should really learn to hide your thoughts. Being so transparent is only going to get you in trouble."

I cradled my arm to my chest, hissing at the brush of cloth against the sensitive skin. That hurt.

"How can something that simple be an agreement?" I asked through gritted teeth. "We didn't even discuss terms."

"Any verbal agreement is enough to bind you into a contract. You said you'd do it, hence the mark. It's not my fault you failed to clarify things before you agreed. This is magic 101. Do the vampires teach their young anything anymore?"

They probably did, but since I was never trained, I'd missed out on all the basic knowledge. Wish Jerry had taken the time to explain that little tidbit before sending me off on this job.

Not that it mattered. It didn't change the fact I wasn't going after the murderer. He'd gone through some of the highest members of the supernatural community like they were tissue paper. It's why hysteria was building in the city after every attack. If some of the most powerful beings in the city couldn't do anything about him, there was zero chance I'd be able to apprehend or kill him. I'd take the forfeit over certain death, thank you.

"I'm still not going after him," I told the sorcerer.

"I hope you'll reconsider," he said. "The tattoo will kill you otherwise."

"I thought you said it was fifty years of servitude?"

"It's double or nothing now. You do this, and you're free to go on your merry way. Fail and you owe me a hundred years. If you don't even try, you'll die."

He hadn't said anything about a hundred years or death in any of our dealings. I cursed my lack of knowledge. If I'd known that a simple slip of the tongue could get me committed to something, I would have guarded my words much more carefully.

He watched me with a nasty smile on his young face. "Guess you know now why everyone gives sorcerers such a wide berth. I'm not used to being able to bend someone to my needs so easily. I could get used to this."

After this, I would be joining the masses in keeping away from sorcerers.

"Guess I'll be working with you after all," I said, with a grin that was closer to a baring of teeth.

There was no real choice. I just had to hope I could figure some way to take out the murderer. My entire life had been a series of triumphing against stacked odds. Why should this be any different?

"Somehow I knew you'd come around to my way of thinking."

Yeah, yeah. He was smarter than me.

"Let's get on with it. If you know who the murderer is, oh smart one, point me in the right direction."

"I didn't say I knew who it was. The package you were to deliver was supposed to help the werewolf put the last of the pieces together."

"Okay, so if it had everything he needed, you should be able to put the clues together to come up with a name."

He folded his arms over his chest and scuffed one shoe against the cement. "If I knew what that information said, you would be right. As it stands, I don't."

I didn't get it. He'd put the information together. Shouldn't he be able to remember what it said?

"How can you not know?" I asked. "You said you were the one who recovered the clues."

"That may have been a bit of an overstatement."

"How big of an overstatement?"

"I wasn't actually the one who assembled the information. Someone else did that."

Unbelievable.

"So it should be easy to find that person and ask him what we need to know."

"Yes. It should be easy for you to find him."

He looked at me meaningfully. I narrowed my eyes at him. Parts of his story didn't add up. If this was as important to him as he said, shouldn't he want to keep a much closer eye on things? I know I would be supervising closely a job of this magnitude. Especially if I thought my employee had already screwed up a critical piece of the job. For that matter, why was he asking me, the person who'd already failed once, to do this? He had to have others waiting in the wings. Why a baby vamp?

"And where will you be while I'm questioning this guy?" I asked.

He lifted one shoulder. "Around. It's not really any of your business is it? That's why you're my employee for the moment. I tell you what to do, not the other way around."

Hm. I'd already been burned by this guy once. Twice if you counted the cluster that was the delivery time and place.

It was clear he wasn't to be trusted. My gut told me he was hiding a lot. For the moment, I didn't have a lot of choices so I'd go along with his plans until I could figure out a way to get out of this fool agreement.

"Here." He tossed me a small metal charm. I caught it and turned it over in my hands.

"What's this? A necklace. Not sure it'll do me a lot of good with the killer."

He rolled his eyes. "No, you twit. It's an amulet. Break it and it'll call me to your side."

Hm. That could come in handy.

The teenage looking sorcerer gave me the name and address of where I could meet his guy and took off to wherever sorcerers went in their spare time.

Picking up Cherry was easy compared to last night. If there were any werewolves around, they were well hidden when I strolled up to the bright red mustang. Even better, there wasn't a single scratch on her. Jerry would leave my head in place for another day.

The address the sorcerer gave me was on the edge of the Arena District, close to the heart of downtown. Prior to my change, I had spent many a night on the town down here with my friends. It was the entertainment center of the city and some of the hottest clubs and restaurants made their stand along Park Street, which ran down the middle of the district. A lot of the bigger companies kept apartments and condos in the area as temporary housing for employees looking to relocate to the area.

I had avoided it since moving back to the city. I'd heard vampires had their fingers in every club down here. It was the perfect place for hunting. Plenty of young, healthy and inebriated people looking for a good time and not particularly on their guard.

The sorcerer's contact lived and worked in one of the condos, so despite my misgivings, I found myself parking in one of the garages and walking the three blocks there.

The complex was one of the new builds. The brick was beautiful, and the land around the four story building charmingly landscaped. Nestled down a brick walkway, it was off the main thoroughfare and had its own underground parking garage. I couldn't help being impressed and slightly disgusted at the same time. The place was nice and in the heart of everything. You could step out your door and find yourself at any point downtown in just a few minutes. For someone who loved being in the middle of everything and wanted to be surrounded by a lively atmosphere, the place was perfect.

It was also obscenely expensive. My parents had looked at a couple of these when they were first built, thinking that with two kids in college it might be nice to move closer to everything. They quickly changed their mind at the price tag.

My guy was on the third floor, condo 315. Getting in had been as simple as waiting for a resident to happen along and then asking them to hold the door. I had several shopping bags filled with tissue paper and rocks to help sell the image.

The lady hadn't even questioned me. All this fancy security and it didn't' mean squat unless the residents were willing to follow the rules. I could have been a serial killer for all she knew.

I knocked on the door and waited, looking up and down the hall. When no one answered, I knocked again. I already knew it was useless. If anybody had been home, I would have heard them moving around.

I didn't really want to wait around all night in vamp territory. I couldn't lurk outside in the hall all night either. Even if this place had lax security, they were bound to get suspicious of someone lingering in the hall for hours. I couldn't even wait outside for him to come home because I had no idea what he looked like.

That left breaking in.

I reached into my back pocket and grabbed my library card. It didn't get as much use these days and if it broke I could easily get a new one. It turns out, TV had it semi right when they showed people breaking into houses with the use of a credit card. I discovered this trick after locking myself out of my apartment for the third time in less than a week. It didn't work on every lock, but the generic, cheap ones were too easy to get through. If his deadbolt was engaged, I was screwed. This trick wouldn't get me through a deadbolt.

My mad breaking and entering skills turned out to be unnecessary; the door knob turned easily in my hand before I could use the card.

The door swung open. I lingered outside not liking this one bit. There were only a few reasons for someone's door to be unlocked. The first, they were one of those idiotic people who left their doors unlocked against all common sense. Or they just left for a moment and thought it would be safe as long as they came right back.

Given my luck recently, I had a feeling it was closer to someone had already beaten me to breaking in.

The smell of old decay reached me.

It could also be that my contact was already dead.

This was becoming a theme with the sorcerer's errands.

From the smell of things he'd died quite a while ago. The scent was faint so I doubted a body was still in the condo. If he was already dead, there wasn't much he could do to me. I doubted the killer was waiting in there for me either. His work was already done. Might as well see what I could find. Maybe my dead contact had a helpful flash drive labeled 'murder clues'.

I stepped inside and shut the door after me, taking the time to glance around. This was a nice place. I could see why people were willing to pay a premium for a spot in this building. The floors were a dark hardwood, so new there wasn't a scratch on them. The space was very modern with an open floorplan. You could stand in the kitchen and still converse with people in the dining and living room areas. The kitchen was twice the size as mine, with oak cabinets running all the way to the top of the vaulted ceilings and an island in the middle of the space. Every appliance was stainless steel.

Whoever lived here had money and taste. If the location hadn't screamed 'well off', the furniture would. My aunt had a slight obsession with nice quality furniture, and as a result, rotated her living room furniture out several times. For that reason, I knew a little about what this stuff must have cost. Nothing in this room was under a thousand dollars. Well, maybe that book.

Must be nice to be able to afford all this. I'd pinched pennies for so long now I couldn't imagine throwing a single one away for indulgences such as these.

Too bad whoever owned this place was no longer around to enjoy it.

The smell of death permeated the air, but I was having a hard time pinpointing it. Nothing really seemed out of place. There were no blood stains or broken furniture. I was sure I wasn't imagining it. Something had died in here within the last week.

A thought occurred that should have dawned on me much sooner. Just because I smelled death didn't mean that it was necessarily the guy I'd been sent to find who'd done the dying. Perhaps my contact had done the killing.

If that was the case, he might be a little perturbed to find I'd broken into his place. I should report back to the sorcerer and see if he could give me some idea on this new situation.

I took a step to the door only to come to a halt. The knob wiggled back and forth. I backed away. I'd forgotten to lock the door behind me when I came in earlier.

It swung open before I'd even taken two steps, leaving me facing a familiar pair of blue eyes. I blinked, the surprise I felt reflected on his face as well.

He moved so fast I couldn't get out of his way before he had me by the throat. He slammed me against a wall.

"Well, well. What do we have here?"

His face was only inches from mine as he held me effortlessly off the ground. I struggled, kicking and wiggling. It was no use. His fingers gripped my throat with an implacable steel. He wasn't budging.

I settled for grabbing his wrists and using some of my own strength to take some of the pressure off. I didn't know if I could survive if he decided to tear my throat out.

"Which Clan are you from?"

I gurgled, the sound garbled and incomprehensible. His grip made it impossible to form even a word.

"This is the second time I've found you at one of my scenes. You're not one of the Azul, and I highly doubt the Branors would take you for their own."

I had no idea what he was talking about. I'd never heard of any of these 'families' before. He was the vampire from Lou's. What was he even doing here? No, what was he doing there?

He shook me. Plaster dust rained down as I thudded into the wall. I gurgled and rolled my eyes, still not able to talk.

Abruptly, he released me, stepping back and watching with an arrogant expression as I collapsed against the wall, gasping for air. That was the second time tonight someone had watched as I fought to breathe. It was not a feeling I liked.

When I felt like my vocal cords weren't in danger of seizing, I said, "I have no idea what you're talking about."

The vampire looked like he'd been turned in his early 30s. His face was young but without that fresh out of puberty look most people in their 20s had. He was attractive. If you saw him in a bar, you probably wouldn't get the courage to go up and talk to him. With dark brown hair cut short above his ears and cheek bones that could cut glass, he probably starred in many a woman's fantasies. Right now his face was smooth and patronizing as he regarded me.

"Your family clan, girl. Which vampire clan sent you?"

Vampire clan. Crap. Right. I didn't have one. I also didn't want him to know that. Problem was I had no idea what the families were even called.

"The Starett clan?"

Starett was Jerry's last name. Or at least the name that was currently on his business cards. In a way he had sent me and I was part of his organization.

"The Starett's?" he asked.

"Yup. The Starett's."

Maybe he'd buy my desperate gamble.

"Hm. And here I thought I knew every vampire family there was."

"We're relatively new. You probably haven't heard of us yet."

I edged sideways along the wall, cursing inwardly when he slid along with me.

He regarded me as a predator does its prey, like he was wondering how I would taste, like he was enjoying the hunt. I wasn't fooling anyone, but I had to try.

"It's funny that I don't remember. I'm sure a name like Starett would have caused some gossip when they petitioned to be recognized as their own clan."

"Perhaps it did and it just never reached you."

His eyes seemed to darken, the colors shifting. I glanced away, not wanting to get caught and mesmerized like last time. I didn't know if that's how the mesmerizing worked but it seemed as good a guess as any.

"That would be very difficult as I make a habit of keeping tabs on every upstart clan."

Okay. Sounded like this guy took intelligence gathering rather seriously.

I shrugged at him. "I don't know what to tell you. Maybe your tabs keeping isn't as good as you thought."

Yes, let's insult the lethal vampire who is capable of upending my entire world. That is a brilliant plan.

He smiled at me. It did not engender feelings of relief, reminding me instead of a dragon smiling at its next meal. This smile said its owner was a slightly deranged psychopath willing to swallow whole anything that got in his way.

He reached out, grabbing me by the back of my neck, not even noticing my puny punches as they bounced off his chest. A feather could have been fluttering against him for all the attention he gave my struggles.

He held me still as he leaned close, running his nose along my neck and sniffing. I stayed motionless, wanting to see how this played out before I did anything. He was stronger than me, but I had a few tricks up my sleeve that might even the playing field.

"Is there a reason you're smelling me?" I asked in the voice I used to use when trying to make a private feel about two inches tall.

"You are lying to me. I thought to cut through your deceptions to the source of the matter." He raised his head, looking at me with penetrating eyes. "I do not recognize any of the scents clinging to your skin. I will need to take blood to get a better picture."

The captain had warned me about letting a vampire take my blood again. He said anybody would be able to tell immediately that I was unclaimed. In rare cases, it might even give them some small claim on me, enabling them to track or compel me.

"I do not give my permission for this," I said. I didn't know if that would work as it hadn't sounded like he was asking permission.

He smiled, showing the tip of one fang. "I do not remember asking."

Yep. That's what I thought. Arrogant asshole.

Several things happened simultaneously after that. He bent to my neck. I palmed one of the slim, silver blades hidden in my belt. He held me too closely for a heart blow under his ribcage and his ribs protected many of his vital organs. That left back or neck.

I buried the blade as deep as I could in his back, praying I hit something important enough to slow him down and then twisted the blade.

A snarl of rage greeted my efforts. I flew through the air and crashed into the kitchen island. Something cracked in my back when I hit. The granite countertop crumbled under the force, spilling me to the ground in a bloody, broken mess.

Pain consumed my being, making it hard to breathe. Blood bubbled out of my mouth. A rib had probably punctured the lung. What worried me more was the hideous agony in my lower back and the crack I'd heard. I didn't think even my accelerated regeneration would be able to fix this. Looked like I wouldn't owe that sorcerer any time, after all.

A silver blade clattered on to the tile next to me.

Boots came to stand beside my head and a pair of blue eyes glared into mine. "That was unwise."

Yeah. I'd gotten that message.

He gave me a confused look. "What is taking so long? Fix yourself."

Would love to but I didn't think this was something I could fix. Maybe the sorcerer could. Did sorcerers have the ability to heal? That would be such a cool super power, much better than an addiction to blood and an allergy to sunlight.

The world was going fuzzy around the edges. My thoughts were starting to slow. I was losing consciousness. After all my struggles to survive, I couldn't believe this was how I would go.

His face reflected puzzlement. "Why aren't you healing yourself?"

I wondered what my parents would think of this. Jenna. She'd be so upset that our last conversation ended in an argument.

Fresh pain jolted me back to the present. I screamed as it slammed through my body.

Angry eyes glared down at me. "I don't know what game you're playing at but whatever it is won't work. Now fix yourself so we can be off."

It took effort and wasn't pretty, but I managed to get the words out. "Don't know what you're talking about."

He cocked his head and his eyes flared with suspicion. "What clan are you?"

I snorted at him. No way was I answering any questions from the man who killed me. It felt good to deny him in this even if it wasn't much of a rebellion.

"You don't have to die. Just tell me what I want to know."

"Wh- What do you mean?" I gasped out.

His face was grim as he reached out and a cool power danced across my skin, raising goosebumps in its wake. It felt good, the way a wet cloth on a hot summer's day did. Abruptly, the cool gave way to burning pain, searing through the flesh all the way down to the bone. I screamed, a long, thin sound.

Deep inside, in a sensation I never wanted to experience again, tissue knit together. Breathing got easier and it felt like a weight had been lifted off my chest.

"Now, my answer please," the vampire said.

I gaped at him. He'd healed me. How had he healed me? Not everything was healed. My body was still broken and hanging by a thread, but whatever he'd done had fixed my lungs, making speaking a lot easier.

"You still have a lot that needs fixing. I would take advantage of the situation before I get impatient."

I didn't want to give up my secrets, but I didn't want to die. I'd seen enough in my life to know that my injuries would kill me if left alone.

"I don't have a vampire clan." The words felt odd on my tongue. I wanted to pull them back as soon as they'd left my mouth.

The man looked surprised. It was the first real emotion I'd seen besides anger or predatory interest.

"Impossible. You can't be more than a few years old."

"Surprise." My voice sounded weak to my ears. Even with what he'd done, I wasn't going to last much longer.

He heard the weakness and shifted to touch me again. I flinched. Whatever he'd done before had hurt, even if it'd helped. The pain had rivaled what the sorcerer had inflicted on me. I was not looking forward to experiencing it again.

"Feel what I do," he told me.

His power caressed my skin before once again turning to searing heat. This time though, I concentrated, following it with my senses as it swept through looking for the broken bits of me. I saw what it was doing as it forced things to regenerate and then knit together the parts that had been damaged.

Something inside me swelled, rising to meet his, helping where it could. It wasn't much. My power was so much weaker than his, awkward and fumbling where his was graceful and efficient. Between the two of us, we repaired the damage.

By the time we were done, sweat beaded on my forehead and even the vampire was looking a little ragged around the edges.

When the worst of the damage was healed, his power withdrew. He sat back with a sigh. I took the opportunity to sit up, amazed that I could with only a twinge of pain. This was amazing. It almost made up for getting beat all to hell to learn this skill was in my repertoire. It didn't make me any more dangerous, but it might make me a lot harder to kill.

I probably couldn't do a full repair as he had. I was too young for that, but it did up my chances of surviving.

I looked up to find him studying me.

"Your power is extraordinarily weak for a vampire out of her hundred years of service."

I looked down at the scrapes and cuts I still had. He hadn't healed any of the superficial stuff, just the life threatening ones. It meant I had some impressive scrapes and bruises.

My power might be weak for a hundred year old but not a two year old.

"Though if you had reached your majority, I would expect you to have the knowledge and skill to heal such minor injuries. For that matter, a small fall like that shouldn't have caused the damage it did."

I avoided his eyes, staring off into the other room. It was only a matter of time before he arrived at the right conclusion. Or the wrong one for me.

"How old are you?" he asked.

"That's a rude question. Didn't your mother ever tell you not to ask a woman her age?"

He arched an eyebrow. "Should we start this whole process again?"

I grimaced. No thanks. I had no interest in doing that again. "I've been a vampire for two years."

Thunder clouded his face, his eyes turning nearly black and his fangs slid out as he growled.

I scooted back, not wanting to be too close in case he tried to grab me again. As fascinating as it was watching him turn bestial, I thought one flying lesson for the night was more than enough.

"Where is your sire?" he snarled.

I said carefully, "Your guess is as good as mine. I woke up in the morgue and have been on my own ever since."

"You should have been reported to the local clan. They should have taken you in to educate and train."

He made me sound like a puppy.

He grabbed my arm and hauled me up. I struggled in his grasp, my feet sliding among the debris from the island countertop.

"What are you doing?" I snapped, punching him in the ear.

He snarled, showing both fangs. "Stop that."

Like that was going to happen.

I kicked him in the knee. He barely broke stride, giving me an irritated look.

"Let me go," I yelled.

It didn't matter what I did. It was impossible to slow him as he marched me to the door.

"You're coming with me. I must take care of this matter, but when I'm done I'll put out feelers and find a clan to take you."

My struggles doubled until he was pretty much dragging me bodily down the hall. I was not going to make this easy for him. Vampires weren't derailing my life a second time.

One of my feet caught him right in the back of the knee, sending him stumbling into the wall. His grip loosened and I shot past him, running for the door. A tackle sent me crashing to the ground with him on top of me. I turned into a raging typhoon of claws, biting teeth and vicious blows.

He grabbed my collar and lifted me an inch off the ground then slammed me back down, momentarily stunning me. He thrust his face close to mine and said, "Enough. Continue this and I'll break both legs and carry you out of here."

I glared up at him. It was clear he was stronger than me. I needed to bide my time until I could escape. I wouldn't be able to run if my legs were broken. For now, I'd let him think he'd won.

Seeing the surrender on my face, he hauled me up and pushed me in front of him.

"Let's go."

He'd won for now, but one thing I was extremely good at was being patient. I just needed to wait for my moment.

Chapter Five

The vampire pushed me forward, forcing me through the back entrance of a well-known nightclub just off Spring Street in the Arena District. The place was only a ten minute walk from the condo, but the vampire chose to drive, taking nearly a half hour instead. Once again, I'd had to leave Cherry behind.

Like the wolves, the vampire hadn't bothered to tie my hands or disable me in any way. It seemed like he planned to rely totally on his own abilities to keep me contained. I wasn't complaining. It'd make escaping a lot easier. Still, it was a little insulting how nobody seemed to have even a hint of wariness regarding my abilities.

A woman stepped into the hallway and came to a halt when she noticed my presence. Her mouth dropped open when her eyes shot past me to land on my captor.

She stammered, "Enforcer, what are you doing here?"

"I did not realize I had to report my itinerary to a servant," a cold voice said from behind me.

Asshole. I hoped she blistered his ears. I know I would have. There were several sarcastic replies that would be appropriate for the situation.

She blushed bright red and bowed. No shit. A bow. Who did that in this day and age?

"Forgive me. I did not mean to presume."

I snorted. This was unreal. It was like the middle ages had taken up residence in this nightclub.

A shove landed on my back, and I stumbled forward.

"She is unclaimed. See she is fed and any wounds attended to."

Her eyes darted to mine, curiosity and suspicion alive in them.

"Of course. I will make the guest comfortable."

"Oh, don't worry about that," I told her. "I'm not really a guest. More like a kidnap victim."

She gave me a cool look that held none of the deferential treatment the man received. "If you're not a guest, then you're a prisoner."

"Works for me," I said with a smirk.

There came a sigh behind me. "Make sure you keep an eye on her. I have a feeling she's a runner."

The woman nodded again.

"I will be reviewing the tapes of the attack. When I've finished, I will come for the yearling."

Yearling. Like I'm a horse or something.

She murmured an agreement and dipped her head as he passed.

She watched as he disappeared down the hall. I looked back at the exit. It was only a few steps away. She didn't look that strong. Perhaps I could make a run for it.

She grabbed me by my jacket and threw me up against the wall, lifting me until my feet dangled inches off the ground. Her eyes nearly glowed with a fey light, so bright they cast shadows in the hallway.

I grimaced. Not this again. Perhaps they taught the move in vampire academy. There might even be a "How to subdue other vampires 101 class" and they were graded on how well they threw people against the wall.

"You show great disrespect to your elders, girl," the woman snarled, her fangs coming out to play. I was quite amazed she could speak without the slightest speech impediment. Me, I'd have a thick lisp, making it impossible for my victim to understand me.

"Well, I am a millennial," I told her. "Along with being the boomerang generation, we're known for a lack of respect. Ya'll should really have thought about that before you conscripted me into your ranks."

"There was hardly any force required," she said, her fangs withdrawing with a snick. "Every candidate is carefully vetted and given every chance to reconsider along the way. Every one of you comes to us voluntarily."

My lips quirked in a half smile. "Not all of us."

Her hands loosened on my shirt, and I slid out of them to stand on my own two feet. I smoothed down the jacket, suspecting it was a lost cause. It was ripped and twisted beyond redemption by this point. It was one of my favorites too.

My words had disturbed her more than I thought. "Is it true you were forced?"

"Yup." I drew the word out making it into three syllables.

Her forehead wrinkled.

"Anyways, he said something about you feeding me. Got any chocolate?" I'd been craving it since I woke up.

"You must be joking."

"I never joke about chocolate."

Her lip curled in disgust. I'd take that as a no then. Too bad. It might have made this night a little better. If my entire life was going to be uprooted again, a little chocolate would have gone a long way.

She regarded me as if I was a wayward pupil that needed to be given a certain amount of leeway. I'd been on the receiving end of that look on more than one occasion. I'd really thought I'd never have to be the recipient of it once I left school.

"Let's get you cleaned up and then fed." She gave my clothes another look. "On second thought, perhaps we'll feed you first."

I followed reluctantly, casting a quick glance back at the exit. She was too strong for me to go against her directly. I'd have to wait for a better moment. Best to play the docile yearling before making my move.

The club's non-public parts were much bigger than I'd ever expected. There was practically enough room for a second club behind the real one. I wasn't the best at judging spatial areas, but I was pretty sure the outside size did not match up with the interior. How did they get all this extra space?

There was a soft laugh beside me, and I realized I had said the last bit out loud.

"You have a lot to learn, little sister," the woman said with a smile. "Part of it is illusion, the other half is done with the help of a few spells."

I felt the urge to correct the woman. I wasn't her sister and had no intention of toeing the vampire line, whatever that might be. But I would take every drop of information she imparted even if it meant letting her make certain assumptions.

"What is your name?"

Now that was going a bit far. I had no intention of giving these people my real name. It would be too easy to track me with it. There couldn't be too many Aileen Travers in the city.

I couldn't entirely ignore her, not if I wanted her to keep talking and lower her guard.

They used to call me The Animal when I played sports in high school because I was vicious and scrappy when I went after the ball. Somehow I didn't think that name would work in these circumstances. Same with any of the nicknames I'd gathered in the military.

I could see she was starting to get suspicious of my hesitation. Needed a name. Any name.

"Lena," I said, giving her a shy smile.

It seemed like she bought it because she smiled back.

"I'm Kat."

I hoped the name wasn't too close to my real one. It was all I could think of on short notice. Jenna used to call me that when we were kids. I missed it. She hasn't called me 'Lena' in years now.

"How long have you been a vampire?"

Truth or lie?

"About two years."

This was a rare chance to get some good intel. I'd stick to the truth as much as possible.

She stopped and stared at me in horror. I stopped too.

"Impossible. Vampires have little discipline for nearly a decade after their turn. They require strict control and near constant oversight by a guardian. No newly turned could survive without leaving a massive trail of bodies behind them."

That did not do a lot to inspire my confidence. A shiver skated down my back. If what she said was true, I had posed a much bigger risk to those around me than I had realized.

She could be lying.

"And yet I have managed to not kill a single person since my turn. Maybe those stories about the freshly turned are just exaggerations."

It was possible. I was proof you could do it without the oversight of a clan. Perhaps this was all I needed to convince them to let me go my own way.

"They're not stories," she said with a distinct look in her eyes. Her eyes focused on me again. "We'll make sure your luck holds. I'm glad you don't have to live with the deaths of your loved ones on your hands."

Looked like they weren't going to give up on this claiming so easily. It had been a long shot anyway.

She opened the door we'd stopped in front of. The smell of warm, living blood wafted past me.

Hungry. So hungry. Food. Need. Blood.

A warm neck was in my mouth, my fangs posed to bite down. Distantly, I heard shouting and panic. It was hard to concentrate. The blood was so close, and it had been so long. All I had to do was bite down. It'd be like biting into a grape, a slight pop and then all the blood I wanted could be mine.

My jaw ached with the need.

No. I wouldn't do this. Not this way. Not if I wanted to live with myself. Not if I ever wanted to go home to my family again. I do this and I was the vampires'. I'd turn myself over to them rather than risk going on a killing spree as the woman had hinted at.

I forced myself to straighten. It was the hardest thing I'd ever done. Harder than that time I'd climbed a rope in basic with a broken, swollen hand. Harder than the twenty five mile ruck march I'd done in hundred degree heat.

Peeling back one finger at a time, I eventually let go of my victim. Sweat beaded on my face. It took everything in me to step back.

Only now did I realize it was a man's neck I had been mouthing moments earlier. It was attached to an attractive body, muscled in all the right places, and a handsome face that currently looked terrified of me. His curly brown hair flopped over his ears. He was in his early twenties at the most. Probably a college kid looking for a good time who just stumbled into a situation way over his head.

"Admirable restraint in one so young," an amused voice said from my right.

Kat's hand rested on my shoulder in a claw like grip. It had been her voice I'd heard, though it had a level of panic that probably hadn't helped calm my instincts.

"Patriarch Aiden." Kat sounded shaken but was still trying to keep control of the situation.

It was a struggle to focus on what was happening around me with the delicious blood so near. I practically drooled at the thought of it sliding down my throat.

No. Focus on other things. Ignore the thirst burning a hole in your throat.

I forced myself to take in my surroundings. Anything to get my mind off what I really wanted.

A man with hair so short it was a shadow on his head watched me from across the room. He had a strong jaw and a slightly crooked nose as if it had been broken at some point in his youth.

"It is strange that the Davinish family would let such a young one loose to run about."

"This is not our normal way of doing things, Patriarch. Enforcer Liam brought her in and has entrusted her to our protection as she is currently unclaimed."

"Unclaimed?"

He examined me more closely, like I was a puppy that had done an interesting trick.

"How interesting. I don't think I've seen an unclaimed yearling for the past two, no three, hundred years, not since right after the Clan Wars and then it was a never a woman who was unclaimed."

"What's that supposed to mean? Why is it surprising I'd be a woman and unclaimed?" I asked.

"Quiet," Kat hissed.

You be quiet. I had questions and I wanted answers. This guy seemed talkative.

"Now, that's not very nice," the man told me.

What wasn't nice? My questions?

His lips quirked in a half smile, as if he'd just heard an inside joke.

"To answer your question, it's because women rarely make the transition to our esteemed ranks. They often die without rising. For that reason, they are a bit of a rare commodity and the clans are understandably unwilling to let them face the dangers that being unaffiliated brings."

My eyes narrowed. What a bunch of bullshit. I'd fought my entire life to have the same standing as a man in whatever path I chose to walk. More than ever I was glad to be outside their system. It sounded like I'd get myself in trouble with them sooner rather than later if they thought women the weaker sex in need of protecting.

The other man chuckled as he walked to stand next to us.

"How old are you?"

In vampire years or human? Given how Kat reacted to learning I'd only been a vampire for two years, I didn't really feel like sharing any other personal information.

"Two years? You really are young. Most at your age would have torn the human limb from limb." He flicked Kat a chiding look. She straightened and lifted her chin. "What were you thinking letting her through the door first? If she'd killed him, it would have been your fault."

Mind reader. It was the only way he could have known my age when no one had spoken.

He gave me a sly smile. He was.

Lucky for me it wasn't the first time I'd run into one of these. How did I shield my thoughts last time? Right.

Closing my eyes, I visualized an old, great forest, full of towering oaks, redwoods, birches and spruces. A forest like the one I'd visited in

Yellowstone when I was a child. My forest had twisting paths that winded back on themselves, creating a maze with no center. For added protection I placed briars and underbrush beneath the trees. In my mind, my forest stretched for miles and miles in all directions. Even climbing the tallest tree wouldn't show you the edge of it.

The first time I'd done this I'd pictured an impenetrable wall that the mind reader had no trouble breaching. Since he'd been one of my recurring customers, I'd gotten a lot of practice perfecting this method. I found picturing something living and complex worked better than a structure. Over time I kept adding on to the visualization until I achieved the current incarnation.

It had seemed to work with my customer, but I didn't know if it would work now. I didn't know why it worked or how, just that it did, and that was good enough for me.

Eventually I wouldn't need to close my eyes to pull up my protection. It would just be there, a thought away. I'd been told that practice could keep my shield in place permanently.

"That is an interesting trick," the vampire said, his eyes distant as if his focus had turned inward. "It is quite effective and unexpected."

Something brushed against my mind, testing my invisible forest here and there for signs of weakness. It was uncomfortable. The other mind reader hadn't been skilled enough to make any inroads into my forest. This one, though, felt like he might be able to find the center if given enough time.

"Ah, I see. You've placed the trees to obscure line of sight. Very clever."

His eyes fixed on me, a greediness entering them. It did not give me a good feeling.

"What is your name?"

I kept my thoughts as quiet and still as possible. It seemed like my shield was doing its job but you could never be too careful. The vampire might be misleading me to get me to lower my guard.

"Ah. Lena."

I started.

The vampire's gaze turned to the woman next to me. "Your elder doesn't have quite the same level of skill when it comes to guarding her thoughts."

Kat looked rather displeased by his observation. It made me doubly glad I hadn't given her my real name or any other information.

"Patriarch, as much as we've enjoyed your presence, I'm sure you did not come to supervise a yearling's feeding. I'm sure my elders would be happy to host you and discuss what matters bring you to our club."

I couldn't help being a tad impressed at that eloquent dismissal. Perhaps Kat had a lot more backbone than I'd initially given her credit for.

"I find I am quite happy where I am," the man said.

"Patriarch, this is an unusual request. I am sure you will be much more comfortable in one of our other rooms."

I watched the back and forth, my gaze swinging between the two like it was a tennis match. I didn't know who I wanted to win. The man, who hadn't really done anything threatening yet, or the plucky underdog who was swimming in waters even I could tell were well above her head.

"I will stay and watch. I am curious about the yearling and am contemplating putting in a claim."

Kat went stock still. If I hadn't seen the very faint rise of her chest, I would have thought she was a statue.

"You presume much, Patriarch. This is not your territory. Davinish would have priority in any claim on the yearling."

I assumed they meant me. So great to be talked about like I wasn't even here. Like I was property with no say in what happened.

More and more, my decision to remain hidden was being validated.

The two faced off, the human and I forgotten as the tension ratcheted up.

This was awesome. Perhaps they would fight, and I could slip away in the resulting chaos. I could even take the human for a snack.

Just like that I was fixated on his neck, staring and nearly drooling. Just a sip would go so far in quenching this awful thirst.

Kat hissed at the other vampire. I sidled to the human and bent closer.

A blow knocked me sideways, sending me crashing into Kat. We landed on the floor in a pile of limbs.

"What is this?" the vampire who'd kidnapped me thundered.

His eyes glowed bright blue in the space, his fangs descending and giving him a feral appearance.

My senses returned in a rush now that I was away from the human. I hated referring to him as that. Human. It made me sound like a monster.

Tonight the bloodlust was worse. I kept fixating. If I kept this up, I wouldn't be able to trust myself in my normal life. Even when Jenna had crashed in on me last night, I hadn't been so out of control.

Wait. Last night.

That's the last time I'd had any blood. No wonder I was having so much trouble resisting the human. I was hungry. No. Starving.

I knew better. I never forgot and always made sure to keep myself properly fed. It's the best way I'd found to keep myself from snapping.

How could I have forgotten?

Even if events had been rather distracting in the past two days, my body would have craved it which would have served as warning. When the sorcerer showed up this morning, I should have been jonesing for his blood like a junkie cruising for her next hit.

Why hadn't I? Had he done something to me? And if so, was it something that could be replicated?

While thinking about my hunger problems, I had tuned out of the conversation. With a start, I realized they were talking about me.

"No one is claiming the yearling until I say so."

They both protested.

My kidnapper growled, sounding more like the werewolves from last night than the vampire he was. How was he even able to do that? I never sounded like that when I was mad.

"I don't have time for this. Aiden, I called you here to learn more about the death of your family member. This was the last place I'd been able to trace him to before he was found dead in his apartment. There might be some clue in the tapes."

"It's always business with you, Liam. You never were any fun, even when you were young. I just wanted to get a feel for the girl to see if she would fit in my household."

"I don't have time for your lack of focus. This killer is escalating," Liam said with forced patience. I was surprised when the he didn't turn the glowing eyes back on. He seemed to have a rather short temper. "If you don't mind the death of another of your children, I will be happy to step aside while you fence with words in another Clan's home. Or you could watch the tapes and tell me what you see."

"He needs permission from the club manager before viewing Davinish property," Kat said, shooting Aiden a glare.

She really didn't seem to like this Aiden and was borderline disrespectful towards the end. It was surprising since she'd gone on and on about respecting my elders when Liam turned me over to her. Patriarch, I knew, represented a family head. Same for Matriarch. What one was doing in the back room of a club, I did not know.

The glowing eyes came back on, forcing Kat to bow her head and back down.

"The fact that I said I needed him should be enough," the vampire hissed, his voice hitting notes I'd never heard in a human's voice.

For the first time, I noticed the stack of DVDs in the vampire's hands. I had a sneaking suspicion the man I was supposed to meet in the apartment was on them. It might be worth trying to get a look. The sorcerer would probably want some clues to go on if his contact was dead.

I would also need something to go on if I had any hope of getting out of my fool's bargain. I didn't think even induction into a vampire family could save me from the sorcerer's claim.

"Where did you find the girl?" Aiden asked. "I thought you were checking out Eric's apartment before meeting me here."

"Yes and much to my surprise I found a yearling snooping around."

I found myself the center of two intent stares. Aiden's gaze was calculating and I understood more on why Kat treated him with wariness. In a moment, he'd flipped from easy going to intent and focused as he weighed and cataloged everything he could about me. It was the type of look I'd seen many times on missions as a soldier sized up potential enemy combatants, trying to determine if they carried weapons or IEDs – improvised explosive devices – under their robes. All in the space of seconds.

This time, I was the potential enemy, and I had no doubt Aiden would act with the same aggressive efficiency our soldiers had when we came up against a threat.

I shored up my mental forest in case he decided to go fishing for information.

"You're just full of surprises, aren't you?" Aiden said softly. It didn't sound like a good thing when he said it.

As Aiden turned and walked away, Liam focused on me, "A warning. Vampires are fascinated by mysteries and will do anything to solve them. If you're not careful, you may find yourself torn apart in an effort to get at the secrets you keep hidden inside."

His threat delivered, Liam turned to Kat, "If she kills the human, it will be you I punish. You should have bagged blood on hand for emergencies."

That would have been a nice alternative and given Kat knew my age, it should have been her first choice.

Somehow, despite being nearly prone on the ground next to me, Kat managed to make her inclined head seem graceful as she murmured, "Yes, Enforcer."

She sounded so meek. Totally unlike when she was addressing Aiden. It made me wonder who Liam was.

It also made me wonder if the human had been a test. But why? It's possible she'd counted on me killing him. Maybe to make me feel beholden. No, even that explanation didn't quite fit.

I hated not having enough information to make informed opinions. I knew so little about vampire social interactions that I couldn't even begin to understand any of the motivations at play.

Kat rose with a sinuous grace, leaving me feeling like a lumbering elephant as I scrambled up behind her.

She walked to a wall and pushed aside a picture. Behind it was a safe. She punched in a code and opened it to withdraw a bag filled with red liquid. I stepped slightly to the side to get a better look.

Huh. The safe was actually a refrigerated unit with stacks of blood filled bags. Kind of a weird thing in a club, but it made sense when you realized who owned it.

I wondered if they'd tell me where they got the safe. It would be perfect in my house. No more trying to hide my blood in wine bottles. I also wouldn't have to worry about well-meaning family members stopping by to dispose of the bottles.

There was the faintest evidence of a blush as Kat handed the bag to me. I took it, glancing at the human. It was a little astonishing he hadn't run for the hills with all that had happened in the past few minutes. We weren't exactly guarding our words. I know if I'd heard someone refer to my possible death from exsanguination, I would have been out of here so fast that I'd have left skid marks.

The human gazed back at me with a vacant expression. The lights were on but no one was home. I wondered if Kat had done that mesmerizing thing the werewolves had been talking about. What were the chances she'd show me how to do it?

"You may go," she told the human.

He left without another word, wandering out the door.

"Will he be okay?" I asked.

He still hadn't looked all there on his way out. I hoped he made it home in one piece. It would be rather sad to have escaped death by my bite only to run afoul of some other vampire or supernatural.

"He'll be fine," Kat said, not sparing the door a glance. "He'll go back to the club and then head home where he'll wake up tomorrow not having any memories of the night. I'm sure he'll assume that the night was 'epic' and be no worse off than he was before we interrupted it."

Her tone made it clear that the human had already left her thoughts.

Is that what being a vampire meant? A complete disregard for human life? I didn't want to be that person. The person who couldn't be bothered to care. I would never admit it aloud but part of the reason I joined the Army was to help people. To serve my community and give back to my country. It sounds sappy, which is the reason I never say anything about it.

It could be that Kat was just distracted due to Liam's earlier interruption, but I doubted it. Especially given the blood pack she'd handed me.

It didn't smell nearly as appetizing as the human had. I'd never had blood straight from the source, but if it tasted as good as it smelled, it would be divine. Maybe even better than Black Raspberry ice cream from Graeters. Well, maybe not that good.

In contrast, the blood pack was the equivalent of a stalk of celery. Nutritious and would prevent me from starving but not exactly something you went out of your way to eat. It'd do the job but didn't leave me craving more.

I drained the bag in great big gulps. It was empty too soon, and I looked at it in dismay. I hadn't realized how hungry I was until now, because that one small bag had barely made a dint in my hunger.

"Got any more?" I asked.

She sighed and tossed me another one. I drained that and another before deciding my hunger was under control. I was still a little peckish but didn't want to get too greedy.

Kat had taken a seat and was clicking around on a computer while I finished my dinner.

For the first time since I'd rushed in here intent on a delicious smell, I had the time to devote to taking a look at my surroundings. Half of the room looked like any VIP room, complete with tasteful couches and chairs. They had a very modern shape and were in greys and yellows. Not the colors I would have pegged for a vampire's lair.

There wasn't a drop of red or black in the entire room. I tested one chair. It was much more comfortable than it looked.

The area Kat had availed herself of looked like some high powered executive's office. A heavy wooden desk with a huge monitor and keyboard, an artistic paper weight and antique globe were the only decorations.

I stood and walked over to get a look at the painting behind Kat, stealing a glance at her computer. It wasn't the most subtle of attempts, but it was the best I could do in the circumstances. I forgot about being sneaky as soon as I saw what she was looking at.

"Is that security video?" I asked.

She frowned at me and looked pointedly at the chair I'd just vacated. I chose to ignore the hint and stepped closer.

It looked like it was a video of the club area. It was kind of grainy, and I had no idea what I should be looking for. The date at the bottom was for two days prior.

"Is this what the other two are reviewing?" I asked.

I hadn't noticed her insert a CD or anything into the computer. It was possible it was linked to a secure server that had the videos stored on it. If so, why hadn't she told Aiden and Liam they could watch the video's in here?

Unless I'm the reason that wasn't offered. Maybe they didn't want me seeing what was on the tapes. That couldn't be it as she'd pulled it up where I could easily see it. Also, I doubted they'd take such precautions when none of them saw me as much of a threat. Hence the lack of rope or cage. Even the werewolves had been more cautious than this.

"Do you mind?" Kat asked in a snotty tone.

"No."

She made an angry exclamation and with one click of her nail turned the monitor off.

I was beginning to think there was something she wanted to hide. It made sense. I wondered if Liam had received all of the security feeds.

It was like a modern day Borgia soap opera, full of clandestine meetings, hidden agendas and sneaky plots. Jenna and my mom would be rapt with fascination. Me, on the other hand, I'm much simpler. Give me a clear cut bad guy and good guy any day of the week. Figuring out everybody's convoluted motives are a pain in the ass.

Kat watched me with a calculating look. She wanted something.

"It would be in your best interest to start making friends," she said. "I'd hope you might fit with our Clan. I've always wanted a little sister. I could make a powerful ally."

"Ah hah," was the only response I could give without completely offending her. I don't know where she got the idea that I planned on joining her clan.

"You would, of course, have to prove your worth," she said.

"And how would you suggest I do that?"

I had to give it to her. She didn't let any of the smug satisfaction she was feeling show on her face.

"It'll be easy. I just need you to check in with the Enforcer and Patriarch Aiden and then tell me what you see."

Yup. She was definitely hiding something. Worse, she expected me to spy for her. She must be desperate if she was trying to solicit an unknown vampire to do her dirty work.

"And how would you expect me to do that? Aren't you supposed to be keeping an eye on me?" I asked.

She gave me a bright and completely fake smile. "I will be. The club has cameras in all the rooms. This isn't anything really. Think of it more as that thing college fraternities do to new members. What's the word? I can never remember."

She couldn't really think I was dumb enough to buy this.

"Hazing," I said, playing along.

"Right. It's just a little test to prove your devotion and then we can be Clan." She stepped close and picked up a lock of hair that had slipped loose from my messy pony tail. "I've always wanted a little sister. It'll be so fun. You'll see."

I had a sister and while she annoyed the shit out of me sometimes, I wouldn't trade her for this phony woman and all the blood in the world.

I saw no reason to tell her that though. This was my chance. She might be able to monitor me on the cameras, but every system had a blind spot. If I got close enough to an exit, I wouldn't even need to exploit the system's weaknesses. I'd just high tail it out the door and not stop running until I found a safe place to hole up for the night.

Before I could answer, there was a screech of noise as an alarm sounded. Kat turned back to the computer and brought up the security feeds, not bothering to push me away when I glanced over her shoulder.

From the number of different windows, there were dozens of cameras in the club. It would have been impossible for me to sneak around undetected.

"What are they doing here?" Kat hissed.

At first I couldn't see what she was talking about and then in the top right box on the screen, a familiar face caught my attention. Brax. It was a little grainy and I'd only met him once, but his face wasn't one I would forget.

"Stay here," Kat ordered.

"Is there something wrong?"

"No, of course not. There's just a small situation I need to take care of. I'll be right back."

I could hardly believe it when she hurried out of the room without a backward glance. She didn't actually expect me to obey, did she? Like a dog told to sit. Unbelievable.

Maybe there were guards outside waiting. Unlikely, but possible.

The security feeds were still running on the computer so I enlarged the one containing the hallway leading to this room. Empty. Perfect. Getting out of here would be easy. I probably wouldn't even need to run.

I pulled out my keys and flipped open the small thumb drive I'd carried since I was a freshman in college. I rarely needed it anymore since I didn't really use a computer that often, but I never got around to taking it off after graduating. My laziness was about to pay off. I plugged the USB into the computer and prayed they hadn't disabled the port. A file folder popped up with the USB's name on it. Guess these vampires weren't that concerned about computer security.

It took moments to bring up the files for the past week. I didn't want to chance missing something important just because Kat had been looking at files from two days ago. I dragged them over to the USB folder and winced when I saw the estimated time to download. The files were big. This was going to take a couple of minutes.

The seconds counted down as I monitored all the feeds, keeping an eye out in case someone headed in my direction. The moment they did I was gone. I wouldn't jeopardize my freedom over some files that may or may not be helpful.

It looked like everybody was heading to intercept Brax and a few of his werewolves. I thought I spotted Liam and Aiden on the cameras as well. Good. That should give me enough time.

The files finished downloading. I grabbed the USB, took one last look to make sure my path was still clear, and then headed out.

My footsteps were loud as I walked as fast as I could without running towards the rear exit. In the slight chance someone happened upon me on my way out, I didn't want to immediately alert them that I was up to no good.

No one appeared though, and I was on the street in a very short time, heading back to Cherry.

Chapter Six

The car retrieved, I drove around aimlessly. I couldn't go home in case the vampires or werewolves somehow figured out where I lived. I didn't want to go to Hermes' office partly for that reason and partly because I didn't want to face the interrogation I knew was in store. Going there also meant I'd have to give up Cherry, and I still needed her. I wasn't ready to face the sorcerer again and it was too early in the evening to find a place to sleep through the day. That didn't leave me a lot of options.

Somehow I found myself driving down High Street, past the campus district, through all the college neighborhoods and on down to the Short North area. If I remembered correctly, Elements was near there.

I needed to talk to a witch, and Miriam was the only one I knew. At least the only one I knew how to find and wasn't terrified of. There was that witch on the east side, but I'd vowed never to go near her after her attempt to turn me into a frog had resulted in a week of green skin.

I could use some witchy advice. I needed to know more about the mark on my arm. It also wouldn't hurt to ask a few questions about hiding scents from a werewolf's nose. At the very least, she might have a computer I could borrow.

Parking down here was always a crap shoot. Tonight, being a Thursday, was no different. The college kids were out in force. It paid to have no classes on Friday. Those that did have class probably intended to skip. I know it's something I'd done many times at that age.

The only place I could find to park was several blocks away. After squeezing the car into a spot better suited for a Prius, I pocketed the keys and walked towards the store. It took me a lot longer than I predicted. I'd traveled much further afield in my search for a parking spot than intended, and it was not a relaxing walk with me being convinced Liam or Aiden would materialize at any moment.

Elements had a closed sign in the window when I finally made it. The lights were on and two figures moved in the back. I reached for my phone to check the time. It, along with the bag I normally carried, wasn't there. That's right, I'd left it at Lou's when I'd made my great escape.

With no cell, I had no way of telling the time. I stopped wearing watches years ago when it dawned on me that a cell phone told the time just as well and wouldn't cost me anything extra on my college student budget. It only sucked in the rare times I had no cell phone to check, which almost never happened.

The sign said the store closed at midnight. I did a quick mental calculation. It didn't feel like it was past midnight. So why was the store closed? And how angry would Miriam be if I barged in anyway? In the end, none of my questions mattered. I was desperate, and desperate times called for desperate measures. Even if it did mean pissing off a witch of unknown power.

I tested the door, not surprised to find it locked. Lucky for me, I had increased strength and the locks on this door weren't the heavy duty kind. I briefly considered knocking but didn't want to take the chance she would pretend to be out of the office. It's what I would have done if someone came knocking at my store after I'd hung up the closed sign.

Here's hoping she would listen to my plea before zapping me into the next world.

I gave the door a controlled jerk, smirking as the metal popped off and the door swung open. If this courier business didn't work out, I could always pursue a career as a cat burglar.

I ducked inside, careful not to make too much noise. Forcing the lock hadn't been as loud as I'd expected and by the lack of a chime, it sounded like they had disabled the bell.

On whisper quiet feet, I headed for the sound of voices in the back. I should probably announce myself so I didn't startle Miriam and her shopkeeper, but it had been a rough night. I wanted a chance to observe without them knowing I was here before I announced my presence.

A male voice tangled with the sound of a female's. I paused. Maybe I shouldn't interrupt. It was possible she had closed the store early to entertain a gentleman. It was a weird place to have a date, but what did I know of witches. Maybe 'come see my potions' was a form of foreplay.

Walking in on her and a date would probably not be the best way to gain her cooperation. I could wait outside until the man left. I'd feel like a stalker, but it was better than barging my way in.

"What are you doing here?" Miriam asked right next to my ear.

I shrieked and jumped, giving too much force to my leap and sailing halfway across the room, knocking several items over on the way.

Landing partially on my feet and partially on a plush chair, I looked up to find Miriam regarding me with a tilted head and a bemused expression. She held a large drink in one hand and a familiar looking pizza box in the other. It was from a joint that catered to the after midnight crowd. I sometimes stopped there if I was in the area during a courier run. Their pizza had the perfect balance of grease, fluffy dough, gooey cheese, and mouth-watering toppings.

I straightened, smoothing my hands down my pants.

"Miriam, hi." Oh, that was even more brilliant. If I hadn't impress her with my stellar leaping skills I could wow her with my conversational topics. "What are you doing here?"

"It's my store."

Right. Of course.

"That's not what I meant. You startled me. I thought you were in the back office."

"That's odd, no one should be in here. Angela asked to leave early tonight. It should just be me minding the store. That's why I closed it to run out and get dinner." She waved the pizza box slightly.

I glanced at the curtain of beads. Then who were the two people in the back room.

"Are you the one who broke my door?"

My gaze shot back to her. The softly worded question felt like a trap. Judging from the silvery sheen her eyes had taken, my next answer could decide whether I walked away from this encounter or crawled.

"Um, yes." I rushed on even as I felt the atmosphere take on a disturbing charge. I so didn't want to get electrocuted again. "But only because I saw people in the store and thought it was odd that it was closed early. Given all that's been happening lately with the disappearances and murders, I didn't want to take the chance something else was going on."

Finished, I held my breath. It was a pretty convincing lie given I'd had seconds to come up with it.

The buildup of power paused as she considered my answer. The power retreated. I gave an internal sigh of relief.

"Miriam, what are you doing here?" Angela asked, stepping out of the back.

Her gaze shot between the two of us. She look upset when she saw me but the expression was gone in the next second. I wondered if I'd imagined it.

A man stepped out after her, his gaze cool and assessing as it slid between Miriam and me, noting the damage I'd left in my wake. He was handsome, with one of those faces that would appeal to most women and a body that was fit and lean. His blond hair had that sexy tousled thing going for it, like he'd just gotten out of bed and run his hands through it. He seemed familiar somehow, like I'd seen him somewhere, but for the life of me, I couldn't remember where.

Miriam stiffened as soon as she caught sight of the man behind Angela.

"What is he doing here?" she asked, her voice taking on a deep undertone. It was like it reverberated and echoed back a thousand times in the small space.

Next to the sorcerer's voice, it was pretty impressive.

Whoever he was didn't seemed phased by the suddenly scary witch in front of him.

"I'll see you later, babe," he said, slipping past Angela and heading towards the exit. He gave the broken latch a considering look before slipping away.

Miriam made no move to stop him, keeping her eyes trained on her shop keeper.

"Miriam," Angela began.

"Don't," Miriam said, her voice dropping to normal. "You know I told you to stay away from him. I can't believe you disobeyed me."

"He just stopped by to ask me to look at something."

"And did he just stop by at your house or the store," Miriam asked. "Because you were off tonight, which means you brought him here or you met him here."

I sat on the chair and waited for the argument to burn itself out. It seemed like they'd forgotten me in the drama of the moment.

I didn't really understand what Miriam had against the guy. I could see why Angela had disobeyed, though. That man was fine on the eyes. He was probably a jerk though. He had that air about him. The one that said I'm sexy and know it, but you'll do just about anything I ask even though you know you'll probably end up broken hearted and hurting at the end of it.

"I just. We just." Seemed like Angela couldn't think of a lie quick enough. "It doesn't matter. What I do on my time is my business. You cannot forbid me to see someone just because you're my mentor."

The old defense by attacking. Rooky mistake. It almost never worked but was guaranteed to escalate things. I knew from considerable experience gained through fighting with my mom.

"That's exactly what it means," Miriam said, her voice cold and implacable. "When I took you as an apprentice, you agreed to obey me. This is not obeying. Continue on this path, and I will be forced to dissolve our relationship."

Ouch. That was a little harsh and would no doubt send Angela right into the man's arms.

From the stubborn tilt to Angela's jaw, I guessed she'd be on her way to his door as soon as she was done here. This was like watching one of those teen dramas on TV. Who knew this kind of thing happened in real life too?

As entertaining as it was to watch and dissect where each party was going wrong, I needed this to be wrapped up. My problems weren't going away, and they were a little more serious than Angela getting her heart broken.

"Excuse me. Sorry to interrupt." I stood and stepped forward before Angela could make the situation any worse. "I came here to talk to Miriam, and it really cannot wait. Do you mind if we chat a bit before you guys continue this?"

Angela glared at Miriam before nodding and stalking outside.

"Miriam?" I asked.

Miriam exhaled and it was like she was shaking loose of the anger that had saturated the air since the man stepped into the store.

"Of course. I'm curious as to why you're here as well."

I followed as she walked into the back office. I froze once I pushed past the beaded curtain. This was not the room I'd visited last time I was here. For starters, it had nothing in common with the stereotypical office break room you'd find in pretty much every retail store in America.

There was still a table with chairs around it, but instead of the cheap vinyl folding table and plastic chairs, it had a table burnished a deep cherry brown in its place. It looked like an antique. A very old, very expensive, hand carved antique. Plants, enough to fill a green house, surrounded it, climbing on trellises and clinging to the ceiling. They should be turning brown and preparing for winter but instead they looked like they were caught in the peak of summer, with new buds joining the substantial amount already on them. They were a deep, verdant green almost surreal in the intensity of the colors.

Miriam walked through them, the leaves swaying out of her way as if opening a path. She turned and looked at me quizzically as I gaped at the paradise around me.

"How is this possible?" I whispered. "It wasn't here before, was it?"

I didn't know what would disturb me more. That she'd grown this in the two days since I'd been here last or that it'd been here all along and I just hadn't been able to see it because of a spell.

She looked around in surprise. "Tell me what you are seeing."

"Plants. Lots of them. How are you growing these?" There was a window, but it wasn't nearly big enough to give the plants the type of light they would need to grow to this extent.

Understanding followed closely by suspicion dawned in her eyes.

"Something about you has changed," she said, no question in her voice. "This illusion should have been strong enough to fool a vampire a thousand years older than you. Tell me, have you been marked recently?"

I stopped gaping at the plants. She sounded very sure. Maybe she would be able to help me after all.

"Yes. Some sorcerer claims I'm indebted to him."

I rolled up my sleeve and held my arm out. The lion wrapped in thorns was kind of pretty now that I'd had time to get used to it. I'd always wanted a tattoo but had never been able to figure out what I wanted. If it hadn't been a sorcerer's mark, I'd be tempted to keep it.

"I don't recognize this mark, but it's definitely the reason you can see through the illusion. I'd wager, given the power radiating off of it, you'd be able to see through pretty much any illusion right now," Miriam said. "

"Guy by the name of Barret put it there." That was the name Jerry had given me when he assigned me the job anyway.

"Barret? That can't be right. His mark is an Egyptian eye with a lightning bolt through it."

"I'm pretty sure it was Barret. I did a delivery for him, but there was a complication and I wound up with this."

She raised an eyebrow. "Complication?"

I gave her a smile that was more of a grimace. "Long story."

"I've got time. And more importantly, I won't even consider helping you until I know everything."

I debated how much to share with her.

"Some of it falls under the confidentiality clause. I can't break it," I told her.

Jerry ensured his couriers' discretion by making us all sign a contract with a curse attached to it. As long as we didn't reveal the details of our jobs nothing happened. Break your promise and bad things happened. There were still whispers twenty years later about what happened to the last courier who'd broken the confidentiality clause.

"The contract Hermes had you sign?" Miriam asked.

I nodded. "That's the one."

"If I remember correctly, all you promised was not to reveal the package contents as well as the names of the client or the person to receive the package."

"That sounds about right, but I can't remember the exact language."

She gave me a smug smile and took a seat at the table. "That's okay. I do. Just keep the identities and contents secret and you'll be fine."

"How do you know you're right? Were you a courier?"

She laughed. "No, definitely not. I wouldn't work for Gerald ever. We would have killed each other the first time he told me what to do. I wrote that contract and built the curse into it."

Gerald? I wasn't even going to touch that.

"You wrote it? You mean the current version right."

She gave me a Cheshire cat smile. "There's only ever been one version."

Unless she'd written the thing when she was like seven that would mean she was much older than she looked. Her comments the last time I was here made a lot more sense now.

"Okay, so I wasn't able to deliver the package because its recipient was already dead when I got there," I told her, picking each word carefully. I didn't want to accidently invoke the curse. "The guy's friends happened on me before I could leave and thought I was the killer. They took the package and my phone. I managed to escape but left the package behind."

The next part was tricky. I couldn't say Barret was the guy who hired me. How did I tell her what led to the tattoo without revealing too much?

"And?"

"I'm getting to that. This is harder than it sounds. Everything's wrapped up together, and I don't know how sensitive the curse is."

I'd already mentioned Barret's name and that hadn't set anything off. It had been out of context, which is probably the only thing that saved me.

"Okay, so anyway, the client showed up wanting to know why their package wasn't delivered. He wasn't happy to hear that not only was the recipient dead but his package had been left behind. He had the sorcerer put the mark on me and that leads to now."

Her gaze was enigmatic as she considered me. "Something tells me you're leaving a lot out."

Got that right. I was hoping the vaguer I was the less likely I was to get whammied.

She tapped one finger against her lips. "For a sorcerer to place a mark, you would have needed to agree to it."

"That's what I don't get. All I said was I'd help him. There was no agreeing to terms. No shaking of hands or signing of contracts"

She gave me a scathing look. "You never make an open ended agreement with anyone belonging to the shadow world. By saying you'd help him without any qualifiers, you gave him an open ended contract. You handed him the keys to your life. How could you be so stupid?"

"How am I supposed to know any of this? I haven't exactly had anyone giving me helpful pointers. I'm figuring this shit out as I go along."

"This is why vampires are taken into a clan for the first hundred years. So they can be taught what they need to know. You've been around us long enough to know better. Gerald at the very least should have taught you better."

He hadn't. At least not that I could remember.

Her words made me feel dumber than when my Drill Sergeant made me feel an inch high for getting sun poisoning because I didn't put on sun screen. The military has no sympathy for preventable injuries.

"I did the best I could considering he was torturing me at the time. Can you help me or not?"

"I can't. The sorcerer who put it there is too powerful. Nothing I could do would remove it. I wouldn't anyway. Its bad form to interfere once the agreement is struck. You have to fulfill your part or forfeit the penalty."

I had a feeling that would be the answer. At least Miriam looked regretful she couldn't help me.

"Fine. That's not the only reason I came here. The sorcerer gave me a task, and I need to get a witch's perspective on something." I looked around the room. "Judging by what's in here I came to the right place."

The illusion she constructed was pretty thorough. In addition to hiding any sign of the jungle she had in here, it had wiped away all traces of smell. With it gone, the scent of dirt and growing things saturated the air. I inhaled. Jasmine. How did I miss all of this before?

"How so?" Miriam asked.

From the cast iron pot decorated with a trio of elephants sitting next to her, she poured a cup of tea. She didn't ask if I'd like one.

"If someone wanted to completely mask a scent, how would they go about doing it? And by completely, I mean a werewolf would be able to walk right by an area that smells like a butcher shop five minutes later and not smell a thing."

"That is oddly specific." She took a sip of her tea. "Would this illusion involve sight as well?"

I thought about it a moment. Nothing had appeared amiss in the alley either of the times I'd been in it. That didn't mean anything, though. I could have very easily missed something.

"Illusions are tricky and easily broken," Miriam said. "It's especially hard to trick all of the senses. The stronger the sense, the harder it is to fool. A werewolf's nose is extremely sensitive. One could have walked into this shop and sniffed out my garden in moments. This illusion wouldn't have stood a chance."

"So because my olfactory sense isn't as strong, the illusion held up against me," I said following her logic.

"Yes. Theoretically, it should be easier to fool one sense, for instance smell, but in reality most witches couldn't manage it."

"Could you?" I asked.

She inclined her head.

"I could but it would take me weeks of preparation. If you don't mind me asking, how are you sure that smell was the sense targeted if your hypothetical werewolf missed it."

"Hypothetically, I walked through an area and smelled it, but when the werewolves moved through ten minutes later, all trace of the odor was gone. By your reasoning, that scenario should be impossible, shouldn't it? Since my sense of smell is so much weaker?"

Miriam's face was thoughtful as she tapped one finger against her mug.

"Castings take time to take hold. You may have wandered through the target area in the brief span between whatever created the smell and the casting."

That was pretty much the conclusion I'd come to.

"How many people in the city could make a casting of that complexity?"

Miriam's focus turned inward as she considered.

"Hm. That is a difficult question and the answer is rather imprecise."

"Just give me a ballpark."

An answer would at least give me a place to start.

"All of the sorcerers, of course. Some of the high ranking members of the coven. I'd guess a few of the independents as well. You also have to consider a witch working in partnership with another. I'd say maybe fifteen."

Fifteen? That was too many. It would take forever to narrow it down from there. Still, it was the only clue I had. I figured if I found the person who made the smell dampening spell I'd be able to follow them to the culprit. I do that and my sorcerer problem goes away.

"I don't suppose you'd give me the names of those fifteen?"

Miriam gave me another enigmatic smile. "For a price."

Great. Another deal. The last one had gotten me into enough trouble.

"What's your price?" I asked. This was a bad idea, but I was between a rock and a hard place. I could walk away, but I'd be back to square one. I had video from the security feeds, but there was no guarantee anything was on it.

"This isn't me agreeing to the price," I clarified, quickly. I had learned something since my last interaction with a sorcerer. "I'm just trying to understand the terms."

"Very good. Maybe you're capable of surviving in this world after all." Miriam gestured for me to take a seat beside her. I took the chair and hoped this price was something I could give.

"If I do this, you will owe me a favor to be called upon at a time and place of my choosing."

That was too open ended. I'd read the original Grimm Fairy Tales when I was a child. Not those Disney approved ones that always had happy endings, but the twisted, violent ones. Any time someone agreed to an open ended favor things always went sideways for them. She could demand I carve out my heart or give her my sister's first born child, and by the terms of the agreement, I'd have to comply.

"No, that's too vague."

She inclined her head and smiled. Another test. Miriam seemed content to help me, but equally happy to take advantage of my naivety to trick me into agreeing to something that would benefit her and bite me in the ass. It made her both trustworthy and not. I'd have to be on my guard to not be lulled in by her helpfulness.

She was not a potential friend or even an ally against a common enemy. This was a transaction. Plain and simple.

"One favor, to be called before Jan 1."

"One favor, to be called in the next 30 days. It can't involve a crime, the death of anybody I know, including myself, dismemberment or anything that involves souls or demons."

I remembered her insinuation about using me as ingredients for some of her spells. I had no idea if witches actually trafficked in souls or demons but thought it best to protect myself from even unlikely scenarios.

"How specific," Miriam said. "I see you've been reading some of the Urban Fantasy novels mortals write about us."

I shrugged. There may have been a few movies in there too. It's how I conducted most of my research. There was usually a grain of truth in even the most fantastical of tales.

"Very well. No ingredients, murders, dismemberment, souls or demons. Do we have a deal?"

I paused. Did I really want to do this? I barely knew Miriam. It was highly likely that what she asked of me would be something I could not easily give.

"The favor cannot be called in until after I finish my task for the sorcerer, but yes, we have a deal." I needed help. One thing at a time. I'd worry about what I owed when I got out of my current predicament.

"Wonderful. I'll get a pen and paper."

Miriam stood and walked over to an antique desk hidden behind several potted ferns. She pulled out a notepad and scribbled on it.

What favor could a witch ask of a vampire? I wasn't equipped to do magic and being practically an infant in this world meant I had almost no power. Just strength and healing slightly above that of a human's. Not much for a witch as old as she said she was.

This was such a bad idea. Too late to back out now. The deal had already been struck and judging by the itchy sensation on my bicep, I had a feeling I had a mark to show for it.

I touched the area lightly. It was high enough on the arm that I would have to pull my long sleeved shirt off. I'd have to wait to see what her magic had inscribed in my skin.

She stopped in front of me, looking down with a guarded expression. I waited, wondering if she'd follow through on her end. It would be hard to hand over names of people you've known for years to a person you'd just met. Part of me hoped she'd back out. It would free me up from the favor hanging like an albatross from my neck.

"Some of these names are friends of mine," she told me, setting the paper on the table but keeping her hand on it. I'd assumed as much. "We're a very secretive people. Events of the past have taught us the value of keeping the extent of our abilities hidden from those who mean us harm. I am trusting you will use this information in the way it's intended and not for some other vendetta you or another may have."

I looked at the folded piece of paper. I couldn't speak for the sorcerer, but for my part I only intended to find the witch who cast the spell. After that, I had no use for the rest of the names.

I slid the paper towards me. "I understand. As long as the one who cast the spell means no harm to me, I will not bring harm to him or her. The rest of them don't matter to me."

"Good."

What remained unsaid was that there would be terrible repercussions if I abused this information or if harm came to the innocent as a result of my having these names.

Now that the first part of my plan had been met, I asked, "I don't suppose I could borrow your computer."

"I'm afraid I don't have a computer here, and I'm unwilling to extend further help without renegotiating our terms."

Ah. Yeah, that wasn't going to happen. It would be easy enough to find a computer to use. I had no need to dig myself further into this hole.

"Thanks for your help," I told her.

*　*　*

The breeze was cool against my face when I stepped out of Elements. I pulled my jacket around me by reflex. The cold didn't feel as cold these days, but it was hard to conquer the habits of a lifetime. I still felt the change in temperature even if it didn't affect me as it once did. Or maybe it just wasn't as big a deal as it had been before my transition. I used to hole up and hibernate as soon as fall turned cold. Now I could get by with a long sleeved shirt if I didn't care what normal would think of me.

The moon was nearly full and hung low and large in the sky. Stars winked in the night, more than I'd ever seen as a human.

My feet whispered over the pavement, crunching fallen leaves as I headed back to Cherry.

A hand suddenly gripped my arm, spinning me around. I gaped up at Brax's angry face. How did he find me?

"We need to talk, vampire," he rumbled.

I grimaced. I'd really prefer not to.

"How did you find me?"

"One of my pack saw you slipping out the back after we confronted the vampires in their club. I put it together from there."

Of course he had.

"I do have to thank you for distracting them and giving me time to escape."

His hand tightened, squeezing my arm painfully as he gave a small shake. "You lied to me. You're not from Hermes. You're part of the Davinish clan."

I reached for his hand, digging my fingers into his thumb and jerked, twisting my arm out of his grip at the same time. Military combative training had taught me a thing or two about escaping holds. The thumb was the weakest part of a grip and easier to break if you had surprise and leverage on your side. Even super strength had its weaknesses.

Free, I rubbed my arm and took two steps away.

"I didn't lie to you. I do work for Jerry and Hermes."

"Vampires don't let their yearlings work for people outside the clan, and you're so young you still smell human."

"What do vampires smell like?" I couldn't help but ask, wanting to know if the smell was different for werewolves. I hadn't noticed anything when I was at their club, and my nose was rather sensitive. Not as sensitive as a werewolf's but way better than when I was human.

I waved my question away. "Never mind. It doesn't matter. You could consider me an illegal alien. I'm not part of any of the clans."

His eyes narrowed, but he didn't make any move to attack, instead seeming to settle. He was still alert and stood perfectly balanced, ready to move at a moment's notice. I had no doubt if I attempted to run he would chase me down like a lion would a gazelle. It was not a comforting thought.

"That shouldn't be possible. For all that they're arrogant pricks, they wouldn't turn someone and then abandon them."

I smirked. "Guess I'm special then. Lucky me. Woke up in a morgue and had to figure everything else out by myself." I thought about it. "Well, myself and a few helpful individuals."

"Why should I believe you?"

I shrugged. "I don't really care if you believe me. You can call Jerry, and he'll confirm it."

"I plan to, but for now, you're coming with me."

I backed up as he started towards me. I really didn't have time to be put back in his basement cage.

He blurred as he raced forwards. I dove out of the way, rolled and popped back up to my feet. He crashed into me taking me back to the ground. I grunted as I landed, his weight coming down on top of me and pinning my legs.

I twisted, using my legs to tilt my pelvis up so I could roll him off me. He collapsed his upper body onto mine, making it impossible to get the leverage I needed. The guy was strong, and it had been a couple of years since I'd last tried this move.

"Nice try. I give you an A for effort." His grin was slightly feral.

I elbowed him in the face, grinning happily when he looked back down at me with a bloody lip. How was that for effort?

His tongue darted out to catch a drop of blood, and his eyes turned husky blue.

Maybe it hadn't been such a good idea to bloody him up.

A low pitched growl from our right distracted both of us. A big dog slunk out of the shadows. He looked like a husky but was the size of a mastiff.

"That's a dog right?" I asked.

Brax snarled, his lip lifting to expose a mouth full of fangs. The dog crept closer, his eyes trained on us with strings of drool dripping from his fangs.

"I thought dogs were afraid of werewolves," I whispered.

"That's not a dog."

Brax jackknifed up, dragging me behind him.

"What do you mean it's not a dog?"

He didn't spare me a glance. "I mean it's not a dog."

"Then what is it."

"Werewolf."

Werewolf. I looked back at the beast. It was a lot bigger than any wolf I'd ever seen at the zoo. Bulkier and taller too. His fur was dark brown on top and fading to a creamy white around his legs. He would have been beautiful if it hadn't been for the bald patches and bloody wounds all over his body.

The car was still several blocks from here. I didn't think I could outrun the wolf.

"I thought you were an alpha. Don't wolves have to listen to the alpha?"

"They do have to listen to the alpha." His voice was deep and still managed to sound angry.

"Tell him to go away."

"I would, but he's not listening."

"What do you mean he's not listening? Try again."

We backed down the street as the wolf steadily advanced.

"I have been trying. There's something wrong with him. He's not listening to cues." It sounded like he was talking to himself more than me. "He shouldn't be challenging me like this. All of his instincts should be telling him to run."

That was not ideal. I reached for the silver knife in my belt.

"Is silver as effective on wolves as fiction says?" I asked.

He didn't take his eyes off the advancing threat to see what I was doing.

"Yes."

That was good.

I readied the blade, holding it loose and firm in my hand. I didn't have much practice in knife fighting. Just what friends had demonstrated while goofing around at parties over the years. For some reason, guys always thought I'd be impressed if they did weird things like give me a knife fighting lesson. Once a guy had shown me how to swallow fire. I had to take him to the ER afterwards, but it had been entertaining right up until he started screaming.

"Stay behind me," Brax ordered, running forward just as the wolf leapt.

They came together in a crash of snarls and growls, each one moving almost quicker than my eyes could follow. Brax gripped the wolf's head, preventing it from sinking its teeth in his throat. The wolf raked his claws along Brax's arms and legs, creating long, bloody furrows of torn flesh. A bellow of pain escaped Brax even as his arms tightened around the wolf's neck.

I darted forward, sinking my blade between its ribs, only to withdraw and do it again. Brax held him immobile as I stabbed, again and again. The wolf refused to die.

I changed my angle and stabbed into his abdomen. My knife skated against something hard, before it gave way. The wolf let out a spine tingling howl as he thrashed and heaved, nearly jerking himself loose. Before long, his struggles eased until he hung limp from Brax's arms.

Brax threw the wolf away, sending him crashing into a tree where he lay boneless.

"He really did not want to die," I said. My arms were covered in black gunk. It should have been blood. I sniffed. The black smelled of rot, like the blood had been sitting for weeks and weeks. It smelled like what I'd found in the alley behind Lou's. It wasn't an exact match. This didn't smell nearly as bad, but it definitely had a lot in common with that smell.

T.A. White

"That should not have happened," Brax said, without taking his eyes off the wolf. "He should have bled out much sooner."

"This blood smells similar to what was in the alley," I told him.

Brax's eerie ice blue eyes shifted to me and he leaned forward, inhaling deeply. I held still, not wanting to provoke him. His wolf seemed close to the surface, and I didn't know how good Brax's control was.

"This is wrong. This is all wrong," he growled. "Our blood does not smell like this."

I suspected not many people's blood smelled like this. It didn't change the facts.

I walked over to the body. Somehow, in some way, this wolf had a link to whatever had killed the werewolf at the bar, and all the other deaths that had happened over the summer. I crouched down next to it.

"What are you doing?" Brax asked, coming to stand behind me.

The smell was worse up close. I don't know how I'd missed it while we'd been fighting with the creature. Moreover, Brax should have been able to smell it long before it got close enough to attack.

I picked up a stick and lifted the wolf's head. Its glassy eyes stared vacantly past mine. The pupils were dilated and filmy white, which was strange. It usually took a few hours after death for eyes to gain that appearance.

"Did you notice any type of smell before fighting him? Or even during?"

"No," Brax said slowly as he thought back. "I didn't, and I should have. This smell is distinctive enough that I would have been able to pick it up from several miles away."

Miles? Really? I knew their noses were more sensitive than mine but not by that much. It made sense though. A wolf's nose was a hundred times more powerful than a human's and could outperform a dog's. I just hadn't realized how much of the skill translated over to the human form.

The sound of metal sliding against metal came from the wolf's neck. I leaned closer. There, a piece of chain around it. I picked up another stick and worked it under the chain to lift it free from the fur. It took some work but now that I knew what it was I eventually got the chain and the amulet attached free of the neck. My knife had caught on the chain and snapped it during the fight. I was surprised it had stayed there given Brax tossed him through the air like a Frisbee.

"What is that?" Brax asked, squatting down beside me.

I shook my head, holding the amulet up with the sticks. I didn't want to touch it. Given that I suspected a witch was involved in this somehow, I didn't want to take the chance it was ensorcelled.

The body hissed and crunched. Brax grabbed my arm and pulled me back. I bobbled the sticks, dropping the amulet.

"Wait."

Brax didn't wait, hauling me further away as the body started deteriorating, a fine dust rising in the air.

A face appeared in the dust as a voice hissed, "It's mine. Where is it? Where is it? I know you've taken it. It's mine."

"What are you talking about?" I asked.

"You have it. I know you have it. Tell me where it is. If you don't give it to me, I will curse your family line and hunt all of your descendants down and kill them in their sleep. I will deny you a warrior's death so you languish on this earth, forever denied the halls of your ancestors."

The face morphed between a human's and a wolf's, shifting and changing the features one at a time. Brax grabbed the knife from where I'd stashed it in my belt and threw it. Silver glinted as it spun through the air, dispelling the mist. The voice screamed, the sound enraged and powerful as it echoed through the air before both face and mist disappeared.

"Holy shit. What was that?" I asked.

Nothing I'd read in fiction books or heard from other supernaturals could explain what I'd just seen.

"I don't know."

"You don't know? How can you not know?" I asked.

He was a werewolf. An alpha. He had a better education in these matters than me. He should know what that was.

His face was fierce as he glared at me. "There are more creatures in this world than can be named in any book. I don't know the names of all of them."

"Do you at least have a guess?"

"Not one I'm willing to share with you."

I was betting not. He probably just didn't want to admit he was as clueless as the baby vamp.

It didn't matter if he had a guess or not. If he wasn't willing to share it with me, he wasn't much use.

I walked away. Time to get back to figuring out where I could find a computer.

"Aileen Travers."

I ground to a halt but didn't turn.

"That's your name isn't it?" he asked. His voice sounded like he was right behind me. "Aileen Travers."

I turned around. He was only a step or two away. In easy grabbing distance. I folded my arms over my chest and tried to project a confidence I didn't feel.

"What makes you think that?" I asked.

He gave me a smooth smile and pulled out a phone, holding it up screen side facing me. My phone. I'd forgotten he had it.

He turned the screen towards him. "It's funny. A call came in the day after you escaped. When I listened to the voicemail, I discovered a few interesting things."

Only one person would have left me a voicemail.

"I'm pretty sure I left that locked," I said.

One side of his mouth tilted up in a half smile. "I have a guy."

"And? Is that all you've got? A voicemail?"

"Enough to know your name is Aileen Travers. Your mother is upset with you. Something about scaring your sister?"

That little tattle tale. I'd hoped she would keep our argument to herself, but it sounded like she'd gone running to Mom as soon as I left. That must have been some voicemail my mom left. She gave him everything.

He slipped the phone back into his pocket, his point made. If he had someone good enough to break the security on the phone, it would be possible to find all he needed to know by simply knowing my name.

"There's a reason the vampires pull their newly made out of their prior life," he told me. "Remaining a part of your family's lives puts everybody in danger."

"That's not your choice to make."

"Maybe not but if you don't come with me, I'm going to tell the vampires exactly who you are and how you've been in contact with your family. See how long you last once they know your name and the location of your human family."

He had me. He knew it, and I knew it. I wouldn't risk their safety. I had no quips or retorts. For now, I had no choice but to go with him.

He didn't wait for my agreement, walking towards me and grabbing my arm to haul me after him.

"You don't have to grab," I told him. "You know I'll go with you."

He didn't bother responding, continuing down the street to a car parked in front of a fire hydrant. Brave of him. The meter maids down here went after parking violations with a rabid intensity. He opened the door and shoved me inside, slamming it shut after me.

"Where are we going?" I asked as he got into the driver's seat.

He didn't respond as he started the car and pulled away from the curb. Guess it was going to be a surprise.

Chapter Seven

An hour outside the city, the car's headlights illuminated a two story farm house. We were far enough out that the roads no longer had formal names, just a bunch of numbers.

The house looked like it was built back in the early 1900s. Set back from the road, it had a wrap-around porch with a rocking chair and several potted plants, lending it a warm, homey appearance. An extension had been added to the back with a careful attention to detail, allowing it to blend in with the rest of the house.

It was cute and definitely not what I pictured as a werewolf's den. I had something a little more rustic in mind. Maybe a lodge or even one of those houses that looked like it was falling down around its owners. Not this white picket fence house.

As we pulled up, three men came to stand on the porch, watching us get out.

"See you found the escapee," the one on the steps observed.

He wasn't familiar, but I hadn't gotten a good look at all of the wolves at the bar. The other two were people I recognized. One being Declan, looking mildly interested in my presence. The other was the man from Miriam's shop. The glare he leveled at me was the kind reserved for when someone had mortally offended you, like when they kicked your puppy or took the last piece of pizza. I didn't know what I'd done to earn that level of enmity.

"What's she doing here?" he asked, not taking his eyes off me.

The first man gave him a slow look. "Since when were you high enough in the pack to ask questions like that? Unless you were planning on a challenge, Victor."

Victor scowled at the first man and folded his arms over his muscled chest. "You won't always be beta, Clay."

The first man's easy going manner disappeared. He straightened and stared Victor down.

"Is that a challenge, boyo?"

Victor held his gaze for a minute before breaking eye contact and stalking inside the house.

The group was silent for a long minute after the door slammed shut.

I felt a little awkward as I waited for the tension to fade. I felt a little bad for the guy. He'd asked a simple question, and it had devolved into a dominance game. If this was how every interaction was between werewolves, I was glad I'd dodged that bullet. Guarding every word out of my mouth would be exhausting.

I followed Brax up the stairs, lingering behind by a couple of steps.

Clay had relaxed back against the post with a pleasant expression on his face as he smiled at me. I stared back, not changing expression. I was here under duress. I figured that excused me from having to make pleasantries with my captors.

"Was that necessary?" Brax said.

Clay shrugged. "It'll do him good. Perhaps it'll curb some of his more dickish tendencies."

"Unlikely," Declan observed.

Clay watched me with a tilted head. "You're not what I pictured. Thought you'd be taller and a lot more buff."

"I'm devastated I don't live up to your imagination," I said.

To my surprise, Clay threw his head back and laughed. "That's more like what I pictured. I like her."

"My life is complete. I can die happy." I turned to Brax. "So where is my cage this time? The basement again?"

He watched me with cool eyes. "I think I've properly motivated you to stay so we can forgo locking you up this time. First though, we're going to have a chat." He stepped closer. "And you're going to tell me everything you know about these murders, including why the vampires are so interested."

*   *   *

My interrogation was pretty tame by most standards. There was no waterboarding or sensory deprivation. They simply sat me down in the kitchen and served me a mug of blood.

I sniffed cautiously when the feral woman from the bar set it in front of me. I wouldn't put it past her to put something in it after I pushed her down the stairs.

"Don't worry. I didn't poison it," she told me with a wry smile. "If I wanted revenge, I'd be much more direct. A fist to the face or a couple swipes with my claws."

That was a pleasant image.

"Are you planning on revenge?" I asked. It'd be good to know, though I doubted I could trust her answer.

She shrugged on shoulder. "Not particularly. You were just looking out for yourself. I would have done the same in your place."

"How very understanding." I wrapped my hands around the mug. It was warm and the temptation to down it like a frat boy chugging a beer was nearly irresistible. I didn't want to do that in front of the four gathered around me.

"Of course, if the opportunity presented to shove you down a flight of stairs, I would take it."

I snorted, swallowing my laughter back as I was momentarily distracted from the draw of the blood. That was honest.

"Is the blood not to your taste?" she asked, changing topic with whiplash speed.

"It's fine. I'm just not hungry right this moment."

I wasn't hungry; I was starving. The two bags of blood I'd had at the club weren't nearly enough given all the activity of the last few days.

Declan shifted forward, drawing my attention, "How old are you?"

I debated the merits of telling the truth. From what Brax had said during our argument earlier, it was obvious that most of them knew I was young in terms of vampire years. The question then became how much of the truth I should fudge. The vampire from the club had seemed disbelieving of my age.

"Less than three years, I'm guessing," Brax observed when I let the silence linger too long.

How the hell did he know that?

Reading the expression on my face, he said, "You got out of the Army a little over two years ago. No way would you have been able to serve long term with your condition."

I upgraded his hacker's connections from good to superior. The military's firewalls were nothing to sneeze at so any hacker able to get through them to view a service member's records was extremely good at his profession.

"Two years," I said.

"That won't be enough," the woman said abruptly. She slid off the cabinet she'd claimed as a seat and held her wrist out to me. I caught a tantalizing whiff of dark chocolate and champagne before I jerked my head back.

"What the hell?" I said, glaring up at her.

"You're too young to survive on bagged. You need blood from the source."

She held her wrist out to me again. I shoved it away. She smelled so good.

"No, thank you." It was a struggle to sound polite around the fangs that were suddenly crowding my mouth.

She rolled her eyes. "Don't worry. I've been bitten before. You can't hurt me."

A claw slid out from one of her fingers and she drew a line of blood down one forearm. I leapt to my feet, knocking my chair over in my haste. I backed away, tripping over that chair.

"Are you crazy?" I asked. "I said no."

My teeth ached to bite. Her blood smelled like dessert and alcohol, nothing like the stuff I normally drank. It would taste so good going down my throat.

I shook my head to get my thoughts back online. That way lay danger. I was still too uninformed about this life. For all I knew biting someone was a way to become beholden to them. I was keeping my fangs to myself until I knew for sure whether taking blood could get me in trouble. There was also the small matter of never having bitten a live person before. I didn't want to start now with all these people here.

"It's no big deal," she said, walking towards me.

I backed away and encountered the wall. I slid along it as she kept advancing.

"Don't be such a baby."

She darted forward, grabbed my shoulder, bringing her arm up to my mouth. I slapped one hand over my mouth and the other on her arm, holding it away from me.

"Well that's a new one," Clay drawled. "Never thought I'd see Sondra having to chase down a vampire to get her to feed."

"Definitely not something you see every day," Brax said.

Neither seemed particularly inclined to lend a hand in getting the crazy werewolf off me. I gave up on fending her off and slid down the wall to sit with my knees curled up against my chest, wrapping my arms around them and ducking my head so I was curled into a ball. Not the most dignified position, but it worked in first grade when Billy Lars tried to draw a mustache on my face.

I clung with all my vampire strength to my knees, even as Sondra tried to pry me up or at least smear blood on my mouth.

"As amusing as this is, we need to get back to business. Sondra, let her up," Brax ordered.

"But-"

"Now."

"Fine, fine," she grumbled. Her hands left me as she stood and walked away. I listened for several beats as the sound of her footsteps moved across the kitchen. Only when I heard the slight thud as she jumped back onto the counter did I risk lifting my head.

"Didn't you hear," I said, feeling brave now that there was an entire length of the kitchen between us. "No means no."

Her eyes flashed amber, and she lifted herself as if preparing to leap.

"No, Sondra," Brax warned.

She settled back down. I smirked at her. Not my most mature moment, but I wasn't feeling particularly mature after being chased around the kitchen like a child who wouldn't eat her vegetables.

"Come and sit down," Brax ordered.

I eyed the vacant chair.

"Think I'm good here."

"I didn't ask if you were good there." He kicked the chair slightly further out from the table. "Take a seat."

I glared. My temper had always been kind of short. I'd worked my whole life to manage it and for the most part succeeded. Ever since I got back from Afghanistan, and especially since my transformation, I'd had a lot more trouble keeping the volcano boiling inside me contained.

"I'm not one of your pack. I sit where I choose."

His eyes bled to blue. I held his stare, not willing to back down. It probably wasn't the wisest course to antagonize the deadly predator in front of me, but I wasn't going to let them walk all over me.

"Oh boy," Clay muttered, eyeing the table top. All of the wolves dropped their gazes, looking anywhere but at the pissed off alpha.

I lifted my chin. Go ahead. Let's see what you've got.

"You're not very smart," Brax said, his words taking on a guttural edge.

"So people keep telling me."

The two of us glared at each other while the others avoided looking at us, holding their bodies tense as the aggression poured off Brax.

He took a deep breath releasing it on a long exhale.

"Chair. Please."

The please surprised me and judging by the expressions of the rest of the group, it wasn't a sentiment often expressed by the alpha.

It left me to reconsider my position. It felt safer to keep my distance, even if that safety was only in my head. I had no doubt that if I refused after he said please he would put me in that chair, even if he had to pick me up and tie me to it. He'd win too, being much stronger than me. I also couldn't do any permanent damage to him given what he knew of my family. Did I really want to lose any more face by being forced into the chair? Predators were more likely to attack the weaker members of the herd. Might as well take the out he'd given me.

"Since you asked so nicely."

No one commented when I stood and walked back to the chair, taking a seat as if the past few minutes hadn't taken place.

"Shall we get started?" I asked, folding my arms across my chest and trying to appear relaxed.

Clay inserted himself into the conversation by speaking first, "Who asked you to deliver a package to Franklin?"

"Do you guys not use Hermes at all? You know I can't reveal the name of the person who contracted our services unless you're the recipient. Your alpha refused to sign in Franklin's stead so you don't get to know that information."

It was pretty much what I'd told the alpha earlier.

"What's in the package?" Declan asked.

"Again, that's privileged information."

Brax watched me carefully, as if he was considering a particularly interesting puzzle. I gave him calm eyes. It was the look I used to give my Staff Sergeant when he'd caught me doing something I wasn't technically supposed to.

"Tell me what you know of Liam's interest in all of this."

Sondra jolted.

Liam. It took me a moment, but I recalled he was the vampire who'd practically kidnapped me. The one who broke several of my ribs and nearly killed me. He was also the one standing over the body at Lou's, but I hadn't known his name to give Brax back then. How did he know about him now?

"Not sure who you mean," I said, without taking my eyes off Brax's.

He gave me a chiding look. "Lying doesn't really work with werewolves. We can smell deception."

It wasn't difficult to believe him. Given the stress indicators, pheromones and the like, that a person gave off when telling a lie, it would be easy for his nose to sniff such deceptions out.

"If that's the case, why did you put me in that cage?" I asked, outraged when I realized he'd known I was telling the truth about Hermes and the package the entire time. He could have signed for the damn thing, and I would have been able to avoid this entire nightmare.

He shrugged. "Our noses aren't foolproof. You could have been a sociopath or someone skilled in keeping your stress signals under control. Vampires have always been particularly good at that."

"You all thought I was human."

He ignored that.

"Back to my question. What is Liam's interest in our matters?"

"I don't know. I only met the guy tonight and last night at your bar. It's not like he told me his every thought in that time."

"He was at the bar?" Sondra asked.

"Yeah. He's the vampire who was standing over the body." I couldn't bring myself to identify the lump of parts I'd seen as Franklin Wade. Having never met the guy while he was alive, it was a lot easier to disassociate the dismembered parts from anything that had once been living.

"Could this have been an assassination?" Declan asked.

"We have been having trouble with the vampires straying onto our territory over the last few months," Clay said.

"I doubt it," I chimed in. "Sounded like they had a few people killed over the past few months too. It also wouldn't explain the wolf that attacked us earlier. More likely, whatever did the killings over the summer is responsible for Franklin and the guy the vampires just lost."

My voice trailed off as I noticed I was the subject of four intense stares, each looking at me like I'd grown a second head.

"And you know this how?" a voice asked from the doorway.

Victor stepped inside and lurked against the wall. That was the only word I had for it. He used his size and scowling face to try to intimidate me.

I raised an eyebrow. He'd have to work a lot harder than that. I'd been scowled at by some of the best. Drill Sergeant Richards used to be able to drop an entire platoon with just a shift of expression. Compared to them, this pretty boy was a cake walk.

"I listened. Oh, and I used deductive reasoning," I said.

"What makes you think we'll just take a vampire's word for it?" he sneered.

This guy was really getting on my nerves.

"I don't. Honestly, I couldn't care less if you believed me. You guys are the ones who dragged me here. I didn't come barging in demanding to be heard."

Brax interrupted him before he could say anything else. "Is there some emergency that requires your interruption?"

By the tone of Brax's voice, he made it clear there was only one correct answer. I wouldn't want to be Victor if he'd barged in here for no reason.

"There's been some movement on the perimeter," he said.

Clay turned and looked at him. "I thought Alex was in charge of security tonight. Why are you the one reporting?"

Victor's gaze didn't stray from me.

"I volunteered," Victor said.

I couldn't quite figure out the relationship between the three. Clay clearly didn't like the other man, and it seemed the feeling was mutual. I hadn't known Brax long but I could tell that he tolerated Victor's presence out of necessity rather than any liking on his part. It made me wonder, then, why Victor seemed so intent on putting himself in their way. I'd always favored active avoidance when I suspected someone didn't like me.

"Volunteered? Or acted without Alex's knowledge?" Clay asked with a wry twist to his lips.

Victor ignored the question.

"Thought so," Clay said.

Brax didn't look any happier. "You've reported the news. You can be on your way now. We'll discuss your circumventing Alex later."

The look he cast Victor's way promised there would be a reckoning whenever later took place.

They waited until Victor had departed. Brax shared a look with Clay. He was not happy.

Clay sighed. "I'll take care of it. I think he's just about run out of the rope we've given him."

"See to it."

Their attention turned back to me.

"What makes you think they've recently lost someone?" Brax asked.

Hm. It was a stretch and based loosely on the interactions between Liam and Aiden. Coupled with the smell of death in the condo I'd run into Liam at, it all seemed to add up to one thing.

"Just some things that were said in front of me at the club. Liam seemed particularly interested in some security video. He thought that the club was the last place the vampire had been seen."

Sondra leaned back on her arms as she stared into space. "I wonder if there's a way we can get in there to get the videos. We could try slipping in during the day."

"They employ daylight security and have the place warded to hell and back," Declan said.

Should I let them know that I had the solution to all of their problems in my back pocket? It might go a long way to proving I wasn't the killer. The USB was my first real clue in all this and revealing its presence could cost me potential leverage.

On the other hand, I had no computer and didn't know when the werewolves planned to release me. The sorcerer hadn't put a time limit on finding the creature and his item, but I doubted his patience was infinite.

"About that," I said slowly.

All four sets of eyes zeroed in on me. I fought against the instinctive flinch at once again being the focus of so many predators. I reached into my pocket and withdrew the flash drive. It was becoming clear I couldn't do this on my own. Maybe I could use their interest to help me with the killer. I'd rather try than sit here for who knew how long.

"I may have taken the liberty of downloading their feeds onto this flash drive."

I took another sip out of the mug. My eyes fluttered closed. It tasted so good.

I looked up at Declan's low whistle. Brax looked startled and slightly bemused. No one made a move to grab the USB from me.

"How did you manage to get that?" Brax asked softly.

I grinned. "Told you I had to thank you for your well timed entrance at the club. It distracted them long enough for me to download the feeds, which someone had been kind enough to pull up for me before I escaped."

"You're kind of crazy," Sondra said, grinning wolfishly. "I like it."

"I'm so glad. Now I can die happy."

Clay reached for the USB and I pulled it back.

"One condition. I watch too."

I needed to see what was on there. I didn't know exactly what I was looking for or if it even mattered to this case, but I wasn't going to let the chance pass me by.

"We were counting on it," Clay said, reaching and slowly taking the USB from me.

I let him.

Declan left and returned quickly with a computer. It only took a few moments to pull the first feed up. I'd like to say we found a huge clue that enabled us to immediately deduce who the murderer was. In reality, none of us knew what we were looking for, just that the vampires seemed to think something important had gone down at their club. Hours and hours of staring at a computer screen commenced, threatening to rob me of what little sanity I had left.

By the end of the first hour, I was thoroughly disgusted at today's average twenty something. If the amount of drugs, sex and sheer stupidity I saw in those videos was the normal mode of behavior, our society was screwed. There were several fights, a couple make out sessions between both guy/girl couples and girl/girl couples.

By the third hour, I wanted to wash my brain out with soap. Vampires, I learned, were not shy when it came to feeding and having sex with their victims. Many of them also didn't care if they had an audience. I felt like we were watching a silent porno and couldn't help shifting uncomfortably.

At some point we moved to the living room, where Declan linked the computer with the TV to play the security feeds on. The surroundings were more comfortable than the hard chairs from the kitchen at least.

My stomach gurgled. I reached for the popcorn Sondra had made, grabbing a handful and popping it into my mouth. I hoped it would curb some of the hunger I was feeling, because the mug of blood had long since congealed. I was afraid asking for another would encourage Sondra to offer up her wrist again, and I didn't want another awkward chase around the kitchen.

"This is pointless. We don't even know what we're looking for," Sondra complained. It was the fourth time she'd said something to that effect.

From where he lounged on the couch with his feet propped up on the coffee table, Brax said, "We may not recognize it now but something we see here might make sense when put in context with something else."

Sondra groaned. I felt her pain. There were hours and hours of footage. It covered nearly a week's span. Even eliminating the daylight hours, that was a lot of time, especially since there were multiple cameras and multiple angles. It could take weeks. I didn't think I had that kind of time.

Just then something caught my attention. I tensed but didn't move, not wanting to give anything away to the others.

A familiar figure walked across the screen, stopping at several tables before taking a seat at the bar next to a young man. The guy looked like he'd been a nerd at some point but had grown out of it in his later years.

The quality of the video was decent but not good enough to make out too many details on the guy.

The woman though. I knew her. I thought. It looked sort of like Angela. But that was ridiculous. What would a witch be doing at a vampire club?

The two figures on the screen stood and went into the back room. I looked at the bottom right where that camera's feed should have been. There was nothing. The room still looked empty. I glanced back at the other feed. The two weren't there either. They weren't on any of the other camera feeds either. Now, wasn't that interesting?

Clay yawned and stretched, nearly knocking me in the face. "I'm so tired I don't think I can see straight anymore. We're going to have to take a break, maybe let one of the computer guys look at these and break the feeds into separate screens."

Brax unfolded his long limbed body from where he'd been reclining.

"Tell them to make a few copies. I want several eyes on each in case one of us picks up something the others missed."

I stayed where I was in my armchair as the others stood and stretched.

"Show our guest up to her room," he told Sondra.

I grimaced. There were still a couple hours until dawn. I'd hoped they'd leave me to review the disks on my own. I wanted to get a better look at the Angela look alike to see if I was right. That was unlikely to happen if they stashed me in a locked room somewhere.

"I won't go to sleep for a few more hours. I could stay and review the video until then," I said. It didn't hurt to try.

Brax was shaking his head before I even finished speaking. "No. I don't want you reviewing anything without one of us with you in case you get it in your head to hold something back."

Too late for that. I'd already discovered a semi clue and not one of them had picked up on it. Vampire one, super sniffer zero.

"Come on, you," Sondra said, pausing by me.

I grumbled under my breath but stood. What was I supposed to do for the next few hours? Their paranoia was costing me valuable time.

Sondra led me through the house, heading for the second floor instead of the basement as I'd expected. The rooms had a homey, warm feel, decorated for comfort rather than style. Everything had an easy charm. It made you want to take a seat and relax.

Where the downstairs had an almost masculine feel, the bedroom Sondra led me to had a much more feminine spin to it, filled with lace and flowers. The room was pretty and had that delicate sort of look that made you feel like you might break something if you breathed on it too hard.

"You can get a bath or shower in there," Sondra said, pointing to a door. "The windows have silver bars on them, and the door has been reinforced so don't even think of trying to escape. If we find you outside this room, we will attack. If you're lucky, you might get away with a missing limb, though I doubt it. Our guys have a tendency to kill first and eat the evidence after."

That was a nice visual. I wondered how many times she had given this speech.

"You sure you don't want a bite," she asked, lifting her wrist again.

I wrinkled my nose. I needed to eat but still wasn't sure I wanted to risk the consequences a bite might entail. I also didn't know if I could stop myself once I got started. My hunger had only grown over the last few hours. Being in the same room with all that gloriously alive blood rushing just beneath an easily penetrable surface had been pure temptation.

"I'll take a mug of that blood from earlier," I said.

She sighed and shook her head. "You have to be the weirdest vamp I've ever met. Most would be falling all over themselves to get a sip of a willing werewolf."

"Guess I'm just special," I said.

"I'll send someone up with what you need. Meanwhile make sure to get a shower. Werewolf noses are extremely sensitive."

I sniffed my clothes discretely. There was no smell that I could discern.

Left alone, I did as she suggested. It had been two days since I last had a chance to shower. I was looking forward to getting clean.

The water felt amazing as it washed over my skin. A warm bath or shower at the end of a long day had always been an almost decadent pleasure when I was alive. With my heightened senses, the experience was nearly sinful.

I resisted the temptation to linger, not wanting to miss the knock in case my meal arrived. A bathrobe hung off a hook next to the shower. It was one of the ones you'd find in really nice hotels, long and comfortable and soft to the touch. I put it on, giving my discarded clothes a look of disgust. The bike pants and warm top would have been perfect for biking around the city if Jerry hadn't given me Cherry. They'd been slightly less perfect the second day of wear, and I was glad to be out of them.

I would have to put them on soon, but for now I just enjoyed being clean and wrapped tight in a comfortable robe. Maybe the wolves would do me a favor and wash my clothes during the day.

A small piece of worry bit at me over Cherry's fate. I couldn't remember if the place I parked had a time limit before towing. Jerry would probably have a fit if he found out his baby had been dragged around by her bumper.

Drying my hair with one of the towels, I walked into the bedroom. Sondra hadn't been lying about the windows being barred from the outside. I slid open the window and examined them closer. Remembering what she'd said about silver, I wrapped the towel I'd been using around one of the bars, giving it an experimental yank. Even through the cloth, I could feel a slight burn from the metal. It was pointless anyway. The bars didn't budge, remaining firmly in place.

No way was I getting out of this. Even if I could somehow escape, I had nowhere to go. There wouldn't be enough time to make it back to the city on foot. I'd be forced to take shelter out in the open and hope there was something I could use to shield myself from the sun.

I stepped back and frowned at the windows in dismay. They were covered in a lacy curtain. Even shutting the blinds wouldn't be enough protection.

A knock came at the door mere moments before it opened. A young man, one I hadn't met yet, came in, avoiding my gaze and setting a mug on the antique desk next to the door.

He nodded at me and turned to go.

"Wait, I can't stay here," I said.

The door closed before I could get any further.

"Damn it."

It was an effort not pound on the door in frustration. Swiping the mug off the desk, I turned back to the room, sipping on my meal while I thought. The two windows were big, running nearly the length of the wall. Each had a small recessed alcove with cushy pillows on them. The windows were tall, almost reaching the ceiling, but narrow. The problem was the furniture wasn't nearly big enough to block them. The bathroom was also no good, as it had a small window as well.

My eyes landed on the closet.

That might work. I opened the double doors and looked inside. It would be uncomfortable, but if I used the clothes to line the crack on the floor and sides, it should be dark enough in there that I wouldn't burn to a crisp.

Were they trying to kill me or did they just not think of my light allergy? Sondra had struck me as someone who at least had a passing familiarity with vampires so it was hard to believe they wouldn't realize how dangerous this room was to someone in my condition.

I'd give them an earful tomorrow. Right now, I needed to focus on making my little bed for the day as comfortable and safe as possible.

The blue and white flower patterned bedspread went onto the closet floor first. I threw all of the pillows in there as well and grabbed a couple of the towels I hadn't used from the bathroom. My nest ready, I settled back to wait for dawn.

It's hard describing the feeling of sunrise to someone. The first time I'd experienced a sunrise after my transformation I thought I was dying all over again. It's not like someone goes 'lights out' and then you're asleep. No, I could feel dawn coming as that burning ball of fire slowly ascended and the moon gave way. It always felt like someone had a hand around my chest, slowly squeezing, the grip getting tighter and tighter the closer to sunrise it got. Fatigue would sneak in, making thoughts and movement slow, like trying to move through molasses. Eventually, I would lose consciousness.

I timed it once. Figured out the precise time of sunrise and then stared at a clock until I passed out. Turned out I didn't even make it to the technical sunrise, falling asleep about fifteen minutes prior to lights on.

As soon as I felt the first brush of fatigue, I beat a retreat to my closet resting place. I didn't want to mess something up just because I was too tired to take proper precautions. I tucked the towels against the door and then placed several pillows between myself and the crack. Turning my back to the door, I snuggled down as the sun robbed me of consciousness.

Chapter Eight

Waking up without knowing where I was and why I had a crick in my neck was disorienting, made worse when the closet doors were thrown open. Sondra's puzzled face peered down at me.

"What are you doing in here?"

I blinked up at her, my eyes focusing unerringly on the pulse beating at her neck. My fangs came out. Drool pooled in my mouth.

She sighed and disappeared, returning in moments with a mug full of warm blood.

"Your hunger wouldn't be as bad if you just took it from the source," she informed me waspishly.

I didn't reply, chugging the blood as fast as I could. I gasped as I finished, savoring the taste. One day I wouldn't be at the mercy of my cravings. No way could anybody go through eternity like this. I was like one of those people with low blood sugar. The moment I started getting hungry I needed a top off. I wanted to be like one of those women who could go hours and hours without thinking about food.

"You know the bed's perfectly comfortable," Sondra said, looking disdainfully at the nest I'd made.

"You know I'm a vampire, right?"

"What does that have to do with anything?"

I gave the windows a meaningful look. She looked at them and then back at me. Understanding was absent from her face.

I sighed. How could she not get it? A vampire's susceptibility to sunlight was at the core of any vampire movie or book.

"Sunlight and vampires don't exactly get along."

She stared at me blankly for a minute. Then she burst into laughter. The kind that involves your whole body and makes the muscles in your stomach hurt. She wrapped her arms around herself and gasped for breath, only to dissolve into peals of laughter as soon as she caught sight of my face again.

I glared.

I stood, belting the robe tightly around me. I'd gone to sleep in it, not wanting to give up its plush comfort.

Holding my head high, I stepped past the cackling werewolf. If she didn't stop laughing soon, I was going to plant my fist in her stomach. See if she could laugh around that.

"I'm sorry. I'm sorry," she gasped. "It's just your face. You looked so serious saying that."

Of course I was serious. Who would joke about being barbequed?

She sobered up when she got a look at my face. "You're serious. You actually think the sun will burn you."

I paused. The way she said that made it seem like my belief was wrong.

"Unless you're seriously weakened from blood loss or starvation, you won't go up in flame from the sun," she said. "It can give you a pretty extreme sunburn, but only in direct light. Besides making you weak and extremely tired, it poses no real threat to your safety, definitely not enough of one for you to be hiding out in closets. As you get older, you'll even be able to stay up for part of the day."

Impossible. It was in every myth, every story. The captain and Jerry had been clear about my need to stay out of sunlight. I thought back to what they told me. It was true they had never said anything about it killing me. I assumed, based on everything I'd heard in popular culture and the fact that Jerry only gave me night runs, that it was just something I needed to avoid. If I believed Sondra, it was less about my possible fiery death and more about my inability to stay awake during the day.

"Did your sire not teach you any of this?" Sondra asked.

Once again I was faced with having to tell someone I had no idea who my sire was. It was beginning to make me feel like I was abandoned in the trash at birth, slightly ashamed and defensive all at the same time.

"I have no idea who turned me," I snapped.

She gaped at me. "How is that possible? Vampires are extremely possessive of their children. You're too rare as it is. I can't imagine them turning someone and then tossing them aside."

That made me feel so much better. Not only did my sire totally derail my life, but evidently I wasn't good enough. At least not enough to stick around. A small piece of me felt rejected. A very small piece. So small that I probably would try to kill him if I ever laid eyes on my sire.

I shrugged like the topic didn't bother me. "I seem to be getting along okay without him. Thanks for the tip about sunlight though. I was not happy about never getting to see the world during daylight again."

"Have you thought about approaching one of the clans?" she ventured.

"No. I have no intention of getting involved with them." My voice was cold and steely, signally the topic was closed.

She nodded, catching the hint.

She held up an armful of clothes. "Figured you could use some clean clothes. I think these will fit."

I took the clothes from her and glanced at the sizes in the jeans and black long sleeve shirt. They should fit.

"Brax wants you downstairs to go over the next steps."

Oh did he? So kind of him to include me in that.

"Any new information from the videos?" I asked.

She shook her head. "Not really. There are a few odd things, but for the most part, it's a bust."

I wondered if she was telling me the truth or if that was a lie to keep me in the dark.

*   *   *

Brax and Clay were the only ones waiting for me in the living room. Neither rose as I entered. Brax nodded at the sofa. I took a seat and waited. Both fixed me with intent stares that somehow appeared both threatening and calming at the same time. I stared back, knowing this was a kind of test, giving them a blank expression that said I had all night to play this game.

Tension grew between the three of us and too late I remembered that meeting a wolf's eyes could be seen as a sign of aggression. I couldn't back down now without it being taken as a sign of weakness though. I thought non-confrontational thoughts as I tried to channel soothing peace.

"The videos turned out to be a dead end," Brax said. His voice made it clear that my efforts had been ineffective. It sounded like he would like a more physically violent method of communication.

Inwardly, I smiled. So nice to aggravate my kidnapper.

"Oh?" I asked.

He hadn't picked up on Angela. Though why would he? I wouldn't have either if I hadn't met her through Miriam. Her presence wasn't an indicator of guilt. She could have been out for a night on the town or meeting a friend. For all I knew, she was cheating on her boyfriend, Victor, with a vampire. What interested me was how they'd disappeared from the cameras.

I hesitated to give her name to Brax in case her presence was totally innocent. I didn't know what they planned to do to whoever was killing people, but I had a feeling it wouldn't be particularly kind. I'd keep my suspicions to myself until I had more concrete evidence.

"It doesn't escape me that you seem to keep popping up in all this," Brax said. "First Franklin and then the attack on me."

"This has been going on for months. I've only been involved in two instances. There have been dozens," I defended myself.

"Would you be able to name all those you've heard disappeared or were killed?" Clay asked.

I frowned. I knew a good portion as it was part of my job for Hermes, but I couldn't say I remembered every one. Weeks had gone by before the supernatural community was willing to admit there was serial killer. A lot of the first murders had gone unremarked and unnoticed.

"Not all," I said. "But most."

"Create a list of names and any dates you can remember," Brax ordered. "We'll compare them to those we know."

I saw on the coffee table there was a pad and paper waiting. They planned this. I slid the paper to me and clicked the pen. I saw no reason not to give them what they wanted. Comparing my list with theirs might give me a better idea of the bigger picture and allow me to establish a pattern.

"I think that's it." I slid the list to him, keeping my hand on it. There were nine names I was able to remember, some going all the way back to June, when I first started picking up chatter. "Let's see yours."

No way was this information exchange going to be one way.

Clay held a sheet of paper out to me. I grabbed it and read. Most of the names were the same as mine. I had a few they didn't. They had one I'd forgotten and at the very bottom was a name I hadn't known about. It predated the first name on my list.

Jason Sanders. I wondered who he was and how they knew about him when I didn't.

I grabbed another sheet of paper putting the names from both lists in order of deaths or disappearance.

"Who's Jason Sanders?" I asked when I'd finished.

"He was a werewolf. His death was pretty brutal. It looked like he put up a hell of a struggle when he was murdered. The condition of the corpse was a lot worse too. We could barely tell it was him," Clay said.

That was interesting. I only caught a glimpse of the scene of Franklin's death. Besides the massive amount of blood on the ground, it hadn't looked like there was any sort of struggle to my untrained eyes. The blood had puddled and there had been minimal arterial spray. None of the papers had been disturbed and all of the furniture had been upright.

"How was Franklin killed?" I asked.

Brax lifted his head, his eyes training on me like a predator sensing prey.

"He was torn apart limb by limb."

"Any signs of a struggle?"

His eyes narrowed. "No, there wasn't."

"Interesting." I pointed to Jason's name. "Your weakest wolf put up enough of a fight that he was left almost unrecognizable. Where was Franklin in terms of power in the pack?"

"Five or six, depending on how well he fought in a challenge" Clay said.

I looked at the rest of the names. A pattern began to emerge. The killer's first victims had been weak in terms of power and fighting ability. A dryad, kelpie and a werewolf at the bottom of the pack structure. The more recent kills were a lot more dangerous. A werewolf close to the top of the pack, a vampire decades older than me, I assumed he was much more powerful too, and a sorcerer. All heavy hitters.

"He's growing in power," Brax said.

Yup.

"The kills are getting cleaner and more efficient," I said grimly.

"Shit," Clay muttered.

I wondered if the murders were giving him power. None of the gossip I'd heard had mentioned a ritualistic element, but magic was weird. He could be a monster who absorbed souls to power up, for all I knew.

"Have you fed?" Brax asked.

I blinked at the swift change in topic.

"Yes?" It was almost a question.

"Good. It'll make things easier not having to stop to get you a meal while we're out."

"And where are we going?" I asked.

"We have a theory but no evidence so we're going to examine all of the crime scenes to see if we can pick up anything we might have missed the first time."

Ah ha.

That actually made a lot of sense.

Brax turned to Clay, "Increase the number of patrols and pull in the wolves not on duty. I don't want to lose any others if we can help it."

Clay nodded as Brax stood.

Guess that was our cue to leave.

"Any possibility of grabbing snacks before we go? Maybe chips?" I asked hopefully. The blood had taken care of my blood lust, but now I was craving something salty.

The two ignored me.

I took that as a no. Maybe I could get him to stop somewhere for fries.

* * *

The first crime scene was a bust in terms of potential clues. This wasn't a huge surprise as Jason's house, the scene of his violent death, had been thoroughly cleaned months ago. The house lay empty, any helpful information picked clean by Brax's people. All of Jason's records had been removed and his possessions placed in storage.

The place where the kelpie's body had washed ashore was near the Alum Creek reservoir and was equally unhelpful as it wasn't where the murder had taken place.

Brax remained quiet and uncommunicative as we visited each scene, not sharing his observations.

That was fine by me. It let me think, and the silence was welcome. It had been a long time since I'd interacted with other people this much. It was taking some getting used to. I'd never been a particularly social person, preferring most of my interactions in groups of three or less. I was what you'd classify as an introvert. It drove my sister, Jenna, nuts as she was an extreme extrovert.

Brax made a right off High Street into the Park of Roses. The park was a nice little oasis of nature in the middle of Clintonville, an up and coming neighborhood on the border of the city. The houses were charming but overpriced and every young twenty something couple in the city wanted to live there due to all of the trendy restaurants and shops. It was hip but had poor schools, which was why it was forever on the up and coming list. If you didn't have kids, the neighborhood was great. Those with pint sized replicas who still craved houses with old world charm tended to gravitate to the more upscale neighborhoods of Upper Arlington and Grandview.

The park was right behind a branch of the Columbus Metropolitan Library and backed into the Olentangy River. Bike paths threaded through the woods and for those who wanted something a little tamer, they could take a walk in one of the largest rose gardens in the U.S. which featured nearly 400 varieties. Or so the description on the sign said.

It was a popular venue for senior photos and weddings. It was also home to a tribe of dryads, one of which was the victim of our murderer.

Brax drove slowly through the park, watching the trees carefully. There was a small building on the hill that served as a reception hall or meeting place for those who reserved the venue.

Tonight, we weren't here for the roses. The tree of this particular dryad had been close to the large pond next to the park. The dryad's tree was large and shaped like a mushroom. Even in the dark, I could see its bare branches, which should still be cloaked in vivid red leaves. Without the Dryad that was tied to it, the tree would continue to wither and eventually die.

Brax parked in the closest spot he could. He dropped his keys into the cup holder next to him.

"Aren't you going to take them with you?"

"We're just going right there." He pointed at the tree. It wasn't far, but I'd been raised with security always at the forefront of everything I did. Leaving your keys in the car was just asking for trouble.

"Still."

"No one's going to steal the car," he said. "Right now there's no one besides us in the park. I'll hear anybody coming a mile away."

He shouldered open the door and got out. I unclicked my belt and followed. It was his car. If he wanted to risk it, that was his business.

We crossed over the grass to the tree. I tucked my hands into the pockets of my borrowed jacket and tilted my head back.

The tree wasn't very old, probably no more than fifty years. The normals were probably puzzled at the inexplicable slow decline.

"This was the third death we know of," Brax said.

"Do you know where the Dryad was found?"

He gestured with his chin, "It would have been right next to the pond."

That was a big area to search. Neither of us bothered with flashlights as we circled the area. We had superior night vision and didn't need the additional light giving our movements away.

If I remembered correctly, the Dryad had died at the beginning of August. With October drawing to a close, I doubted we would find anything useful.

I paused at a stone marked with several late blooming flowers. They grew so they framed the stone perfectly. It was strange to find this so far from the rose garden. From my limited knowledge of flowers, these were probably wildflowers and looked untended by any gardener's hand. Despite that, they thrived, growing in a riotous explosion of color despite the late season.

It reminded me of a memorial. Live flowers would be more the dryads' style. They wouldn't want to kill a plant but I could see them encouraging the growth of wildflowers.

I bent down and brushed the flowers away from the stone, uncovering a trio of multicolored pebbles, polished smooth by a river, stacked one on top of each other.

"Find anything?" Brax asked form behind me.

I straightened and gestured at what I found, "I think it's a memorial by the dryad's community. I'd be willing to bet this is where she was found."

He came to stand beside me. "I think you're correct."

I stood and turned in a circle. We were only a few feet from the pond. The dryad's tree was on the opposite side. From what I knew of that species, dryads didn't venture far from the safety of their trees. What was she doing this far from hers?

"This can't be right," Brax said, echoing my thoughts. "What caused her to leave her tree?"

"Maybe someone promised something she wanted?"

Brax shook his head. "Dryad's are relatively simple. They gain satisfaction from tending to their trees and need little else."

"Maybe something scared her."

"Enough to abandon her tree?" Brax raised an eyebrow skeptically. "I doubt it. She could have just merged with the wood to escape."

"Unless it threatened the tree as well," I said, thinking out loud. "Or maybe something lured her a little away from safety and then got between her and it. She might have run at that point."

"That is an interesting theory," a voice said from the shadows of the woods next to us.

Brax snarled and dropped into a defensive crouch. I dropped my hand to my belt and the knives hidden there. Even wearing someone else's pants, I'd insisted on keeping my belt and none of the werewolves had argued with me.

A man stepped from the shadows, the faint light of the moon illuminating his sharp features. Liam's eyes were intense as they observed the two of us. He seemed to be alone, which I was grateful for.

The vampire regarded my growling companion coolly. "Are you done yet or should we give you a few more minutes to get your beast back under control?"

Brax's voice was guttural and barely human when he said, "I am always under control, bloodsucker."

Seemed like the two weren't fans of each other.

"What are you doing here?" I asked, hoping to forestall the coming fight.

Liam shot me a sharp glance. "I did not know I needed permission for a stroll in the park, infant."

I narrowed my eyes. Cute.

"So it just happens to be coincidence that this is the scene for one of the murders and that you, who has expressed considerable interest in these occurrences, just happened to be out for a stroll," I said.

Right. If that was true, I was a sparkly unicorn filled with rainbows and moonbeams.

"The murderer has a debt to pay," Brax spat. "Don't get in our way."

"It's not only werewolves he's been killing, wolf. You had your chance to solve this after the first death. You failed or were just too self-absorbed to take care of business. He's killed several of ours so now it's our turn to clean up your mess."

Brax laughed, a deep ugly sound. "As if your kind could stop squabbling between themselves long enough to solve anything."

Liam's lips lifted, displaying a set of impressive fangs. He hissed, sounding like a pissed off cat, only way larger and more dangerous.

I stepped back, not wanting to get caught between them by accident. It sounded like these two had unresolved issues from before this night.

This is one thing I think the myths had right. It seemed there was no love lost between vampires and werewolves. My treatment at the werewolves' hands had been relatively civil, though that may have been because of my relative youth and lack of danger.

I was tempted to let the two of them duke it out. It would free the way for me to go solo.

"Give me the child, wolf," Liam demanded.

Child? What child? He didn't mean me, did he? That term was familiar from the club so I was thinking, yes. I found myself suddenly wishing Brax would pound his face into the nearest hard surface.

"She is part of no Clan. Your claim on her isn't valid," Brax declared.

"She is well below her majority. That automatically makes her ours," Liam said, coming closer.

That thinking right there is what I'd been afraid of this entire time.

"You can't have her. She has a connection to this. Until I find out how, she's staying with me. You can have her back once I find the killer."

Son of a bitch. That back stabbing dog.

"I don't think so," I said outraged. "No one's giving me to anybody. I decide my own fate, not either one of you."

140

"Hush. I don't agree with vampires about much but you need to be guided or you're going to get someone killed. Probably someone close to you. Like your family."

I didn't like that he'd brought up my family, especially since we had an agreement that I'd help him and he wouldn't mention their existence to any vampires. This right here was mentioning their existence.

"You've had contact with your family after your change?" Liam sounded unhappy about that news.

I threw my hands up, my sleeves falling down.

"What is that?" the vampire asked sharply.

"What is what?" I snapped.

"That on your arm."

Crap. I'd forgotten about the sorcerer's tattoo. Tugging the sleeve back down, I gave him my best dumb private look.

"I don't know what you're talking about."

The werewolf grabbed the arm in question and raised the sleeve, tilting it so the vampire and he could see the lion wrapped in thorns.

"A sorcerer's mark," Brax said. He sounded grim, like he was telling someone they had cancer and only had a few months to live.

"How did you get that?" Liam said.

I tugged my arm free and lowered the sleeve. From the way they were acting, you'd think I had leprosy or something.

"It's no big deal. Once I've completed the task he gave me, the mark will disappear."

"What were the terms?" Liam asked, folding his arms over his muscular chest.

If they were unhappy about the presence of the mark, I doubted they would be any more thrilled to hear what I'd inadvertently promised.

"Answer him," Brax ordered.

I was really getting sick of being treated like a recalcitrant child but refused to lower myself to acting like one.

"A hundred years of service."

Yeah, those words didn't sound any better than they had when the agreement had first been struck.

"What possessed you to make such a shitty deal?" the vampire asked in outrage.

I kept my mouth shut. I doubted the details would incline either one of them to view me in a positive light.

"You're going to have difficulties getting her out of a bargain she struck of her own free will," Brax said sounding sympathetic.

"Her sire is going to have a lot to answer for when I find him." Liam shifted his attention back to the matter at hand. "This doesn't change things. I am still taking possession of the girl and you and your wolves are going to stand back and let us work."

Brax's lip curled. "My stance hasn't changed. You'll get the girl when I get my murderer and it's you arrogant bastards that will stand back."

They traded insults as if they'd forgotten I was standing right here. Unbelievable. You would have thought we were in the dark ages or something, and I was just chattel.

Brax sprang forward, covering nearly the entire distance in a single leap. The vampire shifted, blurring in the air, his hand flashing out and tagging Brax in the arm. Blood flew, the droplets spattering the fall leaves.

"You've got to be kidding me," I muttered.

How did they go from talking this matter through to beating on each other in the space of a few sentences?

The fight continued, the two exchanging blows I could barely follow. I watched for a minute. This was ridiculous, and it was getting us no closer to finding our murderer. I dug the sorcerer's charm out of my pocket. Perhaps it was time to go back to the guy who'd started all this.

The two seemed evenly matched, and I didn't see the fight stopping anytime soon. I also didn't want to wait around for them to remember my existence and decide between themselves how I should be handled. It was time to go solo. I'd work out how to get myself out from under the vampire's threat as I went along.

I walked back to the car, dodging the two as they came barreling past me. The snarling from both men was enough to raise the hair on the back of my neck. I was glad not to be the target.

I slipped into the car and grabbed the keys from the cup holder. I'd told Brax not to leave them in here. His mistake was my gain.

I started the car and pulled away, flooring it as soon as I backed up. I had no idea how fast a werewolf or vampire could run and wanted to be as far away as quickly as possible. The wheels screeched as I shot forward and the distinct smell of burning rubber rose from the tires.

There was a brief thud against the back passenger door, and then the car shot forward. I glanced in the rearview mirror and grinned at the pair of irate males glaring after me. Guess not paying attention to the weak, baby vamp had its drawbacks.

The highway wasn't far from here. I hopped on the outer belt and headed toward the Easton area. I would have to ditch the SUV eventually. Brax struck me as the type to fit his vehicle with an anti-theft GPS, but I could use it to get closer to my destination.

I thought briefly of heading back to Elements and picking up Jerry's car but dismissed the idea. Brax had already tracked me there once. It would probably be one of the first places he'd check. I also didn't want to chance something happening to Jerry's car given how dangerous things had gotten. It'd be just my luck to extricate myself from this situation only to have Jerry knock my head off because I'd damaged his precious baby. No, thank you. I'd find another way.

A phone rang from the compartment next to me. I jumped and opened the console, fishing out the phone. It was mine. Finally, something that was going my way. I was a little surprised Brax hadn't taken the time to move it since last night.

The screen said, "Jerry."

Hm. Should I answer? I probably should. He no doubt had questions. Questions that would be difficult to answer and would potentially place my job with Hermes in jeopardy. He would want to know why I hadn't returned from the run for the sorcerer. The news that the vampires had finally caught up to me and that the werewolves had a marked interest in me would probably signal the end of my career as a courier.

I clicked the ignore button and tucked the phone into my pocket. He could wait a little longer. I was thinking until after I'd solved all of my current problems.

Yeah, that sounded like a better plan.

I dumped the car in a parking garage attached to Easton Town Center, a mall built to resemble a small self-contained town, featuring both an indoor and outdoor shopping center. During Christmas the outdoor portion was lined with lights and a miniature train was set up near the fountain. I headed indoors, hoping to use the crowd and closed in area to hide my scent.

I had no idea if Brax and his people intended to track me down, but I wanted to take no chances. They'd know I ditched the car, but they would have to guess the mode of transportation I took from there.

I walked, stopping at the Graeter's to pick up a scoop of their black raspberry ice cream and then dived back into the mob of shoppers. It wasn't too bad this late at night with the shops closing in the next hour. I hoped there were enough scents to mask my own.

I stabbed my spoon down into the ice cream, trying to break a piece of the giant chocolate chip off as I followed a pair of women into one of the many women's clothing stores. It was a chaotic mess inside the place, clothes everywhere, some on the ground and everything cheap. I knew from previous experience that washing some of these clothes once was enough to disintegrate them.

I admired the top the mannequin was wearing as I thought of my next step. Walking anywhere was out. The wolves would just track me. The bus might work if they were running this late at night. My best bet was one of the smart cars you could rent by the hour. I assumed you needed a credit card to use one, and I didn't want to chance Brax's hacker buddy being able to trace the purchase. I could try to steal a car, but I didn't know the first thing about hot wiring anything.

One of the women I was following dug into her purse, knocking her wallet out at the same time. She kept moving forward, not noticing.

I bent and picked it up, pausing as I started to call out to her. The wallet had several credit cards in it.

I had the answer to my conundrum. I turned on my heel, tossing my empty ice cream container in the first trashcan I came across on my way to the smart car lot.

The lot was on the other side of the shopping center. The street lights were out, shrouding the area in shadows. I slowed. Even if the mall had closed, the street lights would still be on. They stayed on all night regardless of whether the mall was open or not.

I peered into a darkness that was much denser than it should have been. I could barely make out the cars at the end of the lot.

This wasn't right. I should have been able to see just fine even without the light. The last time this had happened had been during the sorcerer's theatrics in his office.

I reached for my belt just as something bowled into me from the right. I crashed to the ground, the raging, spitting thing atop me. It clawed at my face and latched onto the arm I raised to protect me.

"Where is it? You have it. They told me you had it," the thing wailed, milky white eyes staring, unseeing into mine.

It was vaguely humanoid but stretched impossibly long. What I thought were claws were actually long fingernails. It reeked of putrefaction and death, like something fresh from the grave.

I kicked out, knocking it away from me as I scrambled to my feet.

The creature was vaguely familiar, its skin patterned like bark and hair the color of moss. Its limbs were too long for a human's, and it was reed thin. Pieces of it were missing, exposing jagged holes that seeped a white, pus-like substance. It looked like a dryad, one that had been dead for a long time and had already started to decompose.

I reached for the charm the sorcerer had given me and broke it. He said that would summon him. Well, it was time for him to do his part.

The creature lunged at me, and I jumped back and up, landing on top of a car. It was fast, running across the ground on all fours. I leapt to the next car as it landed on the roof I'd just been on.

Its head cocked at an unnatural angle, like it had no bones in its neck. I edged back, stopping when my foot almost slid off the roof.

The car the dryad creature was on buckled, the metal screeching and the glass abruptly shattering. The dryad began growing, turning into a hulking monster three times its size.

I should have run, but I couldn't take my eyes off it. It was like watching a train wreck in progress. The monster shook itself and set one hand on the hood, crushing it and leaving a palm print in the metal. That was going to be difficult for the mortals to explain.

Any time now the sorcerer would show up and bust out some crazy spells to take out this thing.

Any time.

Where was he? I had kind of hoped he'd appear in a puff of smoke.

A dry rattling came from its chest. With a start, I realized it was laughter. I'd have to wing this until the sorcerer got here.

"Very impressive. You can get bigger," I said sarcastically. "Any American with access to fast food and donuts can do the same."

The creature snarled and slapped the car, further crushing the hood until it was a mangled mess. I could not let that thing touch me. One swipe and I'd be dead.

"I will pulverize your bones and feast on your flesh," the thing hissed.

"Yeah, yeah. You'll have to catch me first."

I crouched as it sprang, covering the distance between us faster than I could blink. I leapt to the side at the last moment, rolling once as I hit the pavement and darting in a crouched run behind another set of cars.

I was hoping its added size would slow it enough for me to escape using the cars as cover. A roar sounded behind me. There was a screech of metal and then a car door sailed over my head.

Shit, this thing was strong and possessed a nasty temper.

I moved stealthily, crawling beneath a four door truck and rolling to the other side. Heavy thuds followed me from the row I'd just left. I fitted myself next to the front wheel, making sure I wasn't visible in case the creature leaned down to check underneath the truck.

I held my breath. Please move past. Don't look here.

The footsteps paused on the other side of the truck.

It was over. I was dead. My parents would probably never even find my body. Jenna would think I hated her.

The footsteps retreated down the row.

I exhaled shakily. Safe for now. I needed to find transportation before the thing caught up with me again.

This was the second time I'd been attacked in two nights. The eyes of this thing had the same milky glaze as the wolf. It also had the same smell of death and decay, the kind that stuck around for days. I'd have to throw these clothes away, no way would I ever be able to wear them again without smelling that stench. Luckily, they weren't mine.

There was a connection between the two attacks. It made me question whether Brax had been the intended target. Both monsters accused me of having its treasure. I was beginning to think the two creatures were one and the same despite their different packaging.

What made it keep targeting me? I didn't have whatever it kept ranting about.

I crawled from car to car, keeping an eye out for the dryad monster. Damn sorcerer still hadn't shown up. What was the point of a charm to summon him if he didn't come when called?

Wait. The creature hadn't targeted me until after I accepted this job. Why hadn't the charm worked when the sorcerer had promised it would?

How had the dryad known where to find me? Even the werewolves and vampires hadn't been able to track me down this fast.

I crept along the cars, working my way to where the smart cars were parked.

Unless someone had tagged me like a wild animal. I looked down at the charm still hanging around my neck. Maybe a tracker placed in a summoning charm?

It would explain how it had keyed into me twice now.

No, something didn't add up. The sorcerer needed my help and had the power to kill me outright. Why would he need to send a magical creature when he could just do it himself?

The questions were turning me in circles. All the answers I came up with didn't address the whole picture. None of it made sense.

I needed answers. Making it out alive from those last two encounters with that monster had been luck. I didn't think I would survive a third.

I found a rental car and opened the door, sliding into the seat. I fished the stolen wallet out of my pocket and used a credit card to turn on the ignition. I didn't have long. The engine starting would tell the monster exactly where I was.

I backed the car out of its spot and floored it.

"Come on," I snapped as it scooted forward, making the whir, whir sound of a wind-up toy car.

A roar sounded from three aisles away. Even with the pedal pressed all the way to the floor, the little car took forever to get up to speed. Metal sparked when I scraped the bottom of the carriage against concrete as I flew out of the parking lot.

Yanking the sorcerer's charm from my neck, I rolled down the window and tossed it out of the car. It was time to go off book. I'd been playing by everyone else's rules for too long. Time for people to find out exactly who they were messing with.

Chapter Nine

The receptionist was still at her post despite the late hour. I pulled my phone back. Turning the camera on and angling it around the corner wasn't the best method of surveillance, but it would do in a pinch.

I stuffed the cell phone into my messenger bag. I picked up the bag along with a few other supplies at one of my caches a few miles from here. I had similar stashes all over the city in case of an emergency. This life was dangerous, as my current circumstance attested to. The go-bags were a last ditch plan in case things went to shit, if the vampires ever descended on my life.

The worst of my scenarios had already happened, but I refused to abandon the life I'd created here without a fight.

First step, I needed to get past the receptionist without announcing my presence. In the past half hour of my stakeout, she hadn't moved an inch. A coffee or bathroom break would have made my life infinitely easier. But that didn't look like it was going to happen anytime soon.

How to do this without tripping any wards this guy had? We were on the second floor so I couldn't exactly break a window. Pulling the fire alarm also wouldn't work. Nobody was here to evacuate, and the sorcerer could probably extinguish any flames, making an evacuation unnecessary for the two of them.

What to do? I dug through the bag and pulled out a cuff made of beaten copper. It had faded geometric designs etched into the dull metal. It was a gift from a satisfied client. He told me the thing could suppress the wearer's magic if it was locked around the wrist. Why he thought I'd have any need for the thing as a vampire, I had no clue.

Vampires didn't usually have power that needed to be suppressed. Whatever the reason, it was going to come in handy today.

"What are you doing here?" a teenager said behind me.

I froze. Almost in slow motion, I turned, taking in the sorcerer standing there sipping on a jumbo sized gas station fountain drink and holding a food container from the best late night pizza place in the city.

I just might have been the worst thief in the history of bad thieves. My intended target was standing right in front of me and had managed to sneak up on me despite my superior vampire senses.

That was just great. Maybe next time I could send out invitations to my stake out. It'd probably achieve the same result.

He gave me a look patented by teenagers everywhere, infusing it with a skeptical scorn that drove anybody over the age of twenty five close to homicidal.

I needed a plausible lie.

My mind was blank.

The cuff in my hand clinked against the metal in my jacket. Right. New plan. Sneaking up on him and ambushing him wasn't going to work. I'd have to improvise.

"What's that?" the sorcerer asked, his eyes focusing on the cuff.

I lurched forward swinging my bag at his face. He flinched back, raising his occupied hands to protect his face. I snapped the cuff around one of those hands and danced back out of his reach.

Had it worked? If it hadn't, my goose was cooked.

"What the fuck?" the sorcerer spat, lowering his hands.

The copper shone dully from his wrist. The thing was on. I had a feeling I'd know if it had done its job in the next few seconds.

"What is this?" he hissed, finally noticing his new bracelet.

"I don't know," I said cautiously. "You tell me."

There was no need to tell him I had tried to limit his power if the thing didn't work.

"It looks like a genie's shackle," the sorcerer ground out. "Which would be crazy and suicidal on your part because everyone knows these don't work on sorcerers."

This was going to be painful and deadly, but mostly painful.

He reached for the cuff and yanked. And yanked. The cuff didn't budge, remaining stubbornly attached to his wrist.

"Whatever, I don't need it off to take care of you," he sneered and raised a hand. "That was a big mistake on your part."

Nothing happened.

He blinked at me, his face turning nearly purple with rage. He dropped the drink and pizza and raised both hands, then shook them when nothing worked. He hopped up and down, shaking his hands like a giant bird. If I hadn't been so scared the cuff would stop working at any minute, I would have found his flailing hilarious.

"What did you do to me?" he screeched, his teenage voice cracking.

I shrugged, not feeling too bad about binding his powers after the session in the basement. "Just evened the playing field a little."

"Take it off, vampire."

I folded my arms. "I don't think so."

He shook his arm at me. "Take it off, or I will grind up your parts for use in my spells and when you heal, I will dismantle you to do it all over again and again until you're begging me for death."

Like a threat like that was going to convince me to follow his orders? Right. Let me get right on that.

"Like you wouldn't do that anyway."

"Arg," he screamed and kicked the wall.

I rolled my eyes and waited out his little hissy fit. I had no idea sorcerers could be so temperamental. It was going a long way to detracting from the mysterious air they cultivated. He was beginning to seem more like a person and less like this dark, scary being capable of ending me with a snap of the fingers.

"Take it off," he whined. "I feel like I can't breathe, like a limb has been amputated."

"Uh huh," I said. He was really laying it on thick. "I'll think about it, but in the meantime you're going to answer some questions."

"What? What is it that you want?"

There were many things I wanted but only a few he could help me with.

"What's been doing all this killing? You know more than what you told me."

"Have you encountered it?" he asked, his eyes filling with a feverish light. "Describe it to me. Tell me everything."

That wasn't the reaction I'd expected. Something along the lines of furious denial, yes. Sudden interest and begging for details, no. Perhaps I'd been wrong in my assumption of his involvement in the attacks on me.

"It seemed to reanimate the dead," I said. I had turned events over in my head the whole way here. It's the only thing that made sense. "The things that attacked us had the milky eyes of the dead, and the flesh was in an advanced state of decomposition."

"That's not specific enough," the sorcerer said, biting his thumbnail. "Too many creatures have the same ability. I need more information before I can narrow it down."

"Could they also talk through the dead in the same voice?"

He cocked his head in thought. "The same voice or the voices of the host."

It had been the same. I think. I tried to remember. The wolf shouldn't have been able to form real words, not having the same vocal cords as a human.

"Yes, same voice. It was also able to make itself bigger. It attacked me in the shape of a wolf and what I think was a dryad."

"You think?"

"I've never actually encountered a dryad, just heard them described."

"You are unbelievably useless," he muttered.

Said the man unable to use magic due to a copper bracelet blocking his powers.

He stared at the ground, rocking from side to side like a boxer getting ready for the ring. I could almost see the wheels turning in his head. Something I said must have triggered a memory or provided a clue.

He shot past me, heading past the receptionist desk. I blinked at finding it empty. Where had she gone? Now that I thought about it, it was a little odd she hadn't come to investigate during our argument.

"Where'd your receptionist go?"

He paused and looked at the empty desk, then continued into the next hallway. "She must have gone on break."

"And we didn't see her pass us? There's only one way out of here, and we were standing in front of it."

He sighed. "Why does it even matter?"

I stared at him open mouthed. Was he kidding?

"Uh, maybe because there's a murderer running around the city and your receptionist just disappeared."

His shoulders tightened as he sped up, hitting the double doors at a dead run. Instead of the star filled conference room of before, we stepped into a cozy office lined on three sides with shelves and shelves of books. The carpet in here was the same as the hallway, but that was about the only thing that looked like it belonged.

I turned in a circle. The room looked like it had been crammed with artifact after artifact, some of it quite old.

"Good," the teenager sounded relieved. "I was afraid this had disappeared too."

Disappeared too?

"There never was a receptionist, was there?"

It made sense. I'd known there was something off with her. She'd never moved from the desk, instead repeating the same types of tasks over and over. Kind of like a recording. Even her interaction with me had been one sided, like a prerecorded message. How could I not have seen it before?

The sorcerer shot me a look and hurried to one of the bookshelves.

I was right. I'd stake money on it.

"Ah ha."

Ah ha, what?

I crossed the room as he pulled a book, placing it on the desk with a thud. It was old, the kind of old that looked like it had been put together by monks in a monastery somewhere, complete with intricate drawings and bound by hand. The kind of tome that should be sitting protected in a library archive in a temperature controlled room, handled by people wearing gloves, not being tossed around in some dirty office.

I looked at where he was pointing but couldn't read the words. It might have been Sanskrit to me as it looked like a bunch of chicken scratch. Luckily there were pictures. The hand drawn portrait was of a man in armor, clawing his way out of a grave with purple flowers on it. The man was dead, his nails and teeth black with the flesh hanging in strips from his face. The eyes looked crazy.

"And what is it?"

A picture of a zombie creature told me nothing I didn't already know.

"A draugr." He said it like he expected me to know exactly what he was talking about.

I gave him a blank stare.

"A draugr. You know, the Norse undead."

That didn't really clear things up for me.

The sorcerer must have sensed that. He scrubbed one hand through his hair, leaving it to stick up in all different directions. It would have been adorable if he hadn't followed the action with words.

"I really don't know how you made it through the selection to become a vampire," he muttered. "You're as dumb as a rock. They usually only pick the best."

"Hey, cut me a break. This stuff is pretty new for me. I've only been at this for a little over two years."

"That's plenty of time to learn something. I knew more than this in the first year of my apprenticeship."

"Sorry that my mythical education didn't include Norse mythology. We're in the frickin' states. It didn't exactly make the list of creatures I was likely to encounter. Quit belittling my lack of knowledge and just explain what the damn thing is."

His face was mutinous as he said, "Fine. The draugr can be traced to the Norse. The name literally means 'Again Walkers'. They rise from the dead. Usually they're former warriors, but nobody is quite sure what gives rise to them."

"So they're basically zombies."

"Not at all. The draugr retain their intelligence and aren't contagious. The stories contradict each other but most agree that the draugr possess certain talents, including the ability to change their size, possess animals and drive them mad, ride the dead, walk in dreams and control the weather."

I didn't like the sound of the last two. It'd been hard enough dealing with the draugr when he was reanimating dead bodies and making them two times their natural size. I didn't know what I'd do if he was suddenly able to throw a twister at me or invade my dreams. How did I guard against that?

"How likely is it that a draugr can do all of that?"

The sorcerer bent over the book and flipped several pages before straightening. "It doesn't give a clear answer. If I had to guess, I'd say it's based on the level of power it has obtained and how long it's been dead."

And Brax and I had already established it was getting more powerful with every victim it claimed.

"It couldn't be the draugr," the sorcerer said, snapping the book closed in frustration.

"What? You just said it sounded like one. All of the pieces fit."

"I know what I said."

"Then what's the problem?"

"Draugr don't run through cities attacking people willy nilly. They're bound to their graves and guard their treasure with an obsessive jealousy. No way would one leave its treasure to go on a rampage."

"What if its treasure had been stolen?" I asked, slowly.

The sorcerer frowned. "What makes you say that?"

"Every time I've encountered this thing, he's accused me of stealing something. He seems convinced I have whatever it is."

"That could be it. It would explain why it's not bound to its grave and is free to gallivant around the city. But it still doesn't address how it's picking its victims or how the item in question went missing in the first place."

That was true. Our theory only half made sense. Still it was more than I had before I barged in here.

"We need more information," the sorcerer said.

I agreed.

My phone vibrated in my pocket. I dug it out and groaned. My mother. Shit. Ignoring her would mean repercussions when she finally got ahold of me.

I pushed answer as I stepped away from the sorcerer. "Hey, Mom. It's a little late to be calling."

"Am I on a schedule now, Aileen?"

I cringed at the arch question. No one on Earth could make me feel as stupid or guilty with a single sentence like my mother could.

"No, of course not, Mom. That's not what I meant."

"Oh?"

There was a long pause that I refused to rush to fill.

I loved my mother more than words could express, but I also found her to be one of the most frustrating individuals I'd ever met. She had ways of reducing me to that child I used to be who never felt good enough.

When I was around my family, I tended to forget who I wanted to be and regress to a person I neither liked nor knew. Especially these days. As a result, I limited my interaction with them as much as possible. This would have been easier if I hadn't come back to Columbus when I got out of the military. But this was home. And even if they frustrated the living daylights out of me, they were family.

"Your sister told me of her visit."

Of course she did.

"And?" The confrontational question was out before I could stop it.

"You can't keep doing this. You need help."

"I don't need help. There is nothing wrong with me."

"Aileen," she said in that soft way she had. It was the tone she used when she wanted me to know I was wrong, but she loved me anyway. "You know that's not true."

I couldn't do this now.

"I'm at work. I can't talk."

There was a frustrated sigh. We sat on the line in silence, anger crackling over the line between us.

"Fine. You're coming to dinner tomorrow night."

The refusal was already on my lips when she snapped, "I don't want to hear your excuses. You will be there Aileen Travers."

There was no 'or'. Mom was used to being obeyed.

"I'll try," I finally said.

"Don't try, just do. Dinner will be at 6:30. I expect you to be on time."

She hung up. I stood there with the phone to my ear. My eyes closed, my head tilted back. Looked like I had dinner plans tomorrow. Just what I needed, another distraction. It was another ball to add to the ones I was already juggling.

"This is why most of us cut ties when we join this world," the boy said.

I had forgotten him in the exchange with my mom.

"I'm not disappearing from their lives."

"It'd be easier on everyone. It's not like they'd accept you if they knew. They'd call you a monster and probably try to stake you." He seemed sad as he delivered his advice.

"Is that what happened to you? Your family freaked out when they found out what you could do?"

He lifted one shoulder in a shrug. "You should leave while you still have pleasant memories."

"I'm not doing that."

"Your life."

That's right. It was.

"I've found your murderer. Guess that means my task for you is done."

"Not so fast," he said.

I didn't think it would be that easy. But I had hoped.

"You may have found 'what' has been committing these murders, but you haven't found the 'who' or the 'why'. The 'what' is only a faint possibility at this point. One that hasn't been confirmed. I'm not entirely convinced you encountered a draugr. The thing you described sounds similar but doesn't act in the typical fashion. Not to mention you still have to recover my items."

"About that. You never said what those items you wanted me to recover were."

He studied his nails. "That's right. I didn't."

I gave him a get on with it look. He failed to take the hint.

"Okay, so, how about you do that now? I can't get you this item if I don't even know what it is."

"It's what the draugr, if that's what he turns out to be, is searching for."

My eyebrows snapped down. No. There was no way. He couldn't be that dumb.

"Are you crazy?" I asked. "Have you not heard about what it's doing to people? If we're correct and it's hunting people down that it thinks has its treasure, what makes you think it won't come after you next?"

That was only half my worry, the half he would care about. The other part, the one that I was personally invested in was what the thing would do to me if I tried to get between it and whatever it was after. It'd turn me into an oil slick on the pavement.

"I'm counting on it."

The way he said that made me pause. There was something else. Something he wasn't telling me. He hadn't known the killer was looking for something until I told him, and he seemed determined to make me believe that he could be wrong about what was killing people.

It led me back to thinking he might have some hand in these events.

And just when I'd decided he was just an interested bystander. Damn.

"What's so important about whatever it is?"

"That's for me to know."

And me not to.

I really wanted to smack that smug look off his face.

I had to play the game instead.

"Do you have any idea what it's after?" I asked.

"Some."

Sigh. I wondered if all sorcerers were like this or if I'd just gotten lucky with this one.

"Would you care to share?"

I could tell by the stubborn look on his face that he didn't. I needed to convince him. Flying blind was a good way to fail and if he frustrated me this much after only a few nights, I could only imagine what a hundred years of service would be like.

"My chances of recovering the object would be much greater if I knew what to be on the lookout for."

"Very well," he said, grudgingly. "I can do some research on the likely suspects. It will be something the draugr greatly valued in life. If we can find out who he was before he died, we can narrow the focus."

That wasn't going to be easy. I didn't know how many people were buried in Columbus and the surrounding suburbs each year, but I didn't imagine it was a small number. When you factored in all of the deaths over the last few hundred years, you were left with a mind boggling amount of people to investigate.

"That is going to be impossible," I said.

"Any additional information you can gather would help narrow the search."

"Guess I'm going back into the field then."

This task seemed impossible. I wasn't a detective and it felt like I was bumbling around hoping to trip over a clue. It didn't give me a good feeling as to my chances of remaining a free agent. That plus the vampires closing in combined to make everything seem that much more difficult.

I caught a glimpse of the clock and groaned. Any more research would have to take place tomorrow after dinner with my family. It was too late to head out again tonight. I might not be at risk of going up in flames at my first exposure to sunlight but I still wasn't able to stay awake or protect myself once dawn hit. Finding shelter took precedence. I'd continue the search tomorrow.

"Any chance I can get this off?" the sorcerer said, holding his wrist up and giving me a hopeful smile.

"Any chance you'll take this thing off?" I held up my own arm.

"Can't. It's on until the task is complete. I couldn't remove it even if I wanted to."

"Then guess the answer to your question is no," I said sweetly.

He dropped his arm and grimaced. "I had a feeling that was going to be your response."

I probably wouldn't have taken the cuff off just yet even if he had removed the mark. There was no guarantee that once the thing was off he wouldn't use his power to incinerate me where I stood.

"One last question. Why didn't the charm you gave me summon you?"

"What charm?"

I gave him a look.

"Ah, that charm. I felt it break, but I was in the middle of something and didn't have time to drive all the way to that side of town to answer it."

"Drive? I thought it summoned you. As in you appeared right then and there."

He snorted. "What movies have you been watching? No, it simply acts like a flare, letting me know where you last were. Do you have any idea how much power would be needed to pull my corporeal body across time and space to your side? I wouldn't waste that kind of power on a vampire and a weak one at that."

I inhaled. Then exhaled. Then repeated the breaths. Killing the sorcerer would probably land me in more trouble than the temporary satisfaction it would provide. It was tempting though. So tempting. I'm sure I could turn his face into a lovely shade of red if I could just get my hands around his neck.

"That would have been useful information to know before I used the charm," I said.

"I thought it was obvious."

It was not.

"Right. Give me your phone number."

"What? Why?"

Because I said so was probably not an appropriate answer.

"I'll call you when I find relevant information so I don't have to come back here."

"Fine, fine," he grumbled. He waved his hand. When nothing happened, he spat out a curse then stalked over to a cabinet and pulled out a drawer, slammed it shut and pulled open another one. His goal achieved, he pulled out a pad of paper and pen and scribbled the number on a sheet before tearing it out and handing it to me. "Just make sure you only use it to report back. I don't want you eating into my minutes."

What was this? The early 2000's? Who had a plan that relied on minutes anymore?

"Yes, grandpa. I'll make sure to limit my calls to only the necessary."

*　　*　　*

I came awake at sunset in my home away from home, a bolt hole in a closet of an abandoned shack in the less nice part of town. I picked up one of the two bags of blood I'd arranged next to me. When this was over I was going to start trying to stay awake past the sunrise and waking up before sunset.

It seemed like an easy thing to work on. I might be weak in terms of power, but I'd take advantage of any tool I could put in my arsenal. Not being so tied to the movement of the sun gave me a flexibility I hadn't even dreamed of a few nights ago. It might even make all this worth it in the end.

I took a chance and went back to my apartment, stopping for Cherry on the way. It got dark early now so I had a few hours to kill before I had to be at the family dinner. I circled the block a couple of times before parking several streets away. Clinging to every shadow I could find, I made my way towards my building, skulking a block away as I observed the front.

It looked deserted. But who knew with these people? They might be lurking on a roof a mile away and able to appear seconds after I made my move.

It probably wasn't a good idea to go back to the apartment, but I needed a shower and clothes if I was going to visit my family. If I showed up as I was now, unwashed and wearing clothes from last night, my mom would try to have me committed to a short term care facility. The odor coming off me would scream 'problem' faster than any hysterical outburst from me. I didn't think I could make it through another night stinking of that creature's attack anyway.

I walked nonchalantly up the stairs, using the spare set of keys I kept in my go bag to get inside. Sniffing experimentally, I moved through the tiny apartment with caution. Nothing smelled wrong. No decay or wet dog.

I didn't bother with the light as I walked through the dark rooms. If the vampires were watching and I'd somehow managed to evade their notice, I didn't want to alert them as to their mistake by turning on the lights.

I grabbed a shower, taking my time. I figured if the vampires knew I was here they would already be on me. When this was over, I would have to set up a few safe houses throughout the city in addition to the supply caches.

Getting dressed took only a few minutes. I grabbed a pair of dark washed jeans, a black long sleeved top with a scooped neck and a pair of flat black boots that were scuffed and worn from years of use. The outfit was comfortable, flattering and wouldn't make me stick out like a sore thumb in the dark. Perfect for meeting with the fam and then hunting a murderer afterwards.

I checked the time. Since night fell much earlier these days, I had about forty five minutes until I had to be at their house. It wasn't far by car.

I grabbed my tablet and pulled up a search engine. I typed in 'draugr.' I wasn't entirely sure of the spelling but figured if I got close enough, the search engine would do the rest.

My search brought up 306,000 results.

Hm.

Seemed like the creature was pretty popular in several online games. I clicked on a few of those sites, reading up on the monster's characteristics. Some of it jived with what the sorcerer said but most of it was pretty obviously fantasy.

I went back to the search page, clicking on results that seemed interesting. The chances of my finding anything useful were slim, but I'd never even heard of this creature before. Anything would help at this point.

From what I could tell, most of the sites agreed that the draugr was of Nordic descent. Think Vikings and Iceland. Seemed it could be created from anybody who died, though there was a lot of disagreement over what turned someone into an undead 'again walker'.

A theory I found interesting was that a strong will and an extreme jealousy of the living tied a soul to the body, giving rise to the draugr. No one agreed on how the damn thing could be killed. Some recommended fire, others said you needed a hero to wrestle it back into the grave, while still others said a draugr was one of the few true immortals. Even if it was torn apart, it would just reassemble itself over time.

That was not reassuring.

I clicked the tablet off and tossed it onto the couch next to me. The fishing expedition had been a waste of time. There was no agreement among the sources. I still had no new information that I could count on.

Either way, it was time to go. I headed to my bedroom and knelt before my nightstand, opening the door and typing a four digit code into the safe inside. I tucked the gun and a holster into a backpack I'd grabbed from my closet. My first preference would be to carry the gun in a holster at my hip, as the backpack would present a serious challenge to a timely draw, but I didn't want to carry the gun visibly around my family. They'd accuse me of paranoia. I had legitimate reason to be paranoid, but they didn't know that.

The tablet went into the bag after the gun. I planned to use it for more research later, and I had no intention of coming back to my apartment until I'd settled things.

I locked my front door and tucked the keys into my pocket, hoping this wasn't the last time I would be here.

My parent's house was only fifteen minutes away but was in a much nicer part of town. Their historical four bedroom house was in the middle of Grandview, a small suburb of Columbus that had a certain small town charm. Everything was walkable and had those picture perfect neighborhoods seen on older TV shows. The streets were narrow and lined with trees that I knew from previous visits blossomed with beautiful white and pink flowers in spring and turned an amazing red and orange come fall.

Today those trees cast strange shadows, their branches only containing about half their leaves, which had changed from the brilliant red of a few weeks ago to a lackluster brown. I parked the car on the street in front of their postage stamp yard.

As pretty as Grandview houses were, they didn't come with a lot of land. Mom's love of gardening was present in every plant decorating the front, from the perfectly maintained bushes to the fall flowers still holding strong, despite the quickly plummeting temperatures. It wouldn't be long before even those went dormant for the winter.

The curtains were open, and I could see several figures moving inside. I took a deep breath. This wasn't going to be fun. I didn't know what it was about my family, but even before I'd become a vampire, they had been able to strip me of common sense. They could make me lose control of myself faster than any other force on this planet. For this visit, I couldn't lose touch with my normal, rational self. Not if I wanted to convince them their worry was misplaced.

I knocked on the door and waited. It was odd feeling like a stranger in my family home. They'd changed the locks sometime after I joined the service and never gave me a replacement key. I knew Jenna had one, but it just seemed wrong to ask.

The door swung open.

"Aileen." My mom's calm brown eyes observed me. "You came."

"I said I would."

"You've said a lot of things lately," Jenna's voice came from behind her.

From the glare she was giving me over Mom's shoulder, I could tell she'd rallied since the other night. I sighed. Yup. This was going to be a long night.

"Perhaps you should start listening," I said.

"Girls." Mom's voice had a sharp whip to it. We both backed down, settling for mutual glaring instead. "Aileen, come out of the cold. There's no reason to be standing on the porch."

I stepped inside, welcoming the burst of heat. Mom took my coat, hanging it in the hall closet as I followed Jenna into the living room.

Things had changed again since I'd last visited. There was new artwork on the walls, and if I wasn't mistaken, the couch and rug were new too.

That was mom's thing. Decorating. The furniture and color of the rooms rotated almost yearly. Her house was in a constant state of flux. It used to drive me nuts as a kid. I'd always been the sort of person to get things the way I liked, and then not change them unless forced. I was a creature of habit and my mom just was not.

I paused as Jenna joined the group gathered in the living room. More people had shown up then I'd expected. My high school basketball coach, my aunts and uncles, a few cousins. At least they'd left the children out of this.

"Mom, why didn't you tell me the rest of the family was coming to dinner?" I asked pleasantly. "You even got Donna to show up. How is the team this year? Doing well?"

Donna looked uncomfortable at the questions. "Not as well as when you were on the team."

Uh huh. That's why she continually benched me the moment we started losing. Because I was so good.

"Dinner's almost ready. How about we sit down, and I'll get the dishes on the table?" Mom met Dad's eyes meaningfully, engaging in a wordless conversation that had been a hallmark of my teen years.

"Yes, that sounds like a good idea. I'm starving. Aileen, how about you help me set the table?" he asked.

I could do that.

From the way my mouth was watering, I could tell she had made beef burgundy, a dish she knew I loved. It would probably taste as amazing as always. There might even be conversation, laughter, but the meal hadn't even started, and I was already tired of the game. I didn't want to eat dinner like nothing was wrong, waiting until they decided it was time to do whatever it was they had planned.

"Sure," I said, flatly.

My dad stood, walking with me to the silverware drawer with a slight hitch in his stride. He'd had that limp for as long as I remembered. It was the result of an old injury from when I was a kid. He moved smoothly and easily as if he'd taken the injury and assimilated it into his being. As if it was just another part of him.

We worked silently together, mirroring each other's movements on opposite sides of the table.

"How's work?" he asked.

"Fine."

"Any interesting clients?"

"You know I can't talk about my clients."

His smile was stiff. "You don't have to mention them by name. Who's going to know if you share the unimportant things?"

"I will."

His smile fell away entirely and he bent to lay another setting. I grimaced. Way to make them think you're normal.

"How's your work going?" I asked, trying to keep the conversation going. This used to be so easy. When had I gotten so bad at small talk? We used to have hours of conversation on the smallest of things.

"Great. I got a new project."

"What's that about?" Perhaps I could do this after all.

"We're getting ready to switch our servers over..."

I lost track after that. It wasn't that I didn't care. More that it was a lot of jargon that I didn't understand and had no frame of reference for. Thankfully I was saved when Jenna set down the drinks and Mom followed with the food. The rest of the party, all six of them joined us at the table.

The meal was subdued as if everyone was walking on egg shells, trying not to offend me. I took small portions of the beef burgundy and a roll when they passed. For the most part, I pushed the food around on my plate, bringing my fork to my mouth every now and then but not taking a bite. My stomach wouldn't be able to handle this much food at once. Throwing up didn't really have a lot of appeal with the tension so thick you could cut it with a knife.

"How did Linda's dance recital go?" Jason asked Jenna.

Jason was our age and a cousin on my dad's side. Well, technically a step cousin as Dad had married Mom when I was three. He was skinny and tall and had a mop of curly brown hair. He should look like a giant geek but instead managed to pull off sexy professor. I couldn't remember what career he had chosen, but it was no doubt something brainy.

"She was so cute," Mom said. "Our little bumble bee."

"She had a lot of fun. We have photos if you want to see them later," Jenna said.

"I didn't know Linda had joined dance," I said.

The smile fell from Jenna's face and her eyes cooled when she glanced at me. "You never asked."

Ouch. The glacial tone left no doubt as to her feelings at my distance over the last couple of years.

"I'm glad she's enjoying it. We had a lot of fun dancing when we were kids."

"Yes, we did."

The conversation faltered after that and only the sound of the clink of silverware against plates filled the awkwardness that ensued.

Perhaps I shouldn't have said anything. I hadn't intended to bring the conversation to a screeching halt.

"Your father and I were thinking you could borrow the old minivan," Mom said. "It's just sitting in the garage gathering dust. It would be good for it to get some use. Otherwise it's going to develop problems just sitting there."

Here we go.

"Thanks, but I'm happy with my bike."

Mom's offers of help always came with hefty strings attached and since I had no intention of dancing to her tune it was best to refuse outright.

"It's not safe for a woman to be riding around the city at night," Mom tried.

A lot of things I'd done in my life hadn't been safe. I had yet to let that stop me. If my parents had their way, I'd be cowering in my bedroom, scared of all the dangers the big bad world presented.

"I'll be fine."

"You won't be fine," she snapped, slamming her fork down. "You're an accident waiting to happen."

"Elise," Dad said quietly.

Mom took a deep breath, reigning in her frustration as her guests studiously avoided looking at either of us.

"It doesn't hurt anybody to take the van, and it'd make your mom worry about you less," Dad said.

I set my fork down. "That's not the point."

"What is the point?" Jenna interrupted. "That it wasn't your idea? That you have to refuse just to be difficult?"

No, the point was that I was an adult and could choose how I lived my life. Not having a car was a choice, one made under financial duress but my choice nonetheless. My parents were not going to dictate how I got around the city like I was sixteen again.

"I've already made my position clear on the matter," I said calmly.

Jenna let out a long sound of frustration. "And just like that, case closed. You're done talking, and you don't care if anyone else has anything to say. Always have to have it your way, don't you Aileen?"

My jaw clenched on the words I wanted to spit back at her. It wouldn't help anything to let the frustration I had out. It would just make things worse.

Instead I changed the subject, "Instead of discussing a car I don't want, why don't you tell me why you invited all these people here for a dinner that takes the award for most awkward?" I met my parent's eyes with determination.

"Enough games, just tell her, Mom."

My parents had another one of those wordless conversations.

My mom's lips firmed and she nodded in decision. "Aileen, you know we love you, but ever since you came home you've been distant. Difficult even. You haven't been yourself. We know being over there can be tough and a lot of people need help when they come back."

She paused and looked at my dad.

"We just want what's best for you. There's a place we think can help."

My hands clenched around the table, the wood groaning in protest. There it was. What I was afraid of.

"Help with what, Dad?" I asked, feeling brittle for the first time in a while. "What exactly do you think I need help with?"

"Anger management for starters," Jenna inserted.

"Jenna," mom warned.

"It's true."

"Is it now? So Jenna, how should someone feel if they wake up to someone in their house without permission or prior notice, cooking their food and throwing their stuff away? I think I was entitled to a little anger in that instance."

"It's how you expressed the anger that's the problem," Mom said.

"Yelling? Saying mean words? How is that any different than the ways you and Dad fought the entire time we were growing up?"

"Aileen, we're not the focus right now. You are," she said. "You can't deny that you're different. Hell, you threw away all the hard work you did in school to become a simple messenger. That can't be a stable career with UPS, FedEx and email around."

"Ah, right, it always comes back to that. My job. I like what I do. It's interesting and challenging. I get to see parts of the city that I never even knew existed. Not that I should have to justify any of this to you as I'm an adult who's perfectly capable of making my own decisions."

My mom and I glared at each other, neither of us willing to budge on this issue. The funny thing was that even without my special needs, I wouldn't have gone into the finance field. Being tied to a desk all day, every day, was my worst nightmare. I didn't care if I would have made boatloads in that career. The working conditions would have driven me crazy. Worse, it would have bored me. I got creative in not so good ways when I was bored.

"We just think this place can help you, that's all," my dad interjected. He was ever the peace maker, smoothing over the disagreements my mom and I'd had ever since I was a child.

"So let me see if I've got this straight. Because I'm not the same person I was before I joined the Army, you think I'm broken and need fixing." That was what hurt the most. My family loved me, but they had never understood me. Now it seemed like they couldn't even accept who I'd become. "Of course I'm not going to be that person. I went to war. I had experiences. That changes a person and not always in bad ways. It doesn't mean I'm damaged or that I have PTSD or an addiction of some kind. I'm just a little bruised and scrapped up, not broken."

Not every soldier who went over there came back with PTSD. Something the civilian population seemed intent on attributing to every soldier coming home. PTSD was a real problem. I knew soldiers who suffered from it. They were some of the bravest people I'd ever met. I wasn't trying to down play PTSD or pretend it didn't exist. It simply didn't factor into my situation. I'd come back changed, but didn't that happen to anybody who went through an intense experience?

I pushed back from the table, tired of this conversation. It was times like these that I wondered why I came back at all. Why I decided not to take the easy way out and turn myself over to the vampires.

"Aileen."

I ignored my dad and headed to the coat closet.

"At least let me give you a ride home so you don't have to take the bike," he said as he and my mother followed me into the other room.

I yanked my jacket from the closet, putting it on with angry motions. "I don't need a ride. I have a car."

"Why didn't you say you bought a car? You should have had your father go with you to make sure it was a good one."

Unbelievable. I couldn't win with them.

"It's not mine. I'm using a friend's."

"Why can you borrow from a friend but not your family?" Mom's voice rose, taking on an angry tone.

"Because they don't shove things down my throat and berate me when I don't do exactly what they want," I hissed back.

They both flinched, and I took a deep breath. That had come out a lot angrier than I'd intended. Yet it was true.

The doorbell interrupted my apology.

"Finally," Mom breathed. She threw open the door and gestured inside. "Come in. We've already started but perhaps you can talk some sense into her."

"Of course," a familiar man's voice said.

Liam stepped inside, flashing a charming smile at both of my parents.

Chapter Ten

I took a shuddering breath.

No, it couldn't be. How had he found me? What was he doing here? Was he planning on harming my family?

I couldn't breathe. The walls were closing in on me. I had to protect them.

How? My backpack. The gun in my backpack. It was still in the closet. Too far.

The conversation had continued without me as I flipped out.

I tuned back in as my mom said, "Aileen, I'd like to introduce you to Dr. Locks. He specializes in your sort of problem."

I couldn't move, couldn't blink for fear that any move I made would start a massacre.

"What are you doing here?" I asked, my voice steady despite the shock I felt.

"Do you two know each other?" Mom asked.

Liam turned his smile on her and my dad, his eyes taking on that otherworldly glow I remembered from the bar. "Elise, why don't you and Patrick head back to dinner? I'll take everything from here. Aileen is going to be just fine in my care."

The fear and worry smoothed from their faces, leaving them looking blank but happy.

"Of course, Doctor. You'll take good care of our daughter."

Together, they turned and headed back to the rest of the group in the dining room.

"You will stop that right now," I ordered in a low hiss. If he didn't, I didn't care how dead I was going to end up. I'd figure out a way to take him with me.

"Outside," he ground out, turning and stepping onto the porch without waiting for my agreement.

I grabbed my bag from the closet, following him as he'd known I would. There was really no choice. Not with him putting the whammy on my parents. I didn't know how far that hypnosis thing went, whether he could force them to hurt themselves or others. And I didn't want to find out right now.

"You won't ever do that to them again," I said once the door was shut behind me.

I held the backpack loosely in my hand. His back was to me. I could go for the gun now, blow his head off and be done with this. Killing him would also have the benefit of answering the question of whether vampires turned to dust when they were dead. I'd been wondering that since watching reruns of Buffy the first month after joining the ranks of the fangally challenged.

"You're so young," Liam said, sounding tired. He turned and watched me with shadowed eyes. "Do you think there isn't a reason for the way that we do things? That you're special and can break all the rules that have been in place for hundreds of years?"

I kept quiet. He wouldn't like my response. The truth was, I didn't care about his rules or the reasons. As long as I wasn't a clear danger to my family, which if tonight was any indication, I'd proven I wasn't, I didn't care about his reasons.

He gave me a razor sharp smile as if he could hear the thoughts going through my head. I added to the forest illusion I'd thrown up two seconds after he came in the door.

"I see you're going to insist on doing this the hard way. Very well. Just remember you left us with no choice."

There was always a choice. It didn't always have to be a good one.

I squeezed the gun's hand grip.

"Since you've gotten yourself tangled up with the sorcerer, there is no other option but to have you help me find the creature doing all this murdering. Once that's done, you'll submit yourself to our will. You will join a clan. You will obey our laws. Refuse, and I will kill every last member of your family."

The gun was up and pointing at him. It barked three times, the gunshots reverberating through the air as an afterthought.

He moved as soon as the gun came up, jerking as one of the bullets entered his shoulder. He was beside me in the next moment, slapping the gun down and wrenching my wrist hard. I refused to let go, baring my teeth at him and hissing like a pissed off cat.

The sound surprised me. I hadn't known I was capable of making a sound like that.

"I wish you hadn't done that," he gritted out.

Blood oozed from the bullet holes. I was gratified to see all three had hit, though not in as tight a grouping as I'd like. No doubt because of how quickly he'd dodged. There wasn't as much blood as there should have been with wounds like that. Already the flow slowed and stopped.

He touched his shoulder, his fingers coming away tacky. "I see we're going to have to work on your impulsiveness first."

I jerked against his hold, stomping on his instep and elbowing sharply in his stomach.

"Stop that," he snapped.

I head butted him.

"Aileen," Mom screamed as she burst out of the house, my dad and sister right behind her. She paused when she saw us. "We heard gun shots. Are you all right?"

"You need to make your choice right now," he said in my ear. "Obey or they die."

I jerked away from him one last time. His hold didn't even budge.

"Fine," I snapped.

"Good girl," he whispered. In a louder voice, he said, "Its fine, Elise. Just a car backfiring. Nothing to worry about."

I didn't need to see his eyes to know he'd switched the high beams back on. Bastard was whammying them again. I sent a sharp elbow into the wound in his shoulder and smirked at his pained grunt.

"Good news, your daughter has agreed to come visit my facility."

I jerked away from him, fully aware I only succeeded because he let me. I gave him a nasty glare that said exactly what I thought of his words.

There was a way out of this. I just needed to find it. For now, I had a small reprieve because of the deal I'd made with the sorcerer.

"Oh good," Mom said, that vacant, Stepford wife look on her face.

"Stop whatever it is you're doing," I said harshly.

"I'll do what needs to be done."

"Aileen, you know we love you right? If you truly don't want to do this, you don't have to," Mom said softly.

That right there was why I refused to give them up. Why I came home even knowing it would be difficult. Even with someone screwing with her head, she still fought for what she thought was right for me. Our family might be dysfunctional, and we almost never got along, but we loved each other. The kind of love that meant we'd fight for our family even if we spent the entire time cursing each other up one side and down another.

"It's okay, Mom. It's just a visit. There's no harm in checking it out."

"Oh good." She gave me a relieved smile, a bit of her personality peeking through even under the weight of the vampire's mind control.

He took me by the arm. "Alright, enough. Time to go. I've wasted enough time chasing you all over the city."

"No one asked you to, asshole."

"If you had just stayed put, none of this would have been necessary."

"Not a dog."

He stopped, fixing me with heavy glare. "You are if I say you are."

I sneered. Not even if I lived to be a thousand.

He snorted, obviously unimpressed by my sneer. "I do not envy whoever takes you under their banner."

"Yeah, I'm going to make all of your lives hell until you give me back my freedom."

He might as well know what he was dealing with from the start.

"I wouldn't recommend that," he said, clicking a key fob. The lights on a black Lexus turned on. The car was from this year and top of the line from what I could see. "Our kind don't take disrespect very lightly. If you're not careful, your next hundred years will be very unpleasant."

Only if I got caught. There was more than one way to make your thoughts clear without ever giving the appearance of disobedience. Ask any newly minted lieutenant upon arriving at their first duty station. I'd seen some of the best at this game. If I couldn't find a way out of this mess, I was going to be putting what I'd learned to the test.

"Where are we going anyway? Thought I had until I resolved my debt to the sorcerer before you took me into custody."

"We're going to work together to fix this mess you've found yourself in," he said.

"And how do you think we're going to do that?"

"You're going in a safe house while I go hunting. Once I find the murderer, we can turn him over to the sorcerer, and you'll be free."

That wouldn't work for me. I needed to be out, working things to my advantage if I was going to figure out a way around his ultimatum, not sitting on my ass waiting while he did all the heavy lifting.

Judging from how Liam and Brax were handling the problem, I wasn't convinced either of them would be able to find their way to the bottom of this without my help. Power and strength they might have. The ability to find and decipher clues? Not so much. Neither struck me as having the patience to sift through details. They definitely weren't able to get people outside their supernatural species to talk to them.

"That would be great if that was the only condition for my release," I said, seeing an opportunity.

He stopped. "What do you mean?

I shrugged with feigned nonchalance. "Nothing much. Just that the murderer's capture wasn't the only part of the deal."

He spun me to face him. I gave him a sweet smile, widening it when he flashed the tip of a fang. I'd discovered that fangs, for us, were a good indicator of mood. They could mean we were hungry, or angry, or horny. In this case, I was going with irritated.

"That's not what you said at the park."

He didn't believe me. At least not entirely. He was right to be suspicious. I planned to take advantage of his ignorance as much as I could.

"Well, excuse me for not laying out every aspect of my deal with the sorcerer right before your fight with the werewolf." I wasn't sure how developed a vampire's truth sense was. The werewolves seemed able to accurately identify any lie I told, and I didn't want to expose more than I needed to. Sticking as close to the truth and irritating the life out of him was my best smoke screen.

He visibly struggled for patience. "Tell me everything about your deal with the sorcerer."

Thought he'd never ask.

I went over what I could tell him and what could be twisted to my own purposes. There wasn't a lot of wiggle room. I'd have to tread carefully.

"Finding the murderer is part of it," I said, choosing my words carefully. "But he also needs me to find certain items."

"What items?"

I shrugged. "He didn't tell me. I don't think he knew." That was true enough. "He just said I'd know them when I saw them."

"No. Absolutely not," Liam said, seeing where I was going with this. "You're not assisting. You're going to the safe house where you're going to wait like a good little girl until I can resolve this mess."

I rolled my eyes, not even trying to hide my amused scorn. I didn't even know where to start with that antiquated, chivalrous male bullshit. Wait in the corner like a defenseless woman who needed saving? What century did he think this was?

"Do you even hear yourself when the words come out of your mouth? You sound like you're some ancient geezer who should have been retired about three decades ago. For that matter, do you have any idea what is doing all of this? No? Okay. So don't tell me to go hide somewhere while the big boys pound their chests and stomp around like a herd of idiotic buffalo fucking everything up."

Liam glared at me with irritation. Guess he wasn't used to people, especially women, challenging the edicts that fell from his lips.

"If you don't know what items are to be found, we will meet with the sorcerer, and he can tell us."

"Nope."

"Nope?"

"Yup, nope."

Both fangs appeared as his lips curled back. He looked pretty mad. If he had a human's circulatory system, I imagined he'd be turning bright red right about now. As it was, his pale skin flushed slightly as his eyes took on an otherworldly sheen.

"And why not?"

"He's shy. He'll only work with me."

I clamped down on the thrill of excitement at delivering my coup de grace. He was shy, but he wanted the items bad enough that he might consent to working with Liam, especially if he thought Liam was more likely to get him what he wanted. Right now, the fact that I was the only one who knew the identity and location of the sorcerer was my greatest trump card. I intended to use that to my advantage.

"There is something you're not telling me," Liam said, narrowing his eyes.

I went still, shoring up my mental defenses and projecting calm assurance in case he tried to force his way through to my thoughts. There was a lot I was keeping to myself and a lot of misleading distractions in the information I'd just given him.

"Tell me why you think you know what is doing the killings."

I relaxed slightly, glad he was on a different topic. There was less risk in this line of questioning.

"The thing came after me twice. The sorcerer and I were able to narrow down the culprit based on my experiences."

"Tell me."

Seeing no harm, I told him what I'd seen and experienced. The smell of decay, the appearance of death, the dead dryad and the creature's conviction that I had something of his.

"It sounds similar to a draugr. They're able to possess animals, which would explain the attack on the alpha and you, and the most recent death." Seeing the question on my face, he explained, "Another werewolf was murdered last night."

"That means three wolves are dead."

"Three?" Liam's eyes sharpened. "I've only heard of two."

"The first wolf was murdered before anybody put together the connection between the deaths. It was easy to overlook. There were also a few discrepancies between it and the following victims." I hadn't meant to give him all that. I rushed on, hoping to distract him from what I'd just said. "The sorcerer and I believe it's a draugr as well. One thing I haven't figured out is why it's killing in all of these random places. Everything I've been able to dig up on them said they don't usually leave their place of burial."

And how was it choosing its victims? There was no connection that I could see.

"That's a myth. In the old country, people would put salt in front of their doors and windows to keep the creature from entering in body or spirit. They used to bury their dead with iron scissors on their chest to keep them from rising." He looked thoughtful. "Anything could drive a daugr out from its grave. I'm surprised one is here, though."

"What makes you say that?"

"They've become rare in the past few centuries. This city isn't old enough to have one of the ancients. The young these days are less likely to have the strength of will to cling to life after it has faded."

"Okay, grandpa. I get it. My generation is the source of all ills in the world."

"You are truly an irritating individual."

I grinned at the complement. His next words wiped the smile off my face.

"Nothing you have said has convinced me of the need to have you help with my investigation."

"I never said I wanted to help you," I said. "I want to conduct my own."

"No."

"I'm not really asking. This is my life and future you're gambling with. No way am I going to sit quietly hoping you know what you're doing. The sorcerer said he wanted me out looking." I held up my arm up so he could see the mark. "He also said if I didn't actively search for both the killer and the items, the mark would kill me."

He reached out and brushed one thumb along the vine of thorns. A tingle spread from where his fingers touched.

He sighed, and I knew I had won.

"Fine, but there are rules."

Instead of jumping up and down like a five year old on Christmas morning, I schooled my face to an alert attentiveness. No reason for him to know I planned to ditch his rules in favor of doing things my own way.

"Give me your phone," he said.

I dug it out of my bag and handed it to him. He withdrew his and typed a few buttons into it. My phone rang. He clicked the ignore button, then typed a few more buttons into my phone. He handed it back to me.

"I put my number in there. You're to call every hour on the hour. You're not to make a move unless I approve it and under no circumstances are you to confront the draugr on your own. You don't have the strength or power to survive an encounter like that."

I slid my phone out of his hands. "Sure, Dad."

"Miss a check-in and I'll yank you into the nearest safe house. You'll just have to take your chances that I find the creature before that mark kills you. Remember, if you try to hide, I'll-"

"Yeah, yeah. You'll kill my family," I snapped, walking away. "Don't worry. As aggravated as they make me, I wouldn't put them in danger."

I felt the weight of his eyes on me as I walked to my car and drove away.

I'd managed to get myself a temporary reprieve, but I doubted I could keep him at arm's length for long. His patience was bound to dry up before too long. There was also the deal with the sorcerer to keep in mind. The noose around my neck kept tightening and there were no scissors in sight.

*　　*　　*

I ended up back at my apartment. Now that the vampires had found my family, there was no point in hiding. They only had to threaten harm against the people I loved, and I'd folded like a cheap paper bag.

The sun was still a long ways off as I let myself into my place. I threw my keys and bag on the coffee table then pulled out my laptop and a pad of paper. Time to review what I knew before something else happened, and I needed to go chasing around the city like a crazy person.

I pulled up a map and sent it to the printer, printing sections of it on several pages and arranging them on the coffee table in front of me.

Flipping on the TV, I let the news babble in the background as I grabbed the bowl of M&M's off the end table next to me and placed a yellow candy at the site of the dryad's death. Next I placed red ones at the site of the two werewolf murders. More and more M&M's were added to the map where the murder sites were located that I could remember from Brax's list. The vampire had interrupted us before we'd managed to visit every site. I couldn't mark one of the earlier murders off since I couldn't remember the exact location. I also couldn't mark the most recent death.

Finished, I sat back. No pattern emerged. It looked like someone had dumped the shell coated chocolates on the map and they had just scattered with no rhyme or reason.

I threw myself back and looked up at my ceiling. I made a terrible detective. Couldn't make sense of anything.

I sat back up and hunched over the map. I was missing something. What? Think.

Something should be here that wasn't.

"Another family has been reported missing," the newscaster said in the background.

I looked up.

"This is the fourth family to go missing in this fashion. Columbus police are cautioning people to lock their doors at night."

That was it. The humans. There was an entire set of victims that Brax, Liam or myself hadn't factored into the investigation.

I pulled up news articles from the last few months, searching until I found the ones focusing on the missing. I marked the victims' houses off using the green M&Ms. It took me an hour to be sure I found all references to the human victims.

"I'll be damned."

Where the colors marking the supernatural community's victims were spread all over the city, the green was concentrated in one spot. Right next to one of the older parts of the city. Westgate.

I typed the name into google and scrolled past anything that said apartment or real estate. I paused at a blurb that said "Westgate was partially constructed on a former civil war prison camp." That seemed interesting. I hadn't realized there were any confederate prison camps in Columbus.

Looked like the only thing that remained was a cemetery.

I consulted my map. The cemetery was smack dab in the middle of my green markers, as was Westgate Park and about a dozen other sites.

It was worth checking the human victim's houses out to see what I could find. My visits to the vampire victim's house and the dryad's murder scene hadn't discovered anything, but I had nothing better to do and sitting in my house wasn't going to help me solve anything. I had a good feeling about this.

I grabbed my gun holster out of the bag and wrapped it around my waist, tucking it under my shirt and jacket. It hadn't been very effective against Liam, but I wasn't ready to give up on it yet. I'd used the Walther P22 on him. It was a good little gun but small rounds caused less damage than bigger rounds. In the hands of a professional, it was an extremely effective weapon, but if you didn't know what you were doing, you were just as likely to get yourself killed after shooting someone. I knew what I was doing, but the rules of the game evidently changed when you brought supernatural creatures into the mix. I needed a bigger gun. One that did a lot more damage.

I headed back to my bedroom and grabbed The Judge. It was a .45 caliber long colt with a 410 round. You shoot someone with this and chances were they weren't getting back up. It left a little hole, only about a half inch wide upon entering the body but ripped a hole the size of a fist when exiting the body. We'd see if this would work. Next time I'd make sure to aim for a head and hope it killed the thing. Or at least injure it long enough for me to get away.

My phone rang as I was locking my door. I jogged down the steps as I fished it out of my pocket. The display said "Asshole Calling."

I hit the ignore button and tucked the phone back into my jacket. What he didn't know wouldn't hurt him. I had a feeling he'd try to stop me if he found out what I was planning.

Cherry waited where I left her. I could get used to the luxury a nice set of wheels provided. Jerry was probably going crazy right about now. My one day job had dragged into day three with no end in sight. He was probably cursing my name.

As if my thoughts had summoned him, his name appeared on my phone screen as it chimed with an incoming call. I clicked ignore on that one too. I was beginning to think I should have just left the phone behind. That way I'd at least have plausible deniability when I said I never saw their calls.

I immediately discarded the thought as too dangerous. There was a possibility that I would need back up if I stumbled into something I couldn't handle or found the draugr by accident.

I compromised by turning the phone to silent as I ducked into the driver's seat. I turned the car on and pulled into the street.

Westgate wasn't far from me. Filled primarily with lower middle class homes, the community was nicer than I expected for being in the middle of Hilltop. Most were better maintained than the shithole I lived in. I had never really driven through this part of town even as a Hermes courier. I thought I knew the city and its suburbs pretty well by now, but this was new.

I was only a block off the park when I saw police vehicles and a house covered in yellow caution tape. My guess was this was the scene of the most recent disappearances. It'd be pointless trying to get in there right now with police crawling all over it. Maybe if I had Liam's ability to influence minds, it'd be possible.

I continued past the house, circling the block and heading towards the next name on my list. This house was situated on a road right next to the cemetery. Whoever owned it now would probably have a hell of a time trying to sell it as people convinced themselves it was haunted.

I parked two houses down and looked at the house. The windows were all dark. No one seemed to be home. Nobody was on the streets either. If I wanted to take a look around, this was as good a time as any.

I shouldered open the door and jogged across the street. Sticking my hands in the pockets of my jacket, I walked by the house and called in a soft voice. "Rufus. Here kitty, kitty, kitty."

I crossed the street, repeating the same words, confirming that I was the only one dumb enough to be out this close to midnight with a murderer on the loose.

I crossed back, walking up to the house as if I had every right to be there. I tested the front door. Locked. Of course. Made sense. The lock on this house was much better than the cheap one on mine. The credit card trick wouldn't work on this one.

I looked around for one of those handy rocks people used to hide their keys. Having locked myself out of my apartment several times since moving in, I could attest to how convenient, if unsafe, it would be to have one of those lying about.

Looked like this family had erred on the side of safety because I didn't find anything that could house a key. And I tried several rocks, banging them against the ground in vain hope. That option exhausted, I headed around back, testing the windows I could reach. All of them were locked. So was the back door.

No hope for it. I picked up a rock and broke the back door window, reaching inside to unlock it. Hopefully, I had the right house with no one here to notice my breaking and entering. Glass crunched under my shoes as I walked through the kitchen.

Nobody came running.

Looked like I was right; the place was empty.

The kitchen looked undisturbed. I stopped by the fridge, drawn to a picture of a happy family. Two parents and a toddler. I wanted to believe that what went down had happened when the toddler was out of the house, but knowing what I did of the world, that was unlikely. Shitty things happened to good people, without sparing the young.

The living room was in shambles. There were books on the floor, family photos tossed around, and a chair on its side. I couldn't tell if a struggle had taken place here, or if the police had been really thorough in their search.

I headed upstairs, pausing at a red stain on the wooden rail. I continued, not finding anything in the first bedroom, a child's by the look of it. The smell of old blood lingered in the air outside the bathroom.

I opened the door and staggered back at the stench that struck me across the face. Someone had suffered in there. Fear and pain saturated the air until I could taste it on my tongue. I forced myself inside, feeling a tight feeling in my stomach at the amount of blood in the tub and drain. A little yellow duck sat on the side of the tub, its side freckled with red.

Mother and child surprised in the bath. They never had a chance.

I stumbled out of the room, not able to bear the image my mind created. Panting, I hugged the wall next to the bathroom and counted backwards from 100.

The scene wasn't the worst thing I'd ever seen, not even in the top five. There hadn't been any bodies, just blood leftover from a crime that happened weeks ago.

The murder scenes from the supernatural community had been much less grim. All but the most recent had been washed clean of any sign of violence.

I stepped back into the bathroom. Why hadn't this place been cleaned? The police would have released the crime scene weeks ago. Someone should have cleaned up the blood even if their only goal was to sell the house.

Something didn't add up.

The blood. It wasn't right. It was too new. Not fresh, but also not months old.

Shit. I didn't think this place was empty after all.

There was a sound on the first floor, like something had been pushed across the room. I darted out of the bathroom, keeping as quiet as possible. I found a hall closet and stepped inside, fumbling for my phone and gun.

Footsteps thundered up the stairs and into the hall outside.

The bathroom door creaked as it was pushed open and something thudded. I shifted to the side, trying to see through the crack between the wall and the door. I got the slim image of a body being dragged into the bathroom.

Oh God. Why was he taking one of his victims in there?

I didn't want to know. I didn't even want to hazard a guess.

The sharp crack of bone followed by a loud slurp and then smacking lips answered the question. I cringed back, jerking when something brushed against my shoulder. It was a linen. The draugr wasn't behind me. No reason to have a meltdown or scream loud enough to draw him here.

I hit the contacts button on my phone. Time for back up. Sorcerer, vampire or wolf. I didn't care which as long as they got here in the next thirty seconds. Being eaten alive had just made it into my top three worst deaths possible.

I held the phone up to my ear as it rang. Please answer.

"You missed your last check in. I told you what would happen if you missed your check in," Liam's irate voice said in my ear.

Thank you, God.

"Liam," I whispered, covering both the phone and my mouth with my hand. "5536 Chesterfield Road."

"What? Where?" Liam's voice changed to one of anger as he hissed, "You went after the draugr didn't you."

"5536 Chesterfield Road," I said again, my whisper turning urgent as the sound of chewing stopped. "You need to come now."

"We are going to have another talk about your inability to follow simple instructions."

I looked forward to it. If he made it in time, I would gladly listen no matter how long the lecture.

A shape walked into the hallway, its head cocking this way and that. It was human. At least mostly.

"Hello, little vampire." Its voice wrapped around me, brushing against my thoughts, leaving me with the feeling that maggots were crawling inside my mind. "I had hoped to find you tonight. It's so good of you to come to me. Why do you hide in that closet?"

That was not good. The call was still live. I could hear Liam snapping orders. I just needed to buy time. I could do that.

Either way, staying in the closet was getting less appealing by the second.

I tucked the phone into my pocket and dropped the hand with the gun to my side before I pushed open the door.

The creature watched with black eyes tinged with a cloudy white as I stepped out of the closet. Gaunt and gray, the flesh hung from its bones in ribbons. Its lips parted in a macabre smile revealing sharp fangs with flesh still caught in them. It was hunched over slightly, its limbs thin and gangly. It was tempting to misjudge it as weak until you noticed its eyes, mad and filled with a darkness that threatened to spill into your psyche at any moment.

"Who are you?" I asked, my voice surprising me with its calmness. Yes, I interrogated monsters on a regular basis.

"Does it matter?"

This thing was much more coherent than it had been in my previous two encounters. Was this the creature's real body, or was it possible that I had the wrong monster? There was the smallest of possibilities that the human and supernatural community's crimes were unrelated.

"I'd like to know the name of the person who's been making such a splash lately."

He tittered, his laugh high pitched and grating on the ears.

"Yes. Yes. Everyone should know my name."

He sounded crazy. If he'd been human, I would have said he was high or clinically insane.

"You should tell me so I can share it with the rest of the city. It'll let them know who they should fear. Give you some credit for all your hard work."

"I deserve it. Yes, I do. They didn't even give me my name in death."

"Right." Looked like he was one of the soldiers in the prison camp as I'd thought. He could be buried in an unmarked grave. It might be what kept him clinging to this world long after death.

"Eric Miller," he said abruptly, the person he used to be showing through for a moment with all the vulnerability and sorrow I'd expect in someone who suddenly found themselves back in the land of the living. "Or was it Jackson Baker."

He gave me a sly smile.

"Charlie Flannagan. Victor Dubeaux. I just can't bring myself to remember."

He crept forward a few steps. I edged back. Shit, looked like my attempt to build rapport with him had failed.

"I remember you, little vampire. They said you have my treasures."

"Who said?"

"Filthy little thief, taking what's not yours. They're mine. Didn't you take enough from me during life? They were the only things I had left. Give them back."

He was frothing at the mouth and screaming by the end.

I held up my hands. "Wait. Wait. I don't know what you're talking about."

"Liar," he roared.

He was working himself into a state and would attack at any moment. I needed to keep him calm.

"Tell me what you're looking for and maybe I can help you."

He paused, his head swinging back and forth.

"A watch."

"Good. What does it look like?"

I held my breath. How long had it been since I'd called Liam? I didn't know how much longer I could hold this line of questioning until he exploded.

"My grandfather gave it to me. It's gold, which you know since you took it from my grave. You also took my locket. It held my love's photo. I want it back."

I was losing him. "Okay, okay. We're going to get you the watch and locket back. I didn't take it but I can find them. I have contacts who will help me. Just tell me who told you I had it."

His tongue flicked out to lick his lips. It was black and swollen.

"Or I could just eat you. What use are you if you don't have my keepsakes? Not much." He grinned, the darkness of his mind rushing towards mine, bringing madness in its wake.

Without thinking, I pointed the gun at his head and pulled the trigger. It recoiled in my hand, again and again until it clicked. Empty.

The creature fell, its head half gone. I darted toward him. Already, its head was regenerating, bone and brain growing back. It staggered to its feet, its bony fingers clutching at my shirt and tearing it.

Ki... you... Kill... you.

The words weren't something heard with my ears, instead inserting themselves into my mind. Panic rose, sharp and hot. I burst through the master bedroom's window, glass shattering around me and sharp pain lashing my arms and legs. Then I was falling, falling, landing with an abrupt jolt, my knee cracking hard against the ground.

I lay stunned. No time to cry. Feel the pain later. Get to the car. He's coming.

I staggered to my feet, ignoring the sharp twinge in my ankles and knees. My car wasn't far. I needed to get out of there.

An ululating wail chased me as I ran for my car, fumbling for my keys as I moved.

I was out of time. The draugr was chasing me, and I didn't think I could survive the coming fight without any weapons.

My hand touched cool metal. Got it. I pulled the keys out, my hands shaking as I turned it in the lock. I flung open the door and slid inside, not bothering with the seatbelt.

The wheels squealed as I pulled away from the curb. My eyes widened at the sight in the rearview mirror of the draugr chasing after me on all fours.

"Shit. You have to be kidding me."

I floored the gas pedal, taking the next turn at the highest speed possible. I was not going to die here— and I wouldn't wreck this car. For a tense few minutes, I kept above fifty watching anxiously in the mirror for any sign of the draugr. Only when I was satisfied it wasn't chasing me anymore did I let the car slow to the speed limit.

Holy shit. That was scary.

I knew a lot more about what we were facing. The sorcerer was right. The thing was a draugr, and it was after something that had been stolen from it. I knew why its attack pattern was so random now. I was betting whoever had pointed the draugr in my direction had also been the one to steal its stuff. Whoever it was had been guiding the draugr to its victims. I was betting that there was an end target and the rest had just been collateral damage to hide the real motive. Either way, it was time for research.

I pointed the car toward the university. The best place to find information about a human war was a human historian. It just so happened I knew one of those.

Chapter Eleven

You'd be surprised at how many people are still working hard at a university long after eleven p.m. All of those graduate students high on caffeine, diligently hacking away at their thesis. Some of these kids kept odder hours than me. You had to be a little crazy to spend night after long night in a basement cubby or library.

The Ohio State University's campus was among the largest in the world. As a teenager considering my options for college, its campus had intimidated the hell out of me. It was big and confusing, interwoven throughout Columbus in a sprawling maze of buildings, parks and paths. With roots going all the way back to 1870, OSU walked a fine line between the historical charm in some of its architecture and cutting edge science in modern, state of the art, new buildings.

The person I was looking for would either be in the library or the building that housed all of the history classes.

I parked in one of the many garages and headed downstairs. The library and history department were in opposite directions. If I was a history graduate student on the cusp of finishing my dissertation, where would I be?

Probably the library archives. It fit with what I knew of her. She'd always been a bookworm, more content to bury her head in a make believe world than come out and play with me.

OSU's library was a four floor beast of glass and metal. It was quiet as a grave, with students tucked inside books or hunched over desks. And they said books were dead. Looked like students still had to do their research the old fashioned way here, with musty old books and notepads.

I headed down to the archives, getting turned around a few times. I'd only been there once and that was several years ago. No one challenged me as I meandered through the stacks. To them I was just another procrastinating student, intent on doing some last minute research before a test or paper was due.

It felt weird being back in a college library. Familiar, but weird. This was the life Mom wanted me to embrace. Staying up late, ruining my eyes as I struggled to meet a professor's unrealistic expectations. Somehow I didn't regret getting out when I did. As weird as the path my life had taken, it was at least interesting.

The archive section was under lock and key. I expected that. Some of the manuscripts they kept in the climate controlled rooms were hundreds of years old and priceless. Not something you let just anybody off the street come in to handle.

I headed to the empty library desk and tapped the bell. A sleepy looking college kid peered around the corner. I smiled as the early twenty something boy walked up to me, rubbing his curls, causing them to stick straight up. He looked so young, though he couldn't have been more than five years younger than me.

"Can I help you?"

"Yes, I'm looking for Caroline Bradley."

As long as this wasn't his first day, he'd know who I was talking about. She was hard to miss and was here enough that it could be considered her second home.

"Uh, she doesn't like to be disturbed when she's back there."

Yup. That was my friend.

"Don't worry. I can handle it."

"I'm not really supposed to bother her."

"Either go get her or let me back there. Trust me, she'll want to know I'm here."

He gave the door leading to the archives a worried look. "I'll buzz you back. Just don't tell anybody."

I snorted. What had she done to this poor guy that he was willing to let a complete stranger into the archives unsupervised?

"There are cameras. We'll prosecute to the fullest extent of the law if you touch or damage anything."

The door buzzed.

"Consider me warned."

I shivered. The air was cooler than in the rest of the library.

It was easy to find Caroline. She was hunched over a book as long as my arm and almost as thick as my torso. She handled the pages with white gloves, flipping them with the utmost of care. Her curly blond hair was scraped back from her face into a messy bun.

"I really don't understand what you find so interesting in those things."

Her shoulders tensed.

I waited.

She slid her hands out from under the page she was handling and sat back in her chair. Moving efficiently, she stripped off her gloves and pulled a pair of black rimmed glasses from her face, setting them onto the table next to her.

I fidgeted in the silence.

She made me wait as she tidied up her workspace. Only when everything was in its exact spot and perfectly lined up did she turn.

Her face was calm as she regarded me, her girl-next-door looks making her appear the same as she had the day I'd signed up for the Army. I'd always envied her everyday beauty, the kind that was just there and looked good at any age. Even when we'd been in middle school, she'd been the one all the boys had liked. I wasn't insecure about my looks now, but I had been back then. It'd taken over a decade to grow into all my angles.

"I'm waiting," she said.

I stuck my hands in my pocket. "Don't know what for."

She arched one eyebrow and gave me a cool smile. "Then you can let yourself out, and I can get back to examining this fifteenth century manuscript."

She started to turn back to her work.

"I'm not apologizing," I snapped. "I did nothing wrong. It's my life and joining the military was the best decision I could make at that time."

She spun back around, her calm expression deteriorating enough to leave anger and disappointment in its place. "Is that what you think this is about?"

"What else could it be? You made it perfectly clear what you thought when I left."

"Jesus, Lena. You haven't bothered talking to me in four years."

"You could have reached out. I'm not the one who threw a bitch fit when I decided to become a soldier."

"And look how well that ended up. How did the intervention go? Your parents manage to talk you into getting help?"

I drew back, stung. I hadn't realized Mom reached out to her.

Perhaps it had been a mistake coming here. I didn't think she'd be this angry after all these years. We'd been best friends once. She'd had trouble relating to people, and her ability to say precisely the wrong thing at exactly the right time had made it difficult for her in high school and undergrad. She was so smart, with an IQ that was off the charts, and hadn't bothered with people she thought were a waste of time. I never figured out why she started talking to me. We shouldn't have gotten along but we did until we didn't.

I thought time would help bridge some of the distance that had built between us. Obviously not.

She sighed, sounding weary. "What do you want? I know you want something. You wouldn't be here otherwise."

"I need your help researching something."

She stared at me, her eyebrows rising. "You're kidding me."

Nope. That's what I wanted.

She laughed.

I winced. She did not sound happy, more like disbelieving.

"You know I wouldn't be here unless it was important."

She looked down. I waited. Rushing her would just result in her snapping and throwing me out.

"No," she said. "I don't think so."

She turned back to her desk. I waited, frozen in place. I really hadn't thought she'd refuse.

"Caroline," I started. I didn't know what to say. I sighed. There was really nothing to say. Too much time had passed. And, she'd been the one to flip out, not even trying to understand why I joined the Army. "Take care of yourself, okay?"

I turned around.

"Wait," she ground out, setting her pen down with a thump. "How important?"

I faced her. "An avalanche's worth."

"You're not going to tell me what this is about, are you?"

I shook my head. I could try to lie, but it wouldn't work. She'd always had a particular gift for seeing through deception. It had driven away every guy who tried to date her. She made an excellent liar though. Which had made sneaking outside after curfew easy because all of the adults trusted her innocent expression.

"Fuck. I can't believe I'm doing this."

I blinked. The Caroline I knew hadn't been much of a curser. Said it was the crutch for people who didn't have a good command of the English language.

"You'll help me then?"

"Yes. Yes. Don't keep harping on. What exactly is it you need?"

"I need someone who can do a little research, specifically into a soldier who died at Camp Chase during the Civil War."

"That's it? That's all that you want?"

"Yes?" I made it a question.

"Why not my left kidney while you're at it? Do you know how many soldiers' died during that time period? The records from those places were notoriously bad. Most of the men who died were buried in unmarked graves. Little if any information will have survived."

"Anything you can give me would be a huge help."

"Oh yes, because I live to help you," she said sarcastically.

She gathered up her manuscript and walked it over to a tub, putting it inside and carrying it to one of the shelves lining the wall.

"Come on," she said as she grabbed her notebook. "We'll have to head to the third floor where they keep all the civil war books. If we're lucky, they'll have some of Camp Chase's records. If not, you'd better hope they digitized that crap."

I followed as she strode out of the room. The college student manning the desk gave a garbled greeting that Caroline completely ignored. Seemed like this at least hadn't changed. I gave him a commiserating look as I trailed after her. He rolled his eyes and theatrically gestured at the sky. I snorted back a laugh.

"I heard that," Caroline said, not bothering to look over her shoulder.

"Do you want to at least know the name of the soldier I'm looking for?"

She stopped. "You know it?"

"Maybe. There are a few possibilities."

She considered. "It's a place to start at least. Like I said, records from that time period are sparse and a lot of things have been lost over the years."

I gave her the names the draugr had given me. Maybe we'd get lucky and his name was actually one of them.

The third floor was empty as we walked through the poorly lit halls. Half the lights were off, and the place had an air of abandonment.

"Are we supposed to be up here?" I asked, looking around.

"No, they close this section at ten. I've got special privileges due to my dissertation. If anybody asks, I'll just refer them to my thesis professor."

"Ah."

Caroline tossed her bag onto a table and headed to a computer. Not sure what else to do, I followed.

"How can I help?"

Her fingers paused as they flew over the keyboard.

"You see that couch over there?"

I looked behind us at a sitting area, complete with a bright orange couch and comfortable looking chairs.

"Yup."

"I want you to go sit on it and not talk to me for the next few hours."

Her fingers resumed their typing.

"Okay. I can do that."

I backed away and headed for the couch. It was going to be a long night. I lay back and snuggled my head on the cushion behind me.

My phone bit into my hip, and I dug it out. Eight missed calls and three messages. Wonder who that could be.

I clicked into my messages and listened to Liam's terse voice.

"Aileen, we are at the house. Where are you? The draugr was already gone by the time we got here. Call me back."

That didn't surprise me. I doubted it would return anytime soon now that I'd disturbed its feeding ground. The creature was crazy; not stupid.

I clicked delete and played the next one.

"This is the third check in you've missed, and I have yet to hear from you. Call me now."

I deleted the message and moved to the next.

"Aileen." I sat up in surprise at Brax's voice. "I need to speak with you as soon as possible."

I had a feeling it had to do with the werewolf Liam said he'd lost. Brax had been pretty convinced he didn't need my help earlier. He might just be planning to use the connection he thought I had to the crimes. It might be worth giving him a call back when I was through here.

The last message was from Liam. It was short and to the point.

"Call. Now."

I had no plans to follow his order, knowing his next step would be to yank me off the streets. I couldn't chance that. Not when there was so much on the line.

"You seem happy," Caroline observed from her computer. "More like yourself."

I sat up, thinking over her comment. It was true that some of the general numbness I'd been feeling lately was missing, replaced by adrenaline. I was focused with a laser intensity on the problems in front of me. It was a feeling that had been absent from my life for a while now. I didn't feel especially happy, though.

"Why do you say that?"

She shrugged. "Just a feeling."

I settled back down and fidgeted with my phone.

"Your mom's wrong, you know." The keys clicked in the silence. "You don't have PTSD, and I doubt you're an alcoholic. You're just different."

"Different good? Or different bad?"

I hadn't realized how important the question was to me until I waited with baited breath for her to pronounce her verdict. I trusted her judgement and didn't know what I'd do if she thought something was wrong with me.

"It's too soon to tell."

I released the breath I was holding.

"I've found something you can help me with," she said abruptly. "Wait here."

She grabbed a cart and vanished into the stacks.

"Okay. Guess I'll just wait here."

I waited and waited, finally getting up and walking around the study area. With the lights dim and the stacks cast in shadow, the library had an air of creepiness, like it was just waiting to pick us off one by one. Give me a city back ally or warehouse any day. I didn't know how Caroline could stand spending her evenings here.

The creek of wheels announced Caroline's presence long before she appeared out of the gloom. The cart was piled high with books. There must have been dozens of them.

"What are those?" I asked, eyeing them with distaste.

"I told you. Most of the camp's records were never digitized. These books have parts of those records. We'll have to go through each one to see if we can find what you're looking for."

"We?"

There was a reason I'd refused Mom's offer to send me back to school. Spending my life looking through a bunch of dusty old books had no appeal.

She raised one eyebrow. "You didn't think I was going to go through all of these by myself, did you?"

I had thought that.

"No, of course not. That would be rude of me."

"Right." The tone of her voice made it apparent she didn't believe any of the words out of my mouth. "None of the names on the list you gave came up in my search."

That meant the draugr had never intended to give me its name and had no intention of letting me find its baubles. I really thought he'd given me at least one real name. Given the number of books on her cart, it would be nearly impossible finding one person in all those pages.

"I combined some of the first and last names and had a couple hits," Caroline continued. She slid a piece of paper with three names on them. "It's a long shot, and of course, the original names might be in here but just haven't been referenced yet."

She selected several thick books and slid them towards me. I picked one up and flipped through. Words, words and more words. This was going to take all night.

"Start with those. I'll find the rest of the books on the list and then help."

There were more. I gave the stack a disbelieving look.

She unloaded the rest of the books and then wheeled the cart back towards the library stacks. She had a smile on her face, I realized. She was enjoying this. It made sense. She'd always gotten a perverse thrill out of a challenging project. The more difficult it was to hunt down the information, the bigger the charge she got. For all her protestations, I'd handed her the perfect task.

I slid a chair back and seated myself, pulling the first book towards me and opening it to the first page. The going was tedious and required lots of skimming. It wasn't long before I'd sunk into a rhythm, flipping through page after page and making notes of interesting pieces of information. Caroline joined me, the stack of books she'd gone through growing in front of her at a greater rate than mine.

Several hours passed before the aches and pains in my back and neck forced me to sit upright. I stretched, raising my hands high and twisting back and forth. It felt like I should have a pizza or a frou frou coffee in front of me or something. College students still did that, right? I looked around. Maybe not in the library, though.

The lights flickered overhead. Once, twice and then a third time. Caroline didn't bother looking up from the book she was studying, the lamp she'd turned on enabled her to read despite the flickering.

"Is that normal?"

"Is what normal?" she asked in a distracted voice.

The lights flickered again.

"That. The light flickering."

"They're not flickering," she said looking up.

They flickered again and then shut off, leaving only her lamp on.

"That's odd," she said, marking her page in the book. "I don't think this has ever happened before."

I touched the gun at my hip, feeling only slightly reassured by the feel of metal. Had the draugr somehow found me? I gave Caroline a worried look. If I'd thought coming to her would involve her in the crazy parts of my life, I would have stayed far away.

"Where have you been?" an irate teenage voice asked from the shadows.

I released the gun. As annoying as the sorcerer was, he wasn't on the same level of threat as the draugr. Especially with that cuff still on him.

"Whatever you're doing to the lights, stop."

He sighed. The lights flicked back on. He definitely had a thing for theatrics. His grumpy teenage face glared at me from a few feet away.

"I've been looking all over the city for you since last night. You were supposed to check in. This wasn't what we agreed to when we made our deal."

I gave him a humorless grin. "Since I didn't exactly agree to anything, I'd say we're about even."

"Look, you fanged leech," he started.

I cleared my throat and nodded my head at Caroline. If he wasn't careful, he was going to reveal more than he should.

His gaze swung to my friend's blond beauty and got stuck as he stared, mesmerized.

"Friend of yours?" Caroline asked with a quirk to her lips.

"No."

"Yes," he interrupted, sticking his hand out. "I'm Peter. Peter Barrett. It's so nice to meet you."

Peter? So original. The boy who never aged. Wonder where he got that from.

She gave his hand an arch look and turned to me. "These books won't read themselves."

"Got it."

"You know," Peter started.

"Can I talk to you a minute?" I asked tightly.

"Go talk to yourself," Peter retorted.

I grabbed him by the back of the shirt and hauled him after me. He swore and tried to swat me away, missing me entirely.

"What are you doing here?" I snapped when I felt we were far enough away that Caroline couldn't hear us.

He craned his head back towards Caroline, giving her a charming smile. I shook him a little bit, and he leveled a nasty glare at me.

"What do you think I'm doing here?" he shot back. "I'm checking on your progress."

"And how did you find me? Not to mention how did you turn off the lights? The cuff is supposed to cut off your power."

I flicked the metal attached to his wrist for emphasis.

He jerked his arm away from me. "I have my methods. I'm not entirely helpless with this damn thing on. You should remember that."

"I'm sure you won't let me forget."

We glared at each other.

"So, is your friend seeing anyone?"

"We're not talking about that," I said, folding my arms over my chest. "She's human and not part of this world. You're going to leave her alone."

He gave her an assessing glance. "Are you sure about that?"

"Yes." I didn't know what he was talking about, and I didn't care. Caroline was off limits. "I've verified it was a draugr. It's also responsible for the human disappearances around Hilltop. I think the reason the police haven't found any bodies is that it's been eating its victims."

"But not the supernatural ones?"

"Not that I've been able to tell."

"Interesting."

My eyes sharpened. "How so?"

"Draugrs are known for eating their victims, but to my knowledge don't usually distinguish between humans and those from our world. It should be eating all of its victims, not just some."

"I think it's getting direction from someone."

He tilted his head in question.

"It mentioned someone. I think it's being guided towards its victims. That thing it's looking for? I think someone has whatever it is and is now using it to somehow control where the draugr strikes next."

He bent his head in thought. It was so odd seeing a teenage face deep in reflection. I felt like he should start goofing off any moment now.

"Why are you here then?" he asked.

"Research. If I can figure out who he was in life, then I might be able to find some kind of weakness or at least discover what he wants."

His lip curled. "So you're in a library?"

"You know anybody in the city who can give me details of every prisoner held in Camp Chase? The draugr was human once. I figured my best chance of getting information on him lies with human records."

His face held a grudging respect when I'd finished my explanation. "Fair point." He shot a glance back at the table. "It's going to take you days to go through all those books."

I groaned internally. He was right. I'd been ambitious thinking it would only take one night. Even with Caroline's pile of finished books, we had barely made a dent in the stacks we'd pulled. So far we'd discovered exactly nil.

I slapped him on the back. "That's why you're going to help us."

He gave the books a distasteful look. "It would be so much easier if you took this cuff off. I could do a spell to call any books containing relevant information."

"You could do that?"

That would be a pretty useful skill for any student or researcher. He could patent it and make millions.

"Take this off, and you can find out." He rattled the cuff at me.

"I don't think so. Trust between us pretty much doesn't exist."

I headed back to the table, the sorcerer trailing behind me and muttering insults against me and my ancestors. And he wondered why I wasn't willing to take a chance and release him. Some of those threats were creative and horrible enough that I was tempted to just shoot him and be done with all of it.

There was an idea. I gave him a considering look.

Naw, there was too much risk. I had no idea how this mark would react and no guarantee a bullet would actually kill him. With my luck, the tattoo would burn me alive, and he would survive to dance on my ashes.

"Caroline, Peter is going to help us look through the books."

"Uh huh," she said her gaze intent on her research. "Talking less would result in more work done."

Right. I turned to the sorcerer—I just couldn't bring myself to call him Peter—and gathered up several books, sliding them in front of him. "You take this stack. Here are the names we're particularly interested in."

He selected a book off the top and set it down with a thump, flicking it open with sharp gestures as he frowned at me.

"Don't take your anger out on the books," Caroline ordered without lifting her head.

His cheeks colored slightly, and he handled the pages with more care as he bent to work. I wanted to laugh, but knew I'd be the next one to receive a scolding if I did.

We worked in silence, the stacks of read books growing. It was beginning to feel like this had been a waste of time as I went through page after page with nothing useful gleaned. Perhaps the names had been a red herring. The draugr hadn't exactly proven to be a helpful source of information. More like the opposite.

"I think I've found something," Caroline announced, straightening and staring down at the book in excitement.

"Really?" I said, lifting my head from where it'd been resting on the pages. Despite not needing sleep, all that reading had lulled me into a light doze. I scrubbed at the creases on my face.

"Yes. It was one of the combined names. Here take a look."

I grabbed the book she slid towards me and lifted it to my face, the sorcerer rushing around to read over my shoulder.

"It's a photo of one Jackson Miller and his wife Eva Miller. He was a doctor on the Union side until he was discovered giving Confederate soldiers shelter after a battle. They sent him to Camp Chase," Caroline said.

The photo was of a man and woman in their Sunday best, staring out of the book with serious expressions. He looked austere with his top hat and cravat. She had a slight twinkle in her eye that softened the severity of her hairstyle and made it seem like she was having a laugh with him.

"I can't find any records of him after this. I don't know if he died there or was released back to his wife."

"He died there," I said softly.

Even with the skin whole and unblemished and the beard and side burns, I could tell it was the draugr I'd caught eating a human earlier tonight. His story hadn't had a happy ending. He'd probably died of malnutrition or one of the many diseases that swept through those camps in that period. How did he go from being a healer to a monster feasting on flesh?

"The prison camps were pretty brutal. Chase wasn't as bad as Andersonville, but it wouldn't have been pleasant. As a doctor he may have known about the conditions of the camps and tried to protect the enemy soldiers and was instead discovered and seen as a traitor," Caroline theorized.

"More likely he was playing both sides of the war and got caught," Peter said, dryly.

I looked closely at the photograph, studying the locket around Eva's throat. It seemed familiar. I'd seen it somewhere recently. It was silver and in the shape of a circle with fine geometric details rimming it. A branch with flowers had precious stones where the buds should be decorating the middle of it. The locket was pretty and was the type of thing I could picture a wife giving her husband to remember her by before he marched off to war.

A silver chain was visible going from Jackson's waist to a pocket in his vest. I'd bet anything that was the watch he'd been searching for.

"Look here and here," I said, pointing the two items out to the sorcerer. "Think those could be what he's after?"

The sorcerer's forehead crinkled as he stared down at the items in question. "It's possible."

"The camp guards would have taken anything of value from the prisoners. Anything he had would be long gone by now," Caroline said.

He'd managed to smuggle them past the guards. I was sure of it. There was no question in my mind that the locket and pocket watch shown here were what the draugr searched for.

"Do you think you could devise a…" My eyes shot to Caroline and I changed what I was going to say. "Program that would be able to track these things down?"

"I told you that's impossible." Caroline frowned. "They could be anywhere at this point."

"I could do it if this was off," the sorcerer murmured to me, raising one hand.

I debated the merits of releasing his powers. On the one hand, he could be a powerful ally capable of helping me subdue the draugr. On the other, he was just as likely to try and kill me seconds after it was removed.

"What are you two talking about?" Caroline asked, her gaze shooting between us.

I gave her a brilliant smile. "Nothing important. Thanks for all your help, Caroline. It really saved me."

She gave me a flat stare. "Stop lying. You're not going anywhere until I get some answers."

"I can give you answers," Peter said, shooting her a charming smile.

"Quiet, you," I snapped. "Caroline, I've got to go, and I can't really explain everything."

"Fine," she said, standing and piling the books back onto the cart. "If that's how you want it, I'll just sit here while you go off having adventures. Again. Maybe I'll see you in another four years."

The sorcerer gave me a smile and propped his chin on his fist as he watched the two of us. It was so nice to have an audience for this.

"Caroline."

"Its fine, Aileen," she said. "I understand. You should get going. I'm tired and want to get to sleep before dawn."

"I'll try to stay in better touch."

"I'm sure you will, though I won't hold my breath," she said.

I didn't know what to say to that so I said nothing, stepping away from the desk and gesturing for the sorcerer to follow me.

"I hope to see you again," he told Caroline, giving her another winsome smile before trailing after me.

"Do you have to act like such a creepy old man?" I muttered.

"I am an old man," he whispered back. "Besides, your friend is hot."

"And you will never see her again."

He cast one last look behind us. "I wouldn't be too sure of that."

For my peace of mind and to avoid being totally creeped out, I decided to ignore that statement. I had a feeling forbidding him to have anything else to do with her would be like waving a red flag in front of a bull.

Chapter Twelve

"When are you going to remove this?" Peter asked, sliding into the car next to me.

I shot him a glance as he fiddled with the knob that controlled the windows. He was like a kid in a spaceship, curious about everything and pushing any button he could find. He flipped through every channel on the radio then started through them again, changing the volume up and down at the same time. I cringed as it screeched and buzzed.

"Would you stop that?" I asked, slapping his hand away from the radio. "What is wrong with you? You'd think you'd never been in a car before."

"It's been a while. My method of travel is a little more immediate than this. This looks different than I remember. It's amazing how fast humans have evolved this technology given their limitations."

Yeah, we were just so challenged. I wanted to point out that most supernatural species started out as human. I gave the sorcerer a sidelong glance, wondering if he had. He certainly looked human enough.

My phone rang before I could respond.

"You know you shouldn't mess with your phone and drive," the sorcerer observed as I juggled the wheel and the phone.

"Thanks, I've never heard that one before."

Brax.

Shit, I'd meant to return his call hours ago.

I clicked answer. "Brax, I was getting ready to give you a call."

"Is that the werewolf alpha?" the sorcerer asked, alarmed.

I gestured for him to be quiet.

"Somehow I don't believe that."

I would have. Eventually. Maybe.

"You stole my car," he said evenly.

"I did tell you not to leave your keys in the ignition, and I left it in a safe spot."

"Yes, Easton. The parking garage you left it in charged us a hundred dollars to get it out because it was left overnight."

I grinned. I'd chosen that garage specifically for that reason in the hopes he wouldn't recover it until it'd accumulated some fines. He was lucky they hadn't towed it.

"I heard you lost another wolf," I said.

"Liam told you. I'm surprised he hasn't pulled you from the streets yet."

"You two seem to have a history," I observed. They had gone at it like too guys feuding over a girl's affections or as a part of some long standing male rivalry.

He ignored my comment. "We need to meet."

I shook my head, forgetting he couldn't see me. "The last time we met you kidnapped me."

"I can still find out where your family is," he began.

"Ha, nice try. The vampires already know about them, which means your threat has no teeth."

The silence over the line spoke volumes. I smirked. It was nice for the shoe to be on the other foot. He needed me more than I needed him now. The only question was how much I made him beg before I told him what I knew.

"Nothing to say?" I asked. "That's strange. I thought you wanted to know who was killing your people."

"You're so mean," the sorcerer whispered. "I love it."

I shot him a wry glance. He liked it when he wasn't on the receiving end. I bet if I started threatening to not share my information he'd lose his shit.

"I'd be very careful if I was you," Brax rumbled.

"Nope, not what I want to hear."

I clicked the end button and set it in my lap.

"I can't believe you just hung up on the wolves' alpha," Peter said, looking at me with a hint of respect for the first time. "He's going to rip you to pieces when he finally catches up with you."

The phone rang. I let it ring once, twice and then a third before finally picking it up and saying, "Yes?"

"You little."

Click.

Still not what I wanted to hear.

"Oh man, I'm tempted to let all your transgressions against me go just for the sheer entertainment value of the last few minutes."

"And that's why I haven't taken that cuff off yet."

He narrowed his eyes on me then shrugged. "Fair enough."

The phone rang again.

"Don't you dare hang up on me or-"

"Yup, don't want to hear your threats either." I spoke over him. "How about you call me back when you've calmed down."

I hung up again amidst several loud threats and curses.

I grinned. That felt good. Maybe next time he'd think twice about making threats against someone's family or sharing information that wasn't his to share with the vampires. Petty, I know but sometimes you just had allow your feelings to rule or end up regretting it years down the road. It was good for them to realize I wasn't a doormat. That I had teeth, even if they were small, baby ones.

I was able to listen to two songs on the radio before the phone rang again.

"You ready to be civil?" I asked chirpily.

"Only if you're willing to start following directions," Liam's cool voice said on the line.

Shit. I answered without checking.

"Liam, what a surprise."

The sorcerer's head whipped towards me as he bolted upright. He mouthed the word "crap," echoing my feelings exactly.

"Is it? I don't know why as you were supposed to check in ten minutes ago."

My eyes went to the dash board clock. 3:10. Not that I'd planned on checking in at all, but if I'd known we were so close to a check in time I would have been a little more careful answering my phone. After all, he had called during every other supposed check in.

"Oh gee, look at the time. You're right. I can't believe I missed it. The time has really gotten away from me tonight."

He ground his teeth. There seemed to be a lot of that happening tonight.

I'd be lying if I didn't get a small charge out of his and Brax's aggravation. When you're as low on the totem pole as I was, you take your wins where you can. Pissing them off was about the only thing I could get away with. Trying physical violence would only result in a severe beating or death. I was banking on time and distance blunting the worst of their anger.

"We had an agreement," he said, his voice dropping into a smooth cadence. "You have violated the conditions of your release not just once or twice but many times."

He made me sound like a prisoner on parole.

"I was a little busy running from the draugr and all. I didn't have time to stop and make a call to assure you I was still alive."

"And were you running for the entire four hours?" he asked silkily.

I paused, debating how much I wanted to tell him about my whereabouts. I didn't like the idea of letting him know about Caroline or the research she'd done for me.

"It was more difficult to dodge him than I thought."

"Oh, and so you weren't sitting at the campus library a few minutes ago?"

I gave the sorcerer an uneasy glance. He watched me with wide eyes and gestured as if to say he was as confused as me. How did Liam know where I'd been, and did he know where I was right now?

I looked in my rear view and side mirrors. Was he following me even now?

"It was a handy place to hide," I bluffed.

A white truck turned behind me, following me down another block. I sped up slightly. It sped up.

"For four hours. Hm. You must have been very worried."

"Have you been following me?" I teased uneasily. "I didn't know you cared."

The truck followed me through another turn. The sorcerer shook his arm at me giving me a furious look. I shook my head. I wouldn't release him unless there was no other choice.

"I can't have you getting yourself killed while you're my responsibility."

"You're all heart."

I slowed down as I approached a green light. I needed to time this carefully. The truck came closer and closer. Almost.

The light turned yellow. I floored it, the wheels spinning and smoking as we shot forward. We cleared the intersection just as the light turned red. The truck stopped. Guess it hadn't been following us after all.

Peter released the breath he had been holding and relaxed into his seat, shooting me an unfriendly look.

"Take yourself to Asylum. It's a club downtown."

"I know what it is." Everybody knew what it was. It was popular, but I hadn't realized it was owned by the vampires. I'd been in there in the past year too. From now on I would have to steer clear of it.

Liam continued, "I'll have some vampires I trust take you into custody."

That wasn't going to happen. Despite the panic the draugr had managed to instill in me, my goals remained the same. Find the people controlling him. Get the items for the sorcerer and free myself from his mark. The inkling of a plan was beginning to develop as to how I could extricate myself from the vampires' grasp. It wouldn't happen if I was locked down tight for my own protection.

"I'm thinking that doesn't really work for me," I said.

Liam's voice rumbled in a low bass that I felt in my chest. "This isn't a request."

"Whew, that was scary. I bet most people fall right in line when you use that voice." I don't know what it was about Brax and Liam that brought out my inner bitch, but I decided to embrace her for now. She made me feel powerful and not like I was shaking in my boots at all the things that could go wrong.

"Aileen."

"I'm sorry, but no. I have information you don't, and the fact that it's my life on the line hasn't changed. I'll let you know when I need your help. Until then, pack sand."

For the fourth time that night, I hung up over the other party's protests. The sorcerer watched me with a bemused expression as I threw my phone into the cup holder next to my seat.

"What?" I barked.

He shrugged with a feigned nonchalance. "Nothing. Just calculating your life expectancy."

"Very short if we don't figure out how to find the draugr's stuff."

"I'm thinking with the number of people we pissed off tonight, it's not going to matter whether you find his keepsakes."

I ignored that comment as the phone rang again. This time I made sure it said, "Brax calling," before picking up.

"What?" I snapped.

His words were stiff and formal as he said, "Would you please tell me about what you've uncovered?"

It wasn't the apology I wanted, but it would have to do. Grudgingly, I told him about the draugr who used to be Jackson Miller and my theory that there was a mastermind behind all of the attacks.

"Do you have any proof of this mastermind?"

"Not yet. But I'm hoping to track down those items."

He was distracted as he said, "Until you have more proof, I can't assume there is a mastermind. I'll focus on bringing down the draugr itself to stop these attacks."

"Didn't you listen to anything I said? The wolves have been the focus of all these attacks. You've lost the most people to this thing. Based on the fact that it can take over animals and cause insanity, it would be pure stupidity to go after it directly."

"My people are more than just animals. I think we can handle this 'Again-Walker' as you call it."

Oh, you foolish, arrogant man. You are going to get yourselves killed or worse.

Telling him that would only cause him to dig his heels in further. I'd dealt with enough male testosterone poisoning in the military. I needed to talk him away from the ledge. Lead him to the outcome I wanted. Be diplomatic, the voice of reason.

"Just give me a couple nights to verify my theory. Knowing your enemy's strengths and weaknesses gives you a better chance of surviving."

"Wolves are dying. My people won't just sit idly by waiting to be picked off one by one. We move tonight."

"You're being an idiot. I'm sure they don't want to be slaughtered either. At least give me until tomorrow."

So much for diplomacy.

Brax snarled. "We go tonight. You have a few hours and then me and mine are going hunting."

This time he was the one to hang up.

"Brax?"

I looked at the dead phone in my hand.

Shit.

I threw it in the cup holder.

"Bad news?"

I gripped the wheel tighter and shook my head in frustration.

"The wolves are going after the draugr tonight."

Peter whistled. "They don't stand a chance. With the creature's ability to inspire madness and possess animals, they're fucked. He could take control, or worse strip their control."

"How is that worse?"

"It would leave them mindless beasts with the destructive power of a tank and the disposition of a rabid badger. You ever seen one of those? They're vicious. A bunch of out of control wolves in the middle of Columbus? You're talking a pretty high body count."

And because of me, they knew exactly what they were looking for and his most recent hunting grounds.

"Is there some way to stop them?"

The sorcerer shrugged. "Maybe, but I don't really care one way or the other if they go homicidal on the humans."

I gave him a nonplussed look. "Isn't that why you've had me running all over the city after this thing? To find and stop it."

"That was just to get you on board with hunting it. I just want the two items. Taking care of the draugr was a side benefit. Not the main goal." He gave me a side long glance. "Though maybe I could be convinced if this cuff was removed."

I was tempted. If my inaction caused a bunch of deaths, I was just as responsible as if I'd done the murdering myself. Two things stopped me. First, there was no guarantee the sorcerer would actually help once free. He'd already made it clear his goals didn't really include protecting the wolves. Secondly, I was pretty sure he didn't have the power to do what he was planning, which made his release a moot point and would probably only cause further harm.

"I'll think about it." We drove in silence for a few more minutes. I needed to decide where we were going soon. We were almost out of campus. "Theoretically, how would you help?"

He cocked his head and sent me a sly smile that said he thought he'd won. Not by a long shot, but he didn't need to know that.

"I'd probably cast a summoning spell for the items," he said thoughtfully. "You control those and you'll have some control over the draugr. You might even be able to force him back into his grave. It wouldn't kill him, but it might contain him and lull him back to sleep."

I stared out the window. Earlier he'd been gung ho about getting the items for his own mysterious purposes. Now it sounded like he wanted to use them to contain the draugr. What had changed? Or was this another trick? One meant to lull me into thinking he was working with me when really he had his own agenda.

"Sounds like a difficult spell. You sure you can cast something like that?"

He scoffed. "Any sorcerer or witch who has passed their trial could cast something as simple as that."

I smirked. Just what I'd wanted to hear. I flicked on my turn signal and took a left. Looked like I knew my destination.

He sat up. "Where are we going? All of my supplies are at my office, which is in the opposite direction."

"We're not going to your office."

He lowered his eyebrows. "Then where are we going?"

I gave him a toothy smile. "We're going to see a witch about a spell."

"No. Why? I told you I could cast the spell."

"So can she and I trust her a hell of a lot more than I trust you."

He sputtered, the look on his face making it clear I was right to have my suspicions.

"This is ridiculous. You're making a mistake."

Yeah, yeah. It was my mistake to make. Hopefully, my last visit hadn't totally pissed her off and she'd be willing to help me.

*   *   *

Elements' sign was turned to 'closed'. I stood outside and wondered what I should do. I didn't have Miriam's home address or her phone number. It hadn't occurred to me that she might not be in her shop. I just assumed since she was part of the otherworld that she kept the same hours as me, which was ludicrous. She had no reason to cling to the dark like I did. Her feet were planted much more firmly in the day world than mine.

"What now, oh smart one?" Peter asked sarcastically. "Looks like your plan is a complete dud."

I didn't answer. Time was against me. I only had a few hours left before sunrise, and I didn't think Brax would wait much longer before making his move.

I pounded on the door and stepped back, looking at the windows above the shop. Nothing. No lights turned on, and I could see no movement behind the curtains. I pounded again, my hand smarting from the force. Looked like she didn't live above the shop as I'd hoped.

What kind of witch was this? Shouldn't she be able to sense when people need her?

"She's not here," Peter complained. "Guess you'll have to release me from this cuff."

"Not yet."

I hadn't exhausted all options. There had to be some way to contact Miriam.

"You're the one who didn't want the wolves dying or going ape shit on everyone," he griped.

Wait. I'd made a delivery here. Jerry would have her information on file. There was the slight question of whether he would share that information with me, especially since I'd been actively avoiding him over the past few days. Probably not and definitely not without the most extreme ass chewing of my life.

I grabbed my phone and opened the app for the courier service. Maybe I'd get lucky and her information would still be in my queue. It sometimes took a few days for it to drop off my history. Her cell number should have been included in the contact portion in case I missed the deadline.

Ah ha. It was there. I would be spared from having to go through Jerry after all.

I dialed the number and waited as it rang. And rang. And rang. Then went to voicemail. I hung up and stared at the phone. Was she asleep? During the witching hour?

Peter made a frustrated sound next to me. "Enough of this."

He raised one hand and touched the door. It was like a gong had sounded. I covered my ears, but it wasn't enough to block out the sound. I could feel whatever he'd done in my chest, rattling through my bones. Then it was gone.

"What the hell?" I yelled. "I thought you couldn't do magic."

"That wasn't me," he said with a serious expression, watching his surroundings. "I touched the ward. Think of it like a really annoying doorbell."

A doorbell? I didn't think so. More like a claxon calling up the troops to defend against an attack.

"I touched the door too." I gave the door in question a suspicious glare. "Why didn't it do that when I knocked?"

"I doubt you have enough power to register to the ward. Quite frankly, I'm surprised you were even able to feel the alarm."

I gave him a flat look. Yes. I get it. I'm practically an infant compared to all the heavy hitters around me. No need to keep reminding me. It's shoved in my face every time something new happens, and I'm the only one surprised.

"I had a feeling I'd be seeing you again," Miriam's crisp voice said from behind me.

I spun to see her watching us with cautiously amused eyes. She was dressed casually in lounge pants and a loose, long, white shirt. The kind that draped nicely and was super comfortable but looked effortlessly classy at the same time.

"Really? Because I had no idea I'd end up here again," I said.

She smiled. "Let's go in and you can tell me what spell you need cast."

That was creepy. No matter how many times I encountered it, the whole knowing something before I told them threw me every time.

"I'm surprised you triggered my wards," she said, moving past me.

Peter tried to grab my arm as I followed her. I brushed him off and said, "I didn't. The sorcerer did."

She paused in the act of swinging open the door. Power gathered around her, kind of like a knight readying his shield. It wasn't visible, more like an intangible shimmering in the air around her.

Her eyes were lit with a dark flame as she glared over my shoulder at Peter. He stepped behind me, using me as a shield.

Once again I felt like I'd missed something obvious.

"Sorcerer."

Her voice slithered and swam through the night. I got the sense of something pressing hard on my chest, drowning me even as I drew in air in small, little pants. What was it with everyone pulling power trips at the drop of the hat?

"I wish you hadn't told her that," Peter said behind me.

"If you told me that you two had a history, I wouldn't have."

"We don't have a history. Witches hate sorcerers. Don't you know anything?"

I rolled my eyes. Cowering like a child behind me and he still managed to act like a tool.

"Nope. I don't know anything. Nothing at all. I thought we'd established that by now," I snapped.

"You're Barret's forever young apprentice," Miriam said, her power easing back.

"Apprentice?" I asked raising my eyebrows and turning to face him. "I thought you were a sorcerer."

"I am a sorcerer," he retorted. "I achieved the station right before." He stopped abruptly, his eyes shifting left and right.

"Where is Barret?" Miriam asked, picking up on his tension. "The city has felt different for quite some time now, but his businesses are still operating as they have in the past."

Peter lifted his chin. "He's gone, and he left me in charge until he got back."

She arched one eyebrow. "Really?"

I watched the two of them, trying to read the undercurrents. Sounded like this Barret guy had disappeared and the apprentice had been covering for him for a while now. Miriam's words also confirmed Peter was older than he looked. I wondered how much older. Five years? Fifty? A hundred? How long did it take to become a sorcerer? So many questions and not a one to do with the reason we were here.

"As interesting as this conversation is, it's not why we're here," I interrupted before Peter could fire off the insult I could see brewing. "We need your help."

"You mean you need her help," Peter said. "I told you I was more than capable of doing the spell."

"And I told you I don't trust you as far as I could throw you."

Miriam watched our byplay with an assessing gaze. "He's the sorcerer who owns your mark."

We both shut up, sharing a look before watching her warily. I knew why I was suspicious of her having that information, but why was he. I would have thought he would puff out his chest and claim credit immediately.

"Don't bother denying it," she said, her lips parting in a knowing smile. "I knew that tattoo was familiar. It has a similar style and signature as his master." To Peter, she said, "Do you understand the risk you took in marking her? These things have a way of backfiring. It's why they're so rarely used."

He raised his chin and said snootily, "I know what I'm doing."

She laughed and turned to go inside the store, leaving us staring at each other. Peter's expression said it was all my idea to come to the crazy lady's magic shop and now I had to suffer the consequences.

It had been my idea, and I still stood by my reasoning. It didn't make this situation any easier.

Screw it. I didn't care about the undercurrents right now. I had a task. Find the items and get the draugr back into his grave. Everything else could wait.

I caught the door before it swung fully closed and followed Miriam into the shop, trusting Peter to follow or not as he wished.

Miriam had left the front lights off but the ones in the back were on. In this lighting, her shop took on a sinister edge. Merchandise that had seemed kitschy and harmless earlier in the evening was now vaguely threatening. Or maybe that was because we were hunting an undead monster who could cause madness and rip me apart with its bare hands.

Once again the break room had changed. This time reverting to the back room lunch area found in most stores throughout America.

She shot me a warning look when I opened my mouth to ask why it had changed its appearance. I shut my mouth and glanced back as Peter tugged aside the beads hanging over the entrance.

She didn't want him to know about the other room. The one where she kept all the witchy stuff. She must be pouring some serious magic into it right now to keep him from peering behind the veil.

Either way, it was her secret. If she wanted it kept, I wouldn't go out of my way to expose it. Unless I needed to for some reason.

I took the seat she'd indicated at the table, turning and giving Peter a significant look when he hesitated. He cast an arrogant glance around, comparing it to his own conference room and finding it inferior, before taking the seat next to me. His obvious conviction of his superiority was grating. It made me want to set him straight just to wipe the smug look off his face. Maybe it was the fact he looked like a teenager that meant I found his expressions supremely obnoxious.

Miriam smiled to herself as she shuffled a deck of cards before laying them out in the familiar solitaire pattern.

Time to get this conversation started. I had a feeling it might be difficult to convince her to help us. If I had known she and the sorcerer had such a bad relationship, I would have given serious thought to dropping him off somewhere. His presence would just make this more difficult.

I already owed her a favor and that was for something relatively minor. What was something that used actual magic going to cost me?

"Your help last time was invaluable," I started, hoping flattery would soften her up a little.

I ignored the snort of derision next to me as Peter leaned back in his chair and folded his arms.

"We've found out that the creature is a draugr."

"That's odd," she said, seeming interested for the first time since I'd sat down. "The deaths have been spread all over the city. They don't usually travel so far afield of their gravesite."

I relayed what else we discovered, including the draugr's name and the items he was searching for.

"Interesting. Do you have a photo of these items?" Miriam asked, flipping another card.

I did. Peter had distracted Caroline while I made a copy. Copiers had gotten a lot more complicated in the few short years since I'd been out of school or maybe my skill with them had just gotten rustier.

Whether I wanted to share that copy with her was another matter.

I'd already told her most of it. I pulled the paper out of my pocket and flattened it on the table in front of her.

"Here. We think it's the necklace she's wearing and the watch fob in his vest."

Miriam stared long enough at the locket the woman was wearing that I thought about asking if she recognized it. She studied the man briefly before handing the paper back to me.

"What is it you want from me?"

I shared a glance with Peter. His mouth tightened, and he looked away from me.

"Peter here thinks it's possible to perform a summoning spell that will call the items to us."

I didn't mention how we thought the items would give us some control over the former Jackson Miller. I trusted her but only to a point.

"What good will that do?"

"From my encounters with the draugr, I know it's looking for the things it valued in life. We're hoping to use this attachment to bargain with or trick it."

It was as uncomfortably close to the truth as I wanted to go. Miriam struck me as being sharp so outright lying wouldn't work.

"Hm."

She played several more cards.

"I can do the spell," she said finally.

That's what I needed.

"It'll cost you though."

I was afraid of that.

"How much?" I asked. I'd preferred cash as opposed to a favor this time.

"Not you, him."

The sorcerer unfolded his arms and leaned forward. There was no way she was doing this spell. Not if he had to pay for it.

"What do you want?" I asked, knowing it was pointless but wanting to know anyway.

"I want to know how long Barret has been gone."

I blinked. That was it? I was thinking it would be something big, like the magical equivalent of a kidney.

I gave the sorcerer a cautious look. The question seemed harmless enough, but it'd be in keeping with his character to refuse just to be a pain in the ass.

He glared at both of us, looking like a pissed off cat.

"It's none of her business."

Looked like I was right. He was going to be difficult.

"Is there anything else you'll take in the place of the answer?" I asked Miriam.

She shook her head before moving a king to an empty spot.

"It's an easy enough question," I muttered to him.

"You answer it then. Oh wait, you can't."

I pinched my nose bridge. Dealing with petulant teenagers had never been my forte, and for all that he was older than he looked, he had the teenage act down pat.

"Are you sure you want to go this route?" I asked.

A stony glare was my only answer. I dropped my eyes meaningfully to the cuff around his wrist. His lack of power meant nothing to me besides the promise of my safety. I doubted he wanted that information spread to someone he saw as an enemy.

Seeing where I was looking, he tugged his jacket sleeve down to cover the bronze.

"He's been gone for almost four months," he said grudgingly.

I'd guessed right. The glare he shot me promised retribution. I should have been scared, but I wasn't. After the draugr was taken care of, I'd probably be in the hands of the vampires. I doubted he would want to start a war with them for the indignities he'd endured at my hands.

"Great, you have your answer. How should we do this?" I asked, turning to Miriam.

She swept the cards into a single deck, wiping her game clean.

"First, I'll call my apprentice, then we'll see about summoning your trinkets."

We waited as she made the call, Peter muttering about the ridiculousness of it all. The call placed, Miriam shuffled another hand of solitaire to herself. I fought against the urge to pace. There were still several hours until dawn, but I didn't know how long the wolves would give me before making their move.

Flipping my phone over and over in my hand, I toyed with the idea of calling Liam and updating him about our plans. No, it would be best to wait. If we managed to get the items in hand, we could call him in then. Right now this plan of mine had only a small chance of succeeding.

"Miriam? What's this about?" Angela called from the front room. She didn't sound happy to be here. Surprise registered on her face at seeing us as she stepped into the back room.

"We have customers," Miriam said, abandoning her game of solitaire.

Looking like she had sucked on something sour, Angela gave us a nod before listening to Miriam's instructions.

"We need to perform a summoning ritual. Get what we need from the front room while I set up in back." To me, Miriam said, "He'll need to stay in here. My spells and rituals have been passed down from mentor to apprentice for generations and I have no intention of our knowledge falling into the hands of some barely minted sorcerer."

"Like I have any interest in the backwards, inefficient way you witches do things," Peter returned.

I didn't know if I liked the idea of Angela participating given what I'd seen on the tape from the club, but I didn't know what I could say to Miriam that would be believable. Angela was her apprentice. Chances were she'd trust anything she said over me and in the end I hadn't seen anything that was a red flag.

"That's fine, Miriam." I turned to Peter. "Then waiting here won't be a problem for you."

He shrugged, not giving any of his thoughts away. "Whatever. If you want to trust these two, it's your funeral."

I wasn't too worried. It was just a summoning ritual. I didn't know much about magic, but I didn't imagine there was too much danger inherent in something that sounded relatively innocent.

"What do you need from me?" I asked.

Miriam had watched our interaction with an enigmatic expression. At my question, her expression shifted to amusement.

"Not much. He'll stay here, but you're welcome to watch."

Magic had always interested me. From the time I was no bigger than my dad's knee, I'd sought opportunities to watch magicians and their assistants. I read any book featuring witches and saw all the movies on the subject. Something about the idea of magic just drew me.

When I made my transition, I'd anticipated a life filled with its possibility around every corner. So far, magic had been distinctly lacking in everything I did. From what I'd seen human technology worked just as well and was easier and quicker. I had no idea how either tech or magic worked but their effects were often the same.

"I would love that."

I ignored the sorcerer's snort of derision.

"Follow me," Miriam said.

She stood and headed through a door I hadn't noticed until now. It led to the back, but instead of an empty parking lot, we were in a meadow with a starry, night sky above us.

"Illusion?"

She shrugged one slim shoulder. "One man's illusion is another's reality."

How philosophical. A professor in college had said something similar. That every person's perception of the same experience is slightly different, from the vantage point you see from, to all of your previous experiences that have influenced you until that moment. For that reason, everyone's reality is different from one another in small but significant ways.

Even after all these years, I remembered his words. They had made a certain poetic sense to me up to a point. At the same time, an apple was just an apple even if I was viewing it from above and you from the side. You might hate apples because of something that happened in your childhood, and I might love them, but the apple was still an apple. Its core essence didn't change.

That inability to fully grasp a philosophical concept is probably why I ended up with a C in the class. The only C I'd had my entire time in college.

This illusion was impressive in the level of reality it presented, but it was still just an illusion. It was a waste of effort, in my opinion.

"I have the supplies," Angela said behind me.

I looked away from the stars. Angela bent, her arms full, to set down her items. I tried to catch her eye to thank her. Being woken up in the early morning hours to perform a magic ritual was probably not that fun, but she turned her head away, giving what she was doing her full attention.

"Shall we begin?" Miriam asked before I could speak to Angela.

I nodded and stepped back as Angela straightened and began walking in a circle, dumping a white substance on the ground in a thin, consistent line. I sniffed experimentally. Salt. She was making a salt circle.

Huh. Guess human fiction had gotten something right. Salt always seemed to be used to create wards or keep things out in those books I used to read.

"So how is this going to work?" I asked, stepping up beside Miriam as Angela finished laying the circle.

Miriam gave me a sidelong glance.

"The ritual is one that has been in my family for nearly ten generations. Outsiders have rarely witnessed it."

She moved away after that, leaving me staring after her in bemusement. Well, that was cryptic. I watched as the two of them moved around the clearing with sure, precise movements. It was like watching a dance, one with a music only the two of them could hear.

The trees branches rustled in the light breeze as the grass added their own melody to the night. I closed my eyes, listening. For a moment, it felt like I could hear a very faint strain of the music. That whisper of a melody disappeared when Miriam said, "We're ready."

My eyes popped open. They'd been busy while I'd been entertaining myself with a nonexistent song.

At each of the four corners a candle burned and a small bowl, each one filled with different substance. A map had been set in the middle along with the photo copy of Jackson Miller and his wife.

Miriam and Angela were still in their normal clothes. I had envisioned a crazy scenario of them conducting the ritual skyclad, which I thought was the hippie way of saying naked, or in elaborate ceremonial robes.

Neither of them seemed inclined to strip. I shivered as a sudden breeze whipped by. Being naked in this weather would have been unbearable, anyway. There also wasn't any sign of robes.

"I don't suppose you have anything besides this photo from the draugr?"

I shook my head. Getting close to a creature rather intent on my death had been the last thing on my mind.

"Is that going to be a problem?"

Her head tilted in thought. "It may make things a little difficult."

"Her presence in the circle might strengthen the connection," Angela suddenly spoke up. "The draugr seems to have fixated on her. It could bolster the ritual enough to work."

Miriam gave Angela an assessing gaze, her thoughts shielded and inscrutable. "That is a possibility."

I waited, not sure if she wanted my involvement. Her words hadn't been a rousing endorsement of Angela's idea.

There was an odd distance between Miriam and Angela, one that hadn't been there the last time I was at the shop. I wondered if Miriam was still upset about Angela seeing Victor behind her back. I had a better grasp of why Miriam might want Angela to steer clear now that I knew the man was a werewolf. None of the otherworld sects cared for the other. Miriam probably didn't want a personal association between her apprentice and another group. On the other hand, I'd met Victor and I wouldn't want someone I cared about dating that jerk.

Miriam gestured me forward. As I stepped over the salt circle, I felt a slight buzzing across my senses. I shivered again as the hair on my body stood straight up. It felt like I was continually getting zapped by mild static electricity. It was unsettling and brought my fight or flight instincts to the fore.

I kept moving forward, my anticipation turning into a need to get this over and done with. I stopped next to the map and the copy of the photo as Miriam indicated.

Their voices rose and lifted in a chant, the background buzzing edging from simply uncomfortable to something approaching pain. It felt like a hand had me in a vise grip and was squeezing my insides then relaxing. Again and again.

Was this normal? If so, I'd have to rethink participating in any other magic rituals. This was how I always imagined it felt being in one of those g-force simulators, but instead of a constant gravity, the force surged and receded like a strong wind.

Miriam raised her face to the sky, the words pouring from her mouth faster and faster. I couldn't decipher the individual words, only the cadence of them in the rising melody. That same unseen force gathered around her, tightening like a boa constrictor. Her body was shadowed and hard to see as the force around her strengthened and grew.

I shifted my gaze to Angela, whose voice rose and fell in tandem with Miriam's. In contrast to the older woman's almost holy look, Angela's gaze remained fixed on mine. She seemed determined and victorious as she stared me down. Smug satisfaction oozed from her expression.

My gaze snagged on her necklace. I had seen it before, and recently. A single branch stood out among the fine details. My eyes shot to the photo of Jackson Miller and his wife. I knew where I had seen it.

Everything came together for me. Angela's locket and Victor's hostility. I'd been right when I saw her on the vampire's club tape. I don't know why she'd lured the victim on it to his death, but I had no doubt now that it was the sorcerer's contact I'd been meant to meet.

This was a trap. How could I have been so stupid? Miriam must be in on it too. Her interest in the photo had been pronounced. Now I knew why. She probably fed me that line about the ritual being an old ancestral one to get the sorcerer out of the way.

I advanced forward despite the invisible wind buffeting me. I needed to stop this before it was too late. Pain bit at me. It felt like pieces of me were breaking off and disintegrating into the ether.

I screamed, the sound wordless and full of rage.

This was not how I was going out.

I forced myself an inch closer, darkness eating at the edges of my vision and the song reaching a crescendo.

I reached out, my skin and hand dissolving even as I inched closer and closer to Miriam. Almost. Almost. Just another few inches.

I touched the skin of her face right as her eyes popped open and the song stopped. Silence waited for an eternal minute and then darkness raced in on me. I saw no more.

Chapter Thirteen

My head felt like an Army drill team was performing on it. I lifted it and winced as the matter between my ears throbbed in protest. I hadn't felt this hung over since that one time in college when Caroline decided she wanted to conduct an experiment on which liquor could get us drunk fastest. Tequila won.

How much had I drunk last night? I was too old to party like I used to. My body didn't recover the same.

I sat up, brushing away the paper plastered to my face. Even the crinkle of it as I set it aside hurt my ears.

I looked around. I was in a cemetery and not one I recognized. Tombstones surrounded me, so faded with time that the names were illegible.

Where was I?

This went beyond having a few too many drinks the previous night. I stood on shaky legs and glanced around. The cemetery was deserted this late at night, not a soul to be seen. I walked carefully over several graves, nearly tripping on the uneven ground, until I reached the gravel path.

My memories began to come back to me. Miriam, Angela, the spell. Something had gone wrong.

It was hard to think. My brain felt like it was encased in cotton.

I clutched at the map in my hand. It was a reassuring totem in a world gone topsy turvy. I didn't even know it was possible to teleport people using magic. It violated pretty much every law of physics I'd ever learned in high school.

Unless the spell had simply knocked me unconscious, and Miriam and Angela had dumped me in the cemetery. Or this could be an illusion. Like the one that had covered Miriam's back parking lot.

I thought the spell was supposed to summon the items to me. Not send me to the items. Maybe Angela wearing the locket made the spell go wonky.

I looked around again, the pieces of the puzzle falling into place slower than I'd like. I was in a cemetery. From the looks of it, an old cemetery. Possibly a cemetery circa the civil war time period.

Now what monster did we know derived from that time period and rose from its own grave? Ding, ding, ding. A draugr.

One or both of the crazy bitches had sent me to the same cemetery containing the draugr's grave. Fuck. If the night wasn't already bad enough with my discovery that Angela was at least partially responsible for the murders, I'd also been delivered to the monster's doorstep. This was just hunky dory.

I felt for my pocket. If there was ever time to call in back up, it was now. I had no desire to run into the draugr alone.

I dialed Liam, skulking from headstone to headstone as the phone rang.

Come on, pick up. Pick up. You blew my phone up all night, but you can't pick up the one time I need you?

It went to voicemail. Shit. I dialed again.

I might be a vampire, but walking through a graveyard late at night by myself was still creepy. My skin crawled with the expectation that at any moment something was going to jump out at me.

It went to voicemail again. Liam's terse voice barked at me to leave a message.

"You give me shit about checking in with you and then when I do, you don't answer?" I hissed. "As soon as you get this, get to the civil war cemetery in Westgate. Oh, and I figured out that one of the people responsible for all the recent deaths is a witch named Angela. She's on your recordings in the club meeting with a nerdy guy."

The phone beeped, signaling my time was over. I hung up with a mental curse.

I thought a moment and then dialed another number. Brax had been interested in finding the culprits, and I'd certainly done that. Their possession of the items would just have to be proof enough.

The phone rang and rang before going to voicemail.

Again? This was ridiculous.

Perhaps the sorcerer could help me. I didn't have a phone number for him, but I did have his mark. That's what it was supposedly for, right? Keeping him in touch?

I bared my forearm, and ran one finger along it thinking dire thoughts. I dug a fingernail into it, thinking maybe it needed pain to activate. Nothing. I had no idea if it worked or not.

Looked like I was on my own.

I wasn't prepared to be on my own. I had no weapons. I left those in my car. I had no idea how to defeat the draugr beyond a vague plan of wrestling it back into its grave. I had my doubts as to the effectiveness of that method, even if I could figure out which grave was his.

Stop panicking, soldier. We're still alive. We just need to make it out of the cemetery and back to some sort of highway. From there I could get back to Elements. I actually wasn't too far from it. I just needed to move quickly and carefully and everything would be all right.

I rounded a set of tombstones and came face to face with two wolves. I froze.

Ever unexpectedly come face to face with a predator in the wild? The great wide beyond is its territory and you know if you move, if you even breathe wrong, that it might be the last thing you ever do. Still, you can't help but stare at the majestic beast in front of you, hyper-aware that something so fierce and wonderful can exist in this world. Coming face to face with the wolves was kind of like that.

Time slowed, coming almost to a standstill. Then in the next moment it sped up.

One of the wolves changed, its form folding in on itself as the fur receded, leaving a man crouched in its place.

A naked Brax stood.

He'd got my message. Thank God.

"What are you doing here?" he asked.

Or not.

Wait, if he didn't get my voicemail, why was he standing in front of me naked.

"I told you everything in the voicemail. Didn't you listen to it?"

He gestured at his naked body. "Do I look like I'm carrying around a phone?"

Males. Always picking the absolute worst time to display sarcasm.

"What are you doing here if you didn't get my message?"

No, wait. He'd said something about going hunting. I closed my eyes. Of course he hadn't waited. Why would he do that? He was a big alpha male capable of subduing monsters with a single irate glare. My mistake.

"We're patrolling. I have several teams in the area scouting out the draugr and possible hideouts."

"I thought you said you'd give me a little time to get the proof you needed."

It was getting hard keeping my eyes trained on his face. All that naked flesh, covering miles of ripped muscle, had a way of distracting a person. He was most women's wet dream, cut in all the right places with sharply defined ridges. Guess all that running around on all fours had a nice effect on the body. If all werewolves were built like this, I might want to rethink my policy on fraternizing with beings from the otherworld.

"That was hours ago."

Bullshit. For him to have time to set up patrols and actually deploy them meant he would have had to act shortly after my call. I wouldn't be surprised if he'd already been on the move when I called him.

It didn't matter. It was what it was and no amount of recrimination would change that. He acted, and we now had to deal with the situation as it was.

"It doesn't matter anymore," I said. "I figured out who's behind all this. Do you know a witch named Angela?"

He looked down, frowning thoughtfully. It looked like he didn't. That might make convincing him a little more difficult.

"She's friendly with one of your wolves. The one named Victor. He's the guy who threw a fit in the middle of our conversation in your kitchen and accused me of setting all this up."

A growl so low and vicious that it was almost inaudible came from the wolf standing behind Brax. My eyes fixed on Brax. His face had gone grim and still at the sound of Victor's name. His eyes slid to the right.

I followed them, my breath catching at the sight of a pair of milky eyes peering out at us from the shadow of a tree.

Trap.

"Draugr?" I mouthed.

Brax's head tilted down once. Yes.

Suddenly I was less glad to have happened on Brax. Instead of a possible savior, he was probably going to be the reason I had a one way ticket to that great light in the sky.

The figure near the tree remained motionless. Now that I knew he was there, I could smell the stench of rot. He must have been masking it. I'd been so focused on Brax that I had forgotten to watch my surroundings.

The wolf behind Brax crept forward, the fur on its belly dragging against the grass.

We were at a disadvantage with Brax in human form. How long would it take him to shift back to wolf? Too long if the icy expression on his face was any indication. If he tried to turn back to wolf the draugr would be on him before he could complete the transformation.

I was next to useless in a fight. I didn't even have my knives on me. From the last fight I'd seen between Brax and Liam, I knew I was seriously outclassed. That left running.

I tilted my head in the opposite direction of the draugr.

Brax's mouth tightened, but he nodded.

Like someone had yelled 'play', the wolf sprang forward, and I took off to my right, leaping over headstone after headstone.

There was a yelp then guttural snarls and a roar of pain. I chanced a glance behind me. The stupid man hadn't run, instead turning to face the wolf. He was trying to give me time to get away.

I slid to a stop. Damn it, I really wished he'd run.

He grasped the wolf's shoulders, his arms bulging as he prevented it from latching onto anything vital. The wolf shredded his forearms with teeth and claws, but mostly snapped at the air.

I ran back, bending to pick up a rock the size of my fist as I moved.

Brax tossed the wolf away. It crashed into a tombstone, cracking the marker in two. Victor's wolf stood and shook itself, blood and saliva flying.

There were still twenty feet between me and it. I'd covered much more ground than I thought in my sprint.

I put on a burst of speed as it crouched. Ten feet. It leapt for Brax, paws outstretched and lips curled back from its fangs.

Brax waited, crouched with arms spread.

The wolf landed on him, knocking him back a step. Then I was there, swinging with everything I had, knocking the wolf off him. Victor sailed much further than I'd intended, his pained yelp echoing in the night.

Ha. Not so defenseless after all.

"You were supposed to run," Brax growled.

I gaped at him. Really? That's what he wanted to say after I saved his ass? You were supposed to run? Who said that to someone who had been kind enough to rescue them?

An arrogant asshole convinced of his invincibility, that's who.

My mouth snapped shut, and I narrowed my eyes at him.

"Why thank you Aileen for taking your life into your hands to help me," I said through gritted teeth. "You're welcome, Brax. It was what anybody would do."

He bared his teeth and growled. Actually growled at me. After I'd saved him.

"That's not the point. You should have run."

I rolled my eyes.

"You're an arrogant asshole. Most people would thank me for what I just did."

"Thank you? I had it handled. I didn't need you pulling any misguided heroic stunts."

While we talked, Victor's wolf form receded, leaving a human male behind. His transformation wasn't as clean or quick as Brax's. The snap and crack of bones as his body shifted and changed, his paws becoming hands and his spine twisting as it became a human's made me cringe. It looked and sounded painful.

Brax gave him a lethal glance. I wouldn't want to be Victor once his alpha got hold of him. He probably wouldn't survive the night if Brax's quiet rage was any indication.

My eyes shot to the figure by the tree. The shadows were empty. "Where'd he go?" I asked.

Brax didn't respond, striding forward to grab and jerk Victor up by his shoulder.

I glanced around, turning in circles. No sign of the draugr lurked amid the field of headstones. Why would he run off when his controller was in trouble?

Maybe he didn't recognize Victor while he was in wolf form. I certainly hadn't.

Brax had Victor by the throat and had hauled him close.

"What have you done?" Brax growled.

"Brax." This was making me uneasy. The draugr shouldn't have disappeared like that.

"You've killed so many and your actions may have started another war."

His words were accompanied by another bone rattling shake. Victor's face was turning purple. Brax's grip was so tight he couldn't breathe let alone speak.

"Brax."

I'd feel a lot better if we got out of here. A bad feeling was starting to creep along my skin. I'd learned to pay attention to that feeling. Bad things always ensued when I didn't.

"This isn't our way. You challenge for Alpha. You don't sneak around like a thief in the night. You are the basest of cowards."

"Brax," I yelled. He turned on me, the wolf overlaying his face for just a moment. "That's enough. Either kill him or bring him with us, but we need to go. The draugr is still around, and we're not prepared to fight him."

The wolf stared out of his eyes, the icy blue of his iris holding an alien intelligence. Not beastlike but definitely not subject to human mores and values. He could kill me as easy as look at me. It wouldn't bother him a bit, even if I had saved him moments before. I wasn't pack and therefore he owed me none of the courtesy and affection they were afforded.

I waited, refusing to drop my eyes. It was a definite challenge to his authority, but I was tired of playing games. If he didn't come and come now, I was leaving him behind. He could face the draugr on his own.

The wolf receded, leaving a pissed Brax glaring at me. He released Victor and shoved him in front of him. I released my breath on a shaky exhale. For all my bravado, every muscle in my body had been tensed to flee if Brax had made good on the promise of violence living in his eyes.

Victor coughed and gasped for breath. His shoulders shook. Was he crying? No. A rough chuckle reached my ears. He was laughing.

I took a step back. It was never good when the bad guy gave an evil villain laugh.

Brax stepped forward.

Victor kept his head down, shielding his face. "You should have killed me when you had the chance."

I took another step back. I agreed with him.

Victor lifted his head and turned it to the side. The draugr stepped out of the shadows, his eyes staring blindly at our trio.

"Jackson Miller, you don't have to listen to anything he says," I said.

This wasn't good. This was very, very bad.

I was beginning to think I should have listened to Brax and kept running.

Brax stepped forward grabbing for Victor and missing when the other wolf ducked away.

"Kill them," Victor screamed.

"Jackson," I said. "I know where your keepsakes are. Just stay over there, and I'll get them for you."

"She's lying. She and the wolf have been in on it together the entire time."

The creature who used to be Jackson Miller gaze jumped between us like a spectator at a tennis match.

I held out a hand hoping to keep him calm and reasonable. I didn't want another episode like the house.

"Your name is Jackson Miller, and your wife was Eva Miller. You were a doctor in the civil war."

The draugr's chest heaved at my words, recognition of who he once was seeping into his dead fish stare. Good. Maybe I could turn him against Victor after all.

"Kill her," Victor growled. "How do you think she knows all this? Because she stole your keepsakes."

Brax backed towards me, keeping Victor and the draugr in sight. He herded me back a few steps.

The draugr's eyes turned toward me, the brief moment of sanity fading as madness took its place. I'd lost him. He was hearing, but he wasn't listening. Still I had to try.

"No, he's the one who's lying. He has your stuff and is using it to manipulate you into doing his dirty work."

The draugr screamed, the sound piercing like a thousand needles in your mind. Brax staggered beside me, raising his hands to clutch at his ears.

Whatever was happening affected his balance, and he fell to his knees. He convulsed on the ground, fur crawling over his skin and his limbs and back bulging as the bones ran like water underneath the surface. This wasn't the easy shift of before. This was hideous and painful, torture of a kind I wouldn't wish on anybody.

The draugr's voice faded but Brax's body continued to twist in the throes of the shift. Victor watched with a twisted grin, relishing his alpha's pain.

A gray and white wolf lay on the ground panting in Brax's place. He was a gorgeous specimen, bigger than anything found in the wild, with a luxurious coat and paws the size of dinner plates.

It was tempting to hope that his wolf was enough to turn the tide against our attackers, but I had a feeling things wouldn't be that easy as he staggered to his feet.

"I know what we should do," the draugr sang in a high pitched voice. He giggled and leapt to crouch on one of the headstones, cocking his head like an oversized bird. One whose features were rotting off its body.

The draugr's skin was in worse shape than it had been in his victim's house. Giant patches were missing, showing bone and tendon. Half his nose was gone, leaving strings of flesh and cartilage. A yellow substance, pus perhaps, oozed out of raised boils on his hands and neck.

He looked fragile, but I knew his outward appearance belied the strength resting in his body. The victims showed he was capable of tearing bodies apart. Even those of werewolves in their prime. He'd probably tear through me like tissue paper if I let him get hold of me.

"We'll play a game," the draugr sang, baring a mouth full of decayed or missing teeth in a smile. "Whoever survives will be eaten by me."

"I think I'll pass," I said, taking another step back.

Brax seemed pretty out of it still, his great head hanging and his tail scraping the ground. I tried to catch his eyes. I needed him to run this time, not attack.

"I think the wolf will play." The draugr's head bobbed in a sinuous motion almost like it had no bones constricting its movements. "Yes. Yes. I think he will be most willing."

The low growl focused my attention back on Brax. His teeth were bared as that growl came again. He edged forward on one paw.

"Brax, you don't want to do this," I warned.

The draugr must have messed with his mind. It's the only thing I could think of for him to suddenly turn on me like this.

"I think he does." The draugr giggled and clapped his hands, popping one of the pustules. The yellow liquid slid down his arms and soaked into his coat.

"Brax, you are an alpha werewolf. You can fight this. I know you can."

I backed up, the wolf shadowing me. My foot wobbled on the uneven surface of a grave as his slinking movement brought him even closer.

Victor watched us, his eyes catching and reflecting the light to glow briefly.

I wanted to run. My feet practically itched to take flight. But even if I ran as fast and gracefully as a gazelle through a cemetery strewn with headstones and uneven graves, I would never outrun Brax. He was faster than me. He'd overtake me in a few steps.

My eyes landed on the draugr. He was the source of this. I needed to take him out if I wanted to have even a little bit of a chance.

First though, I needed to create a window of opportunity with Brax.

The wolf's eyes were slightly deranged as they glared at me, his growls getting throatier and strings of saliva hanging from his fangs. His head lowered as he circled to the left of me.

I searched his eyes for some spark of the person he was. I needed him to fight, even if it was only for a few seconds.

I let my attention drift to the draugr for a brief moment, hoping he got the message.

There. A spark. His growl faltered before continuing.

He shook his head, as if to deter a pesky mosquito.

I sprinted forward, using every ounce of whatever vampire speed I might have. There was an enraged snarl and then the thud of paws behind me.

Faster. Faster.

I eked out another two yards.

Victor caught on to my plan and ran forward. I kept my eyes trained on my target.

Come on. Everything you've got. Move.

I flew over the last few yards, before tackling the draugr in as beautiful a leap as any seen on a football field.

The draugr's hysterical laughter was cut short with a grunt as we collided.

I landed on top of him, grabbed him by the throat and banged his head against the ground.

A furry body flew past me, sailing over another headstone and bounding past another. Brax's wolf disappeared into the darkness.

Good. Mission accomplished.

Now I needed to follow him.

I dug a knee into the monster's chest and rose.

A weight bowled into me from the side, slamming me into a headstone.

It cracked under my weight and sent pain screaming through my chest.

My ribs were broken. Again.

Blood bubbled up from my lips as I fought to rise.

Victor sneered down at me, before one bare foot came crashing down on my head.

Darkness sucked me under. Again.

*　*　*

Water dripped onto my face. I flinched and then wished I hadn't. It felt like I'd been run over by a truck. This whole getting knocked out business was turning into a bad habit.

Memories of the events leading up to my loss of consciousness rose. I opened my eyes without turning my head. Where was I, and why wasn't I dead?

A dirt floor greeted my eyes. Cement blocks were only a few feet away from me. Basement. Probably an older house. Another drop of water hit the back of my neck. Probably one with a leak.

I carefully turned my head. Looked like I was alone for now. I stifled a groan as I tried to sit and found I couldn't. Chains were wrapped around my chest and hooked to an old pipe. I gave an experimental yank. The pipe groaned but didn't budge. Just great.

I felt a little nauseous, like I used to when I hadn't eaten. It could also be a sign of concussion, if vampires got concussions. It could be the effect of injury compounded by not getting enough blood in the past twenty four hours.

I forced myself to take stock of my situation.

There was a small window above me. It was glass and not any of the frosted stuff so popular on basement windows. This was the real stuff and looked like it might be original to the house. There was a furnace and water heater in the corner. The rest of the basement just contained boxes of junk, all on shelves.

"Looks like our guest is awake," the draugr said from his position at the top of the stairs. "We had a bet going over whether you would wake up before the sun rose. I thought you'd remain dead to the world." He turned and said over his shoulder, "Looks like you win, as always."

A pair of boots appeared next to the draugr then descended. Victor, wearing clothes this time, came into view.

"You've cost me quite a bit, fang face."

I didn't see Brax anywhere. He must have gotten away.

Not going to lie, wish it had been me to make the escape, but at least Brax knew the whole story. He could round up support and come searching. I just needed to survive until he and his backup got here.

"Did you hear me?" Victor said, kicking my leg.

Pain pulsed up my body. I must have done some damage to the leg and just hadn't noticed with all the other injuries.

He crouched down and grabbed my hair, hauling my face up to his.

"I've been planning this for years, and you've managed to nearly ruin everything."

"What do you want me to say? I've got a knack for throwing a wrench in things."

One thumb caressed my cheek as he crooned at me, "Don't worry. I'm sure we can think of something as payback."

He tapped my rib. I swallowed the pained sound, biting my lip hard enough to draw blood. He got off on my pain. I wasn't giving him any more than I had to. He pressed harder, the pain like a band around my chest, tightening and tightening until a small sound escaped me.

He dropped my head, stepping back. I glared at his boots as I panted. A cold sweat broke out over my skin.

Bastard.

"I don't get you," I said. "Why do all this? Why go through the trouble of attacking the dryad and the vampire, if you just wanted to take Brax out?"

"Not many can grasp the genius of my plan," Victor said. "I've been laying the groundwork for years. The wolves never even suspected the person responsible for everything was one of their own."

I edged forward in my chains, searching for a more comfortable position.

"Why not just challenge Brax directly?" I asked.

"He's too strong. He's one of the strongest alphas of the last two centuries. Even if I won, I would never have been able to hold the pack. He has too many loyal followers. He has them eating out of his hand. Anyone who won that challenge would be dead by the next day. They would have issued challenge after challenge until I was tired and made a mistake. No, I needed to weaken the entire pack. Sow fear and dissention until they were ripe for the plucking."

"Probably didn't hurt that your chosen weapon wouldn't have been strong enough when he first woke up."

Victor gave me a sidelong look. "Yes, that was a consideration. The creature was much weaker than legends had indicated. He needed a few kills and to consume the flesh of humans before his power could grow enough to where he could carry out my wishes."

I was surprised he'd admitted that much with the draugr sitting so close. The draugr might have been a tool for Victor's master plan, but he wasn't a mindless tool.

"I have to thank you, though. Your presence has been an unexpected bonus." He crouched in front of me. "I had planned to start a war between the werewolves and the vampires, thin the herd if you will, with a few murders on each side. Each would blame the other, and in the ensuing chaos I would take control, making sure that any who might oppose me were killed in the fight."

"Boy, you must have been pissed when that didn't take effect," I said. The pain was getting worse.

"Thanks to you. Franklin's death should have jumpstarted things. I even made sure to time it when the vampire's enforcer was close so he could take the blame. Then you blundered into things and ruined everything. No matter though, we're back on track now. After we stage your death at the hands of Brax, the vampires will blame the wolves and seek revenge. Even if Brax knows I'm behind this, he'll fall in the ensuing war, and if he doesn't, my friend over there will finish him off."

My laugh was ragged and wet, like one of my ribs had punctured a lung.

"You're an idiot if you think anyone will avenge me. I'm nobody. I have no clan or family. The vampires didn't even know I existed until a few days ago. This won't even be a blip on their radar."

"Their yearlings are precious to them. They won't care about your affiliations. They'll avenge you simply because you're one of them." He shrugged. "Even if they don't, I'll find some other way to jump start the war."

I took that to mean he planned to kill me either way. So comforting.

"And the witch? Angela? What's her role in all this?"

He gave a negligent shrug. "She helped me secure the draugr's treasure and then use them to control him. That and a few spells were her sole contribution. It'll be nice to kill her after all this is over. She's a nice fuck, but her whining and clinginess is annoying. Perhaps I'll kill her while fucking her. Send her off with a good memory."

"Such a charmer," I gritted out. Why wasn't my body healing itself? The pain should be getting better not worse.

"Don't worry. This'll be over for you soon enough." He walked back towards the stairs, pausing at the bottom. "See that window. Dawn is just around the corner. I'm sure you can feel it. All you fang heads can."

I searched inside. Sure enough. I felt that great ball of fire lurking just out of reach, sending electricity humming along my nerve endings.

"Sun won't kill me," I said.

Sondra had said it wouldn't. Maybe give me a few burns and put me out for the count, but not kill me.

"Is that what you think?" He smirked. "Judging by the fact you haven't begun healing, I'd guess your last meal was quite a few hours ago. Your youth and injuries will make the next few hours excruciatingly painful. I'd put your chances of survival at about fifty percent." He shrugged. "Maybe less."

Chapter Fourteen

Victor headed up the stairs, leaving the draugr staring down at me with hungry eyes. There was no use in appealing to him. His eyes were glassy as if he'd sunk into his mind and acceded control to his instincts. His body was still moving but nobody was home.

I didn't want to believe Victor. Sondra had seemed much less concerned about the dangers of the sun for my kind. I hadn't gotten the feeling she was lying, whereas Victor seemed to have made a practice of deceiving everyone close to him. On the other hand, Sondra may not have counted on me being this hungry or injured.

Who to believe?

A few hours would answer that question.

"Shit."

I jerked against my chains and whined at the sharp stabbing pain in my ribs. They weren't budging, and my skin was beginning to tingle and itch where the chains were, even though cloth protected my skin from direct contact.

Silver. I'd bet my few remaining hours on it.

I settled back, resting my head on the cold concrete. The window was at the top of the wall. It would be hours before direct sunlight even approached me. I wouldn't be in real danger until midafternoon, when the sun was strongest and the angle was just right.

The only mercy is that I'd probably sleep through my incineration. Thank god for small favors.

Maybe if I could just edge over a few inches, it would be enough to take me away from the danger zone. It was a better plan than just lying here waiting for my impending doom.

Focusing on something helped stem some of the despair beginning to overwhelm me.

Alright, Aileen, focus on the things you can still do and then do them. No wallowing in the possibility of death.

Pep talk finished, I shifted my weight and scooted an inch closer to the wall. The pain in my side spread. Was internal bleeding a problem for vampires, or would my body eventually just reabsorb the blood?

How durable were we anyway? I was really hoping we edged closer to indestructible than destructible.

Otherwise, given how scrambled my insides felt, daylight would be the least of my concerns.

I made it about a foot before coming up short. I twisted, looking behind me. A chain trailed from me like a metallic tail. I followed the path to where the links wrapped around an iron pipe. I wasn't going anywhere unless I rolled back over there and somehow broke the pipe and wrestled the chain free.

My head dropped. Just one thing after another.

Exhaustion wrapped cottony arms around my thoughts. Sun must be coming up. My eyes drooped. So tired.

The concrete was cool against my face. So comfortable. Maybe I'd just take a short nap. Yes, a nap would do me good. I could figure this out afterwards.

*   *   *

A tree shaded path stretched before me. Miles and miles of it. The rounded stones embedded deep in the earth were covered in places by the greenest of moss. So green that it practically glowed. The trees were covered in moss too, creating a faery land of impossible colors.

I walked along the stone path, my feet whispering over the ground. So pretty. I looked up at the bare branches above me. Their interlocking limbs swayed with the wind.

"This reminds me of Ireland," a cool voice said next to me.

"It is Ireland," I said with a small smile. "A part of it anyway."

"You've been?"

I gave a wordless nod. Once. When I was young. Even ten years later, I saw those impossibly green trees in my dreams.

"It's taken me hours to wind my way through your psyche," Aiden said. He was the Patriarch I'd met at the vamp club. The one who was a telepath. "You have quite the fortress set up. It's good that I started infiltrating it the last time we met or you'd be in hotter water than you already are."

My feet took me off the path, the bushes and trees just magically parting to let me pass.

There was a curse behind me and then crashing as Aidan chased after me, forcing his way past the vegetation that suddenly sprung up in his path.

"Here now, stop that. I'm not going to hurt you."

I kept going. Where, I didn't know. Just away.

He was a minor buzzing irritant that my mind refused to focus on.

"Stop that." There was a buzzing sound. He cursed again.

"Stop. Hey. I said stop," he roared the last words.

I wheeled to a stop, panting.

I focused on him for the first time since I became aware I was walking down the path.

"Aidan, what are you doing here?" I looked around. "Where is here?"

He glared at me, his handsome face scraped and cut with welts swelling on his neck, cheek and hands. I gave him a puzzled onceover and then looked down at myself. My clothes gave no sign that I'd been traipsing through a heavily wooded forest moments before. My bare feet didn't even have a speck of dirt on them, and I was surprisingly uninjured. Not even a cut.

"*Here* is your mind."

"And what are you doing in my mind?"

I looked around. Yes, I recognized this place. It was part of the forest I visualized when I was trying to shield my thoughts from mind readers. Except it was a little more jumbled and realistic than any image I've ever used.

"Doing my best to save you." He gave me a sour look. "Even if you keep attacking me while I do it."

I raised one eyebrow. "I've yet to attack you."

"Try again, sweetheart. You have internal defenses that have been giving me the runaround all day."

Internal defenses? I wanted to ask how that worked and if I could make them stronger. You never knew when you'd need a little help protecting your mind.

"Think of them like an immune system. Everyone has them. It's just that some are stronger than others. In your case, your defenses act like white cells that descend on suspected intruders and try to tear them apart."

That made sense. Sort of. My definition of plausibility had been stretched in recent years. Facing the impossible every day in the mirror had made the nay-sayer inside me keep her own council. I was just glad my internal defenses, as he put it, were good at keeping people out of my head.

Still, it was a little difficult to believe we were having this conversation. More likely it was a dream conjured to give me comfort before my impending death.

"Doesn't explain what you're doing here."

He gave me a censorious stare. I liked that better than the slightly smoldering ones he'd leveled at me during our first meeting.

"I told you. I'm here to save you."

"And how do you expect to do that from my mind. Last I checked I was chained down about to be burned alive. I may be a little slow, but I don't see how you're going to rescue me unless you have a teleportation ability."

He tapped his lips thoughtfully. "Are you in pain now?"

I gave his question serious consideration, turning inward and assessing how I felt. Nothing seemed to be wrong. No heated skin or burning flesh. Distantly I felt an ache in my ribs, but not much else.

I shook my head. "No, but would I even feel the sun burning me while I was unconscious?"

During normal slumber, most people wake immediately at pain. When the sun rose for me, I was dead to the world. Nothing could wake me. At least nothing I'd encountered yet.

"It's hard to say. You're young, which usually means the sun would make you insensible until it sets, but the drive to survive is a powerful thing. You might be aware of it on some level or even wake up as your body attempts to save itself."

Great. Not really good news. I would be forced to experience my death first hand rather than being unconscious for it. Burning to death was supposed to be a pretty terrible way to go.

"Do you know where you are?"

"Basement. Dirt floor. Furnace looks to be one of the older models. Probably about twenty years. I'd guess it was an older home. Definitely not a new build."

"Anything else?"

"It's not like they told me 'you're at 1032 Builder's Drive'. I was unconscious when they dragged me in here so I didn't see anything."

His eyes unfocused as he turned inward, following me as I started walking. Now that I knew this place was an extension of me, I couldn't believe I'd missed that fact before. The paths and scenes were all images I'd seen before, whether in person or in a photo.

I concentrated, trying to turn the forest to spring. The light dipped and then the trees shifted, rustling their great branches and shedding leaves.

There. A bud. I'd swear to it, and it hadn't been there before. Looked like Aiden had been right. This place was something my mind had created.

"Stop that," he said querulously.

"Why? It's kind of cool. I can move things around to create any sort of place I want."

"Your mind created this, but it did it on a subconscious level. There is a reason why things look the way they do. You going about and mucking with it could do damage."

I stopped and looked around, noticing shadows that had not been there before and a slight blurriness to trees in the distance, as if I had a camera and a soft focus on them. Damage? To my mind, perhaps.

Uneasily, I let the forest revert to its previous form.

This place was more dangerous than it appeared at first glance.

"We think you're still near the cemetery," he said after several minutes thought. "The wolves are searching, but it's slow as they don't know how many in their pack are part of this treachery so they only have a few Brax trusts with this search."

"He can add the rest. Victor is in this alone as far as I can tell. At least he hasn't mentioned any wolves helping him. There's a witch by the name of Angela, but he's planning to kill her off tomorrow night."

"Do you know what his final game is?"

I shrugged. "Nothing too original. Destabilize the pack or incite a war that ends with him as alpha of the werewolves. I get the feeling he wouldn't mind if the rest of the supernatural community in Columbus tore itself apart as well, but I don't think that's his end goal."

"That's not an insignificant undertaking."

I jerked one shoulder up, my feet silent as they glided over the forest floor. Aidan crunched along noisily beside me. "Story as old as time. Little man wants power and is willing to deceive, lie and murder to get it. I'll admit using a reanimated corpse to do his dirty work is a new one. I'll give him points for creativity in the implementation."

"You're so young to be so cynical," he murmured.

One side of my mouth quirked. Not really. I didn't consider myself cynical or even a realist. Most of the time my head was so high in the clouds that my feet barely touched the ground. Facts were facts, and the truth was that people wanted to stand on top whether or not they deserved to be there. It was only a bad thing when people were willing to do anything, including betray everything they were supposed to stand for, to get there.

"Not that any of this matters," I said. "If I don't figure a way out of being chained to a pipe before the sun hits me this afternoon, I'll be dead and won't care who wins this little battle of yours."

He nodded, his face grim. It was nice that he was taking this as serious as he was. If nothing else, maybe he would take the information I'd given him and prevent Victor from reaching his goals.

"When's the last time you ate?"

I thought back. It couldn't be a good thing that I couldn't remember. Was it last night when I woke up or before then? Usually I wasn't this careless.

"Maybe when I woke up last night or before I slept the night before. It's kind of vague."

"That's not enough. Not by half. You should be drinking blood three or four times a night. Preferably straight from the source."

That knowledge did nothing for me right this instant.

"Well I didn't," I snapped defensively.

"Your reserves will be critically low from what essentially amounts to starvation. I'm guessing your healing is sluggish."

I gave a wordless nod.

"You don't make this easy."

Yes, because I asked to be taken hostage by a deranged werewolf.

His mouth firmed as if he'd come to a decision.

"You need a boost to your base power to counteract the lack of blood. It should be enough to allow you to survive the day."

I opened my mouth to ask how we would do that then paused, not liking the way he watched me. Avidly, like he was waiting to pounce.

I stepped over a fallen log and kept walking, forcing myself to take my fear out of the equation to look at the situation objectively.

Everything I'd heard about vampires said they weren't known for their altruism. They weren't the worst thing out there, but they weren't boy scouts either. It would be in their character to take advantage if they could.

As my mom would say, "beware of people baring gifts. There's always a string attached."

"How would you suggest I get this power boost?" I asked, stopping to turn and watch him carefully.

His eyes narrowed slightly in victory. I would have missed it if I hadn't been looking so closely.

"I could give you a boost," he said, smiling charmingly.

It was a devil's smile, smooth and slick and just waiting to lead me to the path of my own destruction.

"At what cost?" I asked.

His smile turned wide and laughing. "So suspicious already. The cost is minor I assure you."

Sure it was, right until it bit me in the ass.

I tilted my head back. He had me over a barrel and knew it.

Bastard. I leveled a stare at him, my expression saying I wasn't buying his platitudes.

He cocked his head and gave me another cocky grin. "I'll need to intertwine my power with yours. It's been known to have side effects."

My eyes narrowed. "What kind of side effects?"

"Does it matter? You're facing death if you don't do this. Whatever reasons you have for refusing contact with us, they'll be moot if you're dead."

He was right, as much as I hated to admit that fact. I could refuse and take my chances with the sun, even I could admit death was almost certain if I took that route, or I could take what he was offering and hope I figured a way out later.

Any promise obtained from me would be given under duress. My conscious would be clear breaking that promise at a later date.

"Guess not."

"Knew you would see it my way," he said. "Don't worry, you'll like being part of my clan."

I stepped back. Clan. Oh, hell no.

No way was I letting him get his hooks in and reel me into the fold with this.

He raised one eyebrow as if to ask if my situation had changed in the last few seconds. I growled. It hadn't.

He held out a hand. I eyed it distastefully. Just do it. I didn't know how long I'd been wandering in my mind, the sun could march across my skin at any moment.

"If this is how you force people to become part of your little 'family,' I wouldn't be surprised if you end up dead before too much longer."

He gave me a smug grin. "Don't be ridiculous. The others weren't nearly so melodramatic when I asked them to join."

Guess I'm just special then. Yay me.

"Let's just get this over with," I said.

"This may be a bit painful," he warned.

I opened my mouth to tell him to get on with it, but the words froze on my tongue as a wave of pain crashed into me. I sucked my breath in to scream, but the sound never escaped. It felt like I burning from the inside out. My skin was peeling, my insides boiling. A thousand hot needles being stabbed deep inside.

The most pitiful sounds assaulted my ears. A high pitched keening that just never stopped. It was me. I was making that horrible sound.

Finally, the sensation ended, leaving me a shaking mess huddled on the ground. My eyes cracked open. What was left of the forest lay in embers. The great trees burned down to soot covered nubs and a thick ash enveloped everything.

"What the hell?" I croaked.

Aidan stared down at me, his arrogant face shaken.

A bit painful? That was agony on an epic scale.

"It didn't work," he said. He looked slightly scared and very unhappy.

"What do you mean it didn't work?" I asked from my position on the ground. I hadn't gotten all the sensation back in my limbs, and I couldn't stop shaking. "How could it not work?"

"I mean it didn't work. I couldn't establish the connection."

Connection?

"I thought this was just supposed to give me a boost. Enough to survive the sun."

"It would have," he defended.

That didn't sound like what he promised.

I fought my way to standing, still shaking like a leaf. I wasn't intimidating anyone like this.

"Explain."

"The connection would have brought you into my clan. It would basically give me the same type of connection as if I'd sired you. I would have had limited tracking ability. We would have been able to talk mind to mind and most importantly, share power back and forth."

That sounded close to what he'd promised. I wasn't a fan of the possibility of him being able to track me, but I could deal with that later.

"Okay, so what happened?"

"The connection didn't take. I was forced out. Your mind rebounded to an extent that I've never seen."

"What does that mean? Rebounded? You're not making sense."

"It's like your defenses slammed down by dropping a nuclear bomb on the surrounding area."

"So we need to try it again?"

A sick feeling started in my stomach. I didn't know if I could take that kind of pain again. Burning in the sun wouldn't have been near as bad.

"No, definitely not," he said adamantly. "That would probably kill you and seriously injure me."

Thank God. If that never happened again, it would be too soon.

It left me in the same situation as before, only weaker judging by the destruction to my mental forest.

"Then what do I do?" I couldn't help but ask.

Please don't say nothing. Please tell me you have a plan.

"I don't know."

I bent my head. Not what I'd wanted to hear at all.

I was dead. All that fighting to get home from Afghanistan, then fighting to manage this thing that had happened to me. It was all for nothing. All that struggle so I could burn to death chained in a basement. Talk about crappy endings.

His hand landed on my shoulder. "There may be a way for me to get you awake. It might be enough for you to move out of the sun's path or at least try to seek shelter."

It could also ensure that I stayed awake for my death. Something I would definitely have preferred to sleep through.

Still, survival was survival. I'd take my chances. I wasn't one of those who planned a graceful exit from this plane of existence. There would be no going silently into that good night. Death would have to drag me kicking and screaming all the way.

"Let's do this," I said, before I could lose my courage.

"This time instead of trying to push power into you while pulling some of yours out, I'll just try to redirect yours. I don't know how much time I can give you so move as quickly as you can."

I nodded. I was ready.

He raised his hand and pressed against my chest. At first I felt nothing, and I was sure whatever he was trying wasn't working.

Then something shifted, unfurling and growing while pushing other things out of its way. The pressure grew and swirled, finding no outlet as it rose, like a tsunami coming ashore or a hurricane gathering force. My head pounded and something inside me buckled, my forest starting to weave and swim.

I tried to form words. To tell him to stop. That this was killing me, but my brain had suddenly lost control of everything else.

I drooped, darkness spiraling out of the sky to consume everything around me. Perhaps the sun wasn't necessary after all.

With a pop, something inside broke, spilling me out of my forest.

I opened my eyes, blinking at the basement wall.

I was awake.

Hot. My right side was so hot smoke was beginning to curl up into the air.

The sun. Needed to get out of the sun.

I rolled over and crawled as far as the chain would allow away from the deadly beams,.

Damn. That was close.

I pressed myself against the cool cement blocks that made up the basement walls. There were just enough shadows left to provide a temporary shelter. For now I was safe, though I could feel day trying to suck me under again.

I had no idea how much longer until sunset, but there couldn't be more than four or five hours left. I could do that.

I was no stranger to sleep deprivation. The military had seen to that, incorporating it into training and then giving its soldiers a brush up any time there was a field exercise.

Trick was to keep your mind engaged and barring that, practicing physical activity.

Running or jumping jacks was out of the question, given my short chain. I could do pushups though. Or sit ups.

I curled up and collapsed back on the ground, seeing stars. Pain marched through my side and forced tears from my eyes. Nope. Not doing that again.

Sit ups were out. Pushups too.

That left keeping my mind occupied.

What to think about.

Routes. Easiest way to get from my house to work, from work to my mom's house. Best roads to take if I wanted to avoid the highway.

On and on I went, imagining scenarios, finding paths I would have to try when I got out of here to see if they would actually save time. When that got boring I pictured all the food I wanted to eat again. Perhaps I'd take up cooking. I used to like it even if I wasn't very good at it. I once burned a potato. In the microwave. The firemen had to come and everything. Mom didn't let me in the kitchen after that.

When the sun encroached on my space, I edged out of its way. We performed our little dance for hours. The sun advancing, me retreating the bare inches the chain allowed. It was almost like being at a ball. Only without the music or fancy dress.

Any time I began to nod off, all I had to do was remind myself of what I'd gone through to get this chance. That helped perk me back up for a few more minutes.

That's how I found myself promising to stay awake one more minute. Then when that minute was done, telling myself I could make the next one. And then the next. And the one after that.

Somehow I managed, watching as the sunlight turned from bright yellow to orange and then finally began to fade, inch by inch, from my basement cell.

Shuffling footsteps slowly descended the steps. I was too tired to even raise my head. My skin felt as insubstantial as two thousand year old parchment exposed to the air for the first time in millennia. I felt like it would crumple, and I'd float away at any minute. My tongue lay thick and dry in my mouth. The Grand Canyon had nothing on the cracks running across my tongue and lips.

"You're still alive," the draugr rasped.

Way to go, Sherlock. Want a cookie?

"Victor was sure you would be dead by now."

So sorry to disappoint.

My head rested weakly against the cement wall. If only I could get up the energy to attack. To do something.

"You don't have my treasure, do you?"

Finally. He was finally getting it.

Too bad that epiphany had come too late.

The draugr had sounded mournful when he made his pronouncement. If I hadn't been so exhausted and in pain, I might have scraped up a smidgeon of sorrow. As it was, I could only exist and wait.

The door at the top of the stairs opened. Victor's boots appeared. This was my last chance.

"Y-" I licked my lips, trying to dredge up even a little moisture for my mouth. "You should get a look at his girlfriend's necklace. You might find something you've been looking for."

The draugr's dead fish eyes searched mine before he turned away.

"Oh my, you're still alive," Victor drawled. "We had a bet going on whether you'd make it through the day. Didn't we?" He gave the draugr a derisive look. "Looks like you were right, and she managed. Doesn't really matter though. Just postpones the inevitable."

"Honey, where are you?" a female voice said from the top of the stairs.

Angela. I'd recognize that slightly whiny, smug little twat anywhere.

Victor's face turned mean. Angela thudded down the stairs. I stayed where I was, not wanting to waste any precious energy.

"What are you doing here? I thought I told you to stay away until I called for you."

Angela came to a stop a few feet away, her overly makeup-caked face turning stricken and unsure. Victor radiated a cold anger.

"I missed you. I just thought that we, that I, could do something to help things along."

"I thought we agreed that you wouldn't do any more thinking after the debacle with the vampire. There's a reason I told you to stay where you were. You've put everything in jeopardy by coming here."

I almost felt sympathy for her at Victor's shift to heartless prick. Almost. If not for her involvement in the spell, causing it to backfire and sending me across time and space to the draugr's grave.

Angela rubbed her hands on her jeans before taking a step toward Victor and laying one hand lightly on his chest.

"But, babe, I missed you."

I snorted. Really? That was her response? She sounded like a brainless nit wit, not a powerful witch capable of terrorizing the entire supernatural community of Columbus. Where was the deception? The cunning that had tricked me into this trap?

How had I missed the facts right in front of me? A detective I was not.

"What's that, bitch?" Angela's voice changed from cute flirting to hardened steel.

"Nothing, nothing. Just wondering how Victor could bring himself to fuck such a brainless lightweight. He must have a lot invested in his plan to put up with your lame seduction attempts."

I detected blood rushing to the surface of her skin. It was hard to tell if she flushed or turned red with all the powder covering her. My fangs pushed against my gums as my thoughts turned hazy with hunger.

My eyes fixed on her throbbing pulse. Her voice faded into a high pitched drone. I bet she'd taste yummy. I licked my lips. Yes. So yummy.

"-like that? What is she even doing still alive?" Angela was saying as I tuned back into the conversation.

I blinked. Shit, the blood lust was making me lose time. That wasn't a good sign. The sun and the silver must have further depleted my reserves, even more than the blood loss and healing had earlier.

At this rate we wouldn't have to wait for the draugr to drive the wolves into a frenzy. I'd be there all by myself in a few hours if I didn't get any blood into me.

"Enough," Victor roared. "Quit with the harping, woman. I will decide what needs to be done."

I watched with interest as Angela's face crumpled. Things weren't turning out as either of them had planned. I wondered what had changed from last night. Victor had been pretty sure he had everything handled.

Now, he seemed oddly off center. I was surprised that Angela was still alive, given how irritating he found her. The fact he hadn't killed her told me something had gone amiss. He must still need her.

Angela whirled and stomped up the stairs, slamming the door behind her.

The draugr's eyes glinted, briefly reflecting the light, as he watched her go with hungry eyes.

"Uh oh. Looks like trouble in paradise," I said with a half-hearted laugh that ended when my ribs protested. I hadn't fully healed during the day. Possibly because my body had been so busy trying to stay awake while at the same time mitigating the sun's effects.

"You have a smart mouth," Victor observed.

Not usually. It was just that facing hopeless situations brought out the sarcastic in me. I blamed TV. Too many plucky heroines when facing the big bads. It had affected my behavior. I swear.

"I wonder how long that will last."

He turned and headed after Angela with those parting words. I watched him go through narrowed eyes. Truthfully, I wondered that as well.

"He's going to kill you."

Yeah. I'd figured that out all by myself.

The draugr remained in the shadows, but I could feel his mad gaze resting on me. It was a sensation that was hard to put into words. It felt like when you come out of a deep sleep and lie in bed motionless, convinced there was something in the dark watching you. Waiting.

I rolled my head back to gaze in the direction of the draugr.

"Don't suppose you'd like to take care of them. Maybe save both of us a little bit of trouble."

He shook his head. "It's not me they're hoping to kill."

"You never know. You could be next on their list. You already heard Victor say he plans to get rid of Angela the moment he no longer needs her. What makes you think you'll fare any better?"

His lips stretched to reveal dark, rotted teeth. "He doesn't hold the power to destroy me."

"You never know."

Stranger things had happened. Like a doctor who served in the civil war coming back to life and massacring and eating a bunch of people.

"They have your treasures," I tried. "You as good as heard Victor admit it. Why continue to help them?"

He cocked his head, his face as pensive as its grotesque form would allow. "Lier. They have done nothing but help me. Pointing me towards those who've been tempted."

Great.

Really I hadn't expected anything else, but it had been worth a try.

"Though if you were to prove it, I would have no reason to hold back. I bet thieves taste mighty good."

I gave him a look, holding his mad gaze with my own. Could I trust him? The madness lurking behind those brown eyes said no, most definitely not. My shitty circumstances asked if I really had a choice.

Not if I wanted any chance of making it out of this alive or undead.

"I can't prove it here. Any attempt would fail with me chained up like this."

I raised one hand, jingling the chain. My arms and lower legs were numb, the silver's poison deadening everything around it. Sometime during the day my clothes had shifted and the metal now rested against my skin. I really hoped its effects were reversible.

He hopped forward, his head rotating and cocking as if it had no bones to make it obey human limitations. I grimaced and looked down at the chain, not wanting him to see the disgust in my eyes.

"Where? Where should we do it?" his voice hissed with greed.

"Think you can get them to your grave?"

His pupils shifted back and forth. He lowered his head, turning partially away from me. "Not there. I don't want to go back there."

"Only place I can think of," I said. "The wolves will be searching the cemetery. They work as both an incentive and a distraction. You want to get your treasures back, don't you?"

He hissed, full of rage. His eyes deepened to a midnight black, madness ready to spill out and consume everything at any moment.

I jerked back. A fine tremor shook my body.

It took several tries to get enough moisture in my mouth to continue.

"Good, then you'll help me convince him to move this little party to a better location."

His cracked lips parted as his eyes rolled. My stomach twisted. That was not a sight meant for human sensibilities.

"I will think on this."

No, I needed him on board.

"Don't you want your treasures?"

"Enough!" his voice turned inhuman as he lunged at me, his teeth inches from my throat. "Perhaps it's you who's planning to betray me. Perhaps I should save him time and just eat you now. I wonder if you'll taste like the last vampire. He was tough, like jerky, but had a certain spiciness."

I held still as his black tongue forked out, tasting my cheek and sliding up to my forehead. I bit my tongue to keep from whimpering when I felt the edge of teeth.

"It's not me who's betrayed you," I forced out. "How many people did Victor send you out after in search of that locket and watch fob? Ten? Twenty? How long are you going to kill for him?"

He drew back, the madness still very present in his eyes.

How much of the doctor remained? Enough to feel anger at being turned into a weapon? Or was that person gone? Erased by a prison camp and the rage that made him cling to life long after it was time to move on?

He bared his teeth, hissing again.

He spun and loped up the stairs on all fours.

The breath trapped in my chest finally escaped.

When I got out of this, I was going to take up a job with zero danger. No running errands for sorcerers or accepting foolhardy deals. No marks. No magic and definitely no undead monsters.

Chapter Fifteen

People were arguing upstairs. Sounded like Victor and Angela. If I concentrated, I could barely make out what they were saying.

"She should be dead already."

"I have a plan."

"I don't understand why you would keep her alive. She knows everything. If she escapes, she'll tell everyone. Any plan you have won't mean anything if you're too dead to reap its rewards."

I had a feeling the 'she' they were talking about was me. Angela seemed dead set on my death. I knew why, and she was right, as a witness my testimony would damn them with each of their kind.

I didn't know why she needed my death right this minute. I was chained in a basement with silver. Unless I developed super strength or lock picking skills in the next couple of hours, I wasn't going anywhere or telling anyone their secrets.

"Baby, trust me. You know I wouldn't let anything happen to you."

Whatever else Victor said was lost as he lowered his voice. There was a soft giggle and then the two became occupied with other things.

Angela was a lot more naive than I'd thought to be seduced so easily by someone who obviously had a hidden agenda. She'd possibly turned against her own mentor as I still wasn't sure what roll Miriam had played in this. Killed for him. They were a regular Bonnie and Clyde, if Clyde had secretly planned to off Bonnie in the last act.

I put my head back and closed my eyes.

Odd. I was tired. Maybe since I'd been up half the day, my body was now craving the sleep I didn't get.

* * *

Something was kicking my foot. There was a sharp pain in my knee, and I came all the way awake with a start. I jerked forward. The chains wrenched me back.

Angela laughed as I struggled and slapped at what was holding me in place.

I stopped, looking around as the cobwebs began to clear from my brain.

I wasn't in the basement anymore. I was in a cemetery. The same cemetery I'd landed in last night. Gravestones peeked from the ground in military straight lines. Rows and rows of them. It wasn't a huge cemetery, but it was big enough.

My sleepiness in the basement hadn't been natural. Given the smug look on Angela's face, I had the feeling she'd given my rest a magical boost.

I looked up at the sky. The stars were visible, the moon still low in the horizon. I hadn't been out long. Maybe a couple hours at most.

The draugr appeared from the shadows beside me, his stench announcing his presence as effectively as a trumpeted introduction.

Angela grimaced and turned away. Victor's nose twitched, but otherwise he didn't reveal any discomfort.

"Hey buddy, this place work for you?" Victor asked.

The thing that used to be Jackson Miller stared vacantly into the distance.

Victor waited expectantly, the genial look fading from his face as the draugr continued to stare.

"I have no idea why you wanted to do this here. You've had no problem with any of the other locations."

Graves. We were at his grave. The draugr was trying to keep our bargain.

Not that it helped me at that moment. I'd envisioned having my hands free and not being chained to a headstone when I proposed this location.

"Let's just kill her and move on to the next part of the plan," Angela whined.

"No, it has to be by the draugr's hands."

"Why? You said the alpha already knows you're behind this. It doesn't matter who does the killing any more as long as she ends up dead."

He snarled, his eyes flashing to wolf. Angela stepped back from the rage on his face, fear tightening the skin on her face.

"Stupid girl. Do I need to explain everything to you? If I kill her, both the wolves and the vampires will be gunning for us. If the draugr kills her, the vampires will blame Brax for abandoning her in battle."

"And they'll fight amongst themselves," Angela finished.

"Even if the wolves win, they'll be weakened, and it'll be easy for us to take control."

"I don't think it'll be as easy as you think," I said as I tested my restraints. Free, I had a chance. If I remained tied down like this, I was as good as dead.

"What would you know?" Angela asked with a sneer.

"Quite a lot actually. The vampires already know who the mastermind behind all this is. They know you have the draugr's treasures and are using them to control him. There's not going to be a war. Just the execution of two idiots on a power trip."

"That's impossible. The vampires wouldn't trust a word the wolves said," Victor said.

"Maybe not, but they'll trust my word."

They both laughed at that.

"And how will you tell them once you're dead," Angela said. "Vampires don't leave ghosts or shades. This time, you die forever and your secrets go with you."

I shrugged. "That's okay. They already know."

Victor tensed. "What's she talking about?"

"Nothing. She's lying."

"Am I?" My gaze shifted to Victor. "You should be able to tell, right? At least Brax could. You're not weaker than Brax are you?"

265

He closed his eyes and sniffed, drawing scents deep into his lungs. He opened his eyes as they shifted to amber.

"She's not lying," he growled. He whirled and sent a fist into one of the headstones. It broke in half.

"How?" Angela asked, her eyes wide in horror. "When did she have the time?"

I allowed a small smirk.

Their plans were crumbling around them much like that headstone had under Victor's fist. It felt good to be the one responsible for that. Even if I died here, they wouldn't achieve their goals.

"Does it really matter how?" I asked as my gaze shifted to Angela. "I wouldn't be surprised if Miriam knows of your involvement. I told the vampires where she lived so I'm sure they've notified her. I wonder what witches do to misbehaving apprentices. If it's anything like what a sorcerer does when he's upset, you're in for a very painful death. If I was either of you, I'd be making a beeline for the border. Remain around here, you're bound to wind up dead."

"Oh God," Angela said. "Miriam can track me. It's only a matter of time before she catches up to us."

Victor glared at me. He smiled, his mouth turning cruel. "No. We still have the draugr. You said yourself it couldn't be killed. We finish her, and then we strike at our enemies before they have time to regroup."

Damn.

They weren't running. My bluff hadn't worked. I was going to die. Probably horribly painfully.

"Buddy, we're here like you asked. Kill her."

The draugr's mad eyes finally shifted to me, and he smiled. It was a smile that spoke of evil deeds done in the dark. Things that man had forgotten or tried to forget. It sent tremors coursing through my body.

Whatever part of Jackson Miller that had convinced them to move the scene to this graveyard was gone. Only madness and hunger remained.

My back pressed hard into the cool of the headstone. If I could, I would have tried to climb through it to escape what was coming.

I yanked at the chain, hissing as the silver stung my palms. The chain didn't budge.

The draugr crept closer. His head doing that bird thing as his eyes fixed on me.

Fuck. Fuck.

I yanked harder, watching him come closer and closer.

I bared my fangs and hissed and snapped as he reached for me with one bony hand.

A blur came out of the dark and barreled into the creature, spinning him away from me. The draugr landed on the ground with a snapping, growling wolf on him.

Dark ichor flew as the wolf sank teeth and nails in its victim.

"Brax," Victor snarled, his face sprouting fur. His bones shifted and popped as his snout lengthened and ears grew from the top of his head.

I yanked harder at my chain. How did they get this stupid thing wrapped so tightly? At the very least I should have been able to slide it over the headstone.

"Kill the vampire," Victor ordered. His words were crisp and sharp despite the fangs that suddenly lined his gums.

"I would prefer you didn't," Liam said, landing between us.

He appeared to have dropped in from the sky. I looked up. Did he fly? Vampires could fly? Could I fly?

"I understand why you want her dead," he said. "She is rather vexing, but I have business with her later which requires her to be alive and kicking."

Looks like the cavalry was here and working together despite Miriam's certainty that the species couldn't put aside differences long enough to get anything done.

Since Brax was distracting the draugr and Liam was keeping the witch occupied, I turned my attention to getting free.

I examined the headstone. The silver chain wrapped in a loop around the stone and was hammered into the ground by a spike. It made slipping free impossible.

I cringed as rock flew by, followed by the body of a wolf.

Maybe if I broke the headstone, I could slip the pieces free and then use the slack in the chains to slide free myself.

I threw my back against the stone, again and again. It. Wasn't. Working.

Angela raised her hands. They sparked green and purple before the two colors curled up her arms.

With a bored face, Liam watched as she raised them and threw something at him. He dodged. The purplish green landed on a grave two over from me. The stone melted.

I threw myself harder against the stone. Needed to get away from here.

A second wolf flew past me to tackle Brax as he savaged the draugr's arm. He knocked Brax away and ripped at him. Blood flew as angry snarls and pained yelps followed.

"How is it that you continue to find the worst circumstances to insert yourself into?" an irate voice said next to my ear.

"Peter! What are you doing here?"

He sighed and pointed at the mark on my arm. "That mark means I can track you, idiot vampire."

Same old Peter. Good to know he hadn't changed when shit hit the fan.

"Okay, less talking, more freeing," I said.

He seemed in the mood to chat. "Your vampire and wolf friends needed someone to track you, and since they've both seen the mark, they were able to find me and insist I help them locate you."

I gave him a surprised look. And he did it?

He rolled his eyes at me, appearing like the teenager his looks suggested.

"They gave a convincing argument. So here I am."

Yes, but I would prefer he be helping me escape.

"How nice. So glad you grew a pair. Now if you could just help me get free."

"It's not all bad being here. The vampire and wolf alpha have a much better chance recovering my items than you. Of course, since you actually didn't play a part in me regaining them, it means you will still owe me that hundred years."

"Wait, what? No, I'm the one who found the draugr. I'm the one who uncovered the plot, and I'm the one who figured out who had your stupid locket and watch fob. No way can you say I didn't help."

He shrugged. "Since you're a little tied up, you won't be able to assist in their actual retrieval."

That was bullshit.

"That's bullshit."

He smiled.

I really wanted to knock his smug, little teenage-self back on his ass.

"What will it take for you to help me get free?"

He lifted one shoulder and brushed a lock of hair from his forehead. The cuff on his wrist shifted.

"Fine," I said. "I'll undo the first lock if you get these chains off me. It should give you some of your powers back."

He held up his hand and jiggled it. The cuff taunted me.

"Nope. Not doing both locks. It's one or none."

He gave the chains surrounding me a significant look.

I glared, not willing to give up my one piece of leverage but also not seeing another way out of this.

Liam sailed through the air and landed next to us. He didn't move, just lay there with his back to us.

Angela sauntered over with a smirk on her face. "Guess vampires aren't as dangerous as everybody says. One good shot and he's out cold. Pathetic." Her eyes began to glow green as she turned her attention to us. "Now, let's get you taken care of so my honey and I can take this to the next level."

"Both locks. I'll release both locks."

"Deal."

He reached behind me and dropped a liquid onto the stake holding the chains in place.

"Hurry, hurry, hurry," I chanted as Angela stalked closer.

"It's working as fast as it can. The bitch put a spell on the thing so it wouldn't budge."

"She's almost here. Do something."

The sorcerer glanced up as Angela neared. Her glowing eyes gave her entire face a greenish cast. She looked possessed and furious.

"Crap. You're on your own."

He turned and ran, leaving me gaping after him.

"What about our deal?" I yelled.

He waved one hand and kept going.

"You really shouldn't put any trust in sorcerers," Angela said, flicking her hair behind her. "They're not known for being particularly brave."

"Says the woman who plans to kill me while I'm tied down and can't defend myself."

I wiggled against the chains and was surprised when they gave. It wasn't much, just enough slack for me to lean forward.

She gave a shrug of acknowledgement. "Fair enough."

The chains loosened further as I rocked back and forth.

"Why do this?" I asked. There was just enough room to shift one arm free. Whatever the sorcerer had put on that stake was working. My struggles were loosening it. "Miriam doesn't seem that bad. I'm sure she'll forgive and forget if you just go home and apologize."

She made a derisive sound. "That old hag never forgives and she never forgets. I wouldn't go back to her even if I could. There's nothing for me there. For years I've listened to her nag about balance and choices and never once did she teach me about the things she promised would be mine in time."

The chains slipped around my chest as Angela vented. I leaned forward creating more room.

I was beginning to see why Miriam hadn't taught Angela the stronger stuff. The girl was a little crazy. There was a major persecution complex there. Probably made her easy pickings for an opportunist like Victor.

"She'll see, though. I'll make them all see. The one laughing in the end will be me. They will all bow."

"Oh man, come on. Enough with the 'woe is me' shit. No one cares. Life is hard. Blah, blah, blah. It didn't go the way you wanted it to. Whine, whine, whine. God, it's a miracle Miriam was able to teach anything to someone so pathetic."

Angela's face turned murderous. "You bitch. You'll pay for that." She stepped forward.

That's right. Keep coming.

I scoffed. "I bet Victor can't stand touching you. Who can blame him? He probably can't bear all the whining. I know I'm tired of listening to it."

She screamed with rage, the sound ugly and sharp like razor blades.

She rushed forward, hands outstretched. An unseen force pressed against me, trying to force me back through the headstone.

I grabbed a rock lying next to me and hurled it at her face.

She flinched, raising both arms to protect herself.

I slithered free of the chains and flung myself at her, tackling her to the ground. She batted at me with one arm, her fear and anger taking over. I grabbed her hand and pinned it to the ground then grasped the locket around her neck and yanked. It came free.

She screamed again and struggled. It was easy keeping her pinned. Lucky for me, her emotions made it hard for her to concentrate her magic enough for an attack. Without that magic, she was almost human weak. Her strength was no match for my vampire enhanced one.

I grabbed her hair and banged her head against the ground, once. Twice. Until she was unconscious.

The smell of blood pulled at me. Hunger bringing out my fangs as I eyed her pulse. Her blood smelled like dandelions and grass. Saliva pooled in my mouth and I leaned down toward her neck.

"It's about time you made your move," Liam said next to me.

I jolted forward, scrambling off the witch.

He stood relaxed next to us, already turning his focus on the draugr and the two wolves.

I looked between him and where he was supposed to be lying unconscious on the ground. "How are you? I thought- Weren't you unconscious a second ago?"

He gave me a roguish smile, the expression turning his face almost sinfully handsome. "A second class witch isn't enough to take me down."

Well, excuse me. It had certainly looked like she had. That's usually what people assume when someone is lying motionless on the ground.

"The sorcerer seemed to think the mark wouldn't disperse without your direct involvement," he continued, ignoring my glare. "I just manipulated events for the outcome I desired. Now that you've obtained the locket by yourself, there shouldn't be a problem with fulfilling your end of the bargain."

I narrowed my eyes. I didn't know whether to believe him or call shenanigans. If what he said was true, he'd taken an awfully big risk with my life. He could have just knocked her unconscious, freed me and then let me retrieve the items.

He gave her a distasteful glance. "I didn't expect you to try to antagonize her to death or for it to take that long."

He was one to talk. He was absolutely no help. Maybe next time he could do something besides just lie there while everyone else takes care of things. Not just pick apart how I did things.

We turned towards the wolves and draugr.

The tide had turned against Brax. He was out numbered and no matter how much damage he did to the draugr, it refused to go down.

He grabbed one of its arms and jerked, whipping his head violently. The flesh ripped. Before he could finish tearing the arm off, Victor barreled into him, knocking him away.

Brax lowered his head and bared his teeth, his eyes shining with Victor's death.

"Shouldn't you help him?" I asked.

"It's wolf business."

"Didn't the draugr kill a few vampires?" I asked. "What's the rest of the city going to say when they find out it was the wolves who avenged the dead? That the vampires stood idly by while the alpha fought?"

He gave me a glare and snarled, "Fine. I'll help the damn alpha."

I chuckled. Heh, so easy.

While Liam joined the fight in a blur of speed, dealing brutal bunches and kicks to both the draugr and Victor, I limped over to the remains of Victor's clothes.

Where, oh where, is the watch fob?

I picked through the pile, feeling in the pockets, tossing aside the keys and rifling through a wallet.

There was a pained yelp. The brown and white wolf that was Victor dodged unsuccessfully as Brax's dark gray one drove him to the ground, latching onto the throat and holding on. The light in Victor's eyes faded as the white and gray wolf whipped its head back and forth. Blood sprayed and a piece of the brown wolf's throat came away in the other wolf's mouth.

Victor was dead.

The draugr threw its head back and roared. Liam faltered, turning towards the wolf. Brax shook his head and hopped and jumped as if something had bitten him. Tremors shook his body as he turned towards Liam, the fur on his back standing up. He dropped his head into a hunting position and crouched.

My hands felt something hard in the pocket of the shirt I was holding. I fumbled inside. My hands clutched something hard that was attached to a chain.

"Stop," I screamed as Liam and Brax came together in a crash, each landing several blows in seconds. I shouted at the draugr. "Is this what you wanted?"

I held the locket and watch fob up.

His black gaze was suddenly riveted on my hand. "Mines."

He advance on me, his gaze held spell bound by the two trinkets.

I backed away, almost tripping on a root before recovering. I needed to get some distance between him and the other two creatures.

"You've got them. That's good," the sorcerer said.

He stood a few headstone down from me and several rows over.

The draugr's attention shot between the two of us. "No. Mine." He bared black teeth.

"Just toss it here so I can end all this," the sorcerer ordered.

I was tempted. Oh so tempted. It'd be so easy to let someone else handle this. Bonus, it would take care of several birds with one stone. Get the draugr away from Liam and Brax. Cancel out my debt. It would also hand the sorcerer an extremely powerful weapon. What damage could the draugr cause in the hands of someone with a little more power and brains than Victor and Angela?

"Please. It's mine. It's all I have left. She gave them to me." The draugr made a weird waffling sound, black leaked out of his eyes, adding further stains to his pale skin.

He was crying, I realized. Not real tears, but tears nonetheless.

"How?" I asked.

The sorcerer canted his head. "How what?"

"How are you planning to end this?"

"Does it matter?"

It mattered.

The draugr suddenly didn't seem that menacing, just sad and confused, like he'd had his whole world ripped away and didn't know how to handle it.

"Give the sorcerer the trinkets," Liam ordered. "You still have his mark."

Sure enough I could still feel the lion with thorns lurking on my arm, the power stretching in a thin line between me and Peter.

"He'll own you for a hundred years if you don't."

"And you'll own me for a hundred years if I do."

Liam paused in his forward motion. "The vampires will be much kinder than a sorcerer."

"I only have your word for that."

"I do not know why you persist in thinking of vampires as the bad guys. We are not the monsters you have painted us as."

I never thought they were. I just wanted to live my life the way I wanted to live it.

"If I go with you, will you let me live here? Stay in contact with my parents?"

I saw from the expression on his face that the answer to both those questions would be no. They might not be monsters. I might even be able to find a place in their world, but I was done with orders. The sorcerer I could manage. I wouldn't be able to manipulate Liam and his ilk.

"If she dies from that mark, sorcerer, we will kill you," Liam said.

Peter looked alarmed, his gaze shifting between the two of us.

"Wait. No. I don't want this."

I gave him a grin. "Looks like we're going to be best buds for a hundred years."

"No. Please not that. I'm telling you I don't want a servant."

I tightened my grip on the two pieces of jewelry. "If I give this to you, do you promise to get into your grave and not kill or eat any other people?"

The draugr nodded.

Would he keep his word? He had kept our bargain earlier by luring Victor and Angela to the cemetery. He was mad, though. Crazy people weren't exactly known for their integrity.

"You were tied to his headstone," Liam said in an undertone.

I moved sideways, stepping carefully as the draugr shadowed me. I really hoped I was doing the right thing.

"It's mine. It's mine."

Hysteria was rising in the draugr's voice. It wouldn't be long before he snapped.

"You want it?" I asked, raising the items in the air. His head followed them. "Go fetch."

"Son of a bitch," the sorcerer swore.

I flung them on his grave. He darted after them. Maniacal laughter followed me as I backed away. The draugr stood, clutching his treasures to his chest.

"Alright, back into your grave you go," I said.

He threw his head back and roared at the sky. His chest heaved and suddenly his head twisted towards me.

"I don't think so. I'm never going back into that dark space again."

Damn. I had hoped he wouldn't do this.

"Now, witch," Liam roared. He flew at me, grabbing my arm and flinging us both out of the path of the draugr.

A lyrical voice hummed a few words.

Branches burst out of the ground, twining up the draugr's legs. They grew around him.

"No. What's this?" The draugr struggled against the plants, ripping away the branches only to have them grow back. Soon they covered him. He howled, again and again, as he was dragged back to his grave and then under. "No. No. No."

The night was eerily silent once the ground finished consuming him.

I sat up. What had just happened?

A figure moved through the cemetery, her blond hair shining in the moonlight. She arched a brow at the undisturbed grave and then wrinkled her nose at the dead wolf.

Miriam gave her apprentice an inscrutable look before focusing her attention on me.

I watched her carefully.

This woman's apprentice had been in league with Victor and the draugr. Had Miriam been totally unaware of Angela's actions?

Miriam had been in charge of that ritual that had gone so terribly wrong. As had already been proven many times tonight, magic was a very tricky and powerful force. It was possible we'd all been duped by this person.

Miriam arched one eyebrow at me sprawled in the dirt. "You're still alive. How surprising."

"I'm like a cockroach that way. I just keep coming back."

She gave me a crooked smile, then glanced behind me. "Vampire."

"Witch," Liam said.

"I see the spell to find your wayward charge worked."

He inclined his head.

Did she mean me? I thought the sorcerer had been the one to lead them to me.

"The items. How could you give them back to that, that, creature?" the sorcerer moaned, coming to stand beside me.

He stared mournfully at the grave.

"You're welcome to dig the grave back up and get them back," I told him.

"No," both Miriam and Liam said.

Miriam gave a strained smile. "That will just wake the draugr back up. Right now he's sleeping. He'll remain there unless someone takes those treasures from him again or disturbs his grave."

I slapped the sorcerer on the back. "Guess that means you're not getting them back unless you dig them up yourself. Sucks to be you."

He turned to me and held up his hand. "Remove this. I'd like to torture you now."

I scoffed. "Yeah, I'll get right on that."

"You have to. Our deal was that I release you from your chains and you remove this."

"Is that a genie's handcuff?" Liam asked.

I nodded.

He gave me an interested stare. "Where'd you get an item like that?"

I gave him a noncommittal shrug. A girl never reveals her sources.

"Our deal, vampire."

"I don't think so." I gave Peter a nasty smile. "You failed to hold up your end."

"That's a lie. I released you."

"I don't count sprinkling that liquid on the chains and then fleeing as fast as you can in the opposite direction as freeing me."

"You wouldn't be free if not for that liquid, so in essence I freed you," he said, leaning forward and pointing at the headstone in emphasis.

I stared at him through narrow eyes. He had a valid point. The chains would never have loosened enough for me to pull free if he hadn't used whatever that stuff was on them. I also never would have escaped if I hadn't used a considerable amount of brute strength.

"You left the job half done," I said. "No deal."

Good thing too, now that the sorcerer had a claim on me for the next hundred years. Things would be a lot easier on me if he didn't have access to his magic.

"That's not how this works," he said through gritted teeth. "You will release me or I'll declare you an oath breaker. This should be obvious to anyone with any experience in our world, but since you continue to display a considerable lack of intelligence, I'll explain it to you."

I folded my arms. This should be good.

"Being an oath breaker would be what we call a bad thing. You would face a lot of hostility and probably be run out of the city." He thrust his arm out. "Now, if we're done discussing this ridiculous point. Remove these."

Hm.

What to do?

I wondered if there was a certain amount of proof he would need to provide about my oath breaker status or if this like so many other things were somehow established magically, like the sorcerer's mark.

"You might have a point if you had brewed that potion," Miriam's amused voice inserted. "Since you didn't, sorcerer, you have no case. I'm sure the vampire and the alpha will support her in this."

"I will," Liam's strong voice said.

Brax barked once.

He had yet to take his human form again. Considering his change left him nude, it was probably a good thing he still wore his fur.

"Stay out of this witch," the sorcerer snapped.

She gave him a chilly smile. "I refuse. You'll have to find some other way to force her to remove that. I'll enjoy watching you try."

He glared at her.

I released a breath, glad that he had switched his annoyance to her. I didn't know if that had been her intent, but it made things easier for me.

She ignored Peter and turned to me. "I'd like to take my apprentice home now."

I blinked at her, not sure I had heard her right.

She wanted to do what?

Brax growled, the sound a low rumble of menace.

"I'm afraid that I have to agree with the wolf on this one," Liam said. "That is impossible. She was instrumental in a plot to overthrow the werewolf alpha and intended mortal danger to many in Columbus. She must answer for her crimes."

"And she will," Miriam said, turning to stare Liam down. "But not at your hands. She will face a witch's justice. I can promise you it won't be easy or merciful."

Liam frowned at her. "No, her crimes were against all of us. The vampires and werewolves have a greater claim. We lost more people."

"It's not up to you," Miriam challenged. She tilted her head toward me. "It's her decision. She's the one who subdued Angela."

I suddenly found myself the focus of several pairs of eyes.

I really didn't want to get involved in whatever power grab was going on here. My troubles with the sorcerer were enough. I didn't need any more.

"I don't think I should get involved."

"You owe me a favor," Miriam interrupted, her eyes flaring.

I paused. "And this would fulfill the favor?"

I wanted to be very sure before I acted.

She nodded, once. "It would. The witches would also be grateful for your service."

Gratitude sounded nice. I could use some of that right about now.

But I didn't want to act hastily and without thought. That was how I got into this situation in the first place.

On one hand, Liam was right. Angela and Victor had done a lot of damage to the wolves. If I handed her over to Brax, he would kill her, whether it was now or later. I didn't know if I wanted that on my conscience. It was one thing to take someone out during combat or while fighting for your life. It was quite another handing them over to certain death. It was a small thing, but sometimes those small things were the only thing standing between you and the darkness such choices can bring.

"You'll make sure she can't do this again?"

Miriam nodded.

"Fine, take her."

Brax huffed. Even as a wolf, he managed to convey his disgust. I shrugged at him. A favor and a semi clear conscious was a good trade to me. He'd just have to be satisfied with Victor's payment.

He threw his head back and howled, the sound hauntingly powerful.

I jumped.

Standing so close to a wolf howling was entirely different to hearing them from several miles off. It was wondrous and terrible, beautiful and deadly.

When his howl trailed off, Brax dropped his head, staring at me for one timeless moment before he loped away.

"We'll be off then," Miriam said, turning and using her magic to lift her apprentice. Her feet glided over the grass soundlessly as she moved through the cemetery, Angela floating behind her like some oversized balloon.

Sometime during the wolf's howl and Miriam's departure, the sorcerer had stalked off, leaving Liam and me in the cemetery alone.

"Now, time to discuss our unfinished business," Liam said, his voice grim.

Chapter Sixteen

I stuck my hands in my pocket and braced. I'd had a feeling this was coming.

"I don't remember any unfinished business."

Giving the draugr his trinkets back had been both calculated and impulsive. He deserved to keep the mementos from his human life, but I was lying if I said I didn't see the opportunity such a chance offered me. I hadn't examined all angles before deciding. There was a chance I'd missed something and the vampires still had a claim on me.

Liam arched one eyebrow, saying without words he knew what was going through my head.

I gave him my inscrutable face. I've been told people had found it intimidating in the past. Liam didn't seem too impressed.

"You've only delayed the inevitable."

I breathed an internal sigh of relief. Delayed sounded an awful lot like my plan had worked. I'd take it over being forced from my home. There was also the fact that Aiden hadn't been able to cement the bond when he'd tried earlier. I did not want to go through that pain anytime soon.

"We'll eventually find a way around the mark. You've made an enemy of the sorcerer so I'm sure he'll be most helpful in that pursuit."

"Not if he ever wants that cuff off," I returned.

He inclined his head, conceding I had a point. "You haven't won this, just gotten a reprieve."

"Yeah, yeah. I hear the warning. What you're not understanding is that when that time comes, I'll figure something else out." I gave a wry grin. "It's what I do."

"Why? From what I can see, you've never had any real encounters with us. What makes you so sure you can't thrive under our care?"

I tilted my head back and stared at the stars. How to put this into words he would understand? I didn't even know if I understood all of my motivations.

"I'm guessing you're old. At least a couple hundred years."

His mouth quirked in a small grin.

"Something like that."

I mentally added a few hundred years to the two I'd guessed.

"You grew up in a different age than me. Totally different mentality and social values. I'm not sure my reasons will make sense to you."

"Try."

"My first encounter with a vampire was at a club two days after I got home from Afghanistan. He didn't ask if I wanted this. Didn't even try to help me understand why this happened. Just threw me in a dumpster with the garbage." I held up a hand forestalling his argument. "I don't blame all vampires for his actions. I've seen enough of what that type of thinking can cause."

I rubbed my neck. "I guess what it boils down to is I just don't want to. I like my life. I like my family. I won't be told what to do, how to live, to give up the people I love. I just won't do it. I don't care if you think that's ridiculous or childish. It's my life. I'll live it the way I want as long as I'm not a direct danger to those around me."

Said out loud it did seem like something a kid would say. I don't want to so I'm not gonna. I didn't care. If there was one thing I'd learned, it's that life is short, even for vampires. I wasn't going to waste time doing what others expected of me. I'd already wasted my human life as it was.

It might be messy. It might be difficult, but I was going to live this life the way I wanted to.

"You do sound like a child."

Figured. I hadn't really expected him to feel any other way.

"You're a weapon. One that can explode and kill everyone around you. I've told you before that there's a reason we do things this way."

282

Yes, he had. Just like before, I called shenanigans.

I gave a humorless smile. "Tell me. When are vampires the most dangerous to those around them?"

His nostrils flared, and his eyes took on a slight sheen.

Thought so.

"Could it be when they're first turned? The first year maybe?"

A vein throbbed in his jaw.

Gotcha.

"I've been a vampire for over two years. In that time, I've never had an accident, never killed anyone. Hell, I haven't even bitten anyone."

"You should be biting people. Not drinking from the source is slowly starving you of nutrients you need. If you weren't so stubborn and convinced you know right, you would know this."

I took a deep breath, trying to master the spark of anger that flared to life. He had a point, even if he was being an ass while making it. Hadn't I lamented my lack of knowledge about my situation several times over the last few days?

"Stop being a fool," he said.

I huffed, biting back the words that I wanted to say. No, I needed to be calm.

"You need to-"

"You want me to learn all this, to give vampires a chance?" I asked loudly. "Then you give me a reason. Don't try to force it or threaten my family. Teach me what I need to know, or get the hell out of my life. Try to establish a relationship, because I can guarantee you won't win any other way. I will make life hell for anyone you stick me with and from what I know about your culture that would almost ensure a painful or perhaps deadly time for me. Not really a lot of incentive there for me, is there?"

I stalked off before he could answer.

The sorcerer's deal would hold. For now, the vampires couldn't hurt me or force me into their fold. It wasn't an ideal situation, but it was the best choice I could make.

My anger carried me out of the cemetery and down several streets and several miles before I calmed enough to find my way home.

I climbed the stairs, my legs weary from all the walking. I let myself in, unlocking the door and shutting it behind me without bothering with the light.

I was halfway into the living room when I froze. There was someone sitting in my armchair. The light clicked on. I shielded my eyes, squinting from the sudden brightness after hours of walking in the dark.

"Jerry?"

"Oh, so you remember who I am?" he asked, his voice tight and calm. "I was beginning to wonder since you haven't bothered to return any of my calls."

I cringed and patted my pockets. My phone was missing. I didn't even remember when I'd lost it.

"Uh, yeah. About that. There were some issues with the delivery."

He arched one furry eyebrow. "Oh?"

"Perhaps we could discuss this tomorrow at work."

"No."

My shoulders slumped. I had hoped to have a little time to prepare my defense.

"The person I was supposed to make the delivery to was already dead when I arrived," I said.

Jerry's face darkened. I stepped back, my apartment suddenly seeming small and confining. It would be difficult to dodge his bulk, and I'd locked the door behind me.

"Explain."

And I did. I explained about the werewolves delaying the delivery even after I announced I was with Hermes couriers, about finding the dead guy, my incarceration, the subsequent deal with the sorcerer and everything that had followed in the last few days.

I held my breath when I'd finished, holding myself prepared to flee. I'd never seen Jerry violent, just heard the gossip around the water cooler.

He sighed. "You should have informed me of this situation several days ago. While you failed to meet your deadline, there were mitigating circumstances, and the werewolves share responsibility. You might have avoided a lot of trouble had you simply reported back like you were supposed to."

I blinked. He had taken that incredibly well.

"I'll make sure to do that next time," I said, not quite believing my luck. I had fully expected to be fired at best and dead or maimed at worst after this conversation.

"Now, on to more important things."

I let myself relax.

"Where's Cherry?"

Shit. His car. I'd totally forgotten, what with the kidnapping and all.

His eyes were penetrating as they stared me down. I felt like a teenager facing my dad after putting a scratch down the side of his brand new vehicle.

"About that."

"I didn't hear it before you came in," he said.

"Yes, well, funny story."

"Where is my car, Aileen?" he thundered.

"It's fine. I made sure nothing touched it."

"Then where is it?"

I made a face. "I'm not really sure."

He stood in an explosion of movement. I flinched back. He adjusted his clothes and grabbed his coat, yanking it on in angry movements. I watched with wary eyes.

"I'm going home. That car had better be there before you come into work tomorrow and there had better not be a single dent or scratch."

"Of course, Jerry."

He paused at my door, "Oh, and Aileen." He waited until I looked at him before continuing. "I'll be charging a fee for the past four days use of my car. Think of it as a rental fee. I think a thousand dollars a day is fair, don't you?"

I swallowed my protest. That was nearly half the fee owed me for this job.

"Sounds fair." I gave him a sickly smile. There goes the possibility of getting my own car.

Could be worse. I could have gotten nothing due to how badly I'd bungled this job. I could also be fired. Hell, I could be dead. A few thousand dollars out of my check wasn't too steep a price to pay.

He left, closing the door after him. I locked it, not wanting any other unannounced visitors and leaned back against it.

The doorbell rang.

I opened it, expecting Jerry. Nobody was there, but a white envelope was on the stoop. I bent and picked it up.

'Aileen' was printed in cursive on the front.

I turned it over in my hands. The paper felt expensive with the kind of weight popular with wedding invitations, but no one I knew was getting married.

I opened it and pulled out a piece of paper.

A number was printed on it and beneath it a message.

"Looking forward to furthering our acquaintance – Liam."

About The Author

Writing is my first love. Even before I could read or put coherent sentences down on paper, I would beg the older kids to team up with me for the purpose of crafting ghost stories to share with our friends. This first writing partnership came to a tragic end when my coauthor decided to quit a day later, and I threw my cookies at her head. Today, I stick with solo writing, telling the stories that would otherwise keep me up at night.

Most days (and nights) are spent feeding my tea addiction while defending the computer keyboard from my feline companion, Loki, who would like to try her paw at typing.

Discover More by T.A. White

Pathfinder's Way
Dragon-Ridden

Excerpt for Pathfinder's Way

The Trateri are about to learn a vital lesson of the Broken Lands. Deep in the remote expanse where anything can happen, it pays to be on a pathfinder's good side.

Nobody ventures beyond their village. Nobody sane that is. Monstrous creatures and deadly mysteries wait out here. Lucky for the people she serves, Shea's not exactly sane. As a pathfinder, it's her job to face what others fear and find the safest route through the wilderness. It's not an easy job, but she's the best at what she does.

When the people she serves betray her into servitude to the Trateri, a barbarian horde sweeping through the Lowlands intent on conquest, Shea relies on her wits and skill to escape, disguising herself as a boy to hide from the Warlord, a man as dangerous as he is compelling.

After being mistaken as a Trateri scout during her escape, Shea finds herself forced to choose between the life she led and the possibilities of a new one. Her decision might mean the difference between life and death. For danger looms on the horizon and a partnership with the Warlord may be the only thing preventing the destruction of everything she holds dear.

Chapter One

"For God's sake, woman, the village will still be there if we take an hour's break."

Shea rolled her eyes at the soaring mountains before her. This was the third rest stop the man had called for since setting out this morning.

"We must be half way there by now," he continued.

Maybe if they hadn't stopped several times already or if they had moved with a purpose, but as it stood the group had probably traveled less than two miles. Half of that nearly vertical. At this pace, it would take an extra half day to get back to Birdon Leaf.

And who would they blame for the delayed arrival?

Shea. Even though it wasn't her needing to stop on every other hill when they felt a muscle cramp or experienced shortness of breath. Since she was the pathfinder, it was obviously her fault.

She could hear it now.

The pathfinder sets the pace. The pathfinder chooses when to take breaks. Yada. Yada. Yada.

She hated running missions with villagers. They thought that since they'd gone on day trips outside their village barriers as children, they knew a thing or two about trail signs and the Highlands in general.

It was always, 'We should take this route. I think this route is faster. Why is it taking so long? These mountain passes are sooo steep.'

Never mind it was her that had walked these damn routes since the time she could toddle after the adults or that the paths they suggested would take them right through a beast's nest.

Nope. She was just a pathfinder. A female pathfinder. A female pathfinder who hadn't grown up in the same village as them. Obviously, she knew nothing of her craft.

The man yammered on about how they couldn't take another step. Any reasonable person could see how worn out they were. She wasn't the one carrying the gear or the trade goods.

Whine. Whine. Whine.

That's all she heard. Over the last several months, she'd perfected the art of tuning them out without missing pertinent information.

It was all in the pitch. Their voices tended to approach a higher frequency when they regressed to bitching about what couldn't be changed. As if she could make the switchbacks approaching the Garylow Mountain pass any less steep or treacherous.

"We'll take a rest once we reach the pass," she said for what seemed like the hundredth time.

They had begged for another break since about five minutes after the last one.

She had a deadline to meet. Sleep to catch. Most importantly, she didn't think she could last another half day with this lot.

"We're nowhere near that pass," the man raged.

The rest break obviously meant a lot to him.

"It's just over that ridge," Shea pointed above her.

Well, over that ridge and then another slight incline or two. It was just a small lie, really. If the man knew the truth, he'd probably sit down and refuse to take another step.

"That's nearly a half mile away." The man's face flushed red.

Really if he had enough energy to be angry, he had enough energy to walk.

"Quarter mile at most."

"We're tired. We've been walking for days. First to the trading outpost and then back. What does an hour's difference make?"

Shea sighed. Looked up at the blue, blue sky and the soaring pinnacles of rock then down at the loose shale and half trampled path they'd already traveled.

"You're right, an hour's rest won't make much difference." His face lit up. "However, you've already wasted two hours today on the last two breaks. You also wasted several hours yesterday, and the day before, and the day before that. We should have been back already."

She held up her hand when he opened his mouth.

"Now, we are getting up that pass. We need to be over it and down the mountain by nightfall. Otherwise you're going to have to fend off nightfliers. Do you want to fend off nightfliers when you could be sleeping? Or would you rather suck it up and get over that damn ridge?"

The man paled at the mention of nightfliers, a beast about three times the size of a bat that had a disturbing tendency of picking up its food and dropping it from a high altitude. It made it easier to get to the good parts on the inside.

"We'll wait to take the break." He turned and headed down to the last switchback where the rest of their party waited.

"Oh, and Kent." Shea's voice rose just loud enough for him to hear. "Please let them know that if anybody refuses to walk, I'll leave them here to fend for themselves. Nightfliers aren't the only things that roam this pass come nightfall."

He gave her a look full of loathing before heading down to his friends. Shea kept her snicker to herself. Good things never happened when they thought she was laughing at them.

Idiot. As if pathfinders would abandon their charges. If that was the case, she would have left this lot behind days ago. There were oaths preventing that kind of behavior.

What she wouldn't give to enjoy a little quiet time relaxing on the roof of her small home right about now.

* * *

They didn't make it back to the village until early the next morning. Shea brought up the rear as their group straggled past the wooden wall encircling the small village of Birdon Leaf.

The village was a place that time had forgotten. It looked the same as it had the day it was founded, and in fifty years or a hundred, it'd probably still be the same. Same families living in the same homes, built of wood and mud by their father's, father's, father. Most of the buildings in the village were single story and one room. The really well off might have a second room or a loft. Nothing changed here, and they liked it that way. Propose a new idea or way of doing something and they'd run you out of town.

They didn't like strangers, which was fine because most times strangers didn't like them.

They tolerated Shea because they needed the skills her guild taught to survive. Shea tolerated them because she had to.

Well, some days she didn't.

A small group of women and children waited to welcome the men.

A large boned woman with a hefty bosom and ash blond hair just beginning to gray flung her arms around a tall man with thinning hair.

"Where have you been? We expected you back yesterday morning." She smothered his face with kisses.

"You know we had to keep to the pathfinder's pace. The men didn't feel it would be right leaving her behind just because she couldn't keep up."

There it was. Her fault.

Anytime something went wrong it was due to the fact she was a woman. Even looking less feminine didn't help her. A taller than average girl with a thin layer of muscles stretching over her lean frame, Shea had hazel eyes framed by round cheeks, a stubborn mouth and a strong jaw-line she'd inherited from her father. Much to her consternation.

"What the guild was thinking assigning a woman to our village, I'll never know," the woman said in exasperation. "And such useless trail bait. They must have sent the laziest one they had."

Trail bait. Dirt pounder. Roamer. Hot footed. Shea had heard it all. So many words to describe one thing. Outsider.

Shea turned towards home. At least she would have a little peace and quiet for the next few days. She planned to hide out and not see or talk to anyone.

Just her and her maps. Maybe some cloud watching. And definitely some napping. Make that a lot of napping. She needed to recharge.

"Pathfinder! Pathfinder," a young voice called after her.

Shea turned and automatically smiled at the girl with the gamine grin and boundless enthusiasm racing after her. "Aimee, I've told you before you can call me Shea."

Aimee ducked her head and gave her a gap toothed smile. She was missing one of her front teeth. She must have lost it while Shea was outside the fence.

"Pathfinder Shea. You're back."

Shea nodded, amused at the obvious statement. Of all the villagers in this backwoods place, Aimee was her favorite. She was young enough that she didn't fear the wilds lying just beyond the safety of the barrier. All she saw was the adventure waiting out there. She reminded Shea of the novitiates that came every year to the Wayfarer's Keep in hopes of taking the Pathfinder's exam and becoming an apprentice.

"Um, did you see any cool beasts this time?" Aimee burst out. "Nightfliers, maybe? You said they liked to nest in the peaks around Garylow's pass. What about red backs?"

"Whoa, hold up. One question at a time." Shea took a piece of paper she'd torn from her journal last night in anticipation of this moment. "Here. I saw this one diving to catch breakfast yesterday morning."

Shea handed her a sketching of a peregrine falcon in mid dive. It was a natural animal, but to a girl raised in a village where all non-domesticated animals were considered 'beasts,' it would seem exotic. Shea had sketched it during one of the numerous breaks the men had taken.

"Pathfinder Shea," a woman said from behind them, disapproval coloring her voice. "The elders wish to speak to you."

Shea's smile disappeared as she schooled her face to a politeness she didn't really feel. Aimee hid the drawing in her skirts.

The woman's eyes shifted to Shea's companion. "Aimee, my girl, your mother's looking for you. I suggest you get on home."

Aimee bobbed in place, suitably chastened and followed as the woman swept away, but not before aiming a small smile in Shea's direction.

Shea lifted a hand and waved. Aimee had become something of Shea's shadow in the past few weeks. It was a welcome change, given how most of the villagers pretended she didn't exist or treated her with barely concealed hostility.

Shea looked woefully towards the tightly packed dirt trail leading to her little cottage. Her muscles ached and three days of grime and dirt coated her body.

She wanted a bath, a hot meal and then to sleep for twelve hours straight. She didn't want to deal with the grumpy, blame-wielding elders who no doubt wanted things they couldn't or shouldn't have. But if she didn't deal with them now, they would just show up and nag at her until she gave them her attention. They wanted something from her. Again. Better to deal with things now so she could have an uninterrupted rest later.

Her well-deserved break would have to wait

Her steps unhurried, she turned in the opposite direction of her bed. Even moving as slowly as she reasonably could, she quickly found herself in front of the town hall. It was also a pub and gathering place, basically anything the village needed it to be.

There were only two stone structures in the entire settlement. The town hall was the first and greatest, holding the distinction of being the only building large enough to shelter the entire village in the event of an attack. There was only one entrance, a heavy wooden door that could be barred from the inside. The thin slits in the upper levels kept attackers of both the four legged and two legged variety from slipping inside.

The building was the primary reason the founding families decided to settle here and was the village's one claim to wealth. The rest of the village, small though it was, had sprung up around it as a result.

For a place as backwards and isolated as Birdon Leaf, the town hall was a majestic building they couldn't hope to replicate. Even without the skills to maintain it, they were lucky. Some of the larger towns didn't have a structure this versatile that could act as both gathering place and shelter from danger.

Shea reached the doors and paused to brush the dirt from the back of her trousers and make sure her thin shirt was tucked in and her dark brown, leather jacket was lying straight.

CPSIA information can be obtained
at www.ICGtesting.com
Printed in the USA
LVHW082150140220
647003LV00012B/248